THE TEMPLAR CURSE

A SEAN WYATT ADVENTURE

ERNEST DEMPSEY

JOIN THE ADVENTURE

Visit ernestdempsey.net to get a free copy of the not-sold-in-stores short story, RED GOLD.

You'll also get access to exclusive content not available anywhere else.

PROLOGUE

CHINON, FRANCE | OCTOBER 13, 1307

S ebastian sat in the darkness, waiting. His right hand gripped the handle of his sword with a tight and deadly strength. The weapon had been his friend and savior for nearly five years now. It had seen death in many lands, including this one, where he and others from his order remained in hiding.

He'd joined the Templars as nothing more than a boy, the son of a farmer. His shovel and plow had been traded for the blade in his hand and the shield at his knee. Through battles against hordes of Moors and other heathens, he'd become a hardened man, forged in the crucible of war. A soldier.

He wasn't completely surprised by the attack. Sebastian had known trouble was coming. His superiors had warned this day would come, though they'd refused to leave the country. What was it they'd called it? An act of cowardice?

The Templars weren't accustomed to surrender, much less retreat.

But this wasn't like withdrawing from a battle. It was something else. It was survival, not just for the order but for something far greater, far more important than any one man or group could ever hope to become.

He heard the men rap on the door. A second later, it burst open. Footsteps clacked on the floorboards as the Inquisitors hurried into the room. Tables were flipped over. Bowls, cups, and utensils went flying. The men trashed the place, scouring it for any sign of Sebastian LeMarc.

Sebastian knew who they were. He'd known this day would come. Despite warning several others in his order, they refused to leave the village, hoping that the king and the pope would come to their senses.

Sebastian wasn't so naïve. He knew what drove men: greed and a thirst for power. Neither was ever sated.

With that knowledge in mind, Sebastian had set about protecting himself in case the day did come. His former life on the farm had taught him much about carpentry, too. The secrets the order protected furthered that knowledge. So, he'd created a safe room behind a faux bookshelf. That safe room was a decoy.

Knowing the Inquisitors would be eager to destroy any books the Templars possessed—dubbing them heretical—Sebastian placed dozens of volumes on the shelves for them to remove. The books would be thrown in a sack and taken to the town square for a massive burning. The volumes the men took wouldn't contain anything important. Sebastian had made certain of that. The things he was charged with protecting were safe with him, in the second hidden room. This one was hidden by a rock façade near the fireplace. An iron rod was fixed to the inside of the hearth, placed in such a way that an intruder would have to be looking for it to find it.

One of the men shouted. Sebastian knew the guy had found the decoy. He heard a creak as the man pulled on the book that opened the room.

"It's a hiding place," one of them said. "If he's not in there, he must have left. Find him."

That was the guy in charge, the commanding officer of this witch hunt.

Templars were being rounded up by the hundreds. Every one of them, so far, had been tortured and then summarily executed. The Inquisitors forced confessions of witchcraft, sorcery, and dark magic, none of which were true. That didn't matter. To the people, it was good enough.

Sebastian listened closely as the men collected the books they'd thrown on the floor and finished trashing the place. Then the footsteps faded as the group marched out the door and into the night.

He waited another half hour before pulling the latch and opening the hidden door. He hurried over to the window and eased back one of the drapes, taking a peek out to see if the men were gone.

There was no sign of them anywhere.

Sebastian knew they'd likely moved on to the next target on their list, but could—and probably would—double back to his place sooner or later. The king's men weren't given to quitting easily. They would find their target or face ruthless punishment for failure.

Sebastian was sickened that he'd served with some of those same soldiers in the Crusades. The men had abandoned the order to seek rank and fortune. The latter almost never came for soldiers—although wearing the uniform did afford a precious few certain... benefits...when it came to the fairer sex.

With not a moment to lose, Sebastian set about his vital task. He rushed back to his secret room and began collecting the items given him by the order's leader, a man called Bertrand.

Sebastian hoped for the best, but he knew Bertrand wouldn't leave town. He was probably being carried into the fortress that very moment, shackled and beaten, preparing to be tortured for the remainder of his soon-to-be short life until he confessed his heresy.

The three chests were already loaded on the cart in the stables a few blocks away. It had been a huge risk to put them there, but Sebastian had no choice. It was that or put them in his home and take a chance that the intruders would find everything. He knew there were two others tasked with a similar mission to his own. The only difference between them was the destination.

Sebastian's orders were to go north until he was out of reach of the king and pope's men. He had no idea where the others were going. That was part of the design. If no one knew where the others were going, they had a better chance of staying hidden and fewer odds of being betrayed.

After grabbing his bag and a few additional items, Sebastian secured the belt that held his sword and scabbard and ran down the stairs.

Screams echoed through the dirty town streets. Men howled. Women cried. Children did both.

From the sounds of it, the Inquisitors were several blocks away in the other direction. That was good news for Sebastian as he poked his head out of the door and looked both directions before stepping onto the sidewalk.

He kept close to the buildings as he hurried toward the stables, though he did his best to not look like he was in a rush. The last thing he needed was some casual observer seeing him running down the street and then yelling for the authorities to come get him.

Up ahead, he saw the street that led to the stables on the left. He let out a sigh of relief when he reached the intersection and turned. *Almost there*, he thought.

The stables were nothing more than a rock barn built in the middle of the city. He'd been keeping his horse there ever since he and the others arrived years before.

It was a strange thing to be leaving his home in such a way. He pondered that thought as he pushed open the heavy wooden door and stepped inside. People he'd called friends, trusted, and even cared for were now all too eager to give up the names and locations of men they believed to be Templars.

Sebastian scanned the room in an instant and found the cart exactly where he'd left it, stowed behind a stall door with his horse.

He closed the door to the stables and entered the stall, giving his nag a rub on the nose as a greeting. When he'd served the order in battle, he'd have rather been dead than show up to a fight on that horse. But he wasn't in a war anymore, at least not a proper one. The battle he was fighting now was against shadows, betrayers, and a mutinous king and pope who'd forgotten what the order had done for them.

Sebastian winced at the thought of how many of his brethren had given their lives, spilled their lifeblood on the battlefield for men who now sought to destroy them. And for what?

He knew what.

The cart was loaded with it.

He hurriedly hooked the cart to his horse and finished making preparations. Then he stepped out of the stall and propped the door open so the animal could pass through, giving a click to urge the horse along.

The animal had only taken two steps when Sebastian felt something sharp poke him in the middle of his back.

"Don't move, Sebastian," the nasally voice said.

He didn't have to turn around to know who it was. The stable master, a man named Beauregard, had been hiding in the shadows, waiting for his moment to be a hero to church and crown.

Sebastian twisted his head and glanced over his shoulder. "You don't want to do this, Beau," he said.

"Oh, but I do. They told me what you and your kind are really up to. Witchcraft, sorcery, magic. I've heard the rumors about how your order worships the dark one in secret chambers. They say he's the one who gives you your power. Now, it seems almighty God will have his revenge."

"You believed those lies?" Sebastian asked. "You think that's what we do? We served the pope. Thousands of men died for him and for God. What sense would that make for us to change sides?"

The question caught the stable keeper off guard, but he didn't flinch, not yet.

"I don't know. And I don't care."

Of course he didn't—because he was getting paid, most likely. "How many pieces of silver did they give you, Beau? More than thirty, I hope."

That question threw the other man off as well. "A man has to eat, no?"

"True."

"Now put your hands up where I can see them. Do it slowly."

"You don't have to do this, Beau. You can let me leave, and no one will know."

Beauregard snorted. "I get way more than silver if I turn you in, Sebastian. I promise you that."

Sebastian raised his hands slowly, letting his cloak fall over his back. The sword on his hip hung in full view of the stable master. He breathed calmly through his nostrils. It wasn't the first time Sebastian had been held at the tip of a sword. He'd stared down far worse situations in the past.

But Sebastian knew better than to underestimate an opponent. He wouldn't go easy on Beauregard, but it pained him to consider killing the man that he'd come to call a friend over the years. Clearly, that friendship was only as thick as a dew falling on a fallow field.

"You don't want to do this," Sebastian repeated.

The look on Beau's face was borderline demonic, like he wasn't in control of his own body anymore, possessed by some other-worldly being. His crooked, stained teeth brandished like a wild dog, and Sebastian was pretty sure the guy was salivating, or about to.

"Oh, but I do," Beau said. "All my life, I've been working in places like this. Not anymore. They promised me enough money to buy my way out of this hole."

Sebastian could hear the Inquisitors' horses thundering toward the stables. The hooves on cobblestone and mud grew louder as the group drew near.

Up to that point, Sebastian had been stalling the stable master. Knowing the man enjoyed hearing the sound of his own voice, the plan was to keep him talking until he gave up an opening, a weakness Sebastian could exploit to end the fight quickly and, despite Beau not deserving it, mercifully.

Now Sebastian would have to force the issue. His mind had

already played out how Beauregard would die. That much was a given.

But the Inquisitors would be a different scenario. The outcome was uncertain. There was no way to know how many there were in their horde or what weapons they carried. That and several other factors would play into the coming fight.

Sebastian learned long ago that when he didn't know the strength of the enemy, he should rely on his own strengths to defeat them. He knew what he had at his disposal: his sword (currently still in the scabbard), his bow and several quivers of arrows in the cart and of course, the chests. He also had his horse, but the nag wasn't built for speed like his battle steed. That was something he'd have to remedy when he got to the next town. Buying a second horse for situations like this would probably be a good idea.

The hooves clopping outside built to a crescendo and then slowed.

Beauregard's sickly grin widened. "Looks like our futures have arrived."

The last mistake he made was letting his eyes twitch toward the front door. Sebastian's sword was out of its sheath in a fraction of a second. The perpetually sharp edge sliced through the stable master's wrist, dropping the severed hand to the floor along with the man's weapon.

Beau's eyes flashed wide as he looked down at the bloody stump. It happened so fast that his nerves hadn't even registered the pain yet.

He was about to scream when the blade slashed through his neck. His body shifted back and forth for a second before the head toppled to the floor. The legs gave out then, and his body collapsed.

Several sudden knocks came at the door.

"Beauregard!" a man shouted. "It's me! Let us in!"

The door was locked. Thankfully, the dead stable master hadn't planned on the Inquisitors showing up so soon. Or maybe the guy was just forgetful. Either way, it bought Sebastian more time than he needed.

He swiftly hopped up onto the cart and grabbed his bow and two quivers of arrows. Between that, his sword, and the dagger at his side, he was armed to the teeth. But would it be enough?

Battle was never certain, even for one of the most powerful warriors in the world. There were things he could do to improve his chances, but there were no guarantees.

He'd already seen the ladder to his left that led to the barn's second floor. Sebastian hurried up the rungs, doing his best not to make a sound as he ascended to the higher level. Up there, he'd have the advantage and be able to use the building's main floor as a kill box. He could see into every stable except the ones he was standing over, but if an enemy were to try to get in there to hide, he'd simply maneuver around and get a clear line of sight on the other side of the platform.

The heavy wooden door shuddered again as the man outside pounded it with his fist.

Then everything fell silent. Sebastian knew what was about to happen.

He didn't flinch when the door nearly exploded open. The Inquisitors poured into the room a second later, one of them holding a heavy wooden log carved to look like it had a lion's head. The men charged forward until they saw the headless body on the floor.

One of the men stepped through the door and stopped short at the sight of Beauregard's head at his feet.

The man had a thick, brown mane flowing down onto his shoulders. His skin wasn't like that of the rest of his men. They all had the same pale complexion of most people in this region. While their armor and uniforms were the same, there was no question that this guy wasn't from around here.

Sebastian eyed him warily from his hiding place above. He already had three arrows in his left hand and set about nocking one of them with deadly silent care. There was no question in Sebastian's mind who the leader of this group was. And he had a good idea exactly *what* the man was.

The feud had started years before, a struggle for power between the two most elite fighting forces the world had ever known. The

Christian world produced the Knights Templar. The other side had produced a counter, a group renowned for their stealth, their cunning, and their ruthlessness.

Their name struck fear in the hearts of the weak. It caused people in positions of power to lose sleep. Men had gone mad at the thought of one of these warriors sneaking into their chamber at night and ending their lives without so much as a flutter of air.

He was a member of the Order of Assassin.

Sebastian fought back the anger inside him. He forced discipline to take over. The sight of the Assassin challenged his will to remain calm, but it wasn't the first time he'd seen one. It might not be the last.

Sebastian counted a dozen men, including the leader. He'd faced tougher odds before, though not by much.

The odds would improve soon.

He ducked behind a wooden stall as the Assassin looked up into the second level, scanning the area for any sign of the rogue knight.

His eyes panned beyond Sebastian's position, and the knight pulled back on the bowstring. He could let the men go and assume he'd already left, but he didn't think that would happen. They would search the room; that much was certain. The awkward stalemate was at the Assassin's choosing. He wanted Sebastian to know he was aware of his presence. Sebastian could sense it, like the guy was begging for a fight, thirsting for the adrenaline rush that battle would bring.

No, there would be no letting this brigand and his little band go. They'd done enough to warrant death. How many of Sebastian's brethren had died at their hands or as a result of their actions? If he let them leave, more would perish. He would die here and now if it would save the lives of others.

Then he remembered his mission. He couldn't get shortsighted now. The chests under him, loaded on the cart, were more important than any knight's life.

Suddenly, the Assassin stepped toward the cart. Something had caught the man's eye.

Sebastian drew a long, deep breath and pushed the air out through his mouth. The enemy leader was moving toward the cart. There was no way the knight would let the Assassin lay his filthy hands on his charge. The time for hiding was over.

Sebastian stood up, took aim, and loosed the arrow.

1

Sean stared at the two men's eyes, not at the pistols in their hands. He'd learned long ago that the eyes would give away intention much sooner than any other part of the body. The eyes, Sean knew, would tell him everything he wanted to know about what these guys were going to do.

He'd been chasing down leads for the last ten days, hot on the trail of the lost treasure of the Old West outlaw Jesse James. All the clues had led him to this patch of land on the outskirts of town.

Situated in the heartland of America, Centralia was a small place with only four or five thousand people living in the vicinity. It was surrounded by farms that spanned the rolling plains between Saint Louis and Kansas City.

Sean had seen the two men coming. What he hadn't expected was trouble, the kind that came with two handguns and a pair of menacing faces.

"I'm sorry, guys. Am I trespassing or something?"

Neither said anything.

Their faces were awash with the look of death. Their eyes blinked. Their nostrils flared. Their chests rose and fell. But they looked more like the walking dead than anything else, zombies programmed by a maker who now controlled them from afar.

Both men wore blue jeans and light windbreakers. Their heads were shaved almost clean. Sean imagined they would have been a few days ago but hadn't had access to a razor in at least forty-eight hours.

While a million questions spun in his mind, he knew none of them mattered. The biggest one—who were these guys?—kept resurfacing, and he had to push it away to focus on the moment.

"Look," Sean said, "I'm sorry. I honestly didn't know this was your property. I thought it was public land."

Then he saw the slightest movement in the eyes of the man on the right. If he'd had time, Sean would have sighed. He knew what was coming next. The men were a good ten feet away. Close enough to be unmissable if everything remained unchanged.

Sean knew he didn't have a choice but to change it.

The flinch in the man's eye was a dead giveaway, the precursor to a trigger being squeezed. He's seen it a hundred times, probably more. Sean knew he had less than a second before the firing would begin. The bullets would tear through his body and vital organs. He didn't waste a moment wondering if they'd leave his corpse there in the field next to an outcropping of trees or dig a hole to bury it. That didn't matter because Sean knew his wouldn't be the dead body.

He felt the weight of the pistol hanging inside his jacket, slung over a shoulder in a holster. The cool spring air brushed over him, flicking a loose strand of scraggly hair against his ear. A crow cawed in the trees to his back.

Sean felt and heard everything.

Then he moved.

He dove to his right and rolled as the man on the right fired his weapon. Sean dug his hand into his jacket as he hit the ground and pulled out the Springfield .40-cal. He kept rolling in the tall grass and extended the weapon. The two men were more difficult to see through the green strands. He found a dark outline and squeezed the trigger. His muzzle popped with a flash. The man who'd been on the right yelped as the round smashed through the side of his leg, tearing muscle and tissue, and battering the bone within.

The guy dropped to the ground, out of sight for the moment.

The other man moved quickly and deftly, like a seasoned special operations agent would. Sean had seen it before. Heck, he moved like that himself. Maybe not so quickly anymore, but when he was in his prime he had. Pushing forty had changed things a little.

Age was just a number, he'd told himself. But that number seemed to have a very real effect on his abilities.

He sprang from his hiding spot among the weeds and looked around. The second gunman was nowhere to be seen. He, too, apparently, was using the grass for cover. Sean spun around in a circle and found his opponent. The gunman raised his weapon and fired. Sean dove back down to the ground and rolled again. He felt something hit his right arm and turned to see the first gunman still writhing in pain next to him.

Panic flooded the man's face when he realized he was right beside the target. He lifted his gun to put a bullet in Sean's head, but Sean was quicker. He grabbed the man's wrist as the weapon let out a thunderous boom. The sound was deafening, especially at such close range, but Sean didn't let it weaken him. He didn't grab his ears to stop the ringing.

He twisted the man's wrist as the guy tried to grab the weapon with his free hand, but Sean used his own pistol and rammed the butt of it against the man's temple. The enemy's arms went limp, and the head fell to the side, eyes closed against the bright light of the sun.

Sean pushed himself up to a crouch and swept the area with his pistol. The questions were coming faster now. Who were these guys? What did they want? Why were they trying to kill him?

The truth was, it could have been any number of former enemies coming after him. He'd done a fantastic job through the years of pissing people off. That tended to happen when you got in the way of an evil plan. Typically, the bad guys ended up dead. Now and then, though, one got away. Those were the ones that caused Sean to wake in the middle of the night with pistol drawn, aiming at shadows.

He suppressed the questions once more and forced himself to focus all his attention on finding the second gunman.

Sean caught a slight movement ahead of him to the right. The guy was trying to flank him, moving around low to get the jump on Sean.

That wasn't going to happen.

Sean stood up and aimed his weapon. He fired three shots, pummeling the guy with every round. At such a short range, there was little risk a pro like Sean would miss. The years he'd spent working for the government—the training, the missions for the ultra secret Axis agency—ensured his shots would hit the mark.

The gunman groaned and collapsed.

Sean stalked over to his prey, wading through the tall grass. He kept his pistol on the guy, watching him to make sure he wasn't playing dead to get a cheap, point-blank kill shot.

The man wasn't playing dead. He was tossing around in the weeds, clutching his wounds as blood leaked through his fingers. If he received medical attention, the man would live. At least that was Sean's quick-and-dirty field assessment. There was no way to know for sure. One round had struck the man's hip. Another had pierced his shoulder. The third round had struck him in the side. That last one was the bullet Sean was worried about. Lots of organs just behind that layer of skin and tissue.

He was no physician, but he'd seen enough wounds like that to know. Sometimes the victim lived, and sometimes they didn't.

Sean wasn't going to execute the man. He had too many questions that needed answers.

He nudged the gunman's good shoulder and forced him over onto his back.

The guy grimaced in agony as he rolled over. Sean used his other boot to step on the man's gun, making sure he wouldn't try anything stupid.

"Who are you?" Sean asked bluntly. He pointed his barrel straight down at the guy's face. Sean was standing directly in the sunlight, making him look like nothing more than a silhouette, haunting and monstrous.

The guy said nothing.

"I'm going to ask you again," Sean said, "and I want answers. If you don't give them to me, I can make the pain you're in right now feel like a Sunday drive in the country. Do you understand?"

The guy swallowed and gave a slight nod.

"You know who I am, obviously, so you know what I'm capable of. Yes?"

Another nod.

"Good. Then we understand each other. Now, that bullet in your shoulder and the one in your hip won't kill you. You probably won't ever play pickup basketball again, but you won't die from those. The one in your side, however, is a different story. Maybe it hit your stomach. Or possibly an artery or something else in there that's important. Without medical attention, there's no way to know."

"I'll tell you nothing." The man's voice was grim, determined.

Sean had heard that before, just before they begged to tell him whatever he wanted to know.

He shook his head. "That's a shame. I thought we had an understanding. Now I have to make it hurt more, and I really don't want to do that."

"There is nothing you can do to me that I can't bear."

The guy was brave. Sean had to give him that. Or maybe he was just stupid. Funny how those two things were so often confused.

Sean hesitated, holding the weapon loose in his fingers. He didn't like doing this. It was one of many reasons he'd left Axis, despite the director begging him to stay.

The more he thought about it, the angrier he became. Centralia was a small town. By most people's accounts, it was in the middle of nowhere, surrounded by farms. How these guys found him there was a mystery, but it was one that fed the fire in Sean's gut. He couldn't even take a personal trip to the heartland of the country without getting shot at.

The trigger tensed under the pressure of his finger. The man's kneecap was dead within the weapon's sights.

Knees were a favorite among anyone who'd ever sought to deal extraordinary pain to another, no matter the reason. Whether they were shattered with a sledgehammer or blasted to pieces by a bullet, kneecaps were one of the few certainties in the world Sean came from. It was ironic, he'd thought many times before, that the criminal underworld used similar tactics. Such was the way of things, and one more reason he was running from that life.

In the years since leaving the Axis agency, he'd only done one mission for Emily, the agency's director. He told her he would help her whenever she needed it, despite the deepest desire in his heart not to, because it felt like a sin to keep talents like his in the closet. The world was full of wicked people, people that needed to be eliminated.

He'd thought of an argument against that justification once before, against the notion was that he was playing God, making decisions for others and playing the role of judge, jury, and executioner.

It was a feeble argument: that the men he'd terminated in the past were trying to hurt the innocent. They were the ones trying to play God, or the devil, in their cases. What had to be done, however, always trumped any other argument.

This one at his feet was no different.

They'd attempted to get the drop on Sean and take him out without so much as a fair fight. As he stared down at the man wincing in pain, Sean wondered how many more times this would happen. Who else in the world wanted him dead? There was no way to know. He hoped there weren't any more. Sean also knew that was a vain desire, nothing more than a fleeting wish.

Sean peered into the man's eyes. He could see the resolve. Sean could put a bullet into the guy's tarsals, his shins, knees, and keep working his way up until the man either blacked out from the pain or died from his other wounds. None of it would matter. This dude wasn't saying a thing.

Then he caught a glimpse of something on the man's skin. It was barely visible below the sleeve. Sean loosened his trigger finger and used the toe of his boot to pull back the fabric.

On the inside of his wrist, just above the joint where his forearm met his hand, was a tattoo.

Sean's forehead wrinkled. He twisted his head around to make sure the other guy was still unconscious. Satisfied the other gunman was still down for the count, Sean returned his focus to the ink on the second man's arm.

He knew better than to ask what it was. There would be no answer.

Sean had seen his fair share of tattoos. Many of the former military men and women he'd worked with in the past had several. Then there were the years he'd spent in bars. It had become the en vogue thing to do in the late 1990s and carried on until the present. This, however, was unique.

The design looked like the letter *A*. Instead of the bridge in the center of the letter, however, there was a curved emblem, a tongue of flame perhaps. The right arm of the letter swooped down and bent up at a slight angle, wider at the top than at the bottom. Sean's frown deepened. He'd seen this design before.

"Where did you get this?" Sean asked.

The man spat in response. The spittle just missed Sean's boot.

To a normal person, the act might have incited an angry, violent response. Indeed, Sean's instincts told him to kick the guy in the ribs or shoot him right there. He ignored the temptation, instead leaning over the guy with a determined, almost sinister look in his eyes.

"I have seen this before," he said. "Where did you get it?"

The man's dark eyes narrowed. A sickly grin crossed his lips. "If you had seen this, you'd already be dead."

"That a fact?"

Sean stepped around to the man's left side. The guy watched him closely, wondering what was coming next. He probably expected to receive a bullet to the head. That wasn't going to happen. Killing the insolent man would be useless. Sean had questions, and dead people weren't the best at giving answers, not without a forensics unit around.

"Have a nice nap," Sean said.

The man flashed a puzzled look a second before Sean reared his foot back and struck him in the temple. The guy's head drooped into the grass, and Sean watched him for a moment to make certain he was out.

Satisfied both assailants were unconscious, Sean pulled his phone out of a pocket and found Emily's name in the contact list.

He held the phone to his ear. It only took two rings for her to answer.

"What prison and which country?" she asked.

Sean snickered. "I'm not in prison. And I'm in the States."

"Oh? So, you looking for a job?"

She'd bugged him forever about coming back. He figured that would never stop. "No, but thanks for the offer."

"I wasn't offering."

"Sure you weren't." Sean flashed a sarcastic grin he wished she could see. "I'm in Centralia, Missouri."

There was a momentary pause. "What are you doing out there? Trying to get off the grid? You in some kind of trouble?"

"Well...."

"It's always something with you, isn't it?"

He shook his head and rechecked the two men. They were still out cold.

"I need a lift."

She let out a sigh. "What happened? Car break down?"

"No. It's not for me. I have two packages that need to be picked up. One of them needs medical attention."

"They both alive?" She immediately understood what he was saying. Years of working together made sure of that.

"Yeah, but one of them is in rough shape."

"Who are they?"

Sean stared down at the tattoo on the guy's wrist, still trying to place where he'd seen it before. "That's what I'm hoping you can help me figure out."

2

ATLANTA

The door opened and Emily walked into her office. The clock on the wall ticked incessantly, which was one of the reasons she did her paperwork with plugs in her ears.

Sean was sitting in one of two leather chairs across from her desk. He'd been there for a half hour, heading to her office after getting her call.

The day before, Emily's people had arrived on the scene within twenty minutes. Paramedics had made sure the man with the stomach wound would survive before he'd been bound and placed in an ambulance with his partner.

After being stabilized in a Kansas City hospital, the men were moved to a more discreet location in Atlanta, with higher levels of security. There were also no prying eyes, and the doctors were on the Axis payroll to ensure no information on the identity or condition of the patients was leaked.

Emily maintained a tight ship; that was certain. She wasn't a micromanager, but she had eyes and ears in place that would give her instant updates if anything went wrong. If something happened to one or both of the prisoners, she'd know how, why, where, and who had done it.

Axis answered only to the president, an ultra-secret agency formed during the Cold War to combat espionage and terrorism. Most of the public didn't know about Axis. Emily intended it to always stay that way.

She eased into her seat and crossed one leg over her knee, then folded her fingers, intertwining them with one another. "Can't seem to stay out of trouble, can you?" she said.

He shrugged and put his hands out wide. "It's what I do."

Sean didn't have to ask for an update. He knew she'd tell him what was going on. From the look on her face, he assumed she'd been unable to get anything useful out of the men.

"They aren't talking," she said.

He smirked. "Yeah, they wouldn't tell me anything either."

"We're running an analysis on that tattoo. Both of them have one, by the way."

Sean figured that too.

"So far, though, we don't know much about them." She exhaled and placed her folded hands on the desk. "They don't have any criminal records, not that we can tell. No matches on their fingerprints."

"That's a tad strange. Don't you think?" He raised an eyebrow with the question.

"It can be. Not really, though. You know that. Most of these international criminal types don't carry ID."

"True," Sean agreed. "How'd they get there? They able to fly or something?"

Emily rolled her eyes. "That theory notwithstanding, we're going to keep working on it. Found an abandoned car nearby. It was rented under a false name, most likely. Our new facial analysis software should be able to pull up something from Interpol. If not, we have a few other tricks up our sleeve. We'll figure it out one way or the other."

Sean wasn't convinced, but he didn't let on. Since getting on the plane to come back to Atlanta, he'd been visualizing the tattoo on the guy's wrist. Where had he seen it before? That question had rattled him the rest of the day and all through the night until he'd fallen into a shallow, troubled sleep.

He knew about the tech Axis had at their disposal. He also didn't have many doubts about Emily's team figuring out who the men were. The problem was who they worked *for*. Their identities didn't mean much in the grand scheme of things. They were goons, nothing more. Dangerous goons but goons nonetheless. Sean doubted it was a case of two guys out for revenge. The people out in the world who wanted him dead wouldn't have been so careful, so calculating. And it was unlikely they would have been able to locate him in the middle of nowhere.

The only people who knew he was in Missouri were Tommy and his lab/field assistants, Alex and Tara—affectionately known as the kids—and Adriana, although she'd been out of touch lately. It had been a week since they'd spoken, which wasn't unusual. It did, however, cause a deep longing in his chest.

Sean missed her, everything about her. While they led separate lives much of the time, the moments he was able to spend with her were his favorite. He wondered what piece of art she was chasing down in some foreign country. As he considered the question, he said a silent prayer for her safety.

"I'll leave you and the rest of your experts to it, then," Sean said and stood up.

"That's it?" Emily's eyebrows knit together. "I thought maybe you'd hang out for a while. We could get lunch in a half hour if you like."

"Thanks, Em. I appreciate it, but I need to get over to HQ. I have a few things I'd like to discuss with Tommy."

Her analytical eyes pored over him. "First of all, *this* is HQ. Second, are you telling him you're coming back to work here?"

Sean cracked a smile. "Love you, Em. Give me a call when you have something."

He didn't look back as he left the room. He didn't have to. He knew the look on her face. She was probably curling her lips and shaking her head, a second before she resumed her normal spy activities, whatever they were.

The drive over to the International Archaeological Agency headquarters was a short one. He was glad Emily had moved Axis HQ to Atlanta several years before. It was far enough away from Washington to reinforce the autonomy with which they operated, but it also kept the agency out of sight and out of mind from the political ambitions and meddling of the would-be kingdom builders in the capital.

Sean parked his car along Centennial Olympic Park Drive and stepped out. The new IAA building's windows glimmered in the sunlight. It was a far cry from the old, gray building that had once stood on the same grounds—destroyed by an explosion targeting Sean and the others who worked there.

He scanned his security card at the front door and walked inside, giving the guard on duty a nod as he passed.

"Morning, Henry," he said.

"Morning, Mr. Wyatt. Baseball's coming. You excited?"

Sean and Henry had discussed the Atlanta Braves more times than either could remember. Their conversations were usually brief, due to the passing nature of their relationship. On occasion, though, they'd paused and discussed trades, pitching and hitting, and a few other aspects of the team that preoccupied true fans.

The truth was, Sean enjoyed the game—and he loved the team—but his hopes weren't high for the upcoming season.

"I told you to call me Sean, Henry. And yeah, it should be a fun year." He lied, thinking the team would underachieve once again.

"I hope you're right, Sean."

"That's better. Mr. Wyatt is my father."

Sean hated the line as soon as it passed through his lips. He detested using clichés, but that one had slipped out. And it was true: Sean didn't yet feel like an "old man." Not like Henry.

"Have a good day, sir," the older man said.

"You too, Henry."

Sean made his way to Tommy's office but found it empty. He

knew that usually meant his friend was down in the lab with the kids, although Tara and Alex had recently been out in the field considerably more than in the past. Tommy felt like it was good for them to get out and see the world, to feel the history they were helping to make. Neither Sean nor Tommy had any concerns about the two handling themselves if things turned sour on a mission.

They were both accomplished marksmen and were more than capable in hand-to-hand combat.

Sean reflected on how they'd made a judgment call a few years back, flown to Japan, and saved his and Tommy's skin at a mountaintop monastery.

Down in the bowels of the building, Sean pushed through a glass door after pressing his thumb to a print scanner. Security in the building had been tightened after a recent attempted break-in. There were more points of entry, each with a different method of verifying who was trying to get in.

It was slightly annoying but understandable. One could never be too careful when it came to protecting some of the most secret and mysterious artifacts in the world. That's why, after all, so many governments and private entities trusted the IAA.

Sean saw Tommy and the other two across the room and made his way through the maze of desks, tables, and countertops.

Tommy was staring down at a small piece of pottery on a desk when he caught a glimpse of his friend approaching.

"Why can't you use the clean-room entry?" Tommy asked, irritated. "That's why we put it in." He stood up straight, crossed his arms, and shot his friend a disparaging glare.

"If you want that to be the only way in, why don't you take out this side door then?" Sean's question was both funny *and* true.

Tommy rolled his eyes. "Vacation to the heartland get cut short?"

"I...ran into some trouble."

"I heard."

Sean stopped next to where his friend and the kids, who were in their late twenties, were working. Sean and Tommy were convinced something romantic was going on between them, but there was no way to confirm it. Besides, it wasn't any of their business.

Sean looked surprised. "You heard, huh? Emily tell you?"

"Maybe," his friend said with a grin.

Sean shook his head. "She can't keep her mouth shut."

"She also said you're leaving me to go back to work for her."

"All these years, and she still won't let it go."

Tommy rolled his shoulders. "I guess she thinks you're good at what you do. I keep trying to tell her you're not, but she won't listen."

Sean chuckled at the barb and turned to Tara and Alex, who were meticulously brushing debris off the clay shard. A stone tablet sat off to the side, carved with a script unlike anything Sean had ever seen.

"What's this? You guys doing actual archaeology stuff?"

They grinned.

Tommy scowled. "You're hilarious," he said.

"That's kind of part of our company name, right?" Tara answered.

Alex looked up. "Hey, did you find anything out in Missouri? I mean other than trouble."

"Ha ha," Sean said. "Sometimes I wonder why we don't just take this show on the road and hit every comedy club in the country." He paused for a second. "And no, I didn't find anything. Kind of left in a hurry."

"That's a shame."

"Yeah, although I did come back with something." Sean reached into his jacket and pulled out a printout of a picture. He set it on the table, careful not to touch the stuff they'd been working on.

The other three crowded around and looked at the image of a man's wrist with a strange tattoo on it.

"What's that?" Tommy asked.

"A tattoo," Sean said.

"Solid burn, Sean," Tara remarked. "Whose is it?"

"Not sure. That's why I brought it to you guys."

Alex looked up in surprise. "Well, it's gonna be kind of difficult to pinpoint an identity with nothing more than a tattoo. That's not really what we do here."

Sean snorted a laugh. "I'm well aware. No, I am wondering if any of you guys recognize the design. It looks familiar, but I can't place what it is or where I might have seen it."

Tommy bent down to get a closer look while his associates examined the image.

"Sure seems like something I've seen before," Tommy said. "I'll have to do some looking around."

"You guys?" Sean asked the other two.

They both shook their heads.

"No," Alex said, "but whoever the artist was did a good job. The lines are clean, ink is dark, no smudging, no fading. If I had to guess, I'd say it was new."

Sean listened and considered the comment, not that it was extremely helpful. He hadn't come here for their critical opinions on skin art.

"Well, I'll be in my office if you need me. I'm going to figure out what this is."

"You know, Sean," Tommy said, "it might just be a design he came up with. People get tattoos. Lots of people, in fact. It's kind of the in thing to do these days. I see random stuff on people's arms, necks, you name it, all the time. Doesn't have to mean anything."

Sean had thought the same thing at first. His friend was right on that count. People came up with all kinds of wild ideas they paid to have drawn on them in permanent ink. This, however, was different.

"I would agree with you except for one important fact."

The other three looked at him with expectant eyes.

"Which is?" Tommy prodded.

"Both of them had the same tattoo, like it was a brand or something."

"Maybe they're brothers?" Tara asked. "Or it could be a friendship thing."

Those were both ideas Sean had considered as well. He'd blown it off. There was more to these guys than met the eye.

"Possibly," he relented. "But they didn't look much like brothers, in spite of their similar haircuts. I don't think those dudes are related."

"Dudes?" Tommy asked.

Sean ignored his friend. "Like I said, I'll be in the office if you need me. Take a look at that when you're done...brushing that piece of clay or whatever it is you're doing."

"Real work, Sean," Tommy's voice escalated as Sean dipped out of the room. "You know, actual archaeology, like you said?" He snickered and shook his head.

3

WASHINGTON DC

Secretary of State Darren Sanders eased into a seat across from the Resolute Desk. He'd been in the Oval Office many times over the last three years, more times than he could count.

President John Dawkins had appointed him upon being elected for a second term after Sanders's predecessor resigned the position due to health reasons.

Sanders had been a rising star in the political arena. He was outspoken and hard-nosed, never taking any bull from anyone. That fact also made him polarizing. He had made both close friends and bitter enemies within days of setting foot in Washington. While Dawkins didn't always agree with Sanders politically, he appreciated strong leadership and felt Sanders wasn't one who could be pushed around, bought or sold.

A kid from the streets of Chicago, he'd fashioned himself into a kind of political force, defying the odds in what many deemed almost miraculous. Some believed he was too ambitious. But Sanders always responded with the same line: "Ambition is necessary for progress."

President Dawkins was a firm but fair kind of guy, while Sanders leaned heavily on the firm part. And if fair happened to come along for the ride? Well, that was a happy bonus. So far, their joint carrot-

and-stick approach to foreign relations had brought real dividends for the nation.

Nobility wasn't something his position could afford. It called for strength, unrelenting decisiveness, and an ironclad will. He'd advised the president on several occasions in regards to tactical strikes on enemy strongholds in Afghanistan, Iraq, and across Southwest Asia. Each time, Sanders knew there would be civilian casualties. And each time, he was forced to lie to the president about that very fact.

Dawkins wasn't a bleeding heart, but he wasn't a callous leader either. He never wanted to be responsible for the deaths of innocent people. He realized there would be collateral damage whenever he ordered a strike somewhere in the world, but keeping civilian casualties to a minimum was a high priority.

Some presidents in the past had viewed civilian losses as inevitable, an unfortunate and unavoidable effect of war. Not Dawkins. He did his best to understand every target inside and out before issuing the order. Bombing a weapons cache could deal heavy damage to a terrorist organization, but Dawkins didn't want to kill an innocent janitor working the midnight shift in the process.

Sanders couldn't care less about some random custodian. Keeping Americans safe was more important. If someone didn't want to die in a tactical hit, maybe they shouldn't live in a country that harbored terrorists.

He looked down at his watch for the third time since arriving. Like most powerful men, Sanders didn't appreciate being kept waiting, even if it was for the president of the United States.

Today, however, Sanders exercised an extra measure of patience. The president had called him the night before, requesting a meeting at 8:30 the next morning. Sanders knew Dawkins had a press conference scheduled an hour after that, so he assumed the meeting would be a short one, though he had his suspicions as to what their engagement regarded.

Sanders made no secret he wanted this office to be his.

He'd set his sights squarely on the presidency long before coming to Washington. Sanders craved power, and the office of president of the United States was the most powerful position in the free world.

Now and then, a flutter of doubt crept into his gut, causing him to question whether or not he'd be satisfied with the position. He quickly dispelled the notion, telling himself that once he was at the top of the mountain, he would finally sit back in that beautiful chair across from him, sip a bourbon, and soak it in.

It was no accident Sanders had been appointed Secretary of State. He'd made himself as visible as possible to Dawkins, catching his eye early on during the president's first term in Washington. He'd made some brash moves, said some things he knew would catch flack in the press but that Dawkins would get behind.

The two had got along almost immediately. Sanders backed Dawkins on every front, speaking out against some of his colleagues in the Senate even though it made a dangerous circle of enemies.

Sanders didn't care. He had one goal, and he knew the easiest path to reaching it was through the position of secretary of state. At least that's what history told him.

Dawkins's second term was almost up. Sanders had been a loyal adviser, at times feeling more like a lackey than anything, but it was all for one cause, a cause he believed was the reason for this meeting.

Rumors swirled about who Dawkins would back to be the next president. Most of the pundits were giving it to the vice president. Sanders scoffed at the notion.

The vice president was one of the weakest men he'd ever met. Born to a wealthy family in Massachusetts, Theodore Hollingsworth had never worked a day in his life. At least that's what Sanders believed. Hollingsworth hadn't been tempered like forged steel the way Sanders had. He would be a pathetically weak leader. Calling him a leader at all was a liberal use of the term. No, Hollingsworth wouldn't be president. That much Sanders knew. Dawkins wasn't stupid.

Everything was starting to fall in place for Darren Sanders, and today was going to be his moment. What other reason could the president have for calling this meeting?

Dawkins was going to tell Sanders that he was about to receive his endorsement for the presidency.

The public, for the most part, would approve. They were tired of people with no political experience. That was one of the reasons Dawkins had won his first term. He understood Washington, knew how to navigate the political land mines. Sanders had absorbed all of that knowledge and used it well.

One of the doors opened and a Secret Service agent stepped through. The man scanned the room for two seconds before stepping aside and letting the president walk by.

Sanders stood up and forced an uneasy smile while shaking Dawkins's hand.

"Mr. President," Sanders said.

"Thanks for meeting me, Darren, on such short notice. Please," he motioned to the seat the secretary had just been in, "sit."

"Yes, sir."

Sanders played the servant role to a T. He wasn't a yes man, not by any stretch. But he knew all the buttons to push, all the levers to pull, and when to step aside and let the boss pretend.

"I guess you're probably wondering why I requested this meeting," Dawkins said as he slipped around behind his desk and eased into his chair. He folded his hands in front of his chest.

Sanders downplayed the comment, acting like he was clueless. He rolled his shoulders. "I figured it was probably about the rumors coming out of North Korea."

Dawkins flashed a short grin and shook his head, almost as if the statement amused him. "The North Koreans don't concern me. I understand we have to keep an eye on them and all that, but they're still in the dark ages when it comes to...well, pretty much everything. Their people are starving. They have no energy. Natural resources are dwindling. It's only a matter of time until they collapse."

"Or until they lash out, sir."

The president cocked his head to the side for a second. He jabbed a finger at Sanders. "That's why I love you, Darren. You're no-

nonsense, cautious, always aware of the dangers ahead. We make a good team. And it's been an honor working with you."

"Thank you, sir. The honor is mine as well."

"Don't worry about the North Koreans. We always have eyes on them. If they do anything stupid, we'll make them pay for it."

Sanders had no doubt the president meant what he said.

"But, no," Dawkins continued, "that's not why I called you in this morning. I requested this meeting because I wanted to let you know who I plan to recommend for this office during the next election." He put his hands out wide as if showing off the room to a first-time visitor.

This was it. It was the moment Sanders had been waiting for since he could remember. He'd climbed from the ditch into the penthouse. Adrenaline coursed through his veins. He wasn't one given to anxiety or nerves, but now he had to fight to keep his hands from trembling. Butterflies fluttered in his gut. Finally, he would achieve his life's goal. He would be the most powerful man in the world.

The opposing party was still weak, scrambling to find a candidate that would appear suitable to the population. They were in disarray, though, a shambled collection of squabbling idiots who couldn't agree on anything, much less who they would nominate.

The media had had a field day with them nearly every single morning for the last six months. The mere fact that their party hadn't decided on a leading candidate yet, with less than a year to go to Election Day, spoke volumes and told the public that they were no longer a viable option.

Dawkins leaned forward, placing his folded hands on the Resolute Desk. "I've given this a lot of consideration, prayed about it, and there is one clear choice. The American people deserve a strong leader. I hope I've been that for them over the last seven odd years."

"You have, Mr. President." Sanders said the words even as he tried to push back a smile, keeping his poker face on as he usually did.

"I appreciate that, Darren. It's that kind of unselfish, honorable support that the world's leaders need. And that's why you're here. I want to ask for your support in the upcoming election."

Support? What did he mean support? A sickening feeling crept into his gut, replacing the nerves that were there a moment before.

"I am going to endorse Speaker of the House Alycia Freeman to be the next president of the United States."

The words hit Sanders like a sledgehammer straight to his chest.

"I'm sorry, sir? The Speaker?" He did his best to sound composed but couldn't help feeling like he'd just asked the love of his life to the prom and been rejected.

"She's a good woman, Darren. And she'll need a good man behind her. That's why I want you to be her running mate. I want you to be the vice president of the United States. She could use someone like you, and I know that you'll be an invaluable asset."

Sanders swallowed hard. He glanced down at the carpet for a second, trying to collect his thoughts and calm his raging emotions. His street instincts from long ago begged him to leap across the desk and beat the man senseless. The Speaker of the House? Why?

Over the last three years, Sanders had done everything the president asked. Meanwhile, Freeman had gone against him dozens of times, often in public. Many in the media claimed their rivalry was deeply rooted. Sanders hadn't paid much attention to the talking heads. Now he wished differently.

The Speaker of the House? The question kept pummeling his brain. It didn't make any sense.

Dawkins was still talking, though the words were muted, unclear in Sanders's ears. "I know that Alycia and I haven't always agreed, but she's a strong leader and will make a fine president, especially with someone like you behind her."

Sanders swallowed hard again and gave a slow, dazed nod. "Yes, sir. I...I don't know what to say." He wasn't lying. He didn't have a clue what to say next. He wanted to yell at the president, tell him he was a fool for not choosing him. Sanders felt the obvious answer was to back him for the office, not the Speaker of the House.

Dawkins's face lengthened, turning almost grave. "Darren? Are you okay?"

"Yes, sir. I...it's just a lot to take in."

"I realize that this is a big step, but I believe you're ready."

It's not a big step, you idiot, Sanders thought. Surely, the leader of the free world couldn't be that stupid. He had to know Sanders was aiming for the Oval Office.

"I...I appreciate it, sir," Sanders managed. "I suppose you'll be making the announcement this morning regarding the Speaker."

Dawkins gave a kind nod. "That is correct. And with your permission, I'd like to recommend you to her myself. I've already spoken to her about my endorsement, and she accepted."

"Thank you, sir. I'm honored."

Sanders stood up and reached across the desk. The president stood and shook his hand vigorously.

"You're going to do well in this new role, Darren. I know it."

Sanders forced a nod of the head. "Well, you have a speech to get ready for, so I'll show myself out. Thank you again, Mr. President."

The secretary stepped out into the next room, full of busy staff members typing memos, sending emails, talking on phones, and discussing the hundreds of issues the White House handled on a daily basis.

The room swirled in Sanders's eyes. He took a deep breath and tried to calm himself. Confusion wasn't something Sanders felt often, but right now he was drowning in it.

But anger also boiled inside him, and after a few seconds of getting his bearings, he strode through the office and stormed out.

He drove through the security checkpoint and out onto Pennsylvania Avenue, a place he'd hoped to call home. The president's actions had virtually guaranteed that would never happen. Vice presidents rarely achieved the highest office in the land. It was a blocking move, whether Dawkins realized it or not.

Maybe the man truly believed he was doing Sanders a favor. The secretary couldn't help but wonder if there was a more sinister intent to the plan.

That couldn't be.

Sanders had the complete trust of the president. He'd worked hard to ensure that through the years. Now, his reward was being placed in a position where he would rot for four to eight years. At the end, sure, maybe he could run for the presidency, but he'd be much older then, and there were no guarantees.

By then, the opposing party would likely have figured things out. It was the way the political pendulum swung in Washington. One party only stayed in control for so long.

He looked into the future Dawkins had set for him and came to one stark conclusion: Darren Sanders would never be president of the United States.

4

ATLANTA

S ean sat up in his bed. He was irritated with himself for not being able to sleep. The events of the last few days had worn him out, so falling asleep had been easy enough. Staying asleep was the issue.

It was a problem he'd had since leaving college. He figured it was anxiety related but had never bothered visiting a shrink or a doctor about it. He treated it with any number of over-the-counter herbs and supplements, but nothing seemed to work.

His dad swore by melatonin, taking up to thirty milligrams of the stuff every night before bed. Sean had given it a go, but it did little to help him stay in deep slumber.

His eyes flashed a quick glance over at the clock on the nightstand. He immediately regretted doing it. The time said 3:30. "Well, that's a few hours earlier than I planned on getting up."

He let out a sigh, pulled back the covers, and let his legs swing over the edge of the bed. A second later, he planted his feet on the cool wooden floors and forced himself up.

Sean padded down the hallway to the kitchen and flung open the stainless-steel door of his refrigerator and pulled out a jug of chocolate almond milk. He did his best to adhere to a vegan diet in most cases, a result of seeing a video about how it was a healthier way to live.

He still enjoyed a bit of cheese now and then, a steak from time to time, and once a month maybe a burger. He kept a jug of milk in the fridge for making hot chocolate with a shot of espresso, but other than that tried to stick to his diet. His doctor approved after seeing the results of his last cholesterol check.

Sean poured the thick brown liquid into a glass and took a sip. It wasn't the same as the chocolate milk he used to drink as a kid, but it was good enough and for a brief moment took him back to that simpler time.

He put the jug back in the fridge and meandered over to the breakfast nook where he'd left his laptop the night before. He plopped down on the wooden chair and flipped the computer open. A second later the screen and keyboard lit up, showing the six tabs he'd left up on the browser.

He clicked on one of the tabs and was presented with a series of images. Before finally falling into a shaky sleep five hours prior, he'd been working his way through dozens of random sites, each displaying hundreds of images of symbols, logos, emblems, and signs.

The tattoos on the two men who'd attacked him in Missouri had been on his mind nonstop for the last two days, nagging at him like a needle scratching at his skin, irritating and borderline painful.

Sean hated not knowing something. It was one of the things that drove him crazy. Little stuff he could let go, like how Native Americans kept insects off their crops three hundred years ago. This, however, was different. It felt imperative that he find the solution.

There was something more to those two gunmen than met the eye, and he wasn't about to subscribe to the notion that they were simply out for revenge, or just random guys in the wrong place at the wrong time.

No, they had been exactly where they wanted to be.

What he didn't understand is why they hadn't just taken him out from a distance. The men weren't armed with long-range weapons, just pistols. If someone wanted him dead, they could have done it with a sniper rifle. The field he'd been standing in was wide open, and a shooter could have been tucked away in the nearby forest. Sean would have never known what hit him.

Was it a tactical mistake on the part of the two gunmen, or were they simply sloppy? He didn't think it was the latter. They must have assumed he was outnumbered and wouldn't put up a fight.

There was another possibility.

They could have been looking for information before they killed him. What, though?

The two men were being held in Washington now. His questions would have to wait until he could get up there and be cleared to speak with them in one of the interrogation rooms.

He scrolled down the page, scanning the different emblems, with nothing coming up that matched what he'd seen on the men's wrists.

More than once, Sean told himself the tattoos were random designs, chosen by two men on a drunken whim. They could have wandered into a tattoo shop one night after too many drinks and decided to get matching ink.

He shook that explanation off multiple times.

These guys weren't the type to do that.

The more likely scenario was that they were part of a gang of some kind, perhaps a secret organization.

Sean clicked another tab and started scrolling through the results on that page. This tab featured images of known gang-related tattoos, mostly Crips, Bloods, and a swath of the newer Latino gangs that had plagued much of the United States in recent years. He'd had a few brushes with the latter during his time in North Georgia, though they typically weren't as violent in that part of the country. Most of their activities involved fist fights and vandalism, maybe the occasional burglary.

But gang tattoos were typically uniform. A skull, a clown face, teardrops, or in the case of Sur 13, three dots usually placed on the wrist or hand. The ink on the two men was a little more elegant, if that was a way to describe a tattoo.

Sean clicked on the next page and kept moving down, eyeing marks that were used by some of the more mysterious groups in history. He noted emblems believed to be associated with the Illuminati, the Freemasons, Knights Templar, Rosicrucians, and others. Nothing, however, matched.

He sighed and took another drink of the chocolate "milk."

He set the glass down and started scrolling again. Nothing there either. He clicked the arrow that took him to page two of the search results and found another page full of pictures. His eyes darted side to side as he worked his way down the listings. At the bottom, he clicked the arrow again.

Halfway down the third page, he stopped. His eyelids pinched together and he leaned forward. He rubbed his eyes for a second to make sure he wasn't imagining things.

There, on the right-hand side of a list of images, was the emblem he'd seen on the two men. It was a perfect match. The tattoo on the man's arm looked like the letter A with flanged legs at each end and a flame in the center in place of a bar.

Sean clicked the picture and was immediately taken to a site that featured all manner of conspiracy theories, myths about secret societies, and histories that were far from the mainstream.

A paragraph next to the image told Sean everything. It briefly described the design and its origins. Sean had to blink several times to make sure he read it correctly.

He hurriedly clicked on the mouse to open another tab and entered a new term in the search bar. A series of results popped up on the screen, and he clicked the first one.

Sean had never been a fast reader. He labored to get through two or three books a year, and that was just the fiction he enjoyed. The research stuff about history, science, and other things related to his job at IAA took longer, though sometimes he could push late into the night if working on an important project. A project like this one.

Technically, he wasn't doing this for IAA, but that didn't matter. He had to know where those guys came from, who they were, and who they worked for. If they found him once, they could do it again.

Sean pored through the paragraphs, studying each line as if he were going to be tested on it. He inspected the images that went along with the text. More than a few of them contained the same emblem the two men had tattooed on their arms.

He'd found it. The answer to the question that had been nagging at him for the last few days was finally right here in front of him.

Unfortunately, the solution didn't bring him any comfort. It brought a deeper concern bordering on worry.

Sean shook his head, still not certain if what he was seeing was accurate or not.

He clicked the back button and selected another listing from the search results. The new site featured different images, but the content was largely the same. The lines suggested the exact things the other site had.

Sean took a deep breath and let out a sigh. "That can't be," he said. "They haven't been around in centuries."

At least that's what he thought.

He'd run into enough secret societies, sects, orders, and whatever else you'd call them to know that sometimes things weren't what they seemed. Actually, they almost never were.

Sean knew better than to blow anything off at this point. He'd seen enough strange things to know that almost anything was possible, including a secret order that had been hiding underground for centuries.

It was a huge leap for most to believe that shadowy groups operated behind the scenes, pulling the world's strings to force governments and populations to do their bidding. Sean, however, had seen it firsthand, and he had a feeling he's barely scraped the surface of the rabbit hole.

This group, however, wasn't some secret handshake order hiding behind the curtain. They were killers. That was their business. While many of the other societies had, no doubt, partaken in their share of murder, the emblem on Sean's screen was connected to a group whose very name was synonymous with killing.

Assassin.

5

WASHINGTON DC

Darren Sanders dragged his feet as he trudged into the office, a full fifteen minutes after eight o'clock in the morning.

Three years in his position, he'd never once been to work late. It wasn't because some supervisor was hovering over his desk, watching to make sure he was there at 8 a.m. every day; he was the boss at State. Being on time wasn't just good policy to Sanders; it was religion.

When his watch's minute hand hit five after the hour, he started receiving text messages from his secretary, wondering where he was. It was only five minutes, but to someone like Sanders it felt like hours.

"Sir, are you okay?" His secretary, a cheery, middle-aged woman named Nancy, stood up from behind her reception desk. She wore a concerned look on her face—eyes wide and lips in a pouting frown.

"I'm fine, Nancy. Had a meeting with the president. That's all." He blew off his tardiness and made his way toward his inner office. "Hold my calls for a few minutes, will ya?"

He'd nearly reached the open door to his chamber when she stopped him. "Yes, sir, but you already have a visitor."

He froze and looked over at her. A confused expression washed over him. "What?"

"He was waiting here when I arrived this morning. Said he had to speak with you."

Sanders's frown deepened. He leaned his shoulders to the right and craned his neck so he could see into his main office. A man was sitting inside, facing the huge desk and the windows behind it. Sanders stiffened and looked back at his secretary. His eyes fired a thousand questions at her, but she knew the one answer he really wanted.

Who was this guy?

She gave a silent "I don't know," with her mouth and shrugged like there was nothing she could do.

Sanders would have to have a talk with Nancy later about her gatekeeper abilities. Maybe she was growing lax toward the end of the president's term.

He turned sluggishly toward the open door and sighed. *Fine*, he thought. *May as well see what they have to say. If it's a reporter, though, I'm going to be looking for another secretary.*

He stepped into the inner chamber and closed the door behind him. The dark-haired man in the chair didn't move, didn't flinch. He didn't even so much as turn to see Sanders come in.

"Hello, Mr. Secretary," the unexpected guest said in a smooth, accented tone.

Sanders couldn't place the accent, but he knew it wasn't from anywhere in the United States. European, if he had to guess. The country, however, was a different matter. Could have been Spain or Portugal, but a nasally hint to it made him think the guy might have been French.

"Good morning," Sanders managed the friendliest greeting he could muster.

He stepped around the desk and slipped into the chair, setting his briefcase down on the floor next to him.

He reached across the table, offering his hand. "Darren Sanders," he said. "Although you already know that. What's your name, and how can I help you today?"

The man took Sanders's hand and shook it once, then let go.

The guest's high forehead reached up to black hair that was cut close to the scalp, nearly shaved. His squashed nose gave the impression he'd been in several fights earlier in life. Maybe he'd been a boxer or some other kind of fighter. The man's slightly tanned skin caused Sanders to think he might be of Middle Eastern descent, but the accent wasn't from anywhere close to those countries.

"My name is not important, Mr. Secretary."

Sanders lowered his eyebrows, almost involuntarily. Almost. What did he mean by that? His name wasn't important? Then why in the world was he here?

"I'm sorry?" Sanders replied.

"I represent an...organization, Mr. Secretary."

"Organization? And please, don't call me that."

For three years Sanders hadn't minded being called Mr. Secretary. That was back when he knew without a shadow of a doubt that the president would pick him to be his successor. Now everything had changed.

"I apologize, Mr. Sanders. I can understand why that title would frustrate you in light of the...recent course of events."

What the...? How did this guy know about that?

Sanders decided to call his bluff. "What recent course of events?"

"The president's decision to offer his endorsement to the Speaker. We know of your designs on the White House, how you've worked your way up the ladder all these years. Your ambition is...admirable."

The man's monotone voice and unwillingness to give up his name were irritating, but the fact that he knew about Sanders's goal was disconcerting to say the least. And how did this guy know anything about what he'd done in the past, about his work, his effort, his ambition?

"I'm sorry," Sanders bluffed, "I haven't heard anything about that."

The crack in his voice said otherwise.

"Do not worry, Mr. Sanders. We have no plans to tell anyone about your goals and your overwhelming disappointment."

Okay, this was getting creepy. Sanders was about to stand up and threaten the guy, but the guest cut him off.

"What would you say if I told you we can get you what you desire most?"

The man's tone hadn't changed since he'd first spoken. It was even, cold, calculating, like he knew his host inside and out. There was something sinister about it, too. Sanders couldn't place that last part.

"What are you talking about?" Sanders asked, still playing dumb. The man couldn't be a mind reader. Sanders had told no one of his aims, not even Nancy. In the political cesspool that was Washington, she was the only person he'd confided in—typically small personal matters—usually after a passionate night in his town home. His ambitions, though, he'd kept to himself.

"There's no need to play coy, Mr. Sanders. The presidency. You want it. And we can get it for you."

There he went again. Talking about "we."

"Who is this *we* you keep mentioning?"

"Sit down, and I'll tell you a story."

Sanders frowned, momentarily refusing to do as ordered.

The guest stood up and peered at him through fiery eyes. The man was at least six feet two inches tall, towering over Sanders at five feet nine inches.

"Please. Sit," the man said again. There was the slightest hint of threat to his voice.

Sanders fumbled with the armrests as he nearly fell back into the chair. He looked more like a frightened child than one of the most powerful men in Washington.

The guest folded his hands behind his back and paced toward one of the windows to his right. He stopped and stared out of the glass at the city beyond.

He drew in a deep breath and paused. "I'm sure you are aware of the many groups and organizations around the world who meddle with the trivial matters of government, economics, and life."

Sanders's frown deepened. "What? What groups?"

"They go by many names, Mr. Sanders. Freemasons are perhaps the most common. Those who are ignorant call groups such as these secret societies. I suppose that is fitting enough—since we operate away from public view."

Public view...secret societies? What was this guy talking about?

The guest spoke before Sanders could ask. "We have been here for over a thousand years, always operating in the shadows, altering the course of humanity in the ways we best saw fit."

"So, you're like a Freemason or something?"

The man's head turned, and he looked across his shoulder at Sanders. There was a slightly irritated glint in his eyes. It was the first sign of any kind of emotion the man had shown since Sanders walked in. Was it something he said?

"No. We are nothing like them. My organization was founded with the goal of bringing truth and light to the world. Unfortunately, much darkness has spread over the last couple of millennia. Those who would hide the truth, who would bury it under the earth's crust, have allowed immorality to run rampant. For centuries, we fought our enemies with the knowledge that the divine would be on our side to help us win the war. We waited, biding our time until our moment of triumph would arrive. It never did."

Sanders eased his finger toward the panic button on the underside of his desk. Whoever this nut job was needed to spend a night in the tank, and probably the rest of his life in a loony bin. He was talking like one of those religious fanatics who'd led a mass suicide, promising the mother ship would pick them up the moment they died.

"That button won't help you," the man said. His head faced the window, his eyes stuck on something outside.

How did he know about that button? This was getting too weird. Time to get out of here.

"Don't worry, Mr. Sanders. I'm not armed. And I mean you no harm. Like I said before, I am here to help you."

"Help me?"

"Perhaps your hearing isn't good. I thought I was clear about that before. You want the presidency. We can help you get that."

Sanders thought for a moment. The clock on the wall ticked like a jackhammer, pounding out the seconds. The guy said he was unarmed. That was probably the truth. He wouldn't have gotten through the security checkpoints. So far, the man hadn't made a threat, only offered some kind of help.

"Okay," Sanders relented. "Let's say you're right and I want to be president. How exactly are you going to do that?"

"My organization is looking for something, something we believe the president has access to."

"Why don't you ask him for it, then? Why bother me?"

"John Dawkins is a fool. He has no idea what it is or where it is."

It? What was this mysterious *it* this guy was talking about?

"The president possesses an item, a relic of great importance to my organization. It is our birthright. And we want it back."

Sanders frowned. "I thought you just said he doesn't know he has it. How can he possess something and not know it?"

The question might have tripped up the visitor, but he didn't show it. "The same way a person has an infectious disease eating away at their organs but doesn't realize it until it is too late."

"Fair point."

"This relic must be returned to us. If Dawkins knew about it, he'd put it in a museum or hide it away in some federal basement, never to be seen again. That is why we need you."

Sanders thought about it. He did his best to process what he was hearing, but nothing made sense.

A stranger showed up in his office and offered to help him win the office of the presidency, and all he wanted was some heirloom?

"What is this...relic you're talking about? Seems like a pretty uneven deal if you ask me. You give me the most powerful office in the world, and all you want back is some artifact? What is it? The Holy Grail or something?"

He chuckled at his own joke, though the laugh was a nervous one. The glare he received from his guest only served to further that anxiety.

"Something like that."

Sanders let out one more snort and then realized the guy was serious. "Wait a minute. You're telling me you think John Dawkins has the Holy Grail and doesn't know about it?"

It was time for this nut job to leave. Sanders reached under the desk and pressed the panic button. It would only take fifteen seconds before the first security guards rushed into the room.

"I told you that button is useless," the man said.

How had he seen that? He was still gazing out the window.

"The Holy Grail is a myth," he went on. "The relic we seek is far more important to our organization. It is...sacred to us. Once you are in office, you will grant us permission to search the premises and remove the artifact. When it is in our possession, we will leave, and you will never hear from us again. You will be free to run your government as you see fit. You will be the most powerful man in the free world."

Sanders thought the way he emphasized the word "free" was funny, but he didn't dwell on it.

"Fine," he said after a minute of thought. "How, exactly, are you going to put me in the White House? The president announced the Speaker is his favorite candidate. Surely, you saw that on the news. I don't have a prayer."

"Leave that to us."

6

ATLANTA

Tommy Schultz barged through his office door, still half-asleep. He'd stayed up late, into the early morning hours, trying to piece together some ancient script they'd discovered on one of the shards he and the kids were working on the day before. He went to sleep unsatisfied. Whatever the script on the clay may have meant would have to wait for another day.

Any hopes of today being that day flew out the window when he found his friend sitting in his chair behind the desk.

Tommy let out a sigh. "You know, you have your own office and desk, right?"

Sean grinned from ear to ear. "Come on in. Have a seat." He motioned to one of the chairs across from him.

"That," Tommy jabbed a finger at him, "is my seat."

"I'll let you have it back in a minute." Sean took a bite of a croissant and slid a little brown wax paper bag across the desk. "I got you one," he said while chewing.

Tommy grumbled and plopped into one of the other chairs. "What's got you so cheery this morning?" He took the bag and pulled out the pastry.

"What's got you so grumpy?" Sean replied. "Late night?"

"I didn't get to sleep until one in the morning. So, yeah."

"Underachiever. I've been up since four."

Tommy frowned. "Why? The anxiety thing again?"

Sean and Tommy had been friends nearly their entire lives. They'd met when they were very young and hit it off immediately. The two shared a love of history, sports, and pretty much everything else. Tommy knew his friend like he knew himself and had worried about Sean's sleeping issues for a long time. Tommy always blamed it on anxiety, though Sean wasn't sure that was it.

"Sort of," Sean confessed. "I figured it out."

Tommy passed a confused look across the table. "Figured what out?"

"Have you had your coffee yet?" Sean said with a wrinkled forehead and lowered eyelids.

"I was running a little late. Figured I'd get some once I was here."

Sean slammed a small stack of photos and printouts on the desk and slid them across to his friend.

"What's that?" Tommy asked, leaning forward. He pulled the sheets closer with his fingertips.

"The tattoos on the men who attacked me in Missouri. They're Assassins."

Tommy's frown deepened. "Yeah...I mean, that's what they were there to do based on what you told me. They were trying to assassinate you. Although, I have to say, usually that term is reserved for those who kill people who are important."

"That hurts, Schultzie." Sean used the nickname he'd given his friend long ago.

Tommy cocked his head to the side and offered his best smug grin.

"No," Sean went on, "that's not what I mean. I mean they're part of the ancient Order of the Assassin." He said the word as it would have been pronounced a thousand years ago, with the third syllable sounding like the word *seen*.

For a second, Tommy sat still, processing what he'd just heard. Then he suddenly snatched the pictures and printouts and leaned back in his chair. He inspected the photos, analyzing every image with wide eyes.

He knew Sean wasn't one to jump to conclusions. He was rational and calculating with almost everything he did in life. If he believed he'd found evidence that suggested the two gunmen were part of an ancient order, Tommy had no doubt his friend wasn't grasping at straws. He'd stumbled onto something concrete.

Tommy studied the images before reading the printouts. He skimmed that part since he already knew a little about the background of the ancient Order of Assassin.

They were a group that originated in Persia, now modern-day Iran—an elite fighting force that came from a sect of Islam called the Nizari. The legend suggests that an old man in the mountains of Persia and Syria formed the group in the late eleventh century as a way to fight competing sects. Soon after, in the twelfth century, the Assassins were used to combat the hordes of Crusaders pouring into Jerusalem.

"Hassan-e Sabbāh," Tommy said and set the sheets back on the desk and crossed a leg over his knee. "He's the one most historians attribute to the founding of the Order of Assassin."

"Right."

"The pictures are interesting," Tommy continued. "But all that stuff is hearsay. No one really knows much about the Assassin. Everything that was written about them, at least in the earliest years, was from their enemies, people who'd been attacked by them. It's conjecture."

"I know," Sean said. "I considered that. Come on, man. You know me better than that. You think I'm gonna just do a quick Google search and take the first thing they throw at me?"

Tommy put up a hand. "You're right. I'm sorry. Please, continue."

"Thank you. So, I did some digging around."

"At four in the morning."

"Yes. And it turns out there have been reported sightings of this same emblem at various incidents around the world."

Tommy's eyes narrowed and his brow furrowed. "Incidents?"

Sean gave a nod and slid one more piece of paper across the desk surface. This one displayed a map of the globe in two parts. It featured several red *X*s in seemingly random places.

"Did you draw the *X*s?" Tommy asked with a hint of humor in his voice.

"Yep."

"So X marks the spot, eh?"

Sean didn't answer immediately, instead letting his friend look over the map for a moment.

"Each one of those red marks is where someone was murdered in the last ten years."

Tommy looked up from the sheet with questions in his eyes. "That's all? Lots of people are murdered every year, man."

"Yeah, but not where witnesses claim they saw this emblem." He tapped his finger on a picture of the same symbol he'd seen on the gunmen's wrists.

Tommy leaned forward, planting both feet on the ground. His eyes darted between the map and the emblem under Sean's finger.

"Okay," he said after a minute of thought. "Let's say you're right, that all of these murders were committed by members of some ancient secret organization called the Assassin. What's the point? I mean, it's not a new idea that there are secret societies out there, pulling strings, making the world turn the way they want it to. I'm not a conspiracy theorist."

"I know," Sean cut in.

"But this group hasn't been around for a long time."

"That map suggests otherwise."

"My point is, why would they kill these people? Who are they? What is their motivation?"

"And more importantly," Sean said, "what do they want, and why are they just now resurfacing?"

"You said that map is from the last decade."

Sean nodded. "Before ten years ago, there was nothing. Not one single sighting of this symbol."

Tommy's head twitched from side to side. "So? Why no sign of them before a decade ago? What were they doing for a thousand years? And why all of a sudden come out of hiding and start whacking people?"

"Exactly." Sean held up a finger to emphasize what he thought was his point.

Tommy looked more confused than ever. "Exactly what? You didn't clear up anything."

"No...I mean, exactly...like, why did they show up out of nowhere ten years ago?"

"Oh, I thought you had an answer for that."

"No. No, that's...you're missing the point."

"Obviously."

Sean exhaled and ran his fingers through his hair. "My *point*," he said, "is that we need to look into this. I mean, they tried to kill me, for crying out loud. If they murdered all these people and tried to get to me, that means they may strike again. We can't let that happen."

For all their joking around, Tommy was taking his friend's theory seriously. His curiosity was certainly piqued, but there were so many questions, so much that needed explaining.

"Who were the targets on the map? You know their identities?"

Sean nodded. "Politicians, businessmen, occasionally a cop or fed."

"So, no ordinary people."

"Not usually."

There was one issue lingering in Tommy's mind that threw a monkey wrench into Sean's theory about the ancient organization of Assassin. "If they're so secretive, so good and being stealthy and all that, how is it that"—he counted the Xs on the map—"so many witnesses saw that symbol?"

Sean's lips cracked on the right corner. "Glad you asked. The victims were left with the emblem."

"Left?"

"Mmhmm."

Tommy got the feeling his friend was holding something back, and he wasn't sure he wanted to know what it was.

"Some of them were found with the emblem cut into their skin. Others had it branded on them."

Tommy grimaced. "That's a tad grisly."

"I know."

"So, why are you smiling about it?"

Sean quickly corrected himself and returned to his stoic expression. "Look, the point is these people were all killed by the same group. They were trying to tell us something."

"Us?" Tommy asked.

"Us. The world. Everyone. You know, us."

"Why would an organization that's been shrouded in secrecy, hiding underground for the last thousand years, doing everything they can to not be discovered, suddenly pop out from their hole and start murdering people? On top of that, why would they leave a calling card for everyone to find them?"

"Right. And before you ask, I know the next one you're going to throw at me."

"You do?" Tommy's eyebrows shot up.

"What's so special about me? Why would they target political types, wealthy businessmen, and others like them and then come after a nobody like me?"

"I didn't want to say it that way, but yeah, that's what I was thinking."

Sean took no offense. "Precisely. And on that line of thought, why didn't they come after you? I mean, you're the boss."

The question took Tommy a little off guard, but his friend was right. Why would they target Sean and not him? That could mean only one thing. It wasn't an IAA issue they were trying to eliminate. It was specific to Sean.

"What did you do?" Tommy asked in a direct tone that bordered on stern.

"That's what I'm trying to figure out."

Tommy scooted his chair closer to the desk. His adrenal glands were firing up, and the blood pumped faster through his body. "Okay, let's start with the obvious. You were in Missouri looking for the Jesse James treasure, right?"

"Yeah."

"But that wasn't an IAA operation. No one called us about that."

"Nope. I was on my own time." Sean could see the gears turning in his friend's mind.

"Okay. So, why Jesse James? What's so special about that treasure that lured you out there? I mean, there are any number of rumored caches of loot out there. Why not D.B. Cooper? Forrest Fenn? The Dutchman?"

"Not sure," Sean said. "I guess I was always interested in outlaw stuff as a kid. When I was young, I read one of my grandpa's books about buried treasure in the United States. Most of the ones that book talked about were from outlaws like Jesse James, Billy the Kid, those kinds of guys."

"Cooper was an outlaw."

Good point. "Yeah, I know, but everyone is looking for that. I wanted to go with something more obscure. So, I dug up some info about the Jesse James loot and started snooping around."

"Who did you tell?"

Sean shrugged. "No one except you and the kids. Oh, and Adriana. Although I left her a voice mail. She's kind of been off the grid lately."

Tommy frowned. "Yeah, June has, too. Strange." He let his concern go for the moment. "All right, let's get back to how these guys might have found you and why. You were in Missouri. You only told a few trusted friends and colleagues where you were going and what you were doing."

A thought popped into Sean's head. "When was the last time we did a sweep of this place?"

"A sweep? You mean for wiretaps and stuff like that?"

Sean responded with a solemn nod.

Tommy rolled his shoulders. "I dunno. Never? Why would I do that?"

Sean picked up his cell phone and scrolled through the contacts until he found the name he was looking for. "Well, I'd say we have a reason to now."

7

NEW YORK CITY

Alain rapped three short times on the rusty red door to the derelict building then followed it with two long knocks. He ran bony fingers through his wavy black hair as he waited to be granted entry. A narrow window panel cut into the entrance slid open. Dark pupils surrounded by yellowish white stared out at him. The window shut abruptly. A second later, locks clicked from inside. Then the door opened.

The putrid stench of the sewers wafted out mixed with the scent of onions, cumin, cayenne pepper, and paprika.

Alain Depricot let the smells waft over him before he stepped inside and into the warm embrace of the old brick building. The guard stood just to the right, holding the door open for the taller man.

The grunt barely stood higher than five and a half feet. He was squat with a belly that told the world he wasn't a big fan of diet and exercise. The curly dark hair on his head was a mess and looked—just like the man—as if it hadn't been washed in a week.

The guard gave a nod as Alain passed by, his cologne wafting over the squat man and momentarily blessing him with the scent of civilization. There was a look of fear in the guard's eyes. As well there should have been. Alain was one of the most dangerous men in the world, yet very few knew that fact.

No one knew how old Alain was. His contemporaries and associates would have guessed mid-forties if pressed, but the truth was he didn't look a day over thirty. Some claimed it was his strict diet and rigorous workout regimen. Then there were the other explanations.

Rumors fluttered through his organization of him being a demon, called forth by some rogue prophet, sent to wreak havoc among the nonbelievers. Others believed he *was* a prophet, a descendant of Mohammad, come to bring the world to its knees and bow to Allah. A scattered few considered him to be a reincarnation of the great prophet himself, though that sect was few and far between.

Only Alain knew the truth, a truth that was much simpler and less convoluted. He was simply a devout believer who'd pursued perfection his entire life.

He strode down the bleak hallway, leaving the guard to his wild fantasies. The door slammed shut, but Alain didn't flinch. His nerves had been trained to be steeled against such things. When his master found him, he had been a spoiled child, raised in a wealthy home with parents who barely had time for him. Barely was an understatement.

His father had been a businessman, a banker by trade. He spent more time analyzing stocks and charts than with his boy. His father's distance had driven Alain's mother into the arms of other men. Alain had even caught her in the act once. The terrible vision of her in rapturous ecstasy with a stranger haunted his dreams for weeks.

Alain never told his father about it. The way he figured, dear old Dad got what he deserved. The betrayal, Alain believed, was to him, not to his father.

His mother was a kept woman. She came and went as she pleased, spending a fortune on clothing, shoes, accessories, and lavish vacations.

All the while, little Alain wished they would give him a fraction of the time and energy they spent so easily on almost everything else the world had to offer.

The only religious experience Alain gained from his parents was a biannual trip to mass in the Bern Minster, a cathedral in his hometown of Bern, Switzerland. Young Alain never found God there. The priest's droning monologues did little to feed his spiritual needs.

He started dabbling with drugs at the youthful age of thirteen. He also took after his mother when it came to attending to his sexual desires, taking multiple partners before he received his driver's license.

His hollow life seemed an endless pursuit of material pleasures that never sated his appetite, or the deep desire for something meaningful that panged at his stomach almost nightly.

It wasn't until he'd met the master that the hunger deep within him was finally fed. He'd blacked out one night, his brain and body beaten by a combination of alcohol, cocaine, and a drug dealer's fists. When the old man found him, Alain was nearly dead. It was the master who nursed him back to health, cared for him unlike anyone ever had, and showed him that life could have a purpose. More than that—that God had a purpose for him.

At first, Alain balked at the notion. He'd given up on any hope of a deity, much less one that cared about him.

The master returned Alain to his parents' home nearly three days later. The only reprimand Alain received was a few lines of ridicule and a tertiary nod from his father.

For all he knew, his parents never realized he was missing in the first place.

Alain returned to the place the master had taken him to recover. He found the old man in prayer with several others. Alain lingered in the shadows as the guy read passages from the Koran and talked with his disciples about the coming war against the nonbelievers.

Initially, Alain frowned upon his savior's ideology. This man was a terrorist, a killer. It was this kind of person who was responsible for the attacks on the United States and other Western cities where so many innocent people were killed. Alain's first instinct was to turn and run, to tell the police, to tell any news outlet that would listen, that here, under the sidewalks and city streets, a madman was planning a war against innocent people.

Alain didn't do any of that. Compelled to remain in the shadows of the underground meeting room, he listened to every word the old man uttered. When the sermon—or whatever it was called—was done, he did his best to shrink back into the darkness and run home.

But the old man had turned and gazed at him with tired eyes hovering over heavy bags of skin. He'd offered a warm, welcoming smile, like he knew Alain had been there the entire time.

Alain turned the corner in the dank hallway and continued walking as he remembered the events that followed that night.

He returned to the secret meeting place, time and time again. Eventually, he joined the other young men at the feet of the master, absorbing everything he could about God and the sins of the nonbelieving world that existed mere feet away from where they were sitting.

It was then Alain learned of the master's true mission, his real intentions, and who he was. The purpose of the Assassin wasn't to terrorize the planet and bring the rest of the world's religions to their knees through coercion and force. It was to influence the balance of things, to alter the course of history by removing key targets that stood in their way.

The old man was the last in a long line of great warriors, a part of a sacred order that had gone into hiding for nearly a thousand years. The Assassin. Their war wasn't one against innocent people, the master said, but with another secret organization that had plagued the earth for centuries, wreaking havoc on the Muslim world and its followers.

Alain had only heard rumors about the Assassin, about the men in ancient times who could move like ghosts through walls, penetrating the most secure places in the world to exact their own brand of justice, vengeance, and murder. The master taught them that the things they did—the killing, instigating political upheaval—was all part of a greater plan. He rebuked the methods of most extremists, calling their acts of terrorism sloppy and animalistic. An Assassin was none of those things.

Terrorists were an improvised explosive device or a plane crash.

An Assassin was a scalpel. And they rarely went after ordinary people. That murderous path belonged to modern-day barbarians.

Days turned into months. Alain came to realize that the master wasn't just giving sermons about purification of the planet. He was training warriors.

Alain was put through a series of rigorous tests before being allowed into the system that would turn him into what he is, one of the most lethal weapons in the world. The early trials he faced were simple enough: movement, motor skills, coordination. As he progressed, however, things became more intense, more difficult. Sparring became a regular part of his day and each bout grew more and more strenuous as he faced tougher opponents.

The final test the master gave him was, for many, a deal breaker. Like the rest of the new batch of recruits, Alain was given a task that would crush his desire to be a part of the order. He was told to murder anyone who was attached to him.

Alain didn't have many friends. Most of the young men in the underground organization didn't. That's how they found themselves there. Killing one's parents, however, proved too much for nearly all of the trainees.

For Alain, it was the easiest part.

He'd been merciful with his father, jamming his knife through the man's closed eye while he slept. He never felt a thing, the only sign of life in him was some muscular twitching as the brain died.

His mother, however, he made suffer.

Her screams echoed through the cavernous bedchamber and down the halls of their mansion. He rebuked her with every cut, every drop of blood he spilled. He called her a harlot, a spawn of darkness, a great temptress.

Alain made certain she took a long time to die.

When the deed was done, he set the house ablaze and never

turned back. It had never been his home. He never had a home, not until the master found him.

Years went by. Alain climbed through the ranks of the order with incredible speed, surpassing Assassins older than him until, when the old man died, he became the one in charge.

The last thing the master asked of him was to finish what had started over a thousand years before: to light the fire that would ignite the final battle against the nonbelievers—and, of course, the heretics.

Now, he turned left in the corridor of the battered brick building and descended a set of concrete steps into its bowels. At the bottom, another guard—this one much fitter than the previous—gave him a respectful nod and pulled open a door.

Alain walked through it. Candles burned on iron sconces along every wall. There were electrical lights, too, though they seemed to cast less light than their more primitive counterparts.

Eight men were standing in a loose circle in the center of the room, talking about something with great fervor. The conversation died as Alain entered. They all bowed their heads respectfully; the ones with their backs turned swiveled around to greet him with the same gesture.

"Good afternoon," he said. His accent was an odd mix of German and French, a result of his parents speaking each.

They all responded with the same greeting.

"What news of our brothers in Missouri? Did they complete the task?"

The eight men looked around at each other as if trying to determine which one would give him the bad news. They were a motley crew, all from different backgrounds, ethnicities, and cultures. Yet they were all of the same mind, each hardened by their training and focused on the same goal.

"Your silence has given me the answer," Alain said. He motioned to one of the men nearest him, a guy with red hair and a matching beard. "What happened?"

The man didn't hesitate. He knew better. To do so would show weakness, fear. The Assassins never displayed either.

"They were arrested, sir. We aren't sure how it happened yet."

Alain frowned. There were at least three things he didn't like about the response, but he gave a commending nod to the man for relaying the information.

"How is it that two of our order came to be arrested by police?" He asked the question not expecting an answer. The others sensed the rage boiling in his voice. He suppressed his anger enough to ask another question. "What do the police know?"

"They won't talk," another said on the opposite side of the circle. "They would die before they betrayed our cause."

Alain gave a nod accompanied with pouted lips. That much was certain. His men and their loyalty could never be questioned. Alain had gone to great lengths to erase any trace of their identities from databases all around the world. For all intents, they did not exist. With the mountainous wealth of resources the order possessed, they would never want for anything, so a need for an identity was superfluous.

"Where are they now?" Alain asked.

"Washington. In a jail."

Alain sniffled. Though spring was sweeping across much of the country, New York was still cold, and the effects of the weather were hitting his nose one last time before the sweltering heat of summer came crashing in.

"Federal or local?"

"Local. But the feds brought them in. They overrode local jurisdiction in Missouri, although we doubt the cops out there had any idea anything happened. More than likely, the feds never even mentioned it to them." His West African accent was heavy and exaggerated with a deep, booming voice.

"Why an ordinary jail, then?"

The dark-skinned man rolled his shoulders. "We pulled that string."

"Ah."

Alain appreciated that answer. Connections were vital for their organization. Across the world, they had more men and women on the take than most of the mobs on Earth combined.

He also understood that while their network was vast, it would never be as simple as paying a prison guard to leave the doors open. Things didn't work that way. It was too obvious. Alain's team, however, could get eyes to turn the other direction when needed, which provided openings for them to complete their task.

"Well then," Alain said, "I guess it's time we go get them."

"What about Wyatt and his friend's agency?" the redhead asked. "You want one of us to go take them out?"

Alain considered the question for a moment before answering. Wyatt and his compadre could be a problem. That much had been proved already. It was one of the reasons Alain had sent two of his men to take care of Wyatt. He didn't need to ask whether his men were able to secure the artifact. That was a definite no. Odds were Wyatt didn't have it on him when the showdown occurred. He would have left it back in Atlanta, where Wyatt and his cronies kept all their loot.

The plan had been solid; that much Alain believed to be true. Getting to Wyatt in Atlanta, a city with a plethora of traffic cameras and too many witnesses would have proved problematic.

Taking Wyatt while he was out on his own in the middle of nowhere, however, improved the odds of success. Alain had orchestrated the plan himself, giving exact details to his men according to the information they'd obtained. Somehow, they'd cocked it up. Now his men were in jail, and Wyatt was still alive. More than that, the man was probably spooked and on full alert.

Wyatt had a reputation of being a difficult man to deal with. A quick read through his dossier demonstrated him to be a lethal adversary. Six years in government service, working for extrajudicial agencies had, no doubt, served to sharpen his already honed abilities.

"No," Alain said after contemplating the issue. "Leave Wyatt and Schultz to me."

8

ATLANTA

Sean waved his metal wand around in the air over his head. He moved slowly, inspecting every corner of the room until he'd checked the entire area. Then he went back into the hall and continued to the next room, checking every square inch of the corridor as he proceeded.

He, Tommy, and the kids had spent the last five hours going through the IAA building with their electronic detection devices. Emily had been kind enough to lend them the equipment, though she didn't have time to help with the actual work. Sean made sure to give her grief about that.

"Anything on three?" Tommy's voice came through Sean's earpiece.

"Not yet. You got anything?"

"No. I'm just finishing up on five. Tara, you?"

"No, sir," she answered. "I still have two more rooms to go."

"I'm clear, too," Alex chimed in.

Sean's face tightened, almost to a frown. He only had a couple more areas to check. So far, no one had found any trace of a listening device or some other type of bug.

It didn't make sense. How had the Assassins known where he was going and precisely where he would be in Missouri? They didn't get the information from any airlines, though he thought about that for a brief second. Normally, Sean would take the IAA jet on a trip like that, but since it was on his personal time he felt it more prudent to use his money and fly commercial. He'd even flown in economy class, though that reminded him of how nice it was to have access to his own plane—well, to Tommy's plane.

He turned into the next room and went through the same mundane process he'd done on the rest of the floor. Still nothing. One room to go, and he'd found zilch. He had the feeling that the last room would produce the same result, which, if the others had the same luck, would put them right back where they started—with no leads.

Sean's suspicions were confirmed after spending five minutes in the final area. He radioed the others to let them know he was done and then headed back down to the main floor via the stairs.

The group reconvened in the lobby when everyone was finished. Tommy was already there when Sean arrived. Alex and Tara showed up a few minutes later.

The kids shook their heads as they stepped off the elevator and strode over to where the two friends were standing by the reception desk.

"Nothing?" Tommy asked, already knowing the answer. It was written on their faces.

"Not a thing," Alex said. "You guys?"

Sean and Tommy shook their heads.

"Well," Tara chimed, "I'm not that surprised. I mean, we have pretty tight security here. If anyone came in and planted something, we'd probably know it."

"Especially after that robbery a while back. We ramped up everything because of that. I'm not saying it's Fort Knox, but it's a lot tougher to get in here unnoticed than before. Heck, I still have problems remembering all the different key codes."

Tommy and Sean knew they were right. They *had* increased security as a result of the break-in. That still didn't help them with the current problem. Someone had found a way to know exactly where Sean would be and when he'd be there.

"Do you think it's possible that somehow they intercepted my email?" Sean asked the two younger members of the agency.

Alex and Tara glanced at each other, both asking the same question and coming up with similar answers.

"I suppose," Tara said. "If someone planted a digital bug in our system, that could be possible."

"Digital bug?" Tommy asked.

"Yeah, it's like spyware on steroids," Alex answered.

Sean and Tommy were familiar with spyware and malware. They routinely ran scans on all their computer systems, both personal and at the agency. Their security systems and firewalls were top of the line, but the guys were also aware that within hours of being updated or released, such software could be made obsolete by an innovative hacker.

"So," Tommy said, "something like that wouldn't be detected by our software defense systems?"

"It's certainly possible," Alex confirmed. "For all intents and purposes, it's unlikely that the agency would be the target of that kind of attack."

"Unless someone was looking for something specific," Tara added.

"Like a travel plan," Sean said.

"Sure. If you had that on the affected computer."

"Or emails I sent."

She nodded a confirmation.

"With something like that, they could have been watching our systems for a while without us knowing, huh?" Tommy asked.

"Sure," Alex said. "I mean, however unlikely, it's definitely possible."

It was good they were getting somewhere, but the new, highly disconcerting information raised suspicions.

"How can we check for that?" Sean wondered.

Tara and Alex thought about it for a second. As far as Sean knew, they were already considering the problem.

"We can set up a scan that will track down any lines of code designed to check email," Tara said after a minute. "It will take some time, but I think we can manage."

"How long?" Tommy asked.

She glanced at Alex before giving a response. "I dunno. If we work on it through the night, probably sometime tomorrow."

"I'll double your pay," Tommy said. "If there's something in our system, we need to know."

Tara smiled at the offer. "You know you don't have to do that. You already pay us plenty."

Alex agreed. "Yeah, and besides, we enjoy this stuff. It's like you pay us to play. Don't worry about it."

Tommy loved the two of them like they were his own kids. Those two were the closest thing he had to family outside of Sean and his own parents.

During the years his parents were missing, Tommy had learned to adapt, to build strong relationships with the people still in his life rather than focusing on what he didn't have.

His parents disappeared when he was young, victims of what he believed to be a plane crash. It wasn't until he was an adult that he learned they hadn't died and were, instead, captured by the North Koreans. Getting them back was one of the best days of his life. Still, things would never be the same with them because of the time that had lapsed. They'd been shielded from modern advancements for decades. Smartphones were something they would have never dreamed of, and that was just the beginning. On top of it all, now that they were back to living a normal life, or a semblance of it, they'd been spending most of their time trying to acclimate. The parents Tommy had known before were dead, replaced by people who were only a blurred reflection of their former selves. Their love for him, however, had not changed.

They'd spent a few months helping him with special projects the agency picked up, but in the end, they wanted to retire. He didn't blame them. They deserved it after all they'd been through.

Now, he was back with the family he'd grown to love, in the house they'd all built.

"Thank you, guys. I appreciate it."

"No problem, boss," Tara said. "We'll get right on it...that is, if the artifacts we were working on can wait for a day or so."

"They can wait," Tommy said with a nod.

The two turned and headed toward the elevator leading down to the basement laboratory where they spent most of their time.

After they disappeared, Sean turned to his friend. "You think they can figure out where that bug is?"

"Yeah," Tommy said. "If anyone can, it's those two. Only problem is that doesn't tell us who put it there. I mean, obviously, we think it was one of the Assassins. They can probably remove it from the system, but that still leaves us without much to go on."

"Except that the two men who came after me are still in custody."

"You thinking of going up there and having a chat with them?" Tommy raised an eyebrow at the idea.

"Wouldn't hurt. I want to find out what they want with me."

"Sounds like murder is what they wanted with you."

"Other than that, smart guy. Think about it. If you want to kill someone, there's always a motive."

"Unless it's because the killer is a psycho. Then motive doesn't come into play."

"Yeah, but that doesn't apply here."

Tommy pondered the question for a moment. "So, revenge, jealousy, money, power, all of those are motives for murder."

"Think deeper," Sean said. "Why would someone want to get rid of me? Sure, revenge might be a reason, but I don't think I've run across those two before. In fact, I doubt I've ever bumped into anyone in their order."

"So, what then?" Tommy paused for a second and then answered his own question. "You think they want you out of the way?"

"That's where I was going."

It wasn't the first time someone had come after one of them. Years before, a madman kidnapped Tommy and forced him to work out an ancient code that ended up leading to one of the greatest discoveries in modern history. There'd been other times, too, more than Sean could recount off the top of his head. He'd grown to accept it as one of the occupational hazards.

Tommy was thinking the same thing. "The tablet," he said abruptly.

Sean bobbed his head once.

They'd been called in to investigate a strange collection of tablets and pottery discovered in the New England area, western Massachusetts to be exact. They excavated the area and brought the items back to the lab for further research. One of those objects was the piece of pottery Tommy and the kids had been looking at the previous day when Sean arrived.

"Maybe this has something to do with the stuff we found in Massachusetts, you know, the tablet and that other stuff you saw me and the kids working on the other day."

Sean knew it was a stretch. He'd seen things, though, strange things since he started working for Tommy many years before. Now, he was willing to keep almost anything on the table.

"I guess anything's possible," Sean said. "But didn't you say you guys hadn't figured anything out about those items?"

Tommy gave an exaggerated nod. "Yeah. That doesn't mean someone else doesn't know what they are."

"Maybe it's time we took a closer look at those artifacts."

"You think that's what they're after?" Tommy asked.

"Those two guys could have killed me if they wanted to. That might have been part of their eventual plans, but you do the math. Two men, probably well trained and part of an ancient society of assassins, sneak up on me but don't kill me? If they just wanted me dead, that would have been easy enough. Even if they didn't take me out with a long-range rifle, they could have just shot me right there in the field and left me to rot."

"They wanted something."

"Exactly. And the only thing you've dug up recently were those artifacts up north."

"All right," Tommy said with a sigh. "Let's see what we can figure out."

The two made their way down into the belly of the facility and into the lab. Tommy led the way through the glass doors and over to the humongous worktable where the items were strewn about on a clean surface. Some of the objects were nothing more than fragments of clay. A few, however, were nearly complete.

The piece Sean was most curious about was a particular stone tablet. It was the length and width of a magazine and about two inches thick. But it weighed nearly twenty pounds. Sean leaned over the tablet and switched on a table light to get a better view. He remembered securing it before the trip back to Atlanta, wondering what its strange engravings could mean.

On their initial inspection, Tommy and Sean had believed the script to be some kind of ancient Scandinavian runes, but further research proved that to be an invalid hypothesis.

The weathered engravings were shallow now, worn down by the centuries. It took a sharp eye to even detect some of the shapes, which made analysis all the more difficult.

"None of those letters or whatever they are show up in any of the databases we have," Tommy said, noticing his friend's interest in the tablet.

"Online or off?"

"Both. We attempted to cross-reference them, even put them out there for a few experts to analyze, but no one could figure it out."

Sean stood up straight and looked over the table at his friend with a perturbed expression. "Wait. Who did you send it to?"

"The usual people," Tommy said.

"Which ones, exactly?"

"Only three."

"Names, Schultzie," Sean pressed.

Tommy did a twitchy combination of a head shake and a shrug. "Doesn't matter. Two weren't any help."

"And the third?"

"Dr. Wilkins."

"In Boston?"

Tommy nodded. "I figured since we found that stuff up there, might be worth it to have him take a look since that's his neck of the woods."

The idea made sense. Wilkins had an extraordinary knowledge of that area's history. Sean's sometimes paranoid mind made him often see conspiracies where there were none. Right now, though he didn't tell Tommy, Sean was wondering if Wilkins was the one who betrayed them.

Tommy turned back to the kids. "We need to double down on translating that tablet. Use anything you have to figure it out. I want to know what that thing says. Cost doesn't matter. Understand?"

"What about trying to figure out how they tapped into our system?" Tara asked.

"Run that check in the background. This is priority one now. They got in. No changing that now. Any investigation into that is to keep things secure going forward, unless you can find a way to track back to their exact location."

There was something in his head; Sean knew that much. It was written on Tommy's face. Sean had the same hunch that whatever was on that tablet had something to do with this whole mess. There was something else playing on Sean's mind, too. He had to find out what Wilkins knew and what he was up to.

"Get the jet ready," Sean said to his friend. "We need to pay Dr. Wilkins a visit."

9

WASHINGTON DC

Four uniformed cops stood in the hallway, waiting for the bars to be opened. The prison guard next to them had to make the request twice in his radio before the controller responded. The heavy-barred gate slid open, wheels and gears grinding and clicking somewhere nearby in the recesses of the building.

"Right this way, fellas," the security guard, a redheaded fellow named Rick, said.

"We appreciate your help with this matter," one of the cops said. "These two are extremely dangerous. It's absolutely vital we make sure the transfer goes smoothly. They must be treated with respect."

"Yeah, we already had a problem with them the first day they arrived. They split one inmate's skull and paralyzed another. Not that I care. The two guys they beat up were bad news: drug dealers and killers in one of the local gangs. If you ask me, your two boys did the world a favor."

Tusun Farmut was one of Alain Depricot's chief advisers and enforcers. It was rare when Alain sent him out on a mission such as this. Usually, the upper echelon of the Assassins directed things. They didn't get out in the field very often. Back in the twelfth century, every man would have been used on a mission such as this, no matter rank or name. Times had changed. The only reason Alain used Tusun was because he knew the mission was of vital importance.

Tusun's family had moved to the United States from Turkey when he was very young. After a neo-Nazi gunman strolled into Tusun's mosque and executed fifteen people—including Tusun's parents—the young man was left with almost nothing except a stern grandmother and a fiery thirst for revenge.

He looked the part of a young cop, fit and ready to do his part for the law. At least that was the impression he gave Rick the security guard.

Tusun's three companions were equally as chiseled, hardened by years of intense training and strenuous missions. That might have thrown off Rick, who was plump around the midsection and clearly didn't get to the gym all that often. Tusun figured, however, the hapless security guard wasn't aware enough to even consider that he and his coworkers were more muscular than the stereotypical cop.

Americans loved their stereotypes. In many ways, it made them easier to deal with. They were predictable. Their fears and behaviors coincided almost flawlessly. In this instance, those same stereotypes could have raised suspicion in a more adept person than Rick.

"Where you guys taking them, anyway? We just got the official paperwork about an hour ago, and I didn't even look that far down."

It hadn't taken much to get clearance for the "transfer." One of the men in charge of the prison was on the Assassins payroll and worked up all the necessary paperwork from his end.

Then all he had to do was send it in a personal email to Tusun, who would then send it from an official-looking government email.

The digital paper trail would look legitimate—if anyone ever bothered to check. By the time they did, it would be too late. Rick would be the fall guy if anything went wrong, but no one would ever find Tusun and his men. That much was certain. "We're making a pickup for the feds," Tusun said. He had no accent. Though his lineage was from the borders of Europe and the Middle East, he'd grown up with other American kids. He despised his grandmother and never wanted to speak the same way she did, so the accent never came.

Rick shook his head. "I can't believe those guys. They can't spare a few people to come make a pickup themselves? So, they send you four down here to do their dirty work. They making you drop off their laundry, too?" The guard laughed at his own joke.

Tusun gave a polite grin and a fake chuckle. Every American thought they were funny. Truth was, most of them didn't have an original joke in their puny brains. For a man trained to kill, Tusun enjoyed laughing now and then. His sense of humor hedged toward the dark side, but who would judge him for that?

The guard turned left down a corridor and then back to the right at the next intersection. He didn't say much else until they neared the block where Tusun's associates were being held.

Some of the inmates rattled their cages as the convoy walked by. More than a few shouted obscenities at the uniformed cops. Others spat at them. One or two made lewd comments that would have made the most hardened sailor blush.

Tusun and his men were too well trained to engage with vermin like these. They couldn't be goaded into a physical altercation. They were warriors and only engaged in confrontation on their terms or as a matter of self-defense.

"Keep it down!" Rick shouted with more than a dash of pepper in his voice.

He led Tusun and his men to the last cell on the block and then turned to face the men inside. He requested the controller open the appropriate door, and a second later a heavy latch clicked and the bars slid open.

Inside, the two men were sitting on the same bed with elbows on knees and hands folded. At first glance, they might have appeared to be praying. Tusun knew they were simply biding their time.

"Up, you two," Rick said in a harsh tone. "You're being transferred."

The nearest inmate stood up. The tattoo showed on his wrist below the short-sleeve orange jumpsuit. Rick probably thought the ink was nothing more than a weekend's drunken mistake rather than a symbol given only to members of an ancient society of killers.

The first inmate, a guy named Syd, sauntered out with a cocky look on his face and an air of untouchability. The second followed close behind. His name was Michel. He was shorter than Syd, slightly more muscular, though that might have been due to the height difference.

Tusun's men cuffed the inmates' wrists and ankles as they stood in the corridor amid a flurry of shouting. When the prisoners were secure, Tusun nodded to the two men in front to head back.

Rick ordered the door shut once more, and it slid closed as the group proceeded toward the exit.

They bypassed the station where inmates retrieved their personal belongings. These two prisoners didn't have anything stored there except the clothes they'd been wearing when they were picked up. They quickly changed out of the prison uniforms and proceeded to the exit. Once they were out of the building, Tusun gave a nod to Rick as his men loaded up their cargo in a white van.

"Thank you for your help," Tusun said.

"Not a problem."

A black sedan pulled up into the closest parking spot, and a woman in a gray business suit got out. Her brown hair was pulled back in a tight ponytail. She looked like she was in a hurry.

"What are you doing with these prisoners?" she asked with a tone of urgency in her voice.

"They're being transferred out, ma'am," Rick said.

"On whose authority?" She was clearly incensed, though the guard didn't know why.

"Paperwork came through an hour or so ago. Feds want them in their place."

The woman shook her head. "I haven't heard anything about this."

She strode over to the two while Tusun's men secured the prisoners in the van.

She held out her badge to the guard and Tusun.

Rick swallowed and his face flushed pale. "I'm sorry, Ms. Starks. I was just following—"

Tusun moved fast. His arm was a blur as he turned to Rick and wrapped it around his throat. A second quick movement brought Tusun's weapon out of its holster. He pressed the gun's muzzle to the side of Rick's skull.

"Put your weapon down," Tusun ordered.

Emily had already reached for her piece, but her reaction was too slow.

"Drop it now."

Reluctantly, she bent down and placed the gun on the ground.

"Kick it away," he said.

She did as instructed. The weapon slid and rattled across the pavement until it stopped a good fifteen feet away.

Tusun pointed his gun at Emily. His vapid eyes displayed a callousness she'd not seen in some time. There was no doubt in her mind this man was a killer. Shooting her would have no impact on his life, just as if he'd squashed a bug on the ground.

His finger tensed on the trigger.

Alarms blared suddenly. Tusun shifted his gaze to the rooftops. Cameras were everywhere. They'd seen the whole thing, and now the facility was on full alert.

He turned back to Emily, but she was in midair, diving for cover behind a concrete wall next to a loading dock.

Tusun fired one shot he knew would miss but would keep her hidden while he made his escape. Then he shoved Rick and shot him in the back as he stumbled forward.

He had no reason to kill Rick, though the wound he'd just given the man might have been mortal. However, shooting the naïve guard would buy some time.

Tusun turned and hurried to the van. The driver had already started it by the time Tusun climbed in.

The back tires barked against the asphalt. Loose bits of gravel kicked out behind the vehicle, and a second later the van lurched forward and disappeared out of the lot.

Emily poked her head out from behind the retaining wall. The men were gone, but the security guard was lying prostrate on the pavement, blood seeping out of his shirt.

He was still moving, groaning in pain. His legs and arms moved, which was a good sign. The round hadn't paralyzed him.

Other prison guards and two cops rushed out of the front door. They surrounded their fallen comrade and started running routine checks on him.

Emily pulled out her phone and made a call. "I need every available agent and officer right now." She relayed the van's information, the tags, description, all of it. Then she ended the call and scrolled down to another name. She drew a short breath, hesitating before she tapped the device to start the call. She exhaled then pressed the screen.

"Hello?" a familiar voice said on the other end.

"Sir, we have a problem."

10

BOSTON

Faint traces of snow dotted patches of grass along the sidewalk and in the corners where concrete met brick buildings, a stark contrast to the warmth of the Atlanta spring Sean and Tommy left behind a few hours before.

People rushed around busily on the sidewalks. The cars were in less of a hurry, due to traffic congestion. The vehicles would move a few feet, stop, then repeat.

A gust of frigid air blew down the street, causing Sean to clutch his coat a little tighter around his shoulders.

Sean loved the city of Boston. It was a town full of fascinating history. Much like when he visited Washington, Sean felt like every step he took was on ground where someone important might have stood hundreds of years before. He viewed it with a sense of reverence and appreciation, often wondering if anyone else did the same. He figured Tommy did, but outside the two of them, Sean assumed that all these people running around to get to work or grab a quick cup of coffee took where they lived for granted.

Another blustery gust smacked him in the face and ripped through his hair. Then again, maybe all these Bostonians in such a hurry were just trying to keep warm.

The two friends turned the corner and, seeing the WALK sign still lit, hurried across the road to the other side.

Red and white signs hung from light posts, staking a claim to that section of town for Boston University.

The college occupied a narrow strip of land along the Charles River to the east of downtown and just north of the suburb of Brookline, home to one of Sean's favorite baseball parks in America: Fenway.

Boston University was a hodgepodge of old historic buildings, bland 1970s architecture, and more modern and contemporary designs. The college stood directly across the river from some of the most prestigious universities in the world: MIT and Harvard, although BU had a stout reputation of its own.

Sean and Tommy turned left and made their way onto the campus. To a first-time visitor, the layout might have been a bit confusing, although it was difficult to get lost between Commonwealth Avenue and the river, even with some of the buildings now on the other side of the street. You could always turn back and figure out where you went wrong without much trouble.

This wasn't their first time visiting the campus, and while Sean and Tommy had only been there a few times prior, they knew where they were going.

The College of Arts and Sciences building stood ahead on the right. An imposing gray edifice with rows of large windows facing Commonwealth Avenue, it gave the impression of strength and power to anyone who walked under its commanding stare.

Sean and Tommy turned onto the sidewalk leading up to the building and made their way to the entrance. Inside, the narrow corridors were full of students scurrying here and there on their way to classes or morning study sessions. The ceilings angled up to a point in the center; the air smelled of books, varnish, and wood.

The two made their way down the passage to the eastern end of the building and then made a sharp left. After climbing the stairs up to the second floor, Tommy led the way to an office on the right where a placard displayed the name of Dr. Cameron Wilkins. The door was slightly ajar, which Tommy took as an invitation to push it all the way open.

The hinges creaked. Inside, a man with deep bags under his eyes, white hair sprouting in a sort of low crown that hugged a bald head, and black spectacles sat at his desk writing something on a piece of paper.

He looked up, momentarily scowling at the intrusion until he realized who it was. Then his frown flipped, and he greeted the two with a broad smile.

"Tommy. Sean. Come in, my boys!" Wilkins stood up with arms open wide. He pulled the glasses off his nose and embraced Tommy first, then shook Sean's hand. It wasn't that Sean wasn't a hugger. He just reserved that for people with whom he had close relationships. Wilkins was more of an associate.

Tommy, on the other hand, had known the old man for several years and conferred with him on numerous research projects. Wilkins had become one of Tommy's go-to guys after the death of Dr. Borringer several years before—a professor at Kennesaw State University just outside Atlanta.

Wilkins was a foremost expert in several areas of ancient history, as well as archaeology and anthropology. Like many in his field, he knew Greek, Latin, and how to interpret Egyptian hieroglyphics. He could read Sanskrit and was, last Tommy heard, working on his understanding of Sumerian cuneiform.

Wilkins had been a friend of Tommy's parents going back to the early 1970s, and the relationship had continued with their son when Tommy founded the IAA.

The old man's crimson blazer contrasted with his khaki pants, but, oddly, matched his socks.

"Please, have a seat," Wilkins said, motioning to two chairs with upholstery that looked like it might be as old as the man himself.

The two guests accepted and eased into the seats while Wilkins returned to his. The man lowered himself gingerly, bracing the armrests with both hands as he sat. Then he leaned back and tapped his fingers together.

"So, to what do I owe the pleasure? I have to admit, you were a bit vague when you called yesterday."

"Sorry about that, sir," Tommy said. He didn't want to tell his old friend the reason he'd held back on the details. Instead, he went straight ahead for the purpose of their visit. "We're working on something pretty interesting, and we really need your help."

"Oh? Another project? That's a surprise. You usually don't come to me more than once a year, and that's when it's really busy." He chuckled to himself.

"Yes, sir. And I'm so sorry to bother you."

The professor dismissed the notion with a wave of the hand. "Please. You're no bother at all, my boy. Now, what can I help you with?"

"Actually, Professor, it's not a new project. We have some questions about the Massachusetts project, the stuff we sent you some weeks back."

"Oh," the man said. "Certainly. What would you like to know? I thought I was clear in my reports on the matter, but perhaps I forgot something."

"No," Tommy said with a shake of his head. "You didn't forget anything. It's just that," he fought off the awkward feeling in his gut, "we were curious who you may have shared that information with." He hated interrogating an old family friend, and a globally respected one at that.

Wilkins's face tightened in surprise. "Shared?" His shoulders raised slightly, and he glanced up to his right for the briefest of seconds. "I don't think I shared it with anyone. I had my assistants do some looking around for a few things, but I did most of the work myself. They never had access to the images of the tablet and the other objects."

The professor went on about his process, explaining to Tommy everything he'd done to try to unravel the ancient code carved into the stone.

Sean's mind wandered. He didn't care about any of that. He knew the professor's methods. They were the same as any other person would use in his profession.

Sean turned his eyes to the bookshelf to his left. It wrapped all the way around to the corner behind him, packed so tight with volumes that he wondered if the sides of the shelf would split apart and cause an avalanche of books, spilling them onto the floor.

He noted classical works by some of the most famous authors of all time. They were philosophical works, mostly, but there were also books about world history, geography, and dozens more in the periphery of those subjects. He stopped his gaze on one book in particular. Putting on his poker face, he didn't show any change of emotion, instead hiding his sudden curiosity from the other two.

He looked farther down the row and found two more books on the same subject. Was it a hobby? Or was Dr. Wilkins an expert on that subject as well? They were each books about the Knights Templar.

"Anyway, I'm sorry if this has been a big waste of your time," Wilkins said. "I can appreciate how valuable it is for you and Sean."

Sean heard his name and snapped back. He played it off like he'd been paying attention the entire time and rapidly switched subjects. "I do have another question for you, Dr. Wilkins."

"Excellent. Inquisitive minds are sharp ones, I always say."

Sean pointed at the bookshelf to the volumes that caught his eye. "Those three," he said, "what's the deal with those? Are you a fan of the Knights Templar, or are you doing a project on them?"

The secretive organization had started off as an elite Catholic military unit. While they weren't officially recognized until midway through the twelfth century, the group had been around long before that.

They were known by many names: the Order of Solomon's Temple, the Poor Fellow-Soldiers of Christ, and the Temple of Solomon. But the Knights Templar was the most common term.

Rumors and conspiracy theories abounded on the group. Books had been written, and movies made, about the order. Some believe they were the ones who possessed the Holy Grail, and others posited that the Templars were the ones who took the Ark of the Covenant from Solomon's Temple and hid it somewhere in Europe. Still others believed they'd crossed the Atlantic and brought it to the New World, hundreds of years before Columbus's famous maiden voyage.

People had spent fortunes trying to find the sacred Ark. Others had paid the ultimate sacrifice in pursuit of it. To date, no one had come close, not that anyone knew of. It was certainly possible that the Ark had been found and the discovery kept secret. Sean doubted that was the case.

The last known sighting of the Ark came from the Bible's Old Testament, in passages that detail events just before the Babylonian siege of Jerusalem. After that, whatever happened to the mysterious golden box was left to the imagination—or the stuff of legend.

Wilkins turned his head to the bookshelf, following Sean's eyes.

"Ah," Wilkins said with crack in his voice, "I've always found the Templars to be a fascinating subject. So little is known about their true identities and purpose. Of course, there is much fiction surrounding them. People want to believe they were heroic bands of secret agents doing their best to rid the world of evil. Pure fantasy, I assure you. The reality of their existence was much simpler than that, and more sinister." He waved his hands around to emphasize his point.

"Sinister?" Tommy asked. He'd done his fair share of research on the Knights Templar, but he was no expert on the subject.

"Yes. You see, the knights used their power and position to build a massive amount of wealth. At one point, they were wealthier than many of the kings in that region, indeed in the entire world. Their vast land holdings put them in the position of almost being a sovereign state. If they'd had their way, I imagine the knights would have pushed for that."

"Like the Vatican."

Wilkins's head bobbed back and forth. "In a way. Except theirs was a military state, governed by martial law. They abused their power, their strength, and took what they wanted. They taxed people heavily, claiming it was in the name of God or calling it tithes. When kings or the pope needed something done, they charged extravagant fees for their services, extorting all who came to their door."

His voice trailed off for a moment, and he reached for a coffee mug on the edge of his desk. After taking a sip, he set the mug down and continued. He shook his head as if he'd just done a shot of whiskey. Maybe there was one in the coffee. "At any rate, they were eventually found out by the king of France and the pope."

"Found out?" Tommy asked.

Wilkins flashed a glance down at his desk and then looked back up, his eyes darting from Tommy to Sean and back again. He folded his hands on the desk top as he leaned forward. "The Templars have this reputation of being upstanding, God-fearing men. They claimed to be servants of the Almighty."

"You don't think they were?" Sean put the question out there even though he had a feeling he knew the answer that was coming.

"I've heard all sorts of things about what happened to the Templars. It's no secret that many of them were publicly executed for heresy. It was a famous date in history, and why Friday the 13th is surrounded by so much speculation and superstition."

To the mainstream and public at large, most people didn't know the real reason behind the irrational fear of this unfortunately numbered Friday. Sean and Tommy, however, were well aware.

"Knights were pulled out of their homes," Wilkins said. "They were tortured, eventually resulting in mass confessions from nearly all of them. Only a few managed to escape."

"Doesn't sound like you feel sorry for them," Sean said, his tone cool and even.

"Pfft. Why should I? Those men were convicted of witchcraft, sorcery, and worst of all, using blood sacrifices in their rituals."

"Blood sacrifices?" Tommy's forehead wrinkled.

"Yes. It eventually came out that the Templars were kidnapping children from other villages and towns to use in their worship of the dark one. Their satanic practices were, thankfully, discovered and rooted out. No one knows what happened to the sparse number of them that managed to evade justice."

Sean listened to the explanation. He'd heard something similar before, and read some of the same things Wilkins was telling them. "What proof did the king's men have to put those knights to death? Surely there was some kind of evidence."

"The evidence was in their confession. Back then, proof was a luxury. It was easier to hide things back in those days. If you knew what you were doing, you could get away with anything."

Wilkins stole a quick glance over at the clock on the wall and abruptly stood up. "Oh dear. Guys, I'm terribly sorry, but I have a class to prepare for. I didn't realize what time it was. I guess I got absorbed in my work before you two came in."

Sean and Tommy stood.

"No problem, Professor," Tommy said and shook the guy's hand.

"Yes, thank you so much for your time," Sean said, waiting his turn for a goodbye handshake.

"My pleasure, fellas. Say, how long are you in town? Maybe we can grab a bite to eat for dinner. My treat."

"Thanks for the offer," Sean said, cutting off his friend before he could accept. "But we really need to be getting back to Atlanta."

Wilkins didn't see the nonverbal exchange between his visitors that let Tommy know to just go with it.

"Yeah, work to do," Tommy agreed. "Perhaps we can come back soon and take you up on that dinner."

"That would be great. I'd love to see you guys and catch up some more."

The two friends showed themselves out and made their way back to the street. The gusty wind had died down, and the sun was doing its best to warm the chilly air embracing the pedestrians.

They walked down the steps and veered back to the left, making their way to the T (what locals call the subway system).

"Well, that was pretty much a waste of time," Tommy said, glancing back over his shoulder at the building as if the professor could hear them all the way out there.

Sean drew a long breath through his nose and exhaled. He shook his head one time. "No, it wasn't."

Tommy looked over at his friend with a confused frown. "It wasn't? You heard Wilkins. Everything he knows about the Massachusetts project was in his reports. And those were fairly useless."

"That part is true. The reports he sent us weren't that helpful."

"So...what are you getting at?"

They stopped at the crosswalk and waited for the sign to change. Sean took a quick look over his shoulder and then stared into his friend's eyes. Tommy knew that look. It was one he'd seen before. It meant that Sean had something serious on his mind.

"Wilkins was lying."

11

WASHINGTON DC

Darren Sanders strode into the receiving room of his office. "Good morning, Nancy," he said with grumble in his voice. "How are you this morning, sir?" she asked. Her tone was polite and way too perky for that time of the morning.

He'd always gotten up early. It was ingrained in his DNA. As the years went by, however, he found himself hitting the snooze button more often, trying to steal a few extra minutes of sleep. Sanders wasn't sure if getting older was the culprit or if he just didn't care as much as he used to. Either way, he was still only half-awake as he trudged into the office.

"I'm fine, Nancy. How are you?"

"Fine, thank you. Your coffee is ready and on your desk, along with several things I need you to sign."

Perfect. No easing into work. It was usually like that: Hit the ground running. One morning, just once, he'd like to walk into work and sit down, sip his coffee, and look out the window at the birds fluttering in the trees outside or the people walking around on the sidewalks. Just a moment of peace would be nice.

Sanders knew that day probably wouldn't come.

He slid into his desk and picked up the mug of steaming coffee and took a sip. He licked his lips and set it back down. Nancy knew how to make coffee just the way he liked it. He wished he knew her trick. Every morning, he made himself a cup at his home, but it wasn't nearly as good as hers. He often dumped out half of his brew before leaving for work, knowing that what awaited him in the office was better than the swill he'd made.

He looked down at the papers and started scanning the first one. Sanders read quickly, which was a huge benefit in his line of work. While he wasn't a legislator anymore, the skill of being able to speed-read had kept him ahead of many other politicians when it came to drafting bills, deciding what to vote for and what to block. He liked to be a step in front of everyone else, which was another reason he was furious about Alycia Freeman being endorsed by the president for the next election.

The thought flipped on the angry switch in his head. He reached for the mug once more and took another sip to calm himself down.

He swallowed the hot liquid and shook his head. "Doesn't do you any good to dwell on it," he muttered.

Sanders signed a blank line at the bottom of the page and moved the sheet to his left, then started reading the next. He was only half-aware of what he was reading. His thoughts lingered on the presidency and the strange visit he'd had from the mysterious visitor just a few days ago.

Since the meeting, Sanders had been able to think of almost nothing else. He wondered when the man would show up again, what he would say or do. The last thing the guy had said to him led Sanders to believe something was about to happen that would give him a chance at the presidency.

That never occurred. The press conference went on as planned, and now the world knew who John Dawkins wanted as his successor.

The more he thought about it, the madder he got. He signed the next piece of paper, stabbing the pen angrily into the sheet, pooling the ink a little in certain places.

He slid the sheet to the side and set the pen down. He ran his fingers through his thinning hair and massaged the back of his scalp.

Sanders took a deep breath and shook his head. There was no use worrying about it.

The mystery guy that had snuck into his office was clearly nuts. He was probably a person who'd abandoned reason long ago. There was something about the man, though, that caused Sanders to believe him. He couldn't put his finger on it. Maybe it was that the guy didn't give off the sense that he was crazy. He was well groomed and clean. In fact, Sanders was certain the visitor had been wearing an expensive cologne.

Then there was the issue of how he'd been granted access. If he remembered correctly, Nancy said he was here when she arrived. Did she mean he was in Sanders's inner office or just waiting in the reception area?

He wished he'd gone back and looked through the security footage. Something told him that wouldn't reveal any answers, however. There was something ghostly about the guy, like he was an apparition that could walk through walls or something. It was a silly thought. Sanders knew that. He didn't believe in ghosts, and he'd never seen anything in life that would push him to believing in men who walked through walls.

Sanders wasn't a religious man. He regarded scriptures of all kinds like ordinary history books, nothing more than an interesting read about people from long ago. The inexplicable miracles, though, he thought were purely allegory or metaphorical in nature.

He snapped his head to the side. Daydreaming again. He often got sidetracked on tangents like that. He needed to sign all these documents before heading off to a meeting with the president later that morning.

He glanced at his $10,000 watch and noted the time. He still had an hour before he needed to be at the White House.

With a sigh, Sanders leaned forward once more and started reading the sheets of minutiae on his desk.

He was halfway down the next page when the cell phone in his pocket started buzzing. He fished it out and glanced at the screen. It was an unknown number.

Usually, Sanders's practice was to ignore callers who blocked their IDs. He didn't have many stalkers—that he knew of—but he'd made plenty of enemies through the years. That was the nature of politics, indeed, of Washington. You could never make everyone happy, and there was no point in trying. The only thing that mattered was pushing through your personal agenda and maybe, along the way, doing a few things that made the majority of your constituents happy.

The phone ceased its gyration. Sanders stared at it for a moment and then laid it on the desk. This second he took his fingers off it, the thing started vibrating again.

Irritated, he picked it up and answered.

"Who is this?" He did nothing to hide his annoyance.

"When I call, you always answer."

He recognized the voice instantly. It was the mysterious visitor from the other day.

"What do you want?"

"When I call, you answer. Do you understand? I'd hate to find another candidate."

Sanders sensed the unmistakable threat in the man's voice. He didn't take kindly to threats. Men in his position were the ones who dished them out, not received them. Yet there was something about this guy that made him keep his feelings deep down. Was it fear? Darren Sanders feared no one. This strange caller, though, was different.

"Fine," he relented, but didn't give the man the answer he sought.

"Turn on your television."

The order caught Sanders off guard. "What?"

"The television hidden in the bookcase across from where you're sitting. Turn it on."

Sanders swiveled around in his chair. A rush of panic flooded his veins. Was this guy watching him? How?

He stepped to the window and looked out, scanning the bushes, trees, and the people walking around outside. The parking lot in the distance didn't reveal any answers to his desperate questions.

"There's no point in trying to find me, Mr. Secretary. Now turn around, and switch your television to the news."

Sanders panted for air as if he'd just finished a 400-meter race. He looked over at his bookcase. A painting hung in the center of it, but that was only a cover. A flatscreen television was hidden behind it, though how the mystery caller knew that he had no idea.

He reached down to his desk and pulled out the middle drawer. A black remote was lying close to the edge. He picked it up and pressed a button. A second later, the painting began moving up into the top of the bookcase, revealing the screen on the wall.

"Atta boy," the man said.

Sanders didn't like being watched, especially by some weirdo who was giving him a play-by-play. He didn't say anything. What was the point? This man on the phone had some kind of power. Sanders didn't know what that power was or how it could affect him, but he had an eerie feeling it wasn't good.

He turned on the television and waited. The TV was almost perpetually on CNN or C-SPAN. The second the screen flickered to life, Sanders understood what the caller wanted him to see.

It was all over the television.

The anchor was interviewing one of their in-house political experts about what it all meant, what was going to happen next, and what the procedures were for such an event.

The bottom chyron line scrolled by almost too fast to read, filled with information about the incident.

"How?" Sanders said, almost involuntarily. His voice was barely above a whisper.

"That doesn't matter. I told you we would handle it."

"What do you want from me?"

"When the time comes, you'll know. For now, let's just say there's something that only the president can give us, and you will be the one to make that happen."

"But what is it? Money? Land? Oil rights?" He fired off all the usual stuff that corrupt men wanted. People who did favors like this weren't easily bought off. It had to be something big.

"Again, when the time comes, I will approach you about that. For now, you must focus on this moment."

Sanders stepped around his desk, still staring at the television. "What am I supposed to do?"

"Nothing, for now. Let the public see your grief. Stand behind the president. Give him your support. Comfort him if you need to. Do everything in your power to be a friend in this time of turmoil and tragedy. He will appreciate that. And then, you will get what you desire."

"But what about what you want? Can't you give me some kind of hint?"

There was no answer. Sanders pulled the phone away from his ear and looked at the screen. The call had ended.

He frowned for a moment, still staring at the device. Then his gaze shifted back to the television. He couldn't' believe what he was hearing, what he was reading.

The Speaker of the House, Alycia Freeman, was dead from an apparent heart attack.

12

BOSTON

"Lying?" Tommy said. His voice was nearly drowned out amid the squeaking and clacking of the T's old wheels and axles.

The subway train meandered along, winding its way like an old green snake through the outlying village of Brookline, nearing the edge of Back Bay.

"What makes you think he was lying?" Tommy asked.

Sean stared out the window. Something wasn't right. He could feel it. There was no way to know for sure what was going to happen next, but one thing he *was* certain of was that Wilkins had lied to them. About everything.

"That entire story was one big lie, Schultzie," Sean said.

Tommy almost looked offended, which for Sean was a pretty tough trick to pull off.

"Sean, Cameron Wilkins has been a friend of my family for over forty years. My parents trusted him. They still do. Why in the world would he lie to me...or to us...about anything? What possible reason could he have?"

Sean knew that question was coming, and he didn't have an answer. Not yet. "I don't know why. And I realize that you and your parents have known him a long time. I'm telling you, though, the guy was being dishonest."

Tommy gave an exasperated sigh. In almost every instance, every scenario, he trusted his friend's judgment. Sometimes, Sean's intuition came across as paranoia. More often than not, however, it ended up being correct. Several times, it had saved their lives. This time, however, was different.

"Buddy, you know I trust you. We've been through a lot together. You've been able to sense when things were wrong when I never did. So, by all means, tell me why you think Dr. Wilkins is lying to us."

Sean's background was in psychology and history. The former had proved to be extremely useful for him as a special agent for the government and later on for Axis. It also came in handy when he was on an assignment for IAA or just playing a game of poker.

"He looked up and to the right, for one," Sean said.

Tommy was befuddled before. Now he was downright lost. "Looked right?"

"It's a tell, a signal. His body language was off kilter."

"Please, elaborate."

"It's psychology, Schultzie. When someone looks up and to the right, it can indicate that person is lying. Of course, that's old school. New research suggests that doesn't give a true indication of deceit."

"Okay...so, why'd you bring it up?"

"It's a piece of the puzzle. The bigger issue was how much he used his hands while he was talking. Did you notice the fidgeting, the hand gestures, the cracks in his voice? All of those things are huge red flags that he was being dishonest."

Tommy let out a long sigh. "So, you're basing this accusation on body language and a best guess?"

Sean sensed the aggravation in his friend's voice. He knew he was walking on thin ice. "It's not an exact science. I know that. Maybe Wilkins didn't do anything wrong. I certainly hope that's the case."

"What you're insinuating is that Dr. Wilkins had something to do with those two men attacking you in Missouri, that he somehow is helping the Assassins. Am I hearing you correctly?"

Sean knew it sounded crazy. He hoped he was wrong. Maybe he was. It wouldn't be the first time. He'd given up any semblance of ego so long ago he barely remembered the year. The exact event that caused it, however, was easy to recall. He'd been a baseball player, and a pretty good one. Problem was, Sean knew it. He'd grown cocky in his prime and almost considered himself invincible.

Then the injury happened.

He tore the labrum in his shoulder. Even after surgery, he knew he'd never be able to throw a ball the way he did before.

It was humbling, to say the least. Sean realized that he wasn't immortal, that he was subject to the whims of fate—or perhaps of a greater power.

As it turned out, the incident brought about a spiritual change in him, one that had guided him through life up to this point. He believed that he'd needed to get injured because it brought about a newfound humility, and a greater appreciation of the things and abilities he had in his life.

Sean buried his ego between physical therapy sessions and became a new person.

He often wondered if God had caused that injury to happen. While he didn't believe in a deity that meted out punishment to people, he did believe that a higher power sometimes guided men and women onto a path that would better serve them.

Sean's intuition had served him well. He knew that, had he never been injured, he would have likely been killed long ago in the line of duty. He would have been brash, arrogant, and most likely dead as a result. His new sense of danger and the realization that he didn't know everything had made him a more effective agent, both for the government and for IAA.

"Maybe I'm wrong," Sean said. "I hope I am. Truly, I do."

Tommy held his friend's gaze for nearly a minute. His eyes pierced Sean's with an intensity Sean hadn't seen from him before, at least not in recent memory.

"Me, too," Tommy said finally.

The train's driver announced the next stop, and the cars

screeched to a halt. Commuters climbed aboard with their briefcases and backpacks. Some swayed or bobbed their heads, listening to music on headphones.

Sean averted his eyes and looked out the window to his left. He gripped the leather strap overhead tighter than he realized, a defense mechanism for letting go of irritation, irritation that would lead to anger.

While he conceded that he could be incorrect about Wilkins, something told him he wasn't, and that his friend was being blinded by family ties that went back decades.

Sean could understand, but he also knew that nothing was out of the realm of possibility. His life had taught him that much.

He scanned the landing outside and caught a glimpse of two men in gray peacoats walking hurriedly to catch the train. He couldn't see their eyes through their dark sunglasses. One of the men was nearly bald. The buzzed hair around the crown of his head was patchy and dark against his pale skin. The other guy had a thick mane of brown hair that flowed down past his ears and fluttered in the breeze.

The men climbed onto the train and slowed their pace in the mob of people already filling the car.

Sean watched as they grabbed on to metal poles to keep their balance as the train lurched forward. The driver's voice crackled in the speaker again, louder this time than before. It startled Tommy and some of the other passengers, but Sean didn't pay much attention. He was focused on the two men gradually making their way toward the back of the train where Tommy and Sean were sitting.

Tommy's back was to the approaching men. He tried to smooth over the awkwardness both were feeling. "Listen, buddy, I'm sorry. I know you probably have your reasons for thinking Wilkins was lying and that he might have something to do with this. It's just that..."

"Sometimes I'm wrong," Sean said.

"Yeah, I mean, sure. Everyone is now and then. It happens."

Tommy noticed his friend was looking over his shoulder and not directly at him. Something had caught Sean's eye.

Tommy's face tightened slightly as concern seeped into his gut.

Then he felt his phone vibrate inside his pants pocket. He fished out the device and looked at the screen. It was a text message from Tara.

The message was huge, at least four paragraphs. Tommy scanned through the lines. His expression changed vividly, and his face flushed pale.

"What?" Sean asked. "What is it?"

Tommy swallowed and looked up from the phone. "It's from Tara. The trace they ran...." His voice trailed off.

Sean shook his head, trying to understand what his friend was saying. "What about it?"

"Whoever was scanning our systems...they...they were here."

"Here, as in Boston?"

"As in Boston University."

Sean's face blanched, too.

"There's a lot of tech jargon in this message," Tommy went on, "but it looks like maybe you were right."

"Well, don't look now, but I think two of Wilkins's guys are coming for us."

"What?" Before Tommy realized what he was doing, he turned his head around and saw the two men.

"And that's why I told you not to turn around."

Sean stared down the man in front. It was the younger of the two, the one with the wavy hair that looked like he should be a model.

"Hold on tight," Sean said.

Tommy's head whipped around, his eyes wondering what his friend was going to do. It only took a second for him to find out.

Sean reached over with his left hand and yanked on the emergency stop cable.

The trains weren't built for speed. They moved along at a steady but slow pace. Occasionally, on some of the longer stretches of track, they'd pick up the pace somewhat, but on the way into the city where multiple stops were required, the trains didn't go very fast.

Momentum, however, was a fickle mistress.

When Sean tugged the cable, the train buckled. Everyone in their seats suddenly leaned forward. Anyone standing up felt their weight pull them forward. Those who weren't holding on tight to the poles or the leather grips above stumbled forward.

The two men coming toward Sean and Tommy weren't holding on to anything, which proved problematic as the train came to an abrupt stop.

A bulbous man in a pinstripe suit to Sean's right hadn't been paying attention, probably thinking he knew all the stops and when to brace himself. That mistake sent him sprawling into the two peacoats. His weight drove both men onto the floor as they struggled to keep their balance and brace their fall.

The second the train stopped, Sean spun around and rushed for the nearest exit. The door was closed but he managed to insert his fingers into the seal and pry them open with both hands. At first, the gap was only a few inches, but Tommy caught up and helped. Once he added his strength to the effort, the doors slid open easily.

The two friends jumped down onto the concrete next to the tracks and took off at a sprint.

"Where are we going?" Tommy shouted, following Sean as he ran across the street in front of traffic.

Angry commuters slammed on their brakes and honked their horns. Sean didn't care, though he put up an apologetic hand to stave off any further ire from additional drivers. It didn't help.

He and Tommy reached the other side of the street and swung to the left.

"Where are you going?" Tommy asked, a bit louder than he wanted. He was running, though, and couldn't worry with being polite when he was panting for breath and trying to get away from danger, potentially life-threatening danger. Tommy had a bad feeling he already knew the answer.

"You know where I'm going, Schultzie."

Tommy didn't protest, though he wanted to. He took a quick look back over his shoulder and saw the two men from the train running after them. They were a few hundred yards back thanks to the head start and to a mob of confused commuters on the train, likely blocking the exits.

Tommy still had his doubts. "You sure you want to go back there?" He still wasn't entirely convinced Wilkins was responsible, though he had to admit the evidence against him was mounting. He also knew he'd never hear the end of it from his friend.

"No," Sean answered without looking back. "But I'm not letting Wilkins get away that easy."

Sean turned the corner of an arched gate fixed into place with stone columns. He never saw the men hiding behind the pillars until they stepped in front of him.

Both men raised pistols to halt Sean and Tommy in their tracks.

Sean's momentum, however, carried him forward. He couldn't stop fast enough and was on the man to the right before he knew it. The guy tried to step to the side, but Sean wrapped his fingers around the barrel of the gun and twisted hard.

It would have been a perfect trap had the men accounted for Sean's speed. The weapon wrenched from the guy's hand even as he pulled the trigger. The muzzle exploded, sending a loud pop across the campus and the parallel street. The bullet smashed into the second gunman's foot, the shoe erupting in a bloody crater.

He screamed and dropped to one knee. Tommy was close behind his friend and saw everything happen in the blink of an eye. He witnessed the second guy being hit by a stray bullet and fall to the ground. Tommy kept running and, like a football kicker, drove the top of his foot into the man's jaw.

The guy flipped over onto his back, out cold.

Sean turned to the first gunman and fired three quick shots into the guy's chest. The shots rang out amid the screams of students and morning commuters.

People ran for cover. Some ducked behind trees. Others sprinted into the buildings to find safety. Cars sped away, tires screeching.

The first gunman dropped to the ground and fell over on his side. Sean looked down at the guy while he caught his breath. He raised his head and gazed out at the chaos of the panicking citizens. Whenever possible, he tried not to let something like this happen. Now he'd just killed a man in front of hundreds of potential witnesses.

Sean tucked the gun into his belt and bent down. He pulled back the guy's jacket sleeve and found the tattoo he already knew would be there. It was the same one the two men in Missouri had and in the exact same location on his wrist. Sean stood up straight and looked over at the unconscious guy. He didn't have to look at his arm to know there would be a matching tattoo.

"We need to go," Sean said.

"What about Wilkins?" Tommy asked, his face full of both confusion and concern.

"We'll have to get to him later."

Then Tommy had another thought. He rushed to the gate and peered around the column. "Where did the other two go?"

Sean stepped next to his friend and looked down the avenue toward the stopped T train. The two men who'd chased them were gone.

13

NEW YORK CITY

The getaway hadn't been easy. Tusun didn't believe in luck, but it had been unfortunate that the woman Emily Starks had shown up at the prison when she did. He didn't bother wondering what she was doing there. She'd obviously come to interrogate the prisoners.

Why she was interested in them was another matter.

Best he could figure, she was still trying to figure out what they were doing in Missouri and why Sean Wyatt had been a target.

Less than three minutes after leaving the prison, Tusun and his men abandoned the van in a warehouse and split up into two SUVs.

The cops would find the van soon enough as their net tightened around a perimeter they'd set up in the area.

The two SUVs made it through roadblocks without any trouble. The cops didn't give them so much as a sniff as they passed by.

They arrived in New Jersey later that afternoon and parked in a garage, changing cars one more time before making their way into Manhattan and the lair where their comrades and their leader would be waiting.

Tusun said nothing as he and the others marched Syd and Michel down the dark corridor, through the additional security doors, and into the underground hideout.

If Syd and Michel expected a welcoming homecoming, they were sorely mistaken.

The second the heavy door closed behind them, they were pushed into the center of the room, surrounded by their brethren. The two stumbled for a second before regaining their balance.

Michel looked incensed. He righted himself and stared around the room, spinning in a circle. "What are you doing?" he asked, his voice bordering on rage.

Syd said nothing, instead watching the others with a curious and wary gaze.

"We are waiting," Tusun said.

"Waiting? Waiting for what?"

"The master."

"Fine. I'd love to speak with him. The plan was flawed. That woman could have ruined everything. Where did she come from? How did she know what we were doing?"

Tusun listened with a stone cold expression on his face. "The plan worked—despite her intrusion. I believe she didn't know what we were doing. It's likely her arrival was an unfortunate coincidence."

"You could have had an equal share in that prison cell, same as us."

"But we got away, and you two are free men...for now."

Syd's face scrunched in a frown.

"For now?" Michel asked. "What's that supposed to mean?"

"What that means is the two of you must prove yourselves in the circle."

"On whose authority?"

"Mine." The new voice resonated from a darkened corner. A second later, Alain stepped into the light. His eyes were darker than normal. He wore black robes that almost resembled those worn by monks or priests. The hood was pulled over his head and added a sinister shade to his face.

He reached up and pulled the hood back, letting it fall between his shoulders with an almost elegant motion.

Syd and Michel spun around to face their leader.

"The circle?" Syd asked. There was only a hint of fear in his voice. "Why?"

Alain approached with his hands folded behind his back. In the flowing black robe, cinched tight around his waist, it almost looked like he was floating, a dark apparition come to haunt every man in the room.

"You failed," Alain said. "You failed to stop Wyatt. Now he and his friend are curious. They're digging in places they shouldn't. You have set in motion a series of events that we must now rein in, a task that will prove more difficult than we planned."

"It wasn't our fault."

Alain raised his right hand, signaling for silence. Michel shut up immediately.

"You were caught. Now people are asking questions. They're searching for answers about you...and us. As a result of your failure, you will face each other in the circle."

Syd and Michel glanced uneasily at each other.

"Only one of you walks out alive," Alain announced.

He turned to a man standing next to Tusun. His head was shaved, his menacing face enhanced by a mustache and goatee.

"Weapons."

The man nodded and produced two katanas from behind his back. He tossed them onto the floor.

The rest of the men backed away, forming a circle around Syd and Michel.

Alain took a step back and put his hands out wide with palms up. "By your failure, you are condemned. By blood, you are freed."

It was an old phrase dating back to the earliest days of the order. The tradition of the circle wasn't one that was invoked often. In fact, Alain had only seen it one time in twenty years. His master had told him that instance was the first in his entire lifetime.

The circle was the punishment of choice for any man or men

who'd done wrong by the order. Theft, unauthorized murder, insubordination, and in this case, failing a mission, were all punishable offenses.

The current master, in this case Alain, chose the weapons. He preferred swords to anything else. Firearms had only been used in the late 1700s and early 1800s when duels were the popular method of dealing with disputes. Alain thought it more appropriate to use more traditional weaponry when it came to something like this. Pistols could misfire. Shooters could get lucky. Swords were precision instruments, more surgical than guns.

"Begin!" Alain commanded.

Syd and Michel looked at each other, then at the swords, then at each other again. The two men had never witnessed the circle before, but they both knew what was at stake. The rules demanded one of them die to absolve their collective sin. It was a barbaric and violent way to set things right. It was also just.

Michel made the first move. He jolted toward the sword nearest him and scooped it up in one swift motion. He whirled around, ready to end the fight in less than ten seconds. Syd, however, reacted almost as fast. He grabbed his sword and dove to the side just as Michel swept the edge of his blade in a vicious horizontal arc.

The sharp metal whooshed over Syd's head, only missing by a few inches as he rolled clear.

Michel stepped back with the weapon held at an angle in front of him. He took a defensive position, ready for Syd to counter.

The men surrounding them said nothing. They didn't cheer. There was no banter. They all knew one of their brothers was about to die. To hope for one or the other to win would be a betrayal of the order. So, they watched in curious silence, only observing as one might observe birds bickering over the last scraps of seed.

Michel shuffled his feet a couple of inches forward. Syd slid to his left. He kept his left hand in front of him, almost like it was a shield. The right hand was cocked back with the sword ready to strike.

The men stared at each other with fiery eyes. Then Michel lashed out. He lunged forward with unmistakable precision that belied years of intense training.

Syd was equal to the task. He moved his back foot behind the other heel and twisted, easily deflecting the first attack, then the second and third.

Michel hacked at his opponent's neck.

Syd parried and countered with a stab that nearly ended the battle right then and there. Michel twisted his body and jabbed his fist into Syd's nose.

The shorter man staggered back, grabbing the wounded appendage with his thumb and forefinger. Blood spurted from his nostrils, but there was no time to tend to it. Michel pounced, launching at his opponent again.

He twisted right, feigning another horizontal slash, then jerked his torso back the other way while flipping the handle in his fingers. He brought the blade down hard at an angle that might have cut his opponent in half from the shoulder down through his pelvis.

Syd wasn't done yet, though, and raised his blade to meet the other. Metal clanked loudly, echoing through the room. The men pushed hard against each other, putting all their weight into the swords.

It was Syd who adapted his strategy first, delivering an elbow to Michel's ribs. One of the bones cracked and sent a sharp pain through Michel's chest. He grimaced but didn't let go of his weapon. Instead, he swept his right foot hard and caught Syd on the heels. The move knocked Syd off balance, and he fell back onto his tailbone. The back of his skull smacked against the hard surface and sent him into a daze.

Michel fought through the agonizing pain from his broken rib and raised his blade high over his head. He brought it down quickly, aiming for Syd's neck.

The room spun in Syd's blurred vision. He blinked rapidly, desperate to regain his senses. He caught a flash of metal above him and realized what was coming. With a last-ditch effort, he stabbed the tip of his sword up, thrusting the sharp point as hard as he could.

The handle shuddered. It hit something solid but malleable. He pushed harder.

Michel groaned and took a step back. The blade slid out of his abdomen, now coated with a thin layer of crimson.

He looked down at the wound as he continued to stagger backward. His katana hung loose in his fingers now, the tip nearly dragging on the floor.

Syd scrambled to his feet. He wavered. The room still spun, though less than before. He saw Michel holding a hand over his gut, blood seeping through the fingers.

Syd took a deep breath. His head pounded and he was disoriented, but he knew what had to be done.

He stepped forward with a sense of caution. While Michel was wounded, Syd knew his opponent was far from finished.

He lashed out with his weapon. Michel took a step back and feebly raised his sword to block the strike. His sword gyrated in his hand. Syd flipped the blade and swiped again. Michel managed to parry the blow, but Syd had set him up like a master chess player forcing an opponent's hand.

Syd spun around and thrust the tip of his sword through Michel's chest. The bloody point protruded out of the man's back for a second before Syd yanked the blade out.

Michel dropped to his knees. A thin trail of blood trickled from the corner of his mouth. He stared ahead with nearly lifeless eyes. His body wavered back and forth, as if he might fall, but he stayed upright by sheer will.

Syd's breath came hard and fast. He wiped his nose with the back of his hand and glanced over at Alain.

The master gave a single nod of approval.

Syd didn't have to ask what to do.

He pulled the blade back over his shoulder and whipped it around in a dramatic arc. Michel's torso fell forward. The second it hit the floor, his head disconnected from the neck and rolled five feet away.

Every eye in the room shifted from the dead body to Syd. No one said anything at first. There was no applause for his victory. They were all equals, and so all had lost as well as gained a brother.

Alain stepped forward from the group and motioned to the dead man. "Give him an honorable burial," he said. Then he turned to Syd. "You are absolved."

Without pomp or formality, Alain swiveled around and walked out of the room with his hands behind his back.

Syd stood there alone in the circle, still panting for air. He wiped his nose again and looked down one last time as the others gathered Michel's body and removed it from the room.

14

BOSTON

Sean and Tommy sprinted to the river. They couldn't take a chance at being caught by the police. Even with Sean's connections, there was no way they wanted to be taken in for questioning.

Killing the gunman had been self-defense. Any witnesses who'd seen the shooting go down would attest to that, but there was something else at play. Sean couldn't risk being taken in. For all he knew, some of the cops were on the Assassins payroll. It was a bold assumption, but he almost always erred on the side of paranoia.

The gunman's weapons plopped into the Saint Charles after Sean and Tommy threw them as hard as they could. Then the two friends took off again, this time at a steady jog. They'd heard the sirens in the distance as the first responders arrived on the scene.

No doubt the campus was on full lockdown and going through all the procedures that were in place for an active-shooter scenario.

The authorities would find the bodies of the gunmen, but there would be no trace of their killers or the murder weapons. Investigators wouldn't bother with searching the river for the guns. It would be too expensive in terms of money and time.

"Where are we going?" Tommy asked as Sean led the way along the riverbank, skirting the edge of the campus.

"We're circling around," Sean answered. "We'll double back once we get a few blocks deeper into Brookline then go back for the car."

Tommy didn't question his friend. Sean knew better how to handle a situation like this, though over the years Tommy had learned a great deal in that regard, too. His friend was a good teacher, even if that wasn't what Sean was trying to do. They'd figured a way out of sticky situations on nearly every continent, and now it was becoming second nature to Tommy, as it appeared to be for Sean.

They slowed their pace when they reached the west end of the college and then hung a sharp left. After crossing Commonwealth Avenue, they continued beyond the thickening traffic and pushed on until they had crossed two more parallel streets. Only then did they turn left once more and make their way back to the car they'd parked earlier.

The entire process took well over twenty minutes, but it was worth it. Cops were everywhere by the time they arrived at their vehicle. Ambulances were on the scene, as well as fire trucks. There was no sign of the students, which meant they'd already been let out of the buildings, or more likely, they were still hiding in various classrooms and study areas until the all clear was given and the active shooter drill ended.

During the escape, Sean kept wondering where the other two hit men were. It was like they'd vanished into thin air, without a trace. One moment, they were sprinting after him. The next, they were gone.

Sean slid into the driver's seat and revved the engine. He rubbed his hands together to warm them for a second before shifting the car into gear.

None of the onlookers surrounding the police-taped area paid any attention to the two men driving away from the scene.

"Find me Wilkins's address," Sean said as he steered the car off Commonwealth and onto a side road.

Tommy looked over at his friend with suspicion in his eyes. "You're not thinking what I think you're thinking, are you?"

"I think so."

"So, we're going over to Wilkins's house to break in? Because that sounds like tempting fate twice in one day."

"Wilkins has something to do with this, Schultzie. I know you don't want to believe that, but it's true."

Tommy sat in pensive silence for a moment before responding. "No," he said finally, "I think you're right. It's the only explanation. How else would those goons have known where we were? And it can't be a coincidence that we left Wilkins's office and stepped right into that mess. They were waiting for us. They knew. And only one person could have alerted them."

"I'm sorry," Sean said. There was no satire in his voice, only sincerity.

Tommy shrugged it off. "It's okay. It is what it is."

Sean's lips curled. "What does that even mean?" He asked in a more lighthearted tone.

"What?"

"It is what it is? What is that supposed to mean? I hear people say it all the time, and it drives me nuts."

Tommy chuckled. "I don't know. I guess it means that things are how they are, and there's nothing you can do to change them."

Sean flicked an eyebrow up. "I suppose."

"Anyway, whatever. My point is, all signs point to Wilkins stabbing us in the back. I can accept that, but breaking into his place...are you sure that's a good idea? What if the cops show up simply because he was there at the college during the shooting?"

It was a stretch. Sean knew that, but his friend wasn't as familiar with process and protocol as he was.

"The cops aren't going to show up at Wilkins's place. I'm not worried about them."

The way he said it told Tommy there *was* something that concerned his friend.

"The other guys?" he said more as a statement than a question.

"Yeah," Sean muttered. "There's a strong possibility we'll find the two from the train at Wilkins's house. First things first. We need to know where he lives."

"I'm on it."

Tommy scrolled through his phone and tapped the screen.

A few rings later, Alex answered. "Hey, Tommy, what's up?"

"We need you to look up Cameron Wilkins's address here in Boston."

"O...kay."

"Can't you do that?"

Alex laughed into the phone. "Of course we can do that. I was expecting something difficult. Hold on a second."

Tommy imagined Alex's fingers flying across the keyboard at his workstation. It took less than a minute before Alex had the address. He relayed the information, which Tommy gave to Sean.

Tommy's memory was good. Sean's was nearly eidetic.

"Made any progress with the tablet translation?" Tommy asked.

"We're working on it. A couple of things came through, but we need more time."

"Stay on it." Tommy paused for a second. "What about the other thing?"

"The trace? It came back to Boston University. That's Dr. Wilkins, right?"

Tommy's face blanched at the truth he didn't want to face. Wilkins had crossed over. He'd betrayed a lifetime of friendships. Now, Tommy needed to know why.

"Thanks, Alex. Give me a shout the second you have something definitive on the tablet."

"Yes, sir. Will do."

Tommy ended the call and let out a long sigh though his nose.

Sean's eyes shifted, and he stole a quick glance at his friend without letting on. He stayed silent for a moment, guiding the car through intersections and weaving through traffic. He made a left turn onto another street that led into downtown. The address of Wilkins's place was in Beacon Hill. That made sense given the professor's affinity for history. Having a home on the edge of Boston Commons was the perfect location for someone of that ilk.

Three full minutes went by before Tommy spoke up. "They said the trace went back to Wilkins."

Sean nodded. "I know."

"I can't believe he would betray us like that. I mean, I know we already figured as much, but hearing it from Alex just now...."

"It hurts." Sean finished his friend's sentence.

"Yeah. He put us in danger. Alex and Tara, too, potentially. I want answers."

"You'll get them soon enough, buddy. We'll be at his place in ten minutes."

Eight and a half minutes later, Sean pulled the car into a parking spot on one of the streets that branched away from Boston Commons. According to the address they received from Alex, the professor's apartment was just around the corner, up the hill toward the Massachusetts State Capitol.

They found the address and hurried up the steps. Sean pulled out a tool from his jacket pocket, while Tommy looked around, making sure no curious pedestrians were paying attention while they effectively committed a crime, breaking into Cameron Wilkins's apartment.

Sean worked quickly with the lock, pushing the little rod into the hole and then fitting the flat piece below it. He twisted and prodded for a second until the mechanism clicked, then he pushed down on the handle and shoved the door open.

The two stepped inside and closed the door behind them before taking a quick look around the foyer. Their brief reconnaissance told them what they already knew: no one was home.

"How'd you learn to do that?" Tommy asked as Sean shoved the tool back in his jacket.

"Part of the job," he said with a shrug.

"Not your current job."

Sean chuckled. "No, I guess not. Although it seems to be coming in handy."

"No question. You gotta show me how to do that one of these days."

"Sure. I'll teach you all about it when we get home." Sean lathered his comment in sarcasm.

Tommy ignored his friend's joke and stepped farther into the foyer. A set of stairs led up to the second floor. To the left, a quaint sitting area featured two plush, high-back chairs with paisley upholstery. To the right, the dining room was furnished with a long oaken table stained in a dark cherry finish. Potted plants were positioned in each corner, and a huge tapestry depicting fruit hung from the far wall.

"His study will be upstairs," Sean said. "We should look there first."

Tommy's eyebrows furrowed. "How do you know that?"

"Where would you put your workspace?"

"I guess upstairs. I'm gonna check down here just to make sure."

Sean snorted and gave nod. "Go ahead."

He tiptoed up the steps while Tommy worked his way down the hall into the living room.

On the second floor, Sean found the master bedroom, a guest room, and, as he suspected, the study.

Wilkins's personal library was immense. The room spanned at least thirty feet across and nearly twenty feet deep. The eleven-foot ceilings made the space feel even more open, which was good because the room had enough clutter in it to make a hoarder blush.

Bankers boxes were stacked four feet high along the interior wall. The bookshelves that lined the other three walls overflowed with volumes on every topic from basic geography to the modern-day implications of the Magna Carta.

Sean's head spun as he took in the incredible amount of stuff Wilkins kept in the study. The desk directly ahead of him had numerous sheets of paper, books, pens, and notes written in Wilkins's handwriting.

Sean moved closer to the desk and looked out the window. The fenced-in backyard wasn't much more than a small courtyard between his abode and the neighbors behind Wilkins. Sean turned his attention back to the desk and started sifting through some of the papers.

He picked up a bank statement, and his eyes went wide with surprise.

Tommy appeared in the doorway and sighed. "I guess you were right."

"I know."

"Nice," Tommy said. Leaving the sarcasm behind, he looked at the paper in Sean's hand. "What's that?" He stepped into the room and made his way to the desk.

Sean handed the piece of paper over to his friend. "How many professors do you know make that kind of money?"

Tommy's forehead immediately wrinkled. "Whoa."

"Yeah," Sean said. "You don't save up that kind of scratch on a professor's salary, not unless you're doing speaking engagements and writing books."

"Dr. Wilkins doesn't do that. I mean, he wrote a few books, but I don't think they sold well."

"Which means he's getting money from somewhere else."

Sean picked through stacks of books on the desk. Many of them were about the Knights Templar. Others were religious texts. A few centered on the topic of religious relics from all over the world. Sean noticed a bookmark in one and picked it up.

He read a few paragraphs and set the book down again.

"His place sure is a mess," Tommy commented, his head twisting around as he took in the collection of seemingly random stuff.

"Intellectuals often use the pile method of storing things. Einstein's office looked a lot like this one."

Tommy knew his friend was right. Often, highly intelligent people were some of the messiest. It made him feel a little humbled at how neat he liked to keep things.

Sean noticed another book on the Templars and picked it up. He thumbed through the pages and then stopped where he found one that had been dogeared.

He scanned the lines of text, absorbing every bit of information.

Tommy picked up a picture frame and stared at it. Dr. Wilkins and Tommy's parents were standing by a palm tree, probably in some far-off land. It tugged at his heart for a second. This man had been a friend for a long time. Now he was caught up in something Tommy still didn't understand.

Sean flipped the page, and his face went pale. He swallowed as he stared into the book.

Tommy noticed his friend's unusual silence and set the picture down. When he looked at Sean, he saw the color absent in his friend's skin. "What? What's wrong?"

Sean swallowed and flipped the book around. The image on the page was of a stone tablet.

On the face of the tablet were rows of symbols. It was an exact match of the tablet in Atlanta.

15

WASHINGTON DC

Darren Sanders loomed in the background, behind the blue curtain, as President Dawkins gave his official condolences regarding the sudden and untimely death of Alycia Freeman.

Sanders didn't pay much attention to what the president was saying. His mind was spinning. The mysterious stranger had come through, at least so far. Now nothing was standing in Sanders's way. He'd be the obvious choice to get Dawkins's endorsement now.

The secretary of state would play it cool, of course. Now wasn't the time to vie for power. His secret benefactor had been right in his counsel. Helping the president grieve, being there as a support for him, that was the best course of action. He wouldn't bring up the presidential election for a few weeks, at the earliest. Things needed to die down, although that could happen quickly in Washington. The president's job was never done, even when he was taking time off at Camp David. The most pressing matters of the world were always on the president's mind, and when he returned to the White House those things were still on his desk, waiting to be tended to.

The president's speech writer and a few other advisers stood to the left of Sanders. Still more interns hung back behind him, farther down the hall, trying to get a view of the press room and the reaction of the people inside.

Sanders wore the most somber face he could muster. It wasn't the first time his job had called for good acting. That was part of being in Washington. The game required it. Every speech he'd ever given to the voters, the press, anyone, had come with an element of dishonesty. That's what acting was, after all: pretending to be someone you're not.

As long as the audience believed it, that was all that mattered.

Cameras flashed in the press room as the president finished his comments and thanked everyone for being there. He'd already told everyone there would be no question-and-answer session at the end, and to Sanders's surprise, all of the reporters respected that wish.

Usually, the sharks were relentless, no matter the situation. They wanted a story, and if they could get a sound bite or some tasty little morsel to put in their next article, they'd do whatever it took to get it. Today, however, they remained silent as the president stepped away from the podium and out of sight behind the curtain.

The staffers—interns included—remained politely quiet with hands folded in front of them, giving respectful nods to the commander in chief as he passed by. Dawkins stopped in front of Sanders, who still wore a downtrodden, somber face.

"How was it, Darren?" Dawkins asked.

Sanders ticked his head to the side and offered a humble smile. "It was perfect, Mr. President."

Dawkins nodded. "I appreciate that. Come with me. We need to talk."

Sanders didn't change his expression despite the invitation being a complete surprise. What did the president want? Why now? Did he know about the phone call with the stranger? Did he know about the visit? A wave of panic rushed through him, but he kept his face stoic, revealing nothing of the turmoil inside.

Dawkins motioned down the hall and started walking. Sanders didn't have much choice. He fell into stride next to the president and followed him through the White House, all the way to the Oval

Office. A team of four Secret Service men followed them to the room. Dawkins closed the door once they were inside and made his way over to the Resolute Desk.

He planted his elbows on the surface and folded his hands, pressing them into his forehead for a moment as if deep in thought.

Sanders stood awkwardly by one of the sofas and then decided it was best if he sit. He eased into a chair across from the president and waited.

Dawkins shook his head slowly. "I can't believe she's gone," he said. His voice carried a beleaguered tone.

Sanders allowed a few short nods, pretending he understood the man's pain. He apparently hadn't realized the connection Dawkins and Freeman had.

"Were you two...close, sir?" Sanders took a chance asking the question, but he didn't mean anything by it. "I didn't realize you were good friends."

"We weren't close, necessarily," Dawkins answered. "Sometimes we disagreed on things, but she was a good woman, and would have made a terrific leader. She would have filled this chair nicely."

He let his hands down to the armrests and rubbed the leather for a second as if mimicking what Freeman might have done the first time she took the seat.

"Now I'm not sure what to do."

"Give it time, sir. It will come."

Dawkins snorted. "Part of being in this chair means you're supposed to know what to do. The words *I don't know* aren't part of a president's vocabulary. We figure things out, sometimes on the fly and without enough information, but we do it. We push ahead." His words trailed off, and he stared down at the desk for a second. "She was a good woman, Darren. A good woman."

Sanders nodded. "Yes, sir, she was. Would have made a fine president."

"You got that right. It's too soon to think about who the party might want to take that place now, but they'll have to figure it out in the coming days. The opponents are already hot on the campaign trail, pushing harder than ever."

"Their candidates are weak, sir."

"I know that. Heck, most of the people know that. But if we don't find someone strong to fill in...well, I'm afraid of what could happen."

Dawkins knew who was running for the other party. They had wild, fanatical ideas. It would be a train wreck from day one if they were elected. According to the polls, that didn't look like a possibility, but now that Freeman was gone anything could happen.

All of John Dawkins's hard work over the last seven years would be flushed down the drain in the first hundred days.

"Sir, with all due respect, now isn't the time to worry about those things. Give it a few days." Sanders spoke with deep sincerity in his voice, never letting on that what he really wanted to say. "Take some time to grieve, to show the world what a great person Alycia Freeman was, what she stood for. Don't worry about the election. You've done your duty as president. Let the committee figure that out. If and when they find someone to take her place, then you can consider your endorsement of that person."

Dawkins's head bobbed. "You're right, Darren. You've always been there for me, ever since I appointed you to your position. You've been a good sounding board and the voice of reason more times than I can count. I owe you a great debt for that. Truly, I do. Your leadership has helped make this administration what it is, what I believe has been one of the best in the history of our great nation." He snickered. "Of course, I'm biased."

Sanders didn't mirror the frail grin. "It has been, sir. No question. And I'm not just talking about approval ratings or any of that crap. You have been a good leader and done more for the people of this nation than anyone I can think of who has occupied that chair."

"I've also screwed up."

Sanders's shoulders raised for a second and then dropped down. "So? You're human. Everyone screws up now and then, but you have led with a sound mind and good judgment. That's all anyone could ask for."

Dawkins listened as his secretary of state finished his comments. He'd carried the weight of the nation on his shoulders for the last seven years. Now that burden was heavier than ever.

For most presidents, things started winding down toward the end of their last term. Some of them coasted to the finish line, preparing to write their memoirs, to start booking speaking engagements, and to play a lot more golf. Others would begin engaging in charitable activities, philanthropy, or simply traveling for pleasure.

Sanders knew Dawkins didn't operate like that. He would work himself hard until the inauguration of the next president, doing his absolute best to make sure the country was taken care of.

He viewed his position as just that, one of a caretaker. He was the shepherd, and the people of the United States were his flock.

"You're right, Darren," Dawkins said after nearly two full minutes of silence passed. "Now isn't the time to think about things like that. It's the time to pay tribute to Alycia Freeman's legacy. That will be a lot easier to do knowing that I already have the perfect person in mind to take her place during next year's election."

Sanders's head twitched slightly, and he looked up to meet the president's gaze. "Sir?"

John Dawkins pointed a bony finger at his secretary of state. "You, Darren. You're the obvious choice. You need to take her place. You have to be the next president of the United States."

16

BOSTON

S ean and Tommy leafed their way through everything on Wilkins's desk. They found notes regarding the tablet, including a few loose translations, though nothing definitive. Apparently, the professor was having the same problem with unraveling the meaning behind the inscriptions.

Tommy snapped a few pictures of Wilkins's solutions and sent them to Alex and Tara. The thought was that the kids might be able to plug in some of the things the professor was able to decipher and thus help in getting additional translations.

It was a long shot, but at the moment that was the best they had.

"He's been working on all this for some time," Tommy said as he rapidly turned the pages in an old notebook.

"No kidding," Sean agreed. "You just sent him the tablet info last week, right?"

"Yeah, but it seems like he's been looking for it forever."

"Not to mention his love affair with the Knights Templar. He's got more books on those guys than anything else in here. I count thirty so far."

Tommy gave an absent nod. "You think he believes there's some kind of connection between the Templars and that tablet?"

"Seems pretty obvious. He's got all this Templar stuff together with the information you sent, plus his own work on the subject. So, yeah, he thinks there's a connection."

Tommy blew off the barb. He'd grown accustomed to it after thirty-plus years of friendship. "The question is, what is he looking for?"

"Yeah. And who is pulling his strings behind the scenes?"

The question lingered for a moment as the room fell silent.

"I know," Tommy said. He slammed the picture of Wilkins and his parents facedown on the desk. "It's clear he's working for the Assassins, if that's who's behind this. I think we both know it is. But why? What do they need him for?"

"And what are they trying to find?"

"That's the big question," Tommy said. "All these years being underground, hiding in the shadows. It's like they were waiting for something."

"Whatever it is, it's big."

"Motive is always tricky," Sean said, "especially with these kinds of organizations. Smoke and mirrors everywhere."

Tommy talked his way through the puzzle. "Originally, they were formed by a radical sect of Islam."

"Correct."

"So, do you think maybe this has something to do with a new holy war?"

Sean blinked rapidly as he considered the question. "A jihad? Maybe. I don't know. It doesn't feel like that's it. There's something else."

"If they're looking for something connected to the Templars, maybe it's the Holy Grail. We've both heard the stories about the Templars taking the grail to Scotland. Then there's the rumors about them sailing across the Atlantic to hide it here."

"Yeah, I know. Oak Island and all that."

"Well, not necessarily there, but yes, that is one potential location."

The mystery of Oak Island had been well documented for over a hundred years. It came to be known as the money pit, a term that started being passed around casually regarding any bad real estate investment down through the decades. The strange pit at Oak Island was anything but a laughing matter.

It was originally discovered by Daniel McGinnis in 1799 while looking for a place to plot his farm. He found a depression in the ground and, thinking it odd, began digging. With some assistance, he claimed he uncovered flagstones several feet down. Later, there were wooden platforms at regular intervals, buried in what he described as loose dirt, much different than the firmly packed soil around the shaft.

He also claimed to find a stone with strange symbols on it, though soon after that he and the others with him abandoned the dig out of fear. Something spooked the men, though they wouldn't say what.

Years went by before the next treasure hunters came along. Some heard all kinds of stories about Captain Kidd's pirate treasure and thought Oak Island to be the perfect location. Still more believed there was something grander down below the surface.

Over the centuries, explorers and treasure hunters had sunk fortunes into the money pit. Six men lost their lives during that span. Some said there was a curse on the island, and that the treasure would only be revealed after seven lives had been sacrificed.

The biggest problem with the Oak Island shaft was that it flooded with ocean water. Whoever built the pit, booby-trapped it with side shafts that branched off to the sea in all directions. People had tried using dye to trace the origin of these offshoot pipelines, but their efforts were unsuccessful.

One crew attempted to get into the shaft under the deepest dig point by going in from the side. They drilled down at an angle, but that only resulted in the bottom of the pit collapsing and flooding the thing all over again.

People formed corporations with dozens, sometimes hundreds, of investors to share the burden of costs that came with trying to uncover the mysterious treasure buried under Oak Island. Every time, the companies, their investors, and the people who founded them lost, sometimes millions of dollars.

Books were written about the bizarre mystery. A television series recently featured one of the newer groups who'd formed in an effort to use new technology. They barely made any more headway than their predecessors.

Sean knew the Oak Island theory was likely a dead end, possibly literally. It wasn't that he didn't believe something was there, but to think that anyone could come up with something that hadn't been tried before and failed was arrogant. Some mysteries, he thought, were better left alone.

He got the impression Tommy felt the same way.

Sean glanced at his watch and then up at his friend. "We need to go. We've been here too long already."

"Okay. Hold on just a few more minutes," Tommy insisted. "Let me look through these last few things."

He flipped the pages faster in a thick volume he'd found on the edge of the desk. Sean stepped over to the window and looked out. He didn't see any signs of trouble, but that burning feeling in his gut told him if they stayed much longer, things would get hairy.

He returned to the desk and pulled open one of the drawers. A jar of old coins, a dark brown leather journal, and a pile of paper clips occupied the inside. He closed the drawer and opened the next one. Stacks of notebooks and files lay one on top of the other. Sean closed the drawer and started to stand up when he had a thought.

He opened the first drawer again and pulled out the leather journal. He wedged a finger under the cover and flipped it open.

"Um...Schultzie?"

"Yeah?" Tommy answered without looking up from the book in his hands.

"I think I found something."

Tommy turned two more pages and then raised his head. "What is it?" he asked. "Looks like some kind of journal."

"Indeed," Sean said, pointing his index finger at the left-hand page. "Look at this."

Tommy narrowed his eyes. He set the book down he'd been flip-ping through and stepped around the desk to get a closer look.

"Is that—"

"It sure looks like it."

Sean set the journal on the desk and the two looked down at the image. It was a crude drawing, but there could be no mistaking the artist's intentions. The rectangular box had what looked like two poles running along each side. Two angels with wings bent forward rested upon the top. Below the drawing were several notes written in different handwriting than Wilkins's other notations. This had been done by someone else.

"No way," Tommy said.

"Yeah," Sean gave an absent nod. "I think the Assassins are searching for the Ark of the Covenant."

A clicking sound came from downstairs. Sean and Tommy snapped their heads toward the open doorway, then glanced at each other with a look of concern on both their faces.

"Wilkins?" Tommy mouthed silently.

Sean didn't answer, only giving a few blinks to neither confirm nor deny his friend's suspicion. Inside, he hoped it was Wilkins. The professor would be easy enough to deal with. They could force him to give some answers. If it wasn't Wilkins, however, there could be problems.

As far as Sean knew, there was only one way in and one way out from their current position, not including the window. He didn't want to consider that. His wretched fear of heights wouldn't allow it—unless there was no other option.

He stepped over to the door, tiptoeing to keep silent. He reached the doorframe and stayed close to the wall, pressing his hand against it to keep his balance as he leaned forward to look down the staircase. The front door was mostly wood with three little square windows on the top. Two narrow brushed-glass windows on either side let light in but kept anyone from being able to see inside the home. Sean could, however, see the dark figures just beyond. He couldn't tell who they were, but there were more of them, at least two.

"It's not Wilkins," Sean whispered over his shoulder. "They're picking the lock."

Tommy let out a disappointed sigh. "Great. What do we do now?"

Sean clenched his teeth. The only way out of the house was down the stairs. Then it was either the front door or the back. Since the men were coming in the front door, he figured they weren't covering the back, though that could be a deadly assumption to make.

Another click echoed up the stairway.

There wasn't another option.

They could stand their ground and fight, but Sean and Tommy only had one magazine each in their weapons. The other problem was they had no idea of the true number of men outside the front door. He could make out two shadows, but there might have been five or six more guys waiting just behind them. If that was the case, the two friends would spend the contents of their magazines and end up sitting ducks.

Sean wasn't a fan of close-quarter firefights, either. He figured he'd lost 5 to 10 percent of his hearing over the years as a result of just such a thing. There were too many unknowns in a gunfight in a house, if that's what it could be called.

Then there was the last element.

Sean never mentioned it to his friend, not that he remembered, though it was possible he'd said something once in a fatigue-induced haze. He hated killing. He only did it when he had to, but if there was another way to handle an issue, he'd take it in a heartbeat.

Over the years, Sean couldn't count the number of people he'd killed. He wasn't like some, haunted by faces and names of the lives he'd taken from this world. His torment was different.

For the most part, he knew what he'd done was justified, necessary even, for the betterment of humanity. There was, however, a deeper guilt that tugged at his heart.

He knew that every person he'd killed had been a child once: innocent, kind, full of hope and joy. Somewhere along the line, that child had taken a turn. Maybe it was from parental abuse or neglect. It could have been a bully at school or a tragedy that rocked their world and turned it upside down. At some junction in the past, they'd chosen to become evil, but before that they were merely children.

Sean wept for that. He hated it.

He understood that, deep down inside, everyone was still a child in one way or another. Some people pushed that child so far away that there was nothing left of them but the tiniest spark.

Sean knew there was no way to get that child back, to bring the person they could have been into the light. And so he killed. He took the lives of those who'd chosen to hurt others, people who'd embraced the good when they were young and taken on a life of relative innocence and normalcy.

In this case, the men downstairs were likely part of the Assassins, a group whose very name carried death with it. Sean would show them no mercy if it came down to him or them, but for now the odds didn't seem like they were in his favor. Sean always tried to leverage the odds.

"We have to go out the window," he hissed as he hurried back across the room.

He pulled one of the locking latches back, and then the second.

"You sure?" Tommy asked.

"There's no other way, and we are outgunned, even with the high ground here. They can keep coming until we run out of bullets. Not to mention the cops will be here in five minutes or less after the first gunshot. I don't feel like explaining why we broke into Wilkins's house."

Tommy scurried across the room to the doorway and eased it shut, save for a narrow crack. He looked down in time to see the front door open. A man in a policeman's uniform stepped into the foyer. He had a pistol in his hand, though he wasn't carrying it like a cop. Cops had certain procedures, training, ways of doing things. Tommy had been around them enough to understand how they'd enter a house in a situation like this. One thing was certain: Whoever was downstairs wasn't a cop. Tommy closed the door, twisting the knob to make sure it didn't click when the thing shut. Then he gently let it go, allowing the bolt to enter the receiver before carefully twisting the lock. It wouldn't keep the men out forever, but it would buy them a few seconds.

He padded quickly back across the floor as Sean slid the window open as silently as possible.

Sean leaned his head out the opening and spied a gutter drain to his left attached to the exterior wall with mounted bolts every five feet.

He pulled himself back into the room and motioned to Tommy. "Go ahead. I'll cover you."

Tommy knew better than to question his friend. Sean was the more capable of the two in a fight, plus Sean was terrified of heights. Even though they were only on the second floor, he had a feeling that his friend wasn't eager to get out on the wall.

Tommy swung his leg over the windowsill and reached out with his right hand. He grabbed the pipe, fitting his fingers in the tiny gap between it and the wall. Then he tugged his weight out the window and planted his feet on either side of the pipe while grabbing hold of it with his left hand. His grip was tenuous at best. His fingers slipped on the smooth surface.

That didn't matter. He wasn't trying to climb. He just needed to slow the descent enough to make it safe.

He shuffled his feet along the wall, letting his hands slide along the pipe until he was about six feet from the ground. Then he let go and dropped to the square patch of grass next to the little concrete patio in the back.

Sean glanced back at the door before he stuck his foot out the window. He took a deep breath and fought the sudden wave of fear that crashed over him. His body suddenly felt heavy. The world twisted. Everything was unstable in his mind. His muscles were Jell-O. He snapped his head to the side to shake off the irrational fear and reached out for the gutter drain.

His fingers gripped it like death, knuckles whitening from the strain. He pulled himself out of the window, but his left heel caught on the sill. Sean lost his balance and swung out too far to the right. His weight tugged him toward the other side of the drain.

Tommy watched below as his friend lost control and nearly fell. Sean's left leg kicked wildly as he grabbed desperately at the pipe with his free hand. Somehow, he managed to get a feeble grip on the drain and steadied his movement enough to slide down a few feet. His boots scuffed the brick wall as he descended rapidly. With eight feet to go, Sean released the pipe and dropped to the ground. He hit with a thud, bending his knees to absorb the landing.

He straightened up and glanced back at the window. "We'd better go."

"Good idea."

They ran across the courtyard to a wooden fence. Sean lifted the clasp on the iron gate and pushed the door open. A second later, they were through and into someone else's yard.

It was surrounded by a fence as well, but there was space between each house, maybe three feet on either side. It wasn't much, but they could fit through and get out to the street.

Sean hurried over to a side gate in the neighbor's fence and started to open it when he had a terrible realization. "The journal," he said. "We left it in Wilkins's study."

Tommy shook his head and pulled open his jacket, revealing the top edge of the leather book in his pocket. "I grabbed it on the way out. Come on. Let's go."

Sean flashed a cheeky smile at his friend and shoved the door open. The two friends disappeared a moment before one of the gunmen popped his head out the open window of Wilkins's apartment.

17

"I understand," Alain said into his phone. "No, it's not your fault. Get back here as soon as you can. We'll figure something out."

He ended the call and slid the device into his jacket pocket where he usually kept it.

Alain reached across his desk and picked up a cigar. The end of it burned slowly, a thin stream of grayish-blue smoke drifting into the air. The man across from him stared straight ahead, his eyes full of fear.

"The journal?" Dr. Wilkins asked.

"They took it."

Wilkins gulped. How could he have been so careless? Now, Sean and Tommy had all his notes. Worse, they knew what he and the Assassins were looking for.

"There's no way I could have known, sir. I took every precaution."

Alain took a drag from his cigar and let a ring of smoke escape his lips as he listened to the professor grovel.

"I locked it away. I swear, I don't even know how they found it. I mean, how did they even know where I lived? They've never been there before." He lied about locking it away, hoping Alain would be understanding and perhaps merciful.

"You underestimated Sean Wyatt."

"No. I swear. There's no way I could have known they'd go to my apartment. Why would they?"

"Because they knew you were lying. Just like you're lying to me now. It's written all over your face."

Wilkins started to defend himself, but Alain raised his hand and gave a subtle shake of the head. He clicked his tongue with the gesture, both a condescending and menacing way of telling his guest to shut up.

"They knew you were lying to them," Alain repeated.

The professor's shoulders drooped. He lowered his head in shame and gazed at his feet for nearly a minute.

"You know what this means, don't you?" Alain asked.

Wilkins looked up. "It means we have to get that journal back. I was on the verge of making a breakthrough, but I need that tablet. The images they sent me were incomplete. Once I have the stone, I can—"

"No." Alain cut him off and took another puff off the cigar. He blew a long stream of smoke through his pursed lips.

"But if we don't get that journal back...they could combine what I've learned with what they have. My notes...they could help Wyatt figure out the language on the stone. Once that happens—"

"No. They won't."

Wilkins appeared confused. His cheeks sagged and his mouth gaped open. "I don't...I don't understand. Is there something you haven't shared with me?" Then it hit him. He should have seen it sooner. How could he have been so daft? Wilkins prided himself on being an intelligent person. Now a sickening realization filled his gut. "Do you know the Ark's location? Have you known all this time?"

"Yes." Alain didn't hesitate to answer the question. He was, after all, the one in charge here, not the professor.

Outraged, Wilkins started to stand up. A strong hand clapped down on his shoulder and forced him back into his seat.

"Get your hand off me!" he protested, a tad louder than he meant. He looked back at Tusun, who was holding him down.

"My second-in-command takes orders from me, not you, Professor," Alain said. His voice was even, cool, like a man who didn't have a worry in the world.

"If you know where it is, why have you had me working on this for so long? I thought we were searching for the thing, and now you tell me you know its exact location?"

"We've always known where it is. We lost track of it for a short time when the Templars brought it here, to the New World, but our agents quickly figured it out. There's only so many places you can hide a relic of such immense power. The colonies were an ideal location to bring the Ark. Population was sparse. Things were much easier to secret away. Your mission wasn't to find the Ark. It was to unlock the code on that tablet. The journal contains that code. And now Wyatt has it."

Wilkins shook his head, momentarily ignoring the part about Sean Wyatt having possession of the journal. "Where is it then? Why haven't you retrieved it?"

Alain allowed a cryptic smile to cross his lips. "It was my opinion that we needed everything in place before we extracted the Ark. The men who hid it placed it in an extremely powerful vault, one that can only be unlocked with a code hidden in both the journal and on the tablet. They're two pieces of a puzzle; we need both to unlock the vault. Your careless actions, however, have forced me to move up the timeline. My intentions were to be patient and wait until all our pieces were in place. Now, things could get...problematic."

The professor looked bewildered. He was trying to process everything his benefactor was saying, but it didn't make sense. "Problematic?"

"Yes." He elongated the word, making it sound more sinister. "Sean Wyatt and his friend have one of the pieces now. Without it, we may not be able to unlock the vault. While we can certainly obtain it, getting the Ark out of it could be an issue."

"A...vault?" Wilkins still didn't see the connection.

"For a man of intellect, you certainly don't seem very intelligent." Alain stood up and placed the cigar on a black ceramic ashtray. He let the insult hang amid the smoky air for a moment. "I'll spell it out for you. We knew Wyatt and Schultz would come to you. There were only a handful of people they would approach about something as curious as the tablet. We made it easy for them to trace the email Sean sent you as well. With the little bug we put in the system, it would be only natural to think you were the one responsible for their betrayal. Our mistake was giving you the journal. That's on me. We hoped that our men would be able to apprehend them there, but apparently they have escaped yet again. I'd have preferred it if you kept the journal in a safe or somewhere a little more secure, perhaps a bank. Alas, now they have it. While they might be able to figure out what we're looking for, it is unlikely they'll track down the location of the Ark, even with both the tablet and the book. Of course, my men will make certain they don't have those items for long."

Wilkins looked hopeful. "So...everything is going to be all right then? You'll let me go?"

"Of course. There would be no point in keeping you here. My associate will show you out."

Tusun loosened his grip on Wilkins's shoulder and allowed the man to stand. Wilkins gave a grateful nod to Alain and turned to leave. He felt like he'd just dodged a bullet. His mind spun with ideas of leaving the country, possibly to stay at his cottage in New Hampshire for a while until things died down. This was getting too sketchy. These men were dangerous, and Wilkins had no doubt they could come after him when it was all over. Men like this didn't strike him as the type to leave a bunch of loose ends lying around.

"Thank you," Wilkins said, stopping at the door before exiting the room.

Alain gave an emotionless wave of the hand.

The metal door slammed shut behind him, and Tusun motioned for his charge to continue down the corridor.

Wilkins startled from the heavy bang of the door closing. Then he nodded and made his way forward. They passed several doors, some open, some closed. Wilkins peered through the open ones and saw simple beds—cots, really—wooden chairs and desks, and basic wooden dressers. The little rooms reminded him of cells in a monastery. Indeed, these men lived a life similar to that of monks. They were devout, dedicated to their cause—whatever that was.

They'd never given Wilkins a real reason behind their purpose. Maybe it was because he was an outsider, a ringer they'd called upon to help with deciphering a code in a two-hundred-year-old journal.

When he'd first been approached, Wilkins had balked at the notion of what the men were searching for. His doubts were pushed aside the moment he started reading the journal. He'd spent days and countless hours analyzing the handwriting to make certain it wasn't a fraud. In his line of work, that sort of thing happened all the time. People came in with books they claimed were penned by the famous hand of a historical figure. In the end, they were almost never authentic.

He smiled at the thought of the time someone, a former student, brought him what she thought was a genuine letter from Abraham Lincoln. Her disappointment was severe when he let her know that it was written by someone around the turn of the century. While the letter was certainly old, it was unquestionably a phony.

People did that sort of thing all the time, trying to make a quick buck from those who would pay for something they thought might be valuable.

That brought Wilkins's thoughts back to the fortune he'd made in the last month. Alain Depricot had paid him extremely well. He'd have enough money to retire now, spending his days on a beach or golf course. For the immediate short term, disappearing was more important. He'd lie low for a while and let things die down before he started enjoying his new wealth. *Someplace warm would be nice*, he thought.

"Please, this way," Tusun said, motioning to a hallway on the right.

They were at the base of the stairs at the second door. The guard who'd let them through earlier was standing in front of it with his arms crossed.

"Didn't we come down that way before?" Wilkins asked.

"They're doing some cleaning up there. We'll have to go out the back." He sensed Wilkins's hesitation. "Please," he urged.

Wilkins reluctantly obeyed and proceeded down the corridor. Straight ahead, another metal door hung open. Another man stood guard just next to the doorframe. Heat rolled down the hallway, pouring out of the open door. Wilkins felt the wave of warmth rush over him and wondered where it was coming from.

The second they passed through the door, he saw the source.

A giant furnace roared against the opposite wall. Wilkins spun around, seeing there were no exits from what he now realized was a type of boiler room.

"What are you doing?" he demanded. Then he saw the other two men standing behind Tusun. They held surgical saws in their latex-gloved hands. The men looked like maskless executioners, wearing black aprons that hung from their necks. Their rubber boots would keep their feet and shins clean.

A sickening feeling shot through Wilkins's body and stopped in his gut. He felt bile surging up through his esophagus, and he nearly vomited right then.

"Please," he begged, "don't do this. You don't have to do this. I can disappear. I swear, I'll never tell anyone about your organization. Please, just don't kill me."

Tusun glared at the man with disgust. He detested weaklings like Wilkins. He was a warrior, ready to die if needed. He had no fear of death, no concerns about his life coming to a sudden end. The only thing that mattered to Tusun was the higher purpose: the order's triumph.

Wilkins's groveling escalated. He dropped to his knees with hands folded so hard his knuckles glowed white in the dim light. "Please. I'll give you money."

"We're the ones who paid you," Tusun said, almost humored by the ridiculous offer.

"No, I have more. You can have it. Take it. I'll give you my account information. Take it all. Just let me live."

"We already did."

Wilkins' pleading, drawn face turned pale. "What?"

"We control everything, Professor. We can access your accounts, anyone's accounts, whenever we please. Do you think us savages?"

"No. No, I don't." Wilkins shook his head vigorously. "You're not savages. So, I beg you, don't do this. Let me go, please."

Tusun had heard enough. Wilkins's lack of courage sickened him. He raised his hand and brought it across the professor's cheek. The ring on his middle finger cut a gash in Wilkins's skin as his head rocked to the side.

He let out a yelp and instinctively reached for the cheek to check for blood.

"This is the price of failure," Tusun said as he drew a pistol from his jacket. He took a suppressor out of another pocket and began slowly screwing it on to the muzzle.

"No! Please!" Wilkins lunged forward and grabbed the bottom of Tusun's coat, pulling on it like a madman.

Tusun planted his heel in Wilkins's chest and kicked him back toward the furnace.

Wilkins felt the searing heat from the open furnace door blast across his face and head. He scrambled, trying to get to his feet, but Tusun was on him and pressed his boot onto the professor's throat. Wilkins wriggled and squirmed, but he couldn't get free. He gurgled for air as Tusun pushed harder on his throat.

"This is the price of failure," Tusun repeated and raised his weapon. He aimed the barrel at Wilkins's nose and pulled back the hammer.

The professor's final protest was a violent shake of his head as he gave one last effort to get free of Tusun's boot. His eyes widened when the killer cocked the pistol. The only solace he could find was that these men, these murderers, wouldn't know about the secret he'd kept from them. He had never told Alain Depricot and his henchmen about the second piece of the puzzle; the letter contained within the journal. He doubted they could interpret the riddle, a riddle he'd figured out in less than an hour. If he was going to die, the secret location of the two keys would die with him. Without those, Alain's plan would fail.

The muzzle flashed. A muffled pop echoed through the room. Wilkins's body went limp.

Tusun took his foot off the dead man's throat and turned to the men in the aprons. He nodded. "Cut him up, and put him in the fire."

He strode out of the room and closed the door behind him as the cleaners began their macabre task.

One loose end tied. Two more to go.

He walked hurriedly down the corridor and turned up the stairs. Once he was outside, he pulled the phone from his pocket and tapped on his contacts list. A second later, he pressed a number on the list and put the phone to his ear.

It rang twice before the man on the other end answered.

"Yes?"

"Status?" Tusun asked.

"Their plane just took off. They're heading to Washington, Dulles International."

"Thank you."

Tusun ended the call and dialed another number. "I need a team in Washington to welcome our troublesome friends. They should be arriving shortly. Dulles."

The voice on the other end didn't mince words. "Understood."

Tusun slipped the phone back in his pocket and hurried back down the stairs. He made his way through the labyrinth of corridors until he found the door to Alain's private chamber. He rapped twice, and two seconds later Alain told him to come in.

The leader of the Assassins looked up from his desk as Tusun entered the room.

"They're going to Washington," he said. "I've made arrangements."

"Good." Alain gave an appreciative nod. "It is paramount that we get the journal back. Without it, we are lost."

"We'll get it, sir, and the men who took it will die."

18

BOSTON

The jet rocketed into the sky and banked hard to the east. Sean and Tommy looked out the windows at the shrinking city below.

They'd managed to get out of Wilkins' neighborhood without any trouble, which Sean considered lucky based on the layout of the area. They could have been cornered at any moment, but that hadn't happened.

When they arrived at the VIP area of the airport, at least that's what Tommy liked to call it, they boarded the plane and hurried to their seats. A call from Tommy on the way to the hangar had given the pilot and crew the heads-up to get things ready for takeoff.

It was Sean's idea for the pilot to submit an alternate destination when making his usual preparations.

For all intents and purposes, air traffic control and anyone else involved with tracking aircrafts would think the IAA jet was heading for Washington. They could reroute once in the air. It was somewhat irregular, but weather or technical issues could make such a drastic measure possible.

Sean's concern was that the Assassins had their fingers in more honey jars than he and Tommy realized, including those monitoring air travel. If there was a mole keeping tabs on their whereabouts, that person would have reported to the Assassins that Wyatt and Schultz were heading to the nation's capital, when in truth they were going farther south.

When they were fifteen thousand feet up, Sean turned to his friend and made a turning motion with his hand. "Let's have a look at what the good professor was hiding in his desk."

Tommy nodded and took the journal out of his pocket. He set it down on the narrow coffee table between them and stared at it for a moment. The cracked leather was worn down in several places, a sign that the book was very old. The pages, too, were weathered, and the ink within was faded to the point of being almost illegible.

They'd noticed that issue before in the brief moments they'd been able to take a look inside the journal. Now they realized just how badly the book had degraded.

"How old do you think this is?" Sean asked as he maneuvered around the table to sit in the seat next to his friend.

Tommy inhaled through his nose and blew the air out of his mouth, letting his lips flap for a moment. "Hard to say," he answered. "Although if I had to guess, I'd say it's at least Civil War era, maybe older."

"I think maybe we shouldn't touch this anymore until we get back to the lab."

"Maybe," Sean said. "Although this plane does provide a sterile, dry environment."

He didn't try to hide the fact that he wanted to know what secrets this journal contained.

Tommy nodded. "Good point. Let me see if I have some gloves in my bag. I usually keep a pair in there for circumstances like this."

"Maybe you should check under your rope," Sean joked.

"Oh, you're funny." Tommy shook his head and pulled his gear bag out from under the seat. "That rope saved our butts more than once."

Tommy had a habit of taking seemingly random things on trips. There'd been a few times when he packed climbing rope, which took up a considerable amount of space and wasn't the lightest material. He had been right, of course. The rope had come in handy on a few occasions. In this instance, however, he didn't have the long cord in his bag, so foraging around for the gloves was significantly less hassle.

"Got 'em," he said and pulled out a Ziploc bag containing two purple latex gloves.

"You steal those from a hospital?" Sean asked with a chuckle.

Tommy unzipped the plastic bag and removed the gloves. "No," he said, and slid them onto his fingers. "You do realize you can buy these, right? They're pretty cheap."

"Yeah, I know, but they sure look like the same ones you'd find in a hospital room."

"You never stop, do you?" Tommy asked. He stared at the drawing of the Ark they'd already seen in Boston, then leaned over the book and carefully peeled the first page over to the cover.

The handwriting, while faded, was pristine. The delicate curves of the letters fluidly traced across the brittle paper with perfect spacing and balance.

"Whoever wrote this sure has better handwriting than me," Sean commented, his voice nothing more than a reverent whisper.

Tommy didn't say anything, instead reading the contents of the first page to himself.

"This *is* about the Ark," Tommy said. "Whoever wrote this is talking about how the Ark was taken from Jerusalem and sent to a faraway land."

He turned the page and found more of the story, though some of the words on the next sheet were more faded than the first and made reading difficult.

"It says the Templars brought the Ark here, to America," Tommy went on. "They thought this would be the perfect place to hide it."

"Like we thought about the Grail."

"Good to see our heads were in the right place."

"Yeah, just thought it was the wrong artifact."

It was an easy assumption to make. The Grail story associated with the Templars was a popular one, though there were nearly as many legends associating the disappearance of the Ark of the Covenant with their order.

The legends were numerous. Some people believed it was in Ethiopia. Others claimed it had been dropped in the bottom of the ocean, in one of the deepest trenches known to mankind. There were other myths, of course. Through the centuries, historians and story-tellers alike had come up with their own theories regarding the disappearance of the sacred Ark.

None of them ever stood up to scrutiny.

One tale suggested that God himself had taken the Ark to heaven after the fall of Jerusalem, though Sean and Tommy didn't lend much credence to that one.

This, however, told the story of how the Templar Knights excavated the earth under the ancient temple and discovered the Ark buried in a secret chamber, surrounded by solid granite. The account went on to describe the chamber as a kind of vault, completely surrounded on all sides. According to the journal's author, the massive box was protected by two seals.

"Seals?" Sean asked. "Like some kind of magic spell or something?"

"I don't know. I've only read as far as you at this point." Tommy made certain his friend caught the hint of venom in his tone.

Tommy turned the page, and the two kept reading. The answer to their question came at the bottom.

"It says they used two keys they found somewhere on the temple grounds."

"Keys," Sean said, more of a statement than a question. "Two of them? Sounds like trying to launch a nuclear missile."

"Yeah, it kind of does," Tommy said with a snort.

He gently took the corner of the next page and lifted it. The old paper tore slightly, and he let it fall back to the main body of the book, fearful he'd damage more. The two friends took a sudden gulp of air and held their breath. Then they exhaled and glanced warily at each other.

"Careful," Sean said, taking his turn as the wise guy.

"Thanks. I got it."

Tommy reached into his pack and pulled out a pair of tweezers, wishing he'd done that in the first place. It would have normally been the tool of choice, but in his hurry to look inside the book and get some gloves on, he simply got careless.

He wouldn't make that mistake again.

He wedged a flat end of the tweezers between the pages and lifted it even more cautiously than before. When the paper reached its zenith, Tommy deftly twisted the little tool and lowered the page to the other side.

The two men let out a sigh of relief and continued reading:

THE KEYS WERE TAKEN to separate locations in order to protect the vault. My father, the great chief, took one. He hid it. I took the other. With an ocean separating the two keys, we believed the relic would be safe. However, when I returned after the death of the great chief, I decided that my key should remain with a trusted friend at his Virginia estate. While he is not an initiate of the order, he is loyal and understands what is at stake. He swore if I ever decided to take it back, I could find it where the hills rise to meet the flowers, hidden beneath where titans rest.

The other was taken by the great chief and hidden in his childhood home. Before he died, my father told me how to find it if such a time arose when it was needed, saying it was concealed beneath the cornerstone.

I pray the day never arrives when the relic is needed to ward off the dark ones. If it does come, however, this cipher will reveal the location of the weapon and how it must be used.

A SERIES of strange symbols ran across the page below the letter, along with the date October 13.

"I guess that was the date he wrote it?" Sean asked. Tommy responded with a bewildered shrug.

The two friends remained silent for a moment in amazed reverence. The signature in the bottom right corner was grandiose, with swooping, curvy letters. Despite the faded ink, there was no question as to whom the autograph belonged.

"Marquis de Lafayette," Tommy whispered, as he would in a church or cathedral during prayer.

Sean gave a solemn nod and echoed his friend's sentiment. "That's unreal. We're staring at the journal of Gen. Marquis de Lafayette."

Both men knew the story about the legendary Frenchman.

The general, known to many as "the Hero of Two Worlds," was born into French aristocracy in 1757. At the time of his birth, Lafayette was named Marie-Joseph Paul Yves Roch Gilbert du Motier de Lafayette, a mouthful to be sure. The lengthy name came as a result of family tradition, one that used monikers of saints and ancestors as a form of protection against evil.

Lafayette was born to one of the oldest families in France. Their heritage was one of great warriors, going back as far as Joan of Arc and the Crusades. Their ancestors were the stuff of legend, winning great battles against the enemies of France and of God.

At the age of two, Lafayette's father was killed by the British at the Battle of Minden. This set events in motion that would determine the young Lafayette's life path.

When he turned thirteen, he was commissioned an officer, an incredible feat by any standard. Then, as a nineteen-year-old, bolstered by the belief in the American Revolution as a just and right-eous cause, he traveled across the Atlantic to offer his help to the American forces.

Initially, they turned him away, but after a great deal of convincing he was given the title of major general. While discreet in the annals of history, it proved to be a defining moment for the young nation.

Lafayette helped turn the tide of the war more than once and was instrumental in designing the three-sided trap that resulted in the capture of General Cornwallis at Yorktown.

George Washington, then commander of the Continental Army,

had taken Lafayette under his wing. They became good friends, and often Washington referred to the younger Frenchman as his son. Washington wrote letters to Lafayette when the two were separated, and no one ever questioned the loyalty of the great French general.

"George Washington took one of the keys," Sean said.

Tommy nodded. "The great chief. That was one of his nicknames."

"And Lafayette referred to his father, but his real father died in France when he was a toddler. It has to be a term of endearment."

"Exactly." Tommy pointed at a specific sentence in the paragraph. "What about this, though?"

Sean read the words out loud, paraphrasing. "A trusted friend at his Virginia estate, not an initiate of the order, hidden behind where titans rest?"

"Childhood home?" Tommy asked. "You think he's talking about Washington's home from when he was a kid?"

"It would have to be, wouldn't it?" Sean cast a sincere, questioning glance over his shoulder to his friend.

"Sure seems like it."

"Where did he grow up? Everyone knows about Mount Vernon."

"Yeah," Tommy said, "but that was his home later in life. He didn't move there until he was an adult."

Sean stared at his friend. He could see that Tommy's brain was trying to access the information, like a computer running millions of commands through files.

"Ferry Farm!" Tommy blurted. "That's it!" He couldn't conceal the excitement in his tone. "George Washington grew up on Ferry Farm."

Sean hadn't heard of it. Every now and then, his friend surprised him with a seemingly random piece of knowledge. This was one of those times.

"Where is Ferry Farm?" Sean asked.

"Fredericksburg, Virginia. I remember now. There was a big archaeological dig there a while back. Took them eight years to find the foundation of Washington's boyhood farmhouse. They tried three locations, eventually locating it in the final spot. They actually reached out to me about transporting some of the artifacts, but we were booked up and I couldn't spare anyone."

"How come I didn't know about that one?"

Tommy let a laugh escape his lips. "I guess because you were running around playing spy hero or something."

"Funny."

"Anyway, I bet I could reach out to the director of archaeology there and see if he'd let us on the grounds after hours."

"They have a director of archaeology? It's an old farm."

"Yeah, but so much history passed through there. The Civil War had several key battles in that area. That spot is a treasure trove of American history."

"Okay, so what about the other one? And if we're looking for the Ark of the Covenant, why would Lafayette refer to it as a weapon?"

Tommy considered the question. He leaned back in his chair and rubbed his forehead with his forearm. "I was wondering the same thing. If you break down the essence of what the Ark really was, I guess you could call it a weapon. I mean, that thing leveled cities and helped the Israelites win major battles. Do you remember the story about what happened when the Philistines took it?"

"Yeah," Sean said. "They put it in one of their temples. The next day, the statue of Dagon, their fish god, was knocked over. They propped it back up, and the next day the thing was over on its side again with the head cut clean off."

"As if it was done with a laser."

"Right."

"Not only that, but the people got sick, terribly sick. If you read the description, it sounds an awful lot like radiation poisoning."

Sean raised a skeptical eyebrow. "Are you saying the Ark of the Covenant is nuclear?"

Tommy quickly shook his head. "No, not really. But you have to admit it sounds similar to the symptoms people experienced for years after Hiroshima and Nagasaki."

"Okay, fine. I'm convinced. The Ark is a weapon. That still doesn't explain the other question. Initiate of the order? Virginia estate? Where titans rest?"

That was another good question but one Tommy had already deduced. "George Washington was a Freemason," he stated.

"Everyone knows that."

"Right, but not everyone knows Lafayette was as well."

"Would make sense since they were basically father and son. Washington must have got his foot in the door."

"Nothing like good old nepotism." The words were coming to Tommy's brain faster than his mouth could say them. "Anyway, they were both members of the order. Do you know which Founding Father from Virginia was not?"

Sean had to think about it for a minute. He shifted his gaze up to the jet's ceiling and stared. He returned his eyes to Tommy. "There were several Founding Fathers from Virginia. I guess the one that sticks out most in my mind is Thomas Jefferson, but he was a Mason...wasn't he?"

Tommy shook his head. "Nope. There has been a good amount of speculation regarding that over the years, but none of the Masonic lodges from that time period have him on the records as being a member. In fact, Jefferson considered fraternal orders like the Masons as sort of a bad thing."

"Bad thing?"

"He didn't like that people were keeping secrets, especially ones that could be mystical in nature. The esoteric traditions in the fraternal orders of the time apparently bothered him."

Sean looked surprised. "Sounds like they were doing dark magic or something."

"I think that's what Jefferson and others believed, that they were tapping into something they shouldn't. At any rate, according to Lafayette's letter here, he seems to be the logical answer."

"So, even though he was against what they represented, Jefferson helped Lafayette?"

"Sure looks that way. Look at the lines. It says that even though he wasn't a member, he was loyal to the cause and someone Lafayette could trust."

If Tommy was right, that answered all of Sean's questions but one.

"What about the thing where titans rest?"

Tommy cocked his head to the side and offered a mischievous grin. "That one I don't know, but there's one way to find out."

Sean sighed. "We're going to Virginia, aren't we?"

19

ALEXANDRIA, VIRGINIA

Secretary of State Sanders got out of his car and hit the button on his fob to lock it. The horn honked once with the flash of yellow parking lights to accompany it. A spattering of rain hit the hood and windshield. The black clouds overhead blocked out the sky, reflecting nothing but artificial light from the city with an eerie, gray glow.

Sanders was still in disbelief. The president had given him his endorsement to be the nominee for the party going into next year's election.

While it wasn't a guarantee of victory, it certainly did more than help. Dawkins was a beloved president, a leader of the people. He'd been strong yet accessible, never rushing into things with foreign policy and always looking to help on the domestic side.

It was a difficult tight rope to walk, and the nation loved him for it.

Sanders didn't care about any of that except for the fact that the people would do pretty much whatever President Dawkins told them. They were his sheep, and soon Sanders would be the shepherd.

He had his own grandiose plans for shaping the nation once he was in office. He'd often daydreamed of the things he would do, who he'd appoint for his cabinet, vacationing to Camp David.

More than that, he thirsted for the power the president wielded. Sanders knew that the job was far from easy, that there weren't many days off in a given week for the most powerful man on the planet. That said, he wanted to be the most powerful man on the planet.

Once he was in the Oval Office, no one would dare stand in his way.

It was a far cry from his upbringing on the streets of Chicago, where he'd had to do things—awful things—to survive.

That was far in the past, though, and Darren Sanders had made a new life for himself that most would have considered impossible.

His memoirs would be best sellers. People loved a rags-to-riches story. They would adore his. Of course, he'd leave out some of those things he'd done as a juvenile: the drugs, the dealings, the killing....

He took in a deep breath of the rain-scented air and exhaled. He stopped on the top of his steps and looked out toward the city across the river. Despite the cloudy skies and the chill in the air, he felt a surge of warmth course through his body.

The night was full of promise.

To celebrate, he'd invited Nancy over. She would be arriving any time now, a little treat to consummate his imminent nomination for the presidency.

Sanders had never allowed her to come to his home. He thought twice about it on this occasion, wondering if it could turn into scandal later on down the election trail.

No one knew of Dawkins's endorsement yet, though, so he could afford one last tryst in the comfort of his own home before having to resume more clandestine means of carnal satisfaction.

He turned around and slid the key into the lock, twisted, and heard the mechanism click like it had done so many times before. He stepped inside and closed the door behind him, hung his coat on the rack by the entrance, and made his way into the kitchen where the bar beckoned.

Sanders kicked off his shoes next to the drink station and

picked up a whiskey glass. He spied the three crystal decanters, each holding a different variety of bourbon or sour mash, and picked the one in the center. It was the most expensive bourbon he had in his modest collection. Why not? Tonight was a night to celebrate. The amber liquid splashed into the glass, rising slightly higher on one side as the wave of alcohol poured into it. He placed the crystal topper back on the decanter and pushed it to its place between the other two. Sure, it was a generous pour, but who was going to criticize him? Besides, he wanted a little buzz before Nancy arrived. It would loosen him up from a stressful day—stressful week, in fact. He preferred not to be so uptight for their little encounters. It made for a better overall experience, for both parties.

He wandered over to the living room and eased into his dark chocolate leather couch and propped his feet up on the matching ottoman. He took a sip of the warm whiskey and let the spicy burn creep down his throat. He let out a low "ah" and looked across at the gas fireplace. *It would be a good night for a fire,* he thought.

Sanders set his drink on the end table and stepped over to the fireplace. He took the remote from the mantel and plopped back into the soft cushion of the couch, then pressed the button to turn on the fireplace.

There was a click, then the sound of a spark. He waited a moment, but nothing happened. He hit the button again, and the clicking resumed, a snappy electric sound that came every time he tried to light the fire. Normally, the flames would have ignited and produced a warm, orange glow.

Something was wrong.

Frustrated, he took another pull from the bourbon and walked over to the fireplace. He jerked back the screen on either side and looked around under the faux logs. He saw the pilot light was out. That was problem number one. Upon further inspection, he noticed the gas knob was turned to the off position.

Sanders didn't remember turning it off. That was why he had a remote. According to his elementary understanding of how the fireplace worked, when he turned it off with the remote control, the valve automatically shut off.

Had he turned this knob off at some point and just not remembered? It had been a while since he had used the fireplace. He wasn't much for cozy comforts. There usually wasn't time. In fact, he couldn't recall the last time he *had* used the thing. Perhaps the maid had turned if off while she was cleaning.

Sanders shrugged off the curiosity and switched the knob back to the on position. He closed the screens and returned to his seat on the couch, picked up the remote, and hit the button again.

The electric sound of sparks clicked in rapid-fire succession a second before the fireplace whooshed. The fake logs erupted in bright orange flames for a second and then died down to their usual steady burn.

Sanders let out a relieved sigh and reached for his drink. Nancy would like the fireplace. It would be a nice touch. He thought about how delighted she'd be and checked his watch. She wouldn't arrive for another half hour. Plenty of time for him to down this drink and pour a few glasses of wine.

He knew her preference when it came to alcohol. Her refined palate came across as demanding, but he didn't mind. He could afford whatever she wanted. Soon, he'd be able to acquire even the most hard-to-get wines in the entire world. The world, he believed, was the president's oyster.

Sanders had thought about the relationship with his administrative assistant. There was no way he could fire the woman. The second that happened, he'd be immersed in a scandal that would destroy everything he'd worked so hard to gain. No, Nancy was going to have to come with him to the White House, one way or the other. He'd find a position for her. Something small, unimportant but that gave her a sense of importance. Whether or not their romantic flings could continue was yet to be seen. He figured those would need to stop, but it was certainly possible he could have a taste now and then.

Of course, as the president he could have anyone he chose—another fringe benefit of the office.

He took another sip of the bourbon. It went down much smoother after the first few tastes. Now he savored the warm oak flavors mixed with a hint of vanilla and leather.

"No need to pour me one, Secretary Sanders."

The familiar voice startled Sanders, and he shot up from his seat. The bourbon sloshed in the glass and spilled onto his pants.

He looked to the doorway, but there was no one there. He stood up and spun around to find the mystery man from his office standing in the hallway between the kitchen and the master bedroom.

"What are you doing here?" he demanded. He tried to wipe the spilled beverage from his slacks to no avail.

"I don't like using the phone for business," Alain said. "In this town, especially."

He was smart to think that way. There was no telling who the FBI or CIA was watching. And the NSA was keeping tabs on almost everyone. Sanders recalled talking to a guy with the NSA a few years before. He'd said they literally had a file on every American in the country, and some who were out of the country.

Sanders expressed his concern about such a boast, but the guy eased his mind, telling him that they didn't pay attention to most people just trying to go about their normal lives.

"Why are you here?" Sanders asked again.

Alain took a dramatic step closer to the living room and stopped near the bar. He turned and examined the small collection of alcohol in expensive decanters and picked up the nearest one. He held it out as if doing show-and-tell at a grade school. "This stuff clouds one's vision," he said in an informative tone. "Makes you weak."

"Yeah? Well, if you'd had the week I have, you'd need a drink, too."

Alain set the container back on its platform and shook his head. "We do not drink alcohol," he said flatly. "It is against our code."

Sanders rolled his shoulders and held out his glass. "More for me, I guess." He tipped the glass up and downed the rest of its contents, then made his way past the uninvited guest to the bar and grabbed the decanter on the right. He poured another generous round and slid the container back to its place without putting the top back in.

This guy gave him the creeps. Now he was standing in his home, appearing again like a threatening apparition.

"I'd ask how you got in here, but I don't think I want to know."

"Doors and locks are for your peace of mind. They do little to deter our order."

"Great. Have a seat." Sanders tried to use a little humor to deflate his overwhelming sense of dread.

"I'll stand."

"Suit yourself."

Sanders stepped over to a club chair near the fireplace and sat down so he could face the intruder. "You wanna make this quick? I've got a...friend coming over in less than a half hour."

"Your secretary. Yes, I know."

Sanders was in mid-sip when Alain made the comment. He nearly spit out the drink but managed to choke it down, though it burned much worse now. Some of it went down the wrong pipe, causing a violent fit of coughing for half a minute.

He wiped his lips with his sleeve and stared across the room at Alain. "What do you want?" he asked for what felt like the hundredth time. "I get it: You're sneaky and can get into any building in the world. So, why are you here?"

"We have to move up the timeline."

Sanders frowned and put one hand out to the side. "What timeline?"

Alain walked slowly around the end of the couch and put his hands behind his back as he stopped next to the end table. "It's time you know more of the details behind my plan."

"I figured you'd eventually come around. Everyone wants something in this town. You're no different."

"Indeed. And we are no different. I need access to the White House."

Sanders raised a befuddled eyebrow. "What, like a tour or something?"

Alain ignored the foolish comment. "We have all but given you the office of the president. You will easily defeat any competitor in next year's election. I'd hoped that we could wait until then before asking you to return the favor. Recent events have caused us to... accelerate our schedule."

This came as a surprise to Sanders. He wondered what could have thrown such a wrench into this man's plans, a man who seemed unfazed by anything.

"Okay...so, why do you want access to the White House?"

"That, Secretary, is none of your concern."

Sanders coughed again, nearly choking up another sip. "Really? Because, you're asking me to get you into the White House. I'm assuming it's not for usual reasons, you know, seeing the Easter decorations and such. That either means you're planning on doing something like—oh, I don't know—killing the president or stealing something. I'm not sure what you'd want to take, so I'm gonna go with assassination." He paused for a second and then added, "Nice work with the Speaker, by the way." He dumped another drink into his mouth, hoping this would be the one that dulled his nerves.

Alain dismissed the last sentence. "I have no intention of harming President Dawkins. If that was my plan, we would have done it already."

The line carried an immense amount of weight. It was no easy feat to kill a president. Only four had done it in the history of the United States. Others had tried and failed. This guy acted like it was nothing more than blowing his nose into a tissue and tossing it in the trash.

"So? What is it?" Sanders nervously poured another shot into his glass. He was on the expressway to Drunkville now.

"There is something in the White House that belongs to us. I'd hoped that this could wait until you were in office. Then the extraction would be much smoother. It, unfortunately, cannot wait any longer. We need you to navigate the red tape and get us access to the building. It could take as long as twenty-four hours to remove the item."

Sanders guffawed. The drink splashed around in the glass as he laughed. "You're serious, aren't you?"

Alain's narrowed eyes and stern expression showed nothing less.

"I mean, twenty-four hours...that's a long time. We're not just dealing with the president here. He has Secret Service everywhere on the property. There are guys in trees with high-powered rifles, cameras all over the place, security gates, metal detectors, the works. You can't just walk in there and hang out for twenty-four hours."

Alain listened patiently while his host explained all the things he already knew. When Sanders was done, he calmly put up his right hand for Sanders to be quiet.

"I know all those things," Alain said. "However, the president will be going out of town on an international diplomatic visit to Brazil on Monday."

"So?" Sanders shrugged. "It's not like the place will be empty. All that stuff I mentioned will still be in place."

"Yes, but every now and then, even the home of the president of the United States needs some repairs."

"Repairs?"

Alain gave a slow nod. "It would be a shame if, say, the basement had a leak that needed to be fixed."

"A leak?"

"I'll let you figure it out. Let me know when it's done. My men will be ready to enter the premises on Monday evening. The president returns Wednesday morning. That window should give us more than enough time to extract the...item."

Sanders took another sip of whiskey and grimaced. He was the secretary of state, not the head of maintenance for the White House. They had people for that kind of thing. Not to mention he was supposed to fly to France on Tuesday with a delegation meeting with the French president.

All of those excuses flashed through his mind in a nanosecond. As he stared at the intruder, he realized none of them would hold up. There would be so much red tape to get through, not to mention he'd have to cancel his trip, which would not go over well. Sanders could come up with an excuse, a national security emergency or something. It didn't even have to be that elaborate. The only thing he knew for certain is this man across from him wouldn't take no for an answer.

"Okay...I think I can do something like that. Will take some finagling, but it's doable. There are some work crews in there now and then. The person in charge of that sort of thing likes me for some reason. If I say the word, they'll listen to a gentle suggestion, although it would take some kind of miraculous play to get the regular crews out of the building." He paused and looked his visitor dead in the eyes. "I gotta ask, though, what is so important that you're willing to go to such lengths? What is it you're trying to steal from the White House?"

He turned to the fire and set his drink on the mantle. "I mean, it's gotta be pretty valuable, right?" He spun back around, but the living room was empty. His guest had vanished like a ghost.

Sanders looked around, suddenly feeling a rush of panic crash over him. He checked behind the couch, in the kitchen, down the hall in the bedroom and guest bath. There was no sign of him.

The stranger had simply disappeared.

20

ALEXANDRIA

Alain made his way down the sidewalk and around the next corner. The area was full of old brick buildings, some of them over a hundred years old. It had become a trendy place to live and work for many younger people, as well as a convenient place for Washington's elite to retire while still staying close to the game they'd played for so long.

Darren Sanders was annoying and a drunk, but he was the order's best chance at getting into the White House. That fact pricked at his nerves as he strode along the concrete toward his waiting car.

No doubt the secretary of state had seethed, trying to figure just how Alain had managed to get in and out of his house undetected. His exit, especially, would have caused the man to wonder if he was losing his mind.

There was no magic involved, simply stealth and anticipation. That along with a deep understanding of how people worked, how their minds processed things, made Alain and his followers seem like nothing more than apparitions, floating in and out of reality with seemingly mystical ease.

That was fine with Alain. Let the mere mortals of the world

consider him supernatural. That only added to their prowess. Once the Ark was in their hands, that mythical notion would only grow.

He hadn't lied to Sanders. He hadn't been exactly forthcoming, either. There was no way he could tell the secretary that the item they were looking for was the lost Ark of the Covenant, the most prized relic of all time.

One, Sanders wouldn't believe Alain even if he told him. And two, if the future president did believe him, he would go to extraordinary lengths to subvert the mission and steal the artifact for himself. Maybe he'd think he could sell it on the black market for a few hundred million. Or perhaps, however unlikely, the secretary would attempt to use it for his own means, perhaps to render American troops invincible on the battlefield.

Alain envisioned the relic being harnessed in a top secret lab somewhere, hooked up to wires, cables, and monitors. They'd run all manner of tests on it, trying to figure out what made it work.

That could never happen. Alain knew the true power of the Ark. He understood why it had been created.

He also knew that it was his order's birthright, not that of the government of the United States, to possess it.

It was all Alain could do to contain his excitement. Despite decades of discipline, elite training, and constant meditation, now and then his human side crawled out from the hole he'd buried it in years ago.

How could he not at least allow himself a moment of joy at the thought of finally getting his hands on the fabled Ark of the Covenant? It would make his order the most powerful organization in the world. Nations would kneel before them, give them anything they desired, simply for mercy...or for their assistance.

With the Ark in their possession, the Assassins would be unmatched by any fighting force on the planet. They could annihilate entire armies in a single stroke.

He recalled the stories from the Bible about how the Israelites had used the Ark to wipe cities like Jericho off the map, how armies numbering in the tens of thousands had fallen before it.

The Order of Assassins had sought the Ark since its inception. They'd chased every lead, followed each possible clue to its end, always finding nothing.

Alain had personally visited several locations in hopes of finding the Ark. He'd been much younger at the time, full of hope and possibility. With each failed attempt, however, his ambitions were blunted with disappointment.

And so the Ark became his obsession. While his teacher, the one who'd brought him into the fold, desired the Ark for religious reasons, Alain's were of a secular nature. He'd played along with the fervor of the other recruits as they bought into the master's plans of toppling the Western world and its heathen beliefs.

Religion was a marvelous tool for such a thing. It brought people without hope into a new realm and gave them purpose like they'd never experienced before. They meant something, and that meaning drove them to work harder, train more fiercely, and push themselves to the absolute limits of their minds and bodies.

Alain's agenda, however, was much less complex.

While he continued to fan the flames of extremism within his ranks, he never let on about the real reasons he wanted the Ark. His men believed that their purpose was to purge the nonbelievers from the world, thus purifying it and making it ready for a new kingdom under the banner of Allah. The truth was, Alain didn't care about any of that.

Sure, in the beginning, when the teacher first found him, it was religious zeal that led him to go back to their underground training facility that fateful night and all the nights after. It was that same zeal that initially drove him to do anything the teacher required.

For Alain, however, it was nothing more than a means to an end.

At an early age, he'd seen what that kind of emotional manipulation could do. He noted how fervent the teacher's followers were; ready to sacrifice their lives at his bidding.

That was a kind of power Alain had never experienced before. It tugged at his internal ambitions, the desire to overcome what he'd been and what he'd experienced. He realized that if he could become the one to take the teacher's place, that power would be his, and he could use it to become a god among men.

The White House was now the only thing standing between him and becoming the all-powerful force on the planet.

The White House, and two idiots from the International Archaeology Agency.

Wilkins had lost the journal, the one item Alain needed to put all the pieces together. Not only did the journal contain clues to the locations of the two keys that would open the Ark's vault, it also possessed instructions as to how the thing must be handled.

The journal was a manual, something that had been handed down through generations of Templar Knights. Marquis de Lafayette had been the last to own it. He'd taken the things he'd learned and put them all into one book that could be handed down to another Templar at the right time.

The book, however, had never been given to a proper heir. Why, Alain didn't know. It was anyone's guess why the heathen knights decided to hide the journal rather than keep it within their ranks.

It had taken years for Alain to track it down, but he'd managed, discovering the little book in a chateau on Lafayette's old family land.

The owners of the property had been less than cordial with his request, so he'd been forced to terminate them. Unfortunate, yes, but not without cause. Once the journal was in his hands, the only thing he needed was the tablet. Only with the cipher contained in the journal, and the symbols on the tablet, could someone activate the holy weapon that would bring supreme power to the one who commanded it.

Despite his lack of interest in most things religious, Alain had pored over the Hebrew scriptures. He read the original Greek version to find answers to the curious methods needed to activate the Ark, but nothing could be found. The original owners, it seemed, had no intentions of conveying the secrets beyond the minds of the high priests who, once a year, were permitted to use it.

Wilkins was dead now. He paid the ultimate price for his carelessness. Alain was going to have Wilkins killed anyway. The timeline for the execution just got moved up as a result of the unfortunate series of events surrounding the journal.

Alain turned the next corner and found his car where he'd left it. The black Jaguar sedan was a little flashier than he'd initially planned on getting, but he liked the power, the style, and the way it made him feel.

It wasn't a sin, he thought, to treat himself to something nice now and then.

Most of the time, he and the others of his order lived a modest life. Their New York home was little better than what a homeless shelter could offer. No one ever complained, least of all him. Alain had been in far worse circumstances in his youth, before his teacher found him.

He winced at the thought of what he called the man who'd saved him. Teacher. Alain had heard of other men who went by that nickname. They were delusional, bent on grand visions of sending their "warriors" into the streets with bombs strapped to their chests. They promised their disciples eternal life in paradise for their sacrifice, something that Alain's teacher had also promised, but with different tactics of achieving their goals.

He never asked any of his men to commit suicide. If they died in battle, it was honorable, like the great soldiers of old who charged into the field against all odds. Suicide, however, wasn't honorable.

Alain appreciated that about the old man, among many things.

He reached out to the door handle of the car and pulled it open. The car sensed he was near with the fob in his pocket and automatically unlocked a few seconds before he grasped the handle.

He slid into the black leather driver's seat and let the smell of the car fill his nostrils. It never got old, and he let himself smile for just a second. Simple pleasures were some of the best.

He closed the door and revved the engine to life as his phone started ringing in his pocket. He glanced at the screen and answered it through the car's speaker-and-microphone system.

"Go ahead," he said.

"Sorry to disturb you, sir, but we've had a situation."

"Situation?"

"Schultz's plane...it didn't go to Dulles."

Alain's second-in-command didn't mince words. He knew better. Beating around the bush was for people who worried about hurting the feelings of others or the blowback that could come with being blunt. Tusun had been around long enough to know what his leader preferred.

"Where did it go?"

"It took a bit of doing, but we tracked it to Reagan International. By the time we figured out what happened, the plane had landed, and the two passengers were gone."

Alain sighed. It couldn't be easy. Nothing in his life had been, or relatively little.

"Where are they now?" He knew Tusun would have the answer. He wouldn't have called to simply relay bad news. Tusun knew better. It was ingrained in him to find solutions to problems before reporting them to his leader.

"Virginia, sir. We have a team moving into place. They're currently under strict orders to observe only until told otherwise."

Alain was impressed, as he always was by Tusun's use of resources and ability to come up with innovative ways to get things done. Still, he was curious. "How did you find them?"

"We checked the rental car records and learned they picked up a late-model sedan. I had the men set up a net within a three-hour radius of the airport. We got a ping a few minutes ago from a hotel in Charlottesville. Would you like me to have the men apprehend the targets?"

Alain weighed the options. He needed the journal back, but if Wyatt and Schultz had it, and were suddenly changing course, that could mean only one thing: they'd discovered something.

His brain raced for what seemed like a minute, though it was only ten seconds or so. He ran through his brittle geographical knowledge of the area but came up with nothing off the top of his head.

"What's in Charlottesville?" he asked, assuming Tusun had already run a quick check of the area.

"University of Virginia. Thomas Jefferson's Monticello estate. James Monroe's plantation. Shenandoah National Park. Those are the main things."

Alain considered the response. Two of the possibilities stood out more than the others. "Two former presidents' homes," he said.

"Yes, sir."

"They must be going to one of those." He pondered the potential reason, and it hit him like a bat to the temple. "They figured out where one of the keys is located."

Tusun waited for a moment to make sure Alain was finished. "You want us to pick them up when and if they find it?"

"No," Alain said. "Keep the men at a distance. We don't want to spook them. Wyatt is savvy to that sort of thing. Remember, we need two keys. Taking them now could delay finding the second one."

"You want us to let them find both keys before we bring them in?"

"Correct."

"Makes sense to me. I'll handle it."

"Thank you. Keep me informed. I'll rendezvous with you soon."

He ended the call and set the phone on the passenger seat. "Well," he said to himself, "this is an interesting development."

21

CHARLOTTESVILLE, VIRGINIA

Sean steered the car down the winding road. The pavement twisted through the rolling Virginia hills leading up to the estate once occupied by one of the greatest leaders in American history.

Monticello's massive footprint covered over five thousand acres, half of which was maintained by the Thomas Jefferson Foundation. The mansion itself is an incredible tribute to the man's skills as an architect. The gardens and property surrounding it represented his love of nature and the desire to cultivate it for the good of mankind.

Tommy gazed out the window as the sun peeked over the hills to the east. A few wispy clouds streaked the clear sky above. The skeletal trees were still mostly barren from a cold winter, but their branches showed hints of tiny green buds, a hint that warmer weather was just around the corner.

Sean found a parking space in the lot where shuttles took visitors up to the mountaintop.

Another car pulled up as he and Tommy got out. It was the museum director.

Tommy had made a call from the hotel in Charlottesville the

night before, explaining that they'd like to have an early look around the property before the crowds started showing up.

The IAA was a known commodity in the historical realm, especially on the East Coast of the United States. So, when its founder called and made a special request, people were always happy to assist.

It was an added benefit Sean and Tommy were grateful for.

The man in the car rolled down the passenger window and greeted them with a welcoming smile. "Hey, fellas. Climb on in."

Tim Pinkton was the museum director and a loose acquaintance of Tommy's. They'd chatted before over coffee at a conference, though Tommy wondered if the guy would remember him. Based on the conversation the night before, he did.

Pinkton looked like any average forty-six-year-old American. He was about two inches short of six feet, not overweight but not in peak physical condition, either. A father of two, he fit the dad-bod to a T.

Once his two guests were in the car, he eased the car around onto the road leading up to the mansion.

"I gotta say, I was a bit surprised to get a call from you," Tim said.

"And on such short notice," Tommy added, "I really appreciate you making quick arrangements for us."

Tim shook his head. "No trouble at all. Happy to help a colleague." He scratched his thin, stubbly beard. "So, what brings you to Monticello?"

It was a question Sean and Tommy knew was coming. They'd already discussed the answer before arriving that morning.

"Sean's never been here before," Tommy answered truthfully. "I thought it would be cool to show him around a bit before all the tourists get here."

"Oh, I didn't realize it was your first time, Sean. I'm Tim, by the way."

"Nice to meet you." Sean did his best to sound sincere, though he was focused on finding the key—if it was still on the property—and getting the heck out of dodge. "Thanks for letting us in early."

"Happy to. Is there anything you would like to see first? I'd love to give you a VIP tour of the place, but I have a meeting here in half an hour."

"No worries," Tommy said. "I'll show him around."

Sean took the reins of the conversation and steered it toward their problem. "I was curious," he said, "where Thomas Jefferson may have spent most of his time here—you know, with friends. Was there a special room where he entertained his honored guests, or did that sort of thing happen pretty much all over the place?"

Tim guided the car up the hill, around a long left-hand curve. He thought for a moment before answering. "Well, there were a few special places Jefferson preferred to entertain the more important people from society. I imagine his favorite place to unwind with powerful friends, however, would be the garden pavilion."

"The garden pavilion?"

"Yeah. It's a little building on the edge of the mountain. The views are spectacular, overlooking the countryside, the surrounding hills, all that. In the fall, it's a remarkable vista. The colors of the leaves make it one of the most beautiful places you'll ever see. Of course, that's just my opinion. Then again, I'd say the fall colors alone are one of the reasons Jefferson chose this spot."

Up ahead, the mansion crept into view around the trees to the left. The grand brick building with white pillars and matching dome stood as a testament to the time of its construction, and to the imagination of the architect who designed it.

Tim drove the car up to the drop-off point where shuttles would be ferrying visitors in less than an hour.

That didn't give Sean and Tommy much time, but if this trip took more than an hour they were likely not going to find what they were looking for.

Something Tim said resonated with the two visitors.

He'd used the phrase "powerful friends" to describe those who would come and socialize with Jefferson. To Sean and Tommy, that phrase sure seemed to fit as a synonym for titans—an explicit reference to Lafayette's journal.

Indeed, great leaders from both past and present were often

referred to as titans. The people who'd forged the Industrial Revolution on down to the modern tech billionaires were frequently called "titans of industry."

They were usually the uber wealthy, the elite of the world. That description would've fit perfectly with the people Jefferson had hosted at his home. According to Tim, those folks would have been shown the garden pavilion, perhaps even sat there with the great leader.

In Sean's and Tommy's minds, that was the perfect place to start.

Tommy remembered his last visit. He'd been standing by the garden pavilion, taking in the view. He never considered he'd come back specifically to visit that piece of the property.

Aside from the spectacular vistas, there wasn't much to the building. It was small, maybe ten feet long and eight feet wide, with old brick and mortar making up the exterior wall. There were big gaps on each side, with railing attached to the floors, allowing people to look out in all directions without being inhibited by windows. In truth, the structure was more like a square brick gazebo than anything.

Tim reminded Tommy that if he needed anything else to feel free to call or send a text message, preferring the latter since he'd be in a meeting and would probably be unable to answer for the next hour.

Sean and Tommy thanked Tim for the lift and watched him drive away, heading back around behind the main building. As soon as he was out of sight, the two made their way toward the little brick structure off to their left.

A garden full of winter vegetables and dark brown soil ran toward the driveway from the edge of the precipice. The end of it abutted a narrow path leading from the pavilion to the mansion in one direction, and along the ridge in the other.

"I can certainly see why Jefferson was proud of this little place," Sean said. "If I was here, I'd want all my friends to check it out."

"So, if this was your property, you and I would hang out in this pavilion?"

"Maybe." Sean winked at his friend, who simply shook his head and kept walking.

"Like you have so many friends."

Tommy wasn't wrong. Sean really didn't associate with many people. Other than Schultzie, Adriana, the kids, and occasionally the McElroys, he was kind of a loner. It was the nature of his career, both in the government and with IAA.

But Tommy's social life mirrored Sean's. He was always either out of the country or so deep in a research project that he barely came up for air. It was a wonder either of them was in a semifunctional relationship.

Luckily for them, the women in their lives walked similar paths.

They slowed down as they approached the building and examined the exterior for a moment before stepping inside.

The bright rays of the early morning sun shone through the opening on the other side, casting a white-yellow square onto the floor. Two wooden chairs, made to look like they were from the early nineteenth century, sat in the opposing corners of the front.

"I know this thing has been renovated," Tommy said, "probably a few times over the years, but it's still cool to know we're standing where Thomas Jefferson and other famous people from that era hung out, talked politics or hobbies, and just enjoyed the simple beauty of this view."

"It's pretty awesome, isn't it? I always get that feeling when I'm in a historic place like this. To tread where great men and women have before us, to touch the soil they touched, it's such a powerful connection to the past."

Tommy nodded. He and Sean both appreciated the same things in life. It was one of the many reasons their friendship had endured over the decades. Most people they came into contact with were surprised to learn the two had known each other so long, often telling them that they didn't have any friends they'd known more than a decade.

That bond had also helped save their necks from time to time.

Sean made his way over to the huge window-like frame and looked over the edge. He did so with caution, concerned that there could be a long drop on the other side of the building. He was relieved to see that the precipice only fell off a few feet beneath the foundation then gradually sloped down the mountainside to the valley below.

Tommy joined him at the window and looked out across the scene. "I'd love to sit here and sip some coffee while we enjoy this view, but we're up against the clock."

"Right," Sean said as if he'd momentarily forgotten why they were there. "So, we believe this is the place where Jefferson would hang out with other titans. The journal said that the key was underneath it."

"Correct." Tommy looked down at the wooden plank floor and scratched his head. "I don't know about you, but I have a feeling Tim won't appreciate us ripping these floorboards up."

Sean chuckled. "Yeah, you're probably right." He took a step back and spied the floor as well. "These boards aren't that old, though. They're not the originals."

"No question. So, that means if there was something under them, the carpenters who did the work would have found anything unusual long ago."

"Yep. Unless the riddle wasn't talking about under the floor."

"What do you mean?" Tommy asked with eyes narrowed in a curious expression.

Sean leaned back out over the window and looked down. The base of the little building was built on the edge of the ridge, but the front half of it had been placed on a foundation made from mountain stone.

"What?" Tommy asked and joined his friend, examining the foundation.

"If the key is still here, it's gotta be behind one of those rocks."

"Gotta be? That's a pretty bold statement. I mean, it could be somewhere else. Maybe even buried in the ground or something."

"You go get a shovel then. I'll take a look around those stones."

Tommy snorted a laugh. While they had several tools in their bags, a shovel wasn't one of them.

"I've got the rope, though," he replied in a dry tone.

Sean's head snapped around. "Seriously?"

"No."

It was Sean's turn to snort. "Come on."

The two walked back out of the building and took a quick look back toward the mansion to make sure no one was watching them. Tim was nowhere to be seen, and the few workers on the premises were busily going about their morning tasks.

Satisfied no one was paying attention to them, Sean led the way around the corner of the pavilion and down the gentle slope to the front. The grounds here appeared to be regularly maintained, the weeds and small trees trimmed low to the ground to allow visitors to enjoy the view unobstructed.

The two stepped carefully around outcroppings of rocks until they were facing the front of the building.

"Well," Sean said, "this is where the hills rise to meet the flowers of Jefferson's garden—assuming we were correct about the riddle."

Tommy leaned forward and braced his right hand on the stone foundation while rubbing his finger along the edge of one of the rocks. "These are the original stones," he said. "This foundation is at least a few hundred years old."

"So, if there's something hidden behind it, there's a good chance it could still be there."

"I guess we'll have to see."

Tommy set his bag down and unzipped it. He pulled out a crowbar and held it up.

"Pretty sure what you're about to do is a felony," Sean said. "I'm no lawyer, but that's my guess."

"Just keep a lookout."

"Hey, you're the one that's always trying to be so careful with artifacts and historical stuff."

"I guess with age I get less and less concerned about things like that." He flashed a witty grin and started tapping on the stones with one end of the bar.

Sean crept around the corner and looked back toward the mansion. Still no sign of anyone remotely interested in what they were doing. He watched as his friend kept tapping on the rocks until he found one that made a kind of hollow sound.

"This is the one," Tommy said.

"The one what?"

Tommy didn't answer. Instead, he took the flat end of the tool and started chipping away at the brittle mortar keeping the rocks in place.

Sean walked around behind his friend and looked down the walking path leading away from the manor. There was no sign of anyone in that direction, but he got the strange feeling they were being watched nonetheless.

Tommy finished work on the first seam of mortar and started on the upper section, knocking the stuff out in chunks. It took less than two minutes for him to clear away the second seam. The end sections were even faster. By the time he was halfway done with the last part, the stone jiggled with every strike of his makeshift chisel.

"Got it," he said after five minutes of intense labor. Sean turned back to his friend and looked at his handiwork. The rock was sitting loose on the one below it, and now a dusty gap remained above.

Tommy took a second to catch his breath and admire the job before he set the bar down and stepped close to the foundation once more. Sean stepped back around to the other side of the pavilion and scanned the property near the mansion again. Still no one around to bother them. In his opinion, it was almost too quiet. The banging and chipping sounds Tommy made could have alerted security or anyone nearby that something unusual was going on, but as of yet no one seemed to notice.

Tommy slid his fingers into the opening above the stone and found the back edge. He tugged on it gently, and the rock slid forward a few inches with very little restriction. He pulled again, working the stone back and forth until half of it was hanging over the lip below. Sean stepped close, watching with intense interest.

"You need some help?" he asked.

"Nah, I'm good. One...more...pull." He jerked the stone again, and it slid out of place with a low, grinding sound.

Tommy's face strained from the sudden weight, but he recovered and carefully lowered the rock to the ground. He stood up straight again and peered into the new cavity in the foundation.

Sean leaned close, too, staring into the darkness. He unconsciously pulled his phone out of his pocket and turned on the flashlight, shining it into the black space.

The two friends craned their necks, putting their faces as close to the foundation as possible without actually touching it.

"There's something in there," Sean said.

"Yeah, I see it."

Tommy bent down and grabbed a pair of white gloves from his bag. "Can't be too careful," he said, slipping a glove on his left hand and then on the right.

"This from the guy who just destroyed a nationally protected piece of property."

"We'll put the rock back," Tommy said. The defense was weak and he knew it. He also knew Sean was just giving him a hard time. Breaking the mortar around the stone was the only way to get the thing out. And getting the rock out of the way was critical to solving this riddle.

He reached into the gap with one hand. When his elbow grazed the edge, he felt something brush against the tip of his gloved fingers. He worked his hand around the anomaly for another second, carefully grasping it with the gentlest of grips. Then he pulled his arm out of the hole.

When his hand appeared in the daylight, it held an unusual-looking object. The thing was made of white stone, engraved with a four-sided cross on a flat end the two men figured to be the handle. On the other end of the cylindrical shaft, it widened to a circle. Tommy turned it over and gazed at the bizarre key.

The surface of the circular end was engraved with two men in armor, riding horses with swords drawn. Other raised symbols encircled the image, though at first glance the two friends didn't recognize them. One emblem, however, was unmistakable.

When Sean spoke, it was in a reverent whisper. "This is the first key," he said, "to the vault containing the Ark of the Covenant."

22

CHARLOTTESVILLE

Tusun watched from the forest. They'd followed Wyatt and Schultz from the hotel earlier that morning, keeping their distance. It didn't take long to figure out where the two were going. The direction their quarry took had eliminated the Monroe plantation, leaving only Monticello.

Once they'd arrived, Tusun and his men split up to cover more ground. They also did that to prevent Wyatt and Schultz from trying anything, like some kind of elaborate escape.

Of course, Tusun was operating under the assumption that Wyatt didn't know he was being followed, a dangerous thing to do considering Wyatt's history. It was entirely possible that the man was toying with Tusun, something he'd considered more than once on the journey from New York to Washington and now to Virginia.

There was no way to know for sure, but he had a hunch that wasn't happening.

He peered through his binoculars while four other men surrounded him, two on either side. Two of them were watching the rear, the other two the flanks. It was a standard formation for this sort of thing, and the men didn't need to be told what to do. They'd been in similar situations before, not to mention the intense training required of every member of the order.

Tusun narrowed his eyes as Schultz and Wyatt made their way into the garden pavilion and looked out the front opening. "What are they doing?" he whispered to himself, too quiet for the others to hear.

The two then left the pavilion and walked around the nearest corner to the lower section. They were inspecting something, but what, he didn't know. The foundation? Tusun hated not having enough information. He was accustomed to having files on everything from targets to locations and everything in between. He was flying blind on this one, and it irritated him. It happened, though, and Tusun would deal with it as he always did.

Nothing was ever perfect. The ability to adapt was drilled into each man long before they ever went out on a mission.

Failure to do so had caused their demise some five hundred years prior. The order had nearly been wiped out as a result; their numbers dwindled to a mere handful. The name Assassins faded to the stuff of legend, nothing more than a morning mist blown away by a dry, easterly wind.

Tusun and his men were far enough away from the targets to remain unnoticed. Their camouflage gear made sure they blended in almost seamlessly with the environment. They were, however, close enough to hear the picking sound as Schultz started chipping away at the outbuilding's foundation. His eyes were already slits but narrowed even more as he stared at the two men, one knocking pieces of mortar from the rocks while the other, Wyatt, kept watch.

At first, Wyatt went around to the other end of the pavilion, probably to make sure no one from the mansion was paying attention. Maybe he was concerned the noise his comrade was making might draw the eye of one of the workers. Tusun wondered how no one else noticed, but the staff and the few people wandering around the grounds didn't seem to offer a reaction.

Then Wyatt shifted his position, coming back to the near corner. There was a moment when the man stared straight at Tusun or, rather, at his position. Had Wyatt seen him, he would have gotten out of there in a heartbeat. Based on the details Tusun had learned about Wyatt, he understood the man wasn't given to panicking. Had Tusun and his men been spotted, Wyatt may have played it cool, pretending he saw nothing, instead letting his friend continue his toil until the job was done.

Either way, Wyatt turned away a few minutes later and assisted his friend as he pulled a piece of stone out of the foundation. Then Tusun watched as Schultz removed something else from the pavilion's base. Even with his powerful, top-of-the-line binoculars, it was difficult to make out exactly what the object was, but he didn't need to see the details to know.

It had to be the key Alain was looking for.

Wyatt and Schultz had figured out the clues from the journal in less than a day, something Wilkins had been unable to do for over a week.

That thought sent a spark of satisfaction through the Assassin's mind. If Wilkins had been an idiot, fine. He deserved what he got. And if the professor had purposely delayed his work to throw off the order from finding the Ark, his execution was even more appropriate, though in that case Tusun wished he'd tortured the man a bit more before giving him the mercy of death.

Tusun stared at the object in Schultz's hands as he turned it over, examining the thing for nearly a minute.

Then he wrapped it in a towel and stuffed it in his gear bag, slung the bag over his shoulder, and the two men made their way back down the hill to the road. They walked over to the mansion and disappeared inside. Why, Tusun didn't know, but one thing was certain: they'd found the key.

With the two targets lost from their field of vision, Tusun ordered three of his men to move up slowly through the woods. The other he told to go back to the parking area and get the car ready.

The team leader had the distinct suspicion that his targets would be making a quick exit despite going into the mansion. It was a ruse and he knew it. Wyatt hadn't seen him, but the guy was paranoid or, at the very least, always on his guard. A hint of respect swelled in Tusun's chest. It was about time he had a worthy adversary.

Sean Wyatt was going to make for good hunting. It was annoying when a target didn't give him at least a little sport. Wyatt would make it interesting. Up until the point Tusun killed him.

23

CHARLOTTESVILLE

Sean and Tommy scuffed their feet on the pavement as they hurried down the road, staying close to the edge to stay out of the way of oncoming shuttles. The bus drivers and early-bird tourists didn't think anything of the two men trudging down the hill with their gear bags slung over their shoulders. They had no way of knowing what Sean and Tommy had just done, or what they carried.

Though they did their best not to look like they were in a hurry, the two men couldn't help but move at a brisk pace. The sooner they got out of there, the better.

Tommy tried to mask their guilt by casually waving at two of the shuttle buses as they drove by. The drivers of both returned the favor, probably assuming the guys were workers.

"Subtle, Tommy. Real subtle," Sean said after his friend did it for a second time.

"What?" Tommy asked, sounding a little insulted. "I'm trying to look like we're not doing anything wrong."

Sean let out a laugh. "It's already done. But try not to draw any attention to us, okay?"

"You mean two dudes walking down this long driveway with a couple of bags that look like something bank robbers would use?"

"Yeah, that."

Sean didn't see Tommy roll his eyes.

They rounded the last bend near the bottom of the mountain, and the parking lot slowly came into view. Cars filed in, filling the empty spots rapidly while a couple of attendants directed them where to park.

"I guess Saturday is a big day for visiting this place, huh?" Tommy said.

"Makes sense. And all the more reason for us to get out of here as fast as possible. We don't need a bunch of people seeing our faces."

He pushed his sunglasses up to the top of his nose. He'd worn a beanie to keep his ears warm against the chilly spring air, which he also hoped would help to conceal his identity.

Tommy had a baseball cap on his head and a pair of aviator sunglasses. They'd be difficult to recognize if it came down to that. Sean hoped it didn't. It would be hard to explain why they'd vandalized a national landmark and stolen an ancient artifact on top of it.

They skirted the edge of the parking lot, making their way toward their rental car. Another bus drove by, this time receiving no friendly wave from Tommy. The two were only thirty yards from the vehicle when they were halted by a familiar voice.

"You guys leaving so soon?" Tim Pinkton asked.

Sean and Tommy whirled around, both hit by a sudden rush of panic. Sean was far less prone to such an emotion than his friend, but there were moments, like now, where he feared being caught. He had the connections to get him out of trouble, though he'd probably made that call a few too many times. What was more of a concern was losing trust. Sean knew that he and Tommy had strong reputations in the historical community. If they were discovered vandalizing a piece of history and stealing, that would be worse than any punishment they could receive.

"Hey, Tim," Tommy spoke first. Sean knew his friend's heart was racing. Somehow, he managed to keep his cool. "Yeah, we had a look around, went to the mansion, saw a few things. We gotta get back to

Atlanta. Just got a call from the lab. My research team apparently found something interesting they want me to see."

"Oh, that's exciting." Tim turned his attention to Sean. "What about you? Did you enjoy your visit? Pretty neat, huh?"

"Yeah," Sean said. "This place is amazing. I love being able to reach out and touch history, real history. This property is full of it."

"I know, right?"

"I mean, sometimes I wish I could just rip a piece of it away and take it home with me."

Tim's forehead wrinkled a tad. "Yeah..., I know what you mean." He said it like he didn't really see where Sean was going.

Sean kept it up, knowing full well it was driving Tommy crazy. "Yeah, like if I could take away a piece of this place, that would be so cool."

"Yeah...but we can't, so you know, I guess you'll just have to come back and visit."

Sean peered into the property director's eyes. "Yeah. I guess I will." He let his voice fill with a sinister, foreboding tone.

"Cool. Well, I gotta get going. Thanks for stopping by, guys." He turned his attention to Tommy, clearly disheveled by Sean's odd behavior. "Give me a call sometime when you're in town again, and we'll meet up."

"Sure thing, Tim. You bet. And thanks again for helping us with the whole early access thing. I really appreciate it."

Tim gave a feeble wave and drove off around the corner, heading down a side road with a sign next to it that warned visitors it was only meant for authorized personnel.

The two friends watched as the man disappeared behind an outcropping of trees. When he was out of sight, Tommy spun around and faced Sean, eyes full of daggers.

"What was that?" Tommy blared. "You want to get us caught?"

Sean chuckled. A smug grin crept across his face. "You should have seen your face," he said. "Actually, you should see it right now. You look mortified."

"I *am*! Are you crazy?"

Sean kept up the appearance for a second until his friend's concerned expression cracked.

"Come on, you gotta admit that was funny."

Tommy shook his head and turned back to the car. He reached out for the door handle and pulled it. The thing snapped out of his fingers, and Tommy's body leaned back momentarily from momentum.

He looked over at Sean with his head cocked to the side, his face wearing the biggest *you moron* expression he could muster.

"It's locked," Sean said and burst out laughing.

"You love messing with me, don't you?"

Sean was still giggling as he nodded and stepped over to the driver's side door. He pressed the button on the fob to unlock the vehicle. "I do. I really do."

"You're a great friend, you know that?" Tommy gently placed his bag in the backseat and climbed into the front.

"The best kind," Sean added with a final wink.

He steered the car out of the parking spot and wheeled it around, driving by the throngs of eager visitors lined up on the asphalt. Sean turned out onto the main road and glanced in the rearview mirror.

Tommy noticed. "What?" he asked. He turned back and looked through the rear window at the cars spilling out onto the road, waiting in line for a parking spot. "Big crowd."

"That's not it," Sean said.

Tommy frowned. He knew that tone. It signaled something was wrong. "What do you see?"

"I don't know," Sean confessed. His eyes flashed to the mirror again. "Just keep an eye on the road behind us."

"Okay," Tommy said. He looked in the side mirror for a moment. "You mind telling me what's going on? You think someone is following us?"

"Maybe. It's probably me just being paranoid."

"You mean you being normal."

"Ha."

"Seriously, though, did you see something suspicious?"

Sean shook his head. He genuinely wasn't sure, but he knew he was going to play it safe. There was something in the woods on the mountaintop. He could have sworn he'd seen a glint of light for a split second while Tommy was working to dislodge the stone from the foundation. At the time, he hadn't said anything to his friend. No sense in causing Tommy to panic when it was probably nothing.

That aside, Sean remained on full alert. It was why he'd suggested they go into the mansion after finding the key. Tommy had protested the idea, suggesting they get the heck out of there as fast as possible.

His exact words had been: "I don't feel like jumping into the lion's mouth."

Sean had insisted. Once they were inside, they roamed through an open section of the mansion and back out the other end, through a door that was meant for staff only.

Satisfied they weren't being followed, Sean led the way back down the road toward the lot.

Now, however, he wasn't so sure.

"I thought I saw something in the forest up there," he said. "It was probably nothing, but just to be safe, that's why I thought we should go into the mansion—and why I want you to keep a lookout behind us."

Tommy straightened up a little. "Okay, buddy. I gotcha." A look of concern washed over his face, causing it to pale slightly. "When were you planning on telling me this?"

"Now," Sean said.

Tommy puckered his lips and nodded. "You thought I'd freak out if you said something up on the mountain, huh?"

"Would you have?"

"Come on, man. You know me better than that." He hesitated.

"You're right. You definitely would have freaked."

Tommy let out a laugh. "Thank you. Glad to see you have full confidence in me."

Sean twisted his head to the side and gave his friend a smirk. "I do actually. Just no sense in upsetting the apple cart if there's no cause." He thought for a moment. "Just in case we are being tracked, though, I have an idea."

"Yeah?"

Sean nodded. "Yeah."

24

CHARLOTTESVILLE

T usun's driver kept a safe distance between his SUV and the targets' vehicle. There was no need to have line of sight at this point. The beacon they placed on the rental car's chassis would lead them straight to Wyatt and Schultz, at which point Tusun and his men would hang back and watch until the second key was retrieved.

He hoped it would be in a remote spot, possibly out in the woods or in a field far away from any potential witnesses who would raise a fuss. If at all possible, Tusun tried to avoid collateral damage. Curious eyes of innocent bystanders could turn into real problems later on.

He recalled having to execute an older man once. The guy had simply been in the wrong place at the wrong time and walked into a side street the second Tusun put a bullet through a traitor's face. It was an event that occurred early in Tusun's run with the order. Ever since then, he'd been more careful.

It wasn't that he cared about the deaths of people who happened to get in his way. Truth was, he kind of enjoyed it—something that made him very dangerous. And very respected.

No, the issue was cleanup. Each body that he left lying around was a potential problem, a hazard that could lead even the dumbest investigators to the order. The scenario was unlikely, but being cautious had kept them safely in the shadows for a long time. Tusun knew his boss wanted to keep it that way, and he agreed.

He checked the screen on his tablet and saw the beeping blue dot stop moving. "Hold here," he said, putting out his hand for the driver.

The man behind the wheel slowed the vehicle and turned into a gravel strip along the road, waiting for further instructions. The SUV behind them did the same, pulling in close to the lead vehicle's back bumper.

The blue dot moved a little more, slowly this time, and then came to a complete stop again. Tusun watched with intense curiosity. He used his fingers to zoom out on the map and analyze the location.

"This area is close to Highland," he said.

"What's that?"

It was no surprise that the driver or any of the other men didn't know. Their knowledge of American history was frail at best. Tusun's wasn't great, either, but he made a habit of trying to constantly learn new things, especially about his enemies. There was an old saying about that he kept close to his heart.

"Former American president James Monroe lived there. It was his estate," Tusun said.

"Two presidents owned property so close together?"

Tusun gave a nod. He didn't feel like giving a history lesson. "It was a part of the country where many wealthy people lived back then." He hoped the quick explanation would sate the driver's sudden curiosity. Before the guy could say anything else, Tusun ordered him to move forward, slowly.

"It looks like they're not going anywhere," Tusun said. "Go to the top of that ridge, and we should be able to see them."

"Won't they be able to see us, too?"

"Not if we stick to the tall grass on the other side of that fence." He motioned to an old wooden fence that ran along both sides of the road, about fifteen feet off the pavement. "We'll park just up there, then go the rest of the way on foot. We'll need to stay low."

The driver nodded that he understood and eased the vehicle back onto the road and up the hill. When they were near the crest, he pulled over and parked the SUV next to the ditch, making sure he was almost a foot off the pavement before putting it in park and turning off the engine.

"Let's move," Tusun said.

He and the other men piled out of the vehicles and jumped the fence. Tusun went first and then waited for his team, keeping an eye on the road behind them to make sure there were no cops or curious onlookers.

The men crouched low once they were in the stands of long, green grass and virtually disappeared within seconds. They crept forward with military precision, each man knowing what was expected of him. The unit was like one entity, tethered together by some invisible force that made them think, react, and move together without much more than a subtle hand signal.

They pushed ahead toward the forest and stopped when they came to where the hill started sloping down. Tusun raised up enough to see over the top of the waving grass and saw Wyatt and Schultz wandering into the forest. A few seconds later, the two men were out of sight.

Tusun lowered back down and thought for a second. The second key must be hidden in the forest; that much was apparent. It also presented a new problem. The trees would help keep Tusun and his men out of sight, but it could also make tracking Wyatt and Schultz more difficult if they didn't hurry and catch up.

He made a quick decision and ordered his men ahead with a quiet whisper into his microphone. His barely audible command didn't need to be so silent. The targets were too far way even if he gave the order in full voice. Old habits were nearly impossible to break, especially for someone as well trained as Tusun. He also preferred to err on the side of caution.

He and the other four moved ahead, carefully navigating the grassy slope as they approached the edge of the forest. Tusun held up his hand, signaling the others to stop. He was out in front, with two men staggered back on either side in a sort of V formation.

Tusun almost always took the lead. He believed it was an honor to do so, to be the first in, and last out, of any combat situation. It was the privilege of his rank in the order, a privilege that could potentially come with great sacrifice.

But he didn't fear death. Why should he? Were he to die doing the will of the Almighty, what would he have to fear? Paradise waited for God's warriors. When the time came, Tusun would welcome it.

He peered across the top of the grass, into the woods. The thick rows of oaks, pines, and poplars made it difficult to see anything other than more trees. *There.* It looked like a piece of fabric from Wyatt's jacket flashed between the trunks. He only saw it for a split second, but there was no question in Tusun's mind what it was.

"Move up," he said into the mic.

He veered to the left, moving toward the forest where the grass ended and the undergrowth began. While the men lost the cover of the field, they now had an infinite number of options for cover. Each of the five took up positions in a jagged line across a thirty-foot breadth, tucking in behind thick trees to stay out of sight. Each man under his command waited for their next order, weapons at the ready.

Tusun poked his head around the tree he'd chosen and looked deep into the woods. There was no sign of the two men. He gave a sideways nod to his team, and the men pushed up to another line of trees. They moved deftly, careful not to step on any loose branches or twigs. The slightest noise—a light snap, the rustle of leaves—could alert the targets to their presence.

He flicked his head and made a circular motion. The men to his right and left spread out. Those on the end darted to cover farther away from the two interior men. The plan was to encircle the targets, flanking them from all sides. It was the obvious move to make, and Tusun knew his men would execute it to perfection.

He spied a thick oak tree directly ahead and sprinted to it, keeping to his tiptoes to stay silent as he moved. The rest of the men fanned out accordingly, pushing up in what had turned into a broad U formation. They would surround Wyatt and Schultz and then move in like a boa constrictor, squeezing the life out of their prey.

Tusun reached the next tree and pushed his back into it. He held his weapon high and tight, like he'd done so many times before on similar missions. Then he twisted around and peeked into the woods ahead. There was still no sign of Wyatt and Schultz.

Something wasn't right. He looked out to his flanks. He could barely see the men on either side, but they were in good positions.

Were the targets moving faster than expected? It was the only explanation, which meant the two men must have found something.

Tusun whispered into his radio. "Move up, slowly. Disable only."

His men knew what the second command meant. It was their version of "set phasers to stun." It meant that they weren't to shoot to kill. If their weapons were used, it was only to disable the targets. Tusun wanted the men alive.

The guys on his flanks moved up again, their weapons pointed ahead like Special Forces taking down a high-value target.

They stopped again as they'd done a few times already. Taking too much ground in big chunks could get them noticed. These men weren't stupid. They didn't have delusions of grandeur, storming ahead and ripping the enemy to pieces. They were precision instruments, scalpels sent to remove a disease.

Tusun leaned against his next tree trunk and breathed slowly. His heart pulsed at a steady, slightly elevated rate from the rapid movement. He wasn't nervous. That sort of thing had been expelled long ago. As he waited for the next run, he stared back through the woods toward the field. It was nearly out of sight now. The canopy above submerged them into shadows, only allowing a few rays of sunlight to streak through like thick, bright lasers.

He swallowed and spun around to keep going.

"That's far enough," a man's voice said from behind him.

Tusun froze for a second. His men to the right and left also came to a sudden halt. They whirled toward the sound. They found nothing but empty forest.

Confusion filled them in an instant. They turned their heads back and forth, suddenly aware that they were not only being watched, but the enemy was nowhere to be seen.

"Tell your men to drop their weapons," the voice said. "Or I kill you right now. There's a .40-caliber hollow point aimed at the back of your skull."

Tusun hesitated. He didn't put his hands up or obey the order. He simply waited for a moment.

"Don't make me tell you again," the voice said, this time with greater menace.

Then Tusun looked up into the treetops and found the source of the voice. Sean Wyatt was standing on a pair of branches about fifteen to twenty feet up. His weapon was at full extension with one arm while the left hand held on to another branch above.

The two men to Tusun's right started to aim their weapons, but another voice stopped them. "Uh, uh, uh," Tommy warned.

The men looked up and found the second target hovering over them, his pistol trained on the guy on the outer flank. They froze.

"Drop those guns," Tommy said. "I'll ice both of you before you get a shot off. And your boss over there will get cut down, too."

"Don't drop your weapons," Tusun ordered.

The four men looked confused, as if they weren't sure who to obey.

Sean knew the leader would be difficult. He didn't know the extent to which the man was willing to take things.

"I'm giving you three seconds," Sean said. He kept the mass of the trees trunk between himself and the other men, a shield nature may not have intended but one he'd use nonetheless.

Sean saw the unrelenting determination in his enemy's eyes. This guy was willing to die right then and there. He had no qualms about it, no reservations. He almost looked at peace, something Sean had no way of anticipating.

Either these guys were crazy, or they were beyond dedicated. Funny how often the two of those could be confused.

"One!" Sean shouted. He sensed the men on the other side of the tree shuffling. "Stay where you are!" The movement stopped. "Two!"

Tusun clenched his teeth, but his eyes were glazed over, ready to accept death. Paradise awaited. His soul was prepared. He blinked slowly as a silent prayer of appreciation filled his mind and echoed through the ether.

"Three!"

25

VIRGINIA

"Stop!" one of the men under Tommy shouted. "Wait!"

Sean's eyes flashed over to where his friend was standing on similar tree limbs, looming over the two other Assassins.

The men were bending down slowly, placing their weapons on the ground.

Sean leaned around the tree, risking a glance over at the two on his side. They were doing the same, putting their guns in the leaves and earth of the forest floor.

"Don't," Tusun ordered.

The men didn't listen. They put their hands in the air and stepped slowly away from their weapons.

"Over here." Sean motioned to them to join their comrade.

The men glanced at each other, wondering if they should obey, and then trudged over to where Tusun stood alone, still armed.

Tommy climbed down and picked up the guns the two guys on his side had left. He stuffed one into his belt and held the other in his left hand as he herded the men over to the little clearing. Once Tommy was behind all five Assassins, Sean hurriedly climbed down out of the tree. His boots hit the ground with a heavy thud, his knees bending in an instant to absorb the landing. Then he stiffened and stared straight ahead at Tusun.

Sean took a step forward and grabbed the gun out of the man's hand. "I had a feeling someone was following us."

Tusun said nothing.

"I don't know what it is, Tommy. Intuition? Gut instinct?"

"Maybe it's the smell," Tommy said, sniffing dramatically.

Sean sniffed, too, and twitched his nose. "Maybe that's it."

"What do you think we should do with them?"

Sean cocked his head to the side as if sizing up an opponent in a bar brawl. "You know, I'm not sure. I mean, we could kill them and leave their bodies for the coyotes and buzzards."

"I was thinking the same thing. I say we ice them right here and let the animals decide what to do with them."

Sean sighed. "Okay, see, that's twice you've used the term *ice*. What are you, a rap star now or something?"

"Seriously? You're gonna give me a hard time about that right now?" Tommy looked around the five heads at his friend.

"Yeah, I mean, no one really says that. How many people do you know that say that?"

Tusun's eyes shifted uneasily. His eyebrows forged together for a moment. His men, too, appeared confused at the sudden disagreement between their captors.

"Can we get back to the topic, please?" Tommy urged. "We have a key to find."

"Oh right," Sean said, as if he'd forgotten. "The key." He took a step to the side and looked over his shoulder at Tusun. "See, that's what I can't quite figure out about you guys. What do you want with those keys?"

Tusun didn't answer. His men also remained silent.

"They sure don't talk much," Tommy noted.

"No. No, they don't, Schultzie. Out here in the woods, I'm pretty sure we could do whatever we wanted to them. I'm talking real gruesome stuff."

"You may torture us if you like," Tusun said through clenched teeth. "We will never tell you anything."

Sean gave a nod and stepped back directly in front of the man. "Nope, I believe you. I don't think you'd say a thing. We could put you through every kind of pain imaginable, and you'd take the answer to your grave. Lucky for both of us, we already know what you're looking for."

The revelation came as a surprise to the five captive men. Sean could see it in Tusun's eyes as well.

"Oh? You didn't know that we knew you guys were looking for the Ark of the Covenant?"

Tusun took a deep breath and exhaled through his nose, giving no answer.

"It's okay. You don't have to tell me. See, we figured it out. Your little organization is trying to find the Ark because you think it's some kind of weapon. I suppose you have a sinister plan on how to use it, too, maybe kill innocent people somewhere in the world. Sound about right?"

No response.

"Well," Tommy cut in, "your jihad, or whatever it is, is over. You lose. And the good guys win."

Tusun snorted. "You think that's what this is?"

"Sure. That's what you extremists do, isn't it?" Sean rolled his shoulders.

"You know nothing."

"Maybe. Or maybe I do know something. See, guys like you are all the same. You're looking to mess things up for the rest of us. We can't have nice stuff because of knuckleheads like you. Everything's fine and happy, and then all of a sudden, you come into a mall and kill thirty people, or at a church, or at a street festival. You take the lives of innocent people for no reason other than your messed-up view of what you think your god wants."

Tusun's nostrils flared.

"All the while you never consider that we all come from the same place, the same maker. You ever heard of the idea that all rivers flow to one ocean?"

Nothing.

"Yeah, I figured as much. Because your kind is focused on one thing: killing off anyone who's different, believes different." Sean felt a boiling rage surging inside him. In the past, he'd been a hothead, easily given to his temper. Some people said he had a short fuse. That was a long time ago, back when he worked for Axis. That temper had served him well in a few instances, pushed his adrenal glands into overdrive and enabled him to do things that bordered on the super-human. However, he'd pushed that urge down long ago, leaving it to the world he no longer wished to be a part of.

"It is our duty to rid the world of nonbelievers," Tusun said. "Only when infidels like you are wiped from the Earth can we once again enjoy true paradise and peace."

Sean nodded as if he'd finally been convinced in a debate. Then he backhanded Tusun across the jaw. The man's head snapped to the side, but he straightened up and offered a toothy grin.

"Now," Sean said, "what do you plan on doing with the Ark?"

"I think that," a new voice said, "is something you'll need to see for yourselves."

Tommy stiffened as the unseen muzzle pressed into his lower back.

Sean's head twitched, and he looked over Tusun's shoulder, between the other men behind him.

There was a new face hovering over Tommy's shoulder. The man looked like he was probably a few years older than Sean, possibly the same age. He was dressed differently than the others, wearing a black tactical outfit with lots of pockets. His boots matched the rest, though they weren't shined, instead giving off a sort of matte appearance.

"Drop your guns," the man said.

Tommy let out a sigh and lifted his right hand out to the side. He let the pistol fall to the ground. It hit with a clack.

Sean hesitated. He ground his teeth, furious they hadn't seen the man approach. He'd been so distracted by their leader that he never considered someone else could sneak up on them. With so many trees, he'd not detected any movement. Now the anger that burned inside him was directed inward. How sloppy he'd become. His eyes turned to slits.

"Who are you?" Sean asked. He kept his weapon trained on Tusun.

"That is of no consequence to you, Sean Wyatt, but I'll tell you anyway. My name is Alain Depricot of the Order of Assassins. You have something we need."

"A boot to shove somewhere special?"

Alain let his lips crease for a moment. "Always the funny one, eh, Sean?"

"Hey, I'm funny, too," Tommy protested.

"No you aren't, Schultzie."

"I can be."

"Shut up, the both of you." Alain raised his voice to the point that it reverberated through the trees. "Drop your gun, Sean. Or I end your friend's life right now."

The threat came with a prophetic hint to it. He had said "right now." Sean caught the meaning, though he wasn't sure his friend did. It meant that this Alain guy was planning on killing them sooner or later, but because he needed them alive for the moment, their impending deaths were going to have to wait...for now.

"You're not the first one to put a gun to my friend's back," Sean said. "The way our luck goes, I doubt you'll be the last."

"If you don't drop your weapon right now, it *will* be the last time."

Sean peered into the man's eyes and saw no lie. There was something beyond creepy in the orbs that stared back. It was a vacant, distant look, devoid of emotion. Sean had seen that look before in men, men who were disconnected from a world of love, peace, and joy. It was a look that belied a lifetime of pain and suffering, an upbringing that did little to foster goodwill to others, instead planting seeds of fear, anger, and hate.

"Fine," Sean relented. He held his weapon by the barrel, pinched between two fingers, and let it fall to the ground.

Tusun took a step forward, reared back his right hand, then smacked the back of it across Sean's face. The blow burned through Sean's nerves. He winced and clenched his muscles to fight off the old rage that instantly shot up through him like a long-dormant geyser ready to erupt.

A few seconds passed before the raw emotion was gone.

"That's for slapping me before," Tusun said.

"An eye for an eye, huh?" Sean asked. "I didn't think you guys read the Bible."

Tusun ignored the comment and bent down. He picked up Sean's gun and inspected it for a moment then stuffed it into his belt.

The rest of the men hurried to rearm themselves, gathering the weapons that had been taken from them just minutes before. Rearmed, they took up a position in a circle around the two prisoners.

"I wonder," Alain said, "how it came to be that the five of you were overpowered by these two."

No one offered an explanation right away.

"I guess your men aren't as good as you thought," Sean offered. "All that Assassins training is no match for a couple of good ole boys from the country."

"I surrendered," one of the men blurted. "I did it to spare Tusun's life."

Tusun flashed a glance over at the man who had spoken. He exhaled slowly, knowing what would come next.

"I see," Alain said. He turned his pistol to the confessor and pulled the trigger. The bullet smashed through the man's head and out the other side. His body collapsed in a heap.

"Need I remind the rest of you, we do not surrender...for any reason." He let his words sink in before adding: "Ever."

Tusun and his three remaining men didn't flinch. They knew the price of failure, and of weakness. Their comrade's well-intentioned gesture would have been applauded by someone outside their organization. To sacrifice one's freedom to save another was the ultimate in courage. In the Order of Assassins, it was a show of weakness, even if it was to save one of their own.

Tusun would have welcomed death. While it may have hindered the overall mission of the order, it would have been an honorable way to go. Others would step into his shoes and fill them well. Every man was trained to take over for anyone above or below him. It ensured the order would carry on in perpetuity. They toed a fine line between operating as a single, cohesive unit that watched over one another and callously forging ahead when a brother fell.

Tommy and Sean were shocked at the sudden murder. They didn't show it, doing their best to hide the revulsion in their minds.

What kind of person would kill his own troops? The question clanged through their heads.

Alain turned his weapon. "Now, you two have something that belongs to me. I want it back."

Sean let out a *pfft*. "We don't have anything of yours."

Tusun slapped him hard across the face again. Instinctively, Sean wanted to reach up to check if there was blood streaming down his face, but he thought better of it.

"My men followed you here," Alain said. "We know the first key is in your car. My question is, where is the other key? I assume that it isn't out here in these woods." He put his arms out wide, as if showing off his newly decorated living room.

"I guess you don't know what happens when you assume, huh?" Tommy quipped.

Alain turned to him and took a step closer. "And you should assume that I have no problem killing you right now. You saw what I did to one of my own."

Tommy took the threat in stride. "You don't scare us."

He barely got the words out of his mouth. Alain reached out and snatched his lower lip with a gloved hand. He pressed his thumb into the fleshy part under Tommy's chin and squeezed. The thumb dug in deep. Then Alain jerked him toward the ground.

Tommy screamed and dropped to his knees in agonizing pain.

Sean started to take a step forward, but the armed men blocked his path.

"The key is in the car," Sean said, risking a step forward. "Okay?"

Alain squeezed harder, bringing a fresh yell from Tommy's throat.

"And the second key?" Alain wasn't falling for any tricks. There was nothing Sean could do now. He had no other play.

"It's in Fredericksburg," he confessed. "All right? Now let him go."

Alain flicked his eyes to one of his men and gave a curt nod. Sean received an elbow to his lower back a second later. He dropped to his knees, grimacing, but he didn't let out a sound other than a low grunt.

"No one orders me around," Alain said. "Do you understand?"

Sean winced as he struggled back to his feet. "Yeah, sure," he said. "Big man with a gun and grunts to do your dirty work."

Alain snorted in derision. "Oh please. You can't goad me into a fight, Sean. Besides, you're no use to me dead." He turned to Tusun. "Get them to the trucks. It appears we're going to Fredericksburg."

26

FREDERICKSBURG, VIRGINIA

The sun dipped below the tree-covered hills to the west, casting pink and orange hues across the sky. The abstract tapestry above did little to soothe Sean and Tommy as they sat in the back of the Assassins SUVs. Ferry Farm was set near the Rappahannock Rover amid rolling hills, trees, and fields of emerald grass, all a stark contrast to the to the busy roads, modern convenience stores, and shopping centers located nearby.

Alain's men had divided up the two friends into separate cars to make guarding them easier. Sean's handler never took his eyes away from him, as well as keeping his pistol pointed straight at Sean's head the entire ride.

The drive to Fredericksburg had taken a little more than an hour and a half. The trip was comfortable enough, other than the career killer pointing a gun at him the entire time. Sean stared out the window, wondering how much longer they were going to sit there.

The two-vehicle convoy arrived more than three hours ago, and nobody had moved a muscle, instead sitting on the edge of a forest that ran along the border of the property.

"Do you guys ever have to take a leak?" Sean asked, abruptly breaking the silence.

Alain looked back at him. The leather seat made a funny noise as he twisted. Alain's glare lasted a few seconds, and then he turned back around.

"Just think it's weird. Seriously, how do you not need to take a leak right now? I gotta be honest, I've been holding it for over an hour now."

Alain listened patiently but didn't acknowledge the further comments. He wouldn't bend to Sean Wyatt's game.

Sean glanced back at the other SUV. Tommy was inside with the other two henchmen, one sitting in the back—presumably getting the same pistol-pointing-at-him treatment.

"And how much longer are we going to sit here?" Sean asked. He knew he was getting on Alain's nerves, whether the man acknowledged it or not.

"We wait until dark," Alain answered, speaking for the first time since they'd left Charlottesville. "Then you will take us to the second key."

"Oh I see. You don't want anyone to notice us snooping around." Sean's eyes gazed out the windows with a sort of contemplative stare. "Smart. I guess it technically is trespassing, so that might cause some concern, especially in a historic place like this."

"You don't shut up, do you?" the man in the back seat sneered.

Sean twisted his head around and snickered. "I was starting to wonder if you could speak. Never know with you secret-order types. I thought maybe they cut your tongues out or something."

The guard gave no response, instead returning to his silent duty. He instantly realized he'd made a mistake engaging.

The last fading traces of light blended to darkness overhead. Stars poked through the blanket above, first one, then two, then hundreds. A few stragglers from the archaeology team finally left the property, driving down the road away from the old farm.

Ferry Farm had long been believed to be the boyhood home of George Washington. It wasn't until recently that crews had managed to locate the original stone foundation of the home. Marquis de Lafayette's decision to hide the second key there had, apparently, been a good one—at least for more than two hundred years. Now it was most certainly in danger of being discovered by the teams of meticulous diggers scraping away at the soil every single day.

The good news was that according to everything Sean and Tommy had seen about the dig, the foundation itself had remained undisturbed. The stones were left in place, just as they'd been laid by Washington's parents.

"Let's move," Alain said.

The driver revved the engine to life and pulled out onto the main road leading into the property. Then they made the short drive down to the gate and pulled off on the shoulder.

"Everybody out," Alain said. "I want to be in and out of here in less than twenty minutes."

"Pfft," Sean said. "You can't put a timeline on this sort of thing. We don't even know the exact location of the key."

Alain opened his door and looked back into the rear seat at Sean. The threat was written all over his face. "You have twenty minutes, or I kill your friend. Am I clear?"

Sean bit his lower lip. "Sure."

"Good."

The men from the second SUV shoved Tommy forward as Sean was stepping out of his ride, the driver already outside waiting and keeping an eye on his every move, with a gun aimed at his chest.

Sean saw his friend approaching with his escorts. "I see you're having the same date," he joked.

"Yeah," Tommy said. "These two are real charmers, too. Haven't said a word since we left Charlottesville."

"Yeah, mine were a pair of real Chatty Cathys, too." Sean fired a derisive glance over his shoulder.

"Enough," Alain said. "You're on the clock."

"Clock?" Tommy asked.

"Yeah," Sean said. "This guy says we have twenty minutes before he kills you."

"Oh." Tommy acted like the ominous threat didn't bother him.

"Did you explain to them that we don't even really know the key's exact location?"

"I tried, but they won't listen. There's no talking to these two."

"Move," Alain ordered. "You have nineteen minutes now."

Sean shook his head. "Take it easy. Take it easy." He put up his hand like he was trying to calm down a wild stallion.

The men slipped through the wind gaps in the gate and made their way down the path. The half-moon cast an eerie glow on the road, giving them enough light to not need the use of their flashlights or phones.

The path meandered down the side of a hill. Toward the bottom, a small white wooden house sat on the slope. It overlooked the valley below and a creek that divided two parcels of the property.

Beyond the farmhouse, the outline of the dig site stood out like a giant impression in the ground.

"That should be it down there," Tommy said, pointing at the square cutout in the land.

The group made their way beyond the little farmhouse and over to the foundation where the original boyhood home of George Washington had once stood. The building's footprint was immense, much larger than the after-hours visitors expected. For a humble farm dwelling, the home must have been pretty large.

"You have fifteen minutes," Alain said.

Sean's eyes darted from the group's leader to the others. The four men with him never let their weapons stray, always trained on the two captives.

"So," Sean said to his friend, "you remember what that clue said about this place?"

Tommy considered the question for a moment. "I thought you were the one with the great memory."

"I am. I just wanted to see if you could recall."

"We're fifteen minutes away from being executed out here in the middle of Virginia, and you're cracking jokes."

"It's probably closer to fourteen now," Sean said with a wink at Alain.

The man wasn't amused.

"Cornerstone," Sean said. "Lafayette's entry said the key was buried beneath the cornerstone. Although, now that I think of it, I wonder how he got it under there."

"Must have dug to it, I guess."

Sean turned to Alain with a smug look on his face. "You guys don't happen to have any shovels, do you? You know, for digging graves and stuff like that?"

Alain turned to one of his men. "Go get some tools out of the back."

The man turned and started up the hill at a steady pace.

"You mind hurrying?" Sean asked. "Your boss is going to kill us in a few minutes, so time is kind of a big deal."

The guy glanced back over his shoulder and increased his stride ever so slightly.

"Thanks!" Sean shouted at him. "Appreciate it!" He looked over at Alain. "Hey, I don't want you to kill either of us. Just trying to do our part, boss."

A few minutes passed before the gopher returned with a couple of tire irons. He dropped them at the prisoners' feet. The heavy metal clanked together when they hit the ground.

"Those aren't shovels," Tommy said.

"Make do." Alain's response came with a tapping of his watch, signaling that the clock was running.

"Yeah, yeah," Sean said. He bent down and picked up the irons, handing one to his friend. "We get it."

They maneuvered around a row of stones and made their way over to the far corner.

"This it?" Sean asked.

"Looks like it," Tommy said. He bent down, using the tire iron as a brace and craned his neck to the side to get a better look. In the pale light of the moon, he discovered the faintest trace of an emblem carved into the rock. It was a W with a sword on either side, tilted in toward the letter.

"This is it," Tommy confirmed.

"What you thinking?" Sean looked into his friend's eyes. "You start on this side and I start on the other?"

"Good enough for me."

Sean stepped over the foundation and onto the grass. He'd have more to dig through, but that was fine. Either way, they were going to have to get the cornerstone loose enough to pull it out.

He set the tire iron on the ground, leaning it against a few rocks, and began removing the stones from on top of the main block. Once those were gone, Tommy started digging in earnest. Sean picked up his makeshift shovel and did the same, ripping away at the grass and soil directly behind the huge stone.

The two men toiled for about six minutes before Tommy stopped to wipe his brow. Despite the chilly night air, he was working up a sweat. Sean, too, was getting a workout.

He looked up from the impressive hole he'd dug and pleaded with his eyes. "You guys mind lending a hand over here? We could go a lot faster if we took turns."

Alain, Tusun, and the other three didn't budge. They simply stood there watching with guns pointed at Sean and Tommy.

Sean tucked his lower lip under the upper and nodded. "I figured as much."

"You should hurry," Alain said. "You have four minutes."

"Four?" Sean said, sounding insulted. "Come on, man. We're going as fast as we can."

"Go faster."

Tommy renewed his effort, scraping away at the soil under the cornerstone with more vigor than before. The metal tools screeched in the night as the two men kept digging, more furiously than before.

With what couldn't have been more than two minutes left, Tommy's iron was the first to hit something other than dirt and rock. It made a hollow, clunking sound. Tommy tapped the end of the tool again and heard something break.

Sean perked up and looked over the edge of the stone at what his friend had discovered.

"I think we found it," Tommy said. "Sean, use your iron like a lever. Maybe we can topple this thing out of the way."

Sean did as instructed and shoved the tool down into the hole on his side. He pushed on it, pressing the metal against the top edge of the cornerstone. Tommy grabbed the lip with his fingers and pulled it toward him. The heavy stone shifted, then it jiggled. The two men grunted, and a second later the cornerstone toppled over onto its face, partially revealing a clay jar underneath.

Tommy didn't wait for the dust to settle. He set to work, brushing away the rest of the soil until the jar was fully visible. He cringed at the hole he'd punched into the container, but upon further inspection realized it wasn't anything special. He felt a little relief at that, even though he'd damaged a piece of history.

He cradled the jar and lifted it gently from its grave.

The two friends stared at it with reverent wonder in their eyes.

"The last person to touch this was Marquis de Lafayette," Tommy said. "Incredible."

Sean nodded, mesmerized.

"Good work, gentlemen," Alain said, interrupting their moment. He stepped close and snatched the jar from Tommy's grasp.

Tommy swallowed hard, concerned the man was going to damage the jar. His concerns were validated immediately when Alain removed the seal from the lid, took out the unusual-looking key, and tossed the clay to the ground. The vase shattered into a dozen pieces.

Sean and Tommy both let out an irritated sigh.

"That was kind of valuable," Sean said.

"Not compared to this," Alain replied. He held the strange key up in the moonlight, eyeing it with a kind of curiosity. He reached into his pocket and withdrew the first key, then held them up together to compare. They were nearly identical on the surface, the only difference between them being the emblem engraved into the circular front.

The second key, the one placed there by Lafayette, was imprinted with a different symbol. This one was familiar to both Sean and Tommy. It was the compass of the Order of Freemasons.

"Load them in the vehicles," Alain said. "We have a long drive ahead of us."

"Long drive?" Tommy asked.

Sean was wondering the same thing, but he wasn't sure he wanted to know.

"Yes," Alain said. "Did you think I was going to leave you here?"

The man's comment came as a surprise to both Sean and Tommy. Why would he keep them around? The two friends figured they were going to be shot and left there on the hillside for some unfortunate grounds worker to discover the next morning.

The guards stepped around behind the two prisoners and ushered them back toward the gate.

"What are they doing?" Tommy whispered out of the corner of his lips.

Alain was several steps ahead and didn't hear the question.

"They need us for something else," Sean said.

"Yeah, but what?" The answer came to Tommy the instant the words escaped his mouth. "Oh."

"Yeah," Sean mouthed. "They need the tablet."

27

NEW YORK CITY

Sean woke up to something cold pressing on the right side of his face. He blinked wearily. He felt the cold surface against his fingers, palms, and forearms. The blurry scene before him gradually cleared, and he realized what he was feeling. He was on a smooth, concrete floor.

He tried to move his hands to push himself up, but his muscles felt like Jell-O and his body seemed to weigh a ton. Everything felt groggy, slow to react, even his brain, though it was the first thing to get back to a reasonable speed.

When it did, Sean realized what had happened.

He and Tommy had been taken to the SUVs and shoved in the back. He'd felt a prick in his arm and then blacked out. Now he was in a room somewhere. It was cold, fairly damp. A musty smell of wet concrete and mold filled his nostrils. Something warm was touching the skin on his right arm, but he didn't know what. He rolled his head over and faced the other direction. Then he saw where the warmth was coming from. The crack under the door allowed a draft of warm air to enter the tiny space. Heat was coming from somewhere out in the hall, if a hall was what was on the other side of the door.

Gradually, his muscles reacted to the commands his brain was sending, and he managed to push himself up onto his backside. The room spun for a second, and he was tempted to lie back down. He fought off the urge and forced himself to stay upright until things balanced out.

Where was he?

Sean tried to recall anything his captors might have said about where they were going, what the plan was, but his mind was nothing but fog and cobwebs. As things continued to clear, he managed to stagger to his feet. He turned around, shuffling his feet to keep steady. He was in a room made from old bricks. The smooth concrete floor also looked to be quite aged, though it was hard to tell for certain. He wondered if he was in an abandoned hospital or asylum. Again, those thoughts weren't helpful. He needed to figure a way out, no matter where he was.

Then another thought occurred to him. *Where's Tommy?*

There was no sign of his friend. Sean immediately feared the worst. As he spun around, almost in a panic, he remembered his training, his years of experience in the field with situations just like this one. He knew better than to freak out. It was a piece of him that he thought had been engineered out long ago. Now he had to consciously force it away, making himself breathe in a constant rhythm. His thoughts shifted to solutions, not problems.

He took inventory of the room in less than ten seconds. There was nothing in there except a metal chair, a beat-up paint bucket that looked like it was from the 1930s, and a grate in the wall near the floor to his right.

Sean rushed over to the metal screen and got down on all fours. He lowered his face so he could see through it and realized there was a similar dim light on the other side. He couldn't tell for sure, but he thought he saw a body on the floor in the next room.

"Tommy?"

The body started and then went limp again.

It *was* Tommy.

"Schultzie," Sean hissed into the vent. "You okay?"

The only answer he received was a low, nearly inaudible murmur.

"Schultzie. We need to get out of here."

"I just want another banana, Mama."

Sean raised an eyebrow. He was clearly still out of it. Perhaps the effects of the drug were still hitting him hard.

"Schultzie," Sean said. "Shut up, and get on your feet. We have to find a way out."

"Out?" Tommy mumbled. "But I just got here. Why would we leave so soon?"

Sean scrunched his eyebrows together, puzzled. For a second, he wondered if his friend was trying to be funny. Then he realized: Tommy was still out of it.

"Hold on," Sean said, "I'll figure out something." He stood up straight, a little too fast, and the room whirled for a second. Whatever they'd put in his bloodstream was still clinging on for dear life.

He forced a few deep breaths and then snapped his head to the side to clear the fog. There had to be a way out. He walked over to the door and tried the handle, knowing full well it would be locked. That would have been too easy. Plus, the men who'd brought them here weren't amateurs.

Everything flooded back into his mind now. The Assassins, the keys in Virginia, and then a terrifying thought: the Ark of the Covenant.

Sean exhaled and scanned the room but found nothing he could use.

Then he heard footsteps in the corridor outside. He paused and listened. They were coming his way.

He considered tucking behind the wall and ambushing whoever was about to come through, but he knew that wouldn't work. These men weren't stupid.

He shuffled back over to the center of the room and plopped down on the floor to wait. A few seconds later, he heard a key sliding into the door, followed by a turn and a click. The portal opened and three men stepped inside. He recognized one from the forest outside Charlottesville. Tusun, was it? Sean wasn't sure where he'd heard the name or why he thought that to be the guy's moniker, but it sounded right. Perhaps one of the other men had called him by name before Sean lost consciousness. It didn't matter. Here he was, imprisoned in some basement in who knew where, and he was rattling his brain about this guy's name.

"He's awake," Tusun said. "Get him up. Take him upstairs."

The two men strutted into the room and reached down to grab Sean under the armpits. He feigned being out of it up until the men were a foot away. Then, as they tried to hook their hands under him, he brought up his fists and smashed them into both men's groins.

They dropped to their knees in nauseating agony, moaning. Sean sprang to his feet, driving his kneecap into one's jaw and swinging the bridge of his hand across the other's cheek. Both men crumpled to the floor and writhed around for a moment while Sean faced the doorway, ready to take on their boss.

He didn't get the chance. Two more men rushed into the room. One of them held a Taser in his hand. He raised the weapon and fired. The two probes hit him just below the neck and sent a surge of voltage through his body.

Sean fell to the floor and twitched from the snapping pain coursing through him, losing all muscle control.

He breathed hard, fighting the blurriness returning to his vision. Then something hit him in the back of the head, and he lost consciousness again.

There was no way to know how much time had passed when he woke for the second time. It could have been nine o'clock in the morning for all he knew. It was daytime; that much was clear from the light pouring in through a single window on the far wall.

He was sitting in a metal chair, his hands bound behind his back, his ankles strapped to the chair's legs. His head throbbed where he'd taken the blow earlier. Instinctively, he wanted to rub it, but that wasn't happening anytime soon. Based on the narrow gauge of the bonds on his wrists, he knew they'd used zip ties. Smart. No way to pick a lock that wasn't there. Not that he had anything he could have used for that kind of escape.

He winced at the bright sunlight coming through the window. It only made his pounding headache worse.

A faded blue metal door in front of him, about twenty feet away, began to open. The hinges creaked their protest. He wondered what kind of derelict building this was. Probably an old warehouse somewhere. Though he could hear cars outside, lots of them. More than once, he'd heard someone honk their horn, which meant he was near a populated area, not someplace out in the sticks. It was difficult to venture a guess as to what city it could be, but it was large. That much was certain. Maybe the men had taken him and Tommy to somewhere in Washington, or somewhere an hour or so away.

Sean lifted his head slowly. It felt like he had a twenty-five-pound weight hung around it. Then he saw Alain walk in with his second-in-command, four other guys, and Tommy. His friend looked like he'd been worked over pretty well. A swollen right eye and a gash on his left cheek told Sean all he needed to know about the treatment his friend had received at the hands of the Assassins.

They dragged Tommy to Sean's right and shoved him down into a matching chair. Tommy looked like he might topple over from exhaustion, but one of the guards propped him up and tied his hands behind his back, then did the same to his ankles, slipping a zip tie around each chair leg.

Sean didn't bother trying to get out. There was no point. For now, he'd save his energy and wait. Patience, he'd learned, was the key to the door of opportunity.

"Glad to see you're awake again," Alain said as he approached. He stopped a few feet away.

Sean could smell the guy's $500 cologne as it washed over him. It was an odd combination when paired with his almost priestly robes —and a stark contrast to the dusty, industrial scent in the room.

Sean didn't bother asking what this man and his goons wanted. He figured that answer was about to come. There was only one reason he and Tommy were still alive: Alain needed something.

"You are a good fighter, Sean," Alain said. "I'm impressed you were able to take down two of my men earlier."

"They were sloppy. Maybe your training methods aren't as good as you thought." Venom dripped from his words.

Alain's head tipped to the side, and he pursed his lips for a second. "Perhaps you're right. It's a shame we can't use your talents. I know you would never join us. You have your own sense of right and wrong, the order of things to which you believe the world should adhere."

"I call a spade a spade."

"Indeed. And I appreciate that about you, as well as your talents as a killer. You would have made a fine Assassin had you been in the right place at the right time." He folded his hands behind his back and paced to the right as if contemplating something philosophical. "But you weren't." He stopped and turned his head to look down at Tommy.

"Your friend wasn't much help," Alain continued. "It seems his resolve is as strong as yours. Wouldn't tell us anything. Not that it matters. We'll get what we want one way or the other."

Sean snorted through his swollen nose. "I guess you're gonna tell me what that is."

"Isn't it obvious? We have two of the three pieces. Only one remains."

Sean fought through the fog and sorted the information in his head. "The tablet?" He said the words, but he already knew.

"Ah, very good! We have a winner!" Alain clapped mockingly like Sean was the contestant on the world's worst game show.

"It won't do you any good," Sean warned. "The translation is incomplete. Your boy Wilkins was the only guy who could have figured it out. But you killed him, didn't you?"

Alain's face tightened into a frown. How did Wyatt know that?

"Oh, you're probably wondering how I know that. Easy. Guys like you are predictable. Once we had the journal, what did you need Wilkins for? Your kind always ties up loose ends. But you made a mistake, didn't you? You failed to realize how much you still needed the good professor."

Sean could see he was digging into the man's stone exterior, so he kept pushing. "Not smart, Alain. Where is he now, I wonder? Bottom of a river? Or did you do something more inventive? Maybe a mulching machine? Seems like I saw that in a movie once."

Alain took a long step toward the mouthy prisoner and drove his fist into Sean's cheek. Sean's head whipped to the side from the blow. A sharp sting shot across his skin. He grimaced but stiffened immediately, clenching his jaw to ease the pain.

"Thanks," he said. "I had a massive headache. Now I can't feel that anymore. Who taught you how to punch, anyway? I had a cousin that punched like that. She was a tough girl, though. Real tomboy."

Alain didn't fall for further antagonizing. He'd trained his men to never get emotional. For a brief second, he'd allowed this pathetic human to get to him. It wouldn't happen again.

"I wonder," Alain said, "if you'd mind taking a look at this." He held out his hand to the right, and Tusun placed a tablet in his palm.

Alain brought the screen around for Sean to see. It was a video feed of the IAA building in Atlanta.

"I think you know where this is," Alain said.

"Obviously."

"Hmm. You see, I know that you're keeping the tablet there. Your little research team has been working on the translations for the past few days. Based on your previous communication with them, it seems they're close to a solution."

"So?"

"So, this is where you come in. You and a team of my men are going to Atlanta to recover the tablet and the translation." He raised a finger. "Before you protest, you need to understand that if you try to resist, I will kill Tara and Alex without a second thought. We know where they live, where they like to eat lunch every day. While they spend a good amount of their day in that building, we know the exact times they leave. You know who we are, Sean. You know what we do. And we're very good at it. Don't make me kill a couple of young people because of your own flawed, self-righteous ideals."

Sean's heart pulsed faster. It was one thing to threaten him. It was quite another to threaten his friends. Tara and Alex could handle themselves. They'd proved that more than once, but these guys were a different caliber. If they wanted to eliminate the kids, there would be no way to stop them. That gave Sean few options at the moment.

"What about Tommy?" he asked. "You gonna kill him, too?"

"That all depends on you," Alain answered.

Sean sensed the lie within the reply. He knew that meant Tommy was a dead man; it was just a matter of how and when. These guys weren't going to let any of them live. However, if Sean could get to Atlanta, maybe he could make something happen. It was worth a shot. Tied to this chair, he had no options.

"So, what, we fly to Atlanta, I get you the tablet and translations, and you'll just go on your merry way?"

Alain's lips creased slightly, no more than a crack in the plaster façade of his face. "I think we both know how this ends, Sean. You and your friend here have to die. I can't have you running amok. You'll get delusions of grandeur, fed by a thirst for revenge. That might get you a few more seconds of life, but in the end you'll lose. The best I can offer is not killing your young friends in Atlanta. They don't have to know who we are or what happened. You and Tommy will disappear. They'll never find your bodies. Who knows, I may even put out a news story about how your plane went down in the ocean or something."

Sean considered the offer. It wasn't the first time he'd faced a choice like that. He twisted his head around to look at Tommy. His friend's chin rested against his chest. He was out cold.

"Fine," Sean said. "Let's get this over with."

28

Darren Sanders walked through the front corridor of the White House and glanced out the big window to the lawn. The president was leaving the next day and he still hadn't figured out what he was going to do to get his benefactor's men into the building.

It wasn't like the White House had to look up handymen in the yellow pages. They had specific crews for stuff like repairs, renovations, and maintenance, people who'd been through an intense vetting process. Most of them were in-house, on the property during normal working hours in case something needed to be fixed. Over ninety people worked full-time on staff. More than 250 worked in part-time roles. They had everything from chefs to plumbers, available at nearly any hour of the day.

This presented a huge challenge for Sanders, who was running out of time. Were he to fail, he knew what the consequences would be. Even for a man of his position and power, there was nowhere he could go to escape. His benefactor had made that impeccably clear.

Sanders turned right and made his way down the adjacent hall before veering onto a staircase and descending deeper into the building.

The White House was an immense structure, much larger than ordinary citizens knew. On the surface, it looked like a three-story mansion. Far larger than a typical home, but not palatial by any stretch of the imagination. Most ordinary citizens didn't realize there were four stories above ground and two more below.

Within the walls, however, the place was gargantuan. There were six floors, including two mezzanine floors that most people didn't know about. It contained hundreds of rooms, dozens of fireplaces, plus multiple staircases and elevators.

Sanders had been overwhelmed the first time he visited. He'd even gotten lost at one point and had to be given directions by one of the cleaning crew.

He rounded the corner at the bottom of the stairs and made his way into the staff break room. Two of the maids were taking their coffee break at a round table next to the counter. The smell of fresh-brewed coffee filled the air and mingled with the scent of toasted bagels.

The break room was probably the most unremarkable space on the entire property. It would have passed as a teacher lounge or a place where factory workers ate their donuts on break. The white cinder block walls let in no natural light, making the room feel more like a bunker than where the servants of the president hung out.

President Dawkins was known to frequent the break room, some said, because he enjoyed spending time with real people after long days with diplomats and politicians. He'd come down, sometimes late in the evening, and enjoy a sandwich or perhaps a cup of coffee with some of the staff, asking about how their day was.

Sanders had no such intentions. The workers here were beneath him, and he found it revolting that the leader of the free world would lower himself to their level.

Things were going to change around here; that was for certain.

The maids gave him a suspicious glance and then continued their conversation while Sanders walked over to the counter and picked up an empty cup. He filled it near the rim with coffee and put the pot back in its place before adding sugar and creamer. He wasn't in the mood for coffee, but he had to fake it to conceal his true purpose for visiting the break room.

He finished stirring the hot brew, fitted a lid on the top, and wandered over to a table in the corner. He eased into the seat facing a small flatscreen television hanging on the wall and pretended to be interested in the breaking news the anchors were ranting about.

Something regarding a new tax proposal. He didn't care. The noise from the television helped drown out the pointless conversation the two maids were having. He sipped his coffee patiently as his mind wandered to visions of waking up in the presidential bedroom, having an entire mansion full of workers waiting on his every desire.

Ten minutes passed before he heard the chairs across the room start scooting over the floor. He didn't look immediately, instead giving the women a few minutes before he turned his head to make sure they were gone.

Then he casually stood up and wandered over to the center of the room and spun around in a circle. The break room was located in the bowels of the White House, not quite the epicenter but a place that—were something to go wrong—would need to be handled quickly.

He'd considered his options when his benefactor made the request. Sanders guffawed at the word. It was hardly a request. More like a direct order.

A leak would have been good, but he wasn't sure how to make that happen. There were Secret Service men stationed all around the main parts of the building, including bedrooms and near bathrooms. Were he to meddle with any of the plumbing, video footage would show him as the last one in the area. After that, pinning the sabotage on Sanders would be elementary.

He'd thought of all that and come to one conclusion: The only room he could attack was this one. There might have been a few other places, but he didn't want to risk it. While he believed he knew where all the surveillance cameras were, it was entirely possible there were other, more secretive ones hidden about the premises.

No, if he was going to make something happen, it had to be here, in the break room.

But what?

He stepped over to the sink, bent over, and pulled open one of the cabinet doors. He spied the pipes inside: the trap, the valves, the knobs that controlled the flow of water. While he had a rudimentary understanding of how plumbing worked, and could easily disconnect some of the hoses, that wouldn't be enough to warrant an entire crew coming into the building to make repairs.

He closed the door and sighed, planting one hand on the counter as he scanned the area for anything he could use.

Sanders rubbed his chin. Frustration started to set in. He had to think of something. Then he heard footsteps clicking in the stairwell outside. Great, another idiot coming in here for coffee or to chew the fat.

Maybe this wasn't the place to make his plan happen. He'd weighed every option, though, and nothing else would work.

The footsteps grew louder, and he scurried back over to his coffee and sat down, pretending to watch the television.

A few seconds later, a man in a white shirt and blue tie walked into the room. He was a young guy with a head of thick, black hair combed over to one side. He didn't look like he could be more than twenty-three years old, though that wasn't out of the realm of possibility. Some of the staff interns were in their early twenties. Sanders wondered if the youngster had any idea the gravity of where he was working.

So many interns like him believed that a position in the White House would lead to greater things. They used it as a stepping stone for their careers. It certainly looked good on a résumé, but it was anything but a guarantee. The only real way to get ahead in Washington was getting your hands dirty. He'd seen a good many young idealists break on that fact like waves on rocks.

Sanders gazed at the television without seeing it. He was focused on his peripheral vision, keeping an eye on the newcomer as he walked over to the counter and took a paper plate from the cabinet. Then came a series of clicks, beeps, and the steady whir of the microwave heating something.

After around forty seconds, intermittent popping filled the room. It grew more frequent and crescendoed into a full rat-a-tat-tat like a stifled and erratic machine gun. The break room flooded with the smell of popcorn.

Sanders rolled his eyes. Kids these days with their popcorn. When Sanders was young, he recalled the few times he'd been able to get popcorn. It was either at a baseball game or at the theater. Maybe he'd had it once or twice when watching a movie at a friend's house.

Now people substituted their breakfast or lunch with it, stealing away the mystique that came with the snack.

The popping slowed, only giving an occasional puff just before the microwave beeped, signaling the food was ready.

The young guy opened the door, and a waft of smoke and steam billowed out. Sanders turned his head slightly. Now the scent of popcorn mingled with a burning smell.

"Aw, man," the intern said as he pried open the popcorn bag and realized his mistake.

Sanders turned his head completely toward the guy and saw him holding the bag. He had a disappointed look on his face like his favorite toy had just been run over by a car.

"Burned it, huh?" Sanders asked.

The young man gave a nod. "Yep. Oh well. I guess I'll just have one of the donuts in the conference room."

He turned, stuffed the still-warm popcorn bag into the trash, and left. His shoes clicked down the short corridor and then faded as he ascended the stairs. Sanders watched the door for a moment, making sure the guy was gone before he stood up and hurried over to the trash bag.

He picked up the popcorn bag and eyed its contents. Sure enough, several of the kernels had turned a charred brown, almost black color. Sanders raised his head and let the popcorn fall back into the basket.

Popcorn. Donuts.

That was it. He rushed out of the room and up the stairs. He knew exactly what he needed to do.

29

ATLANTA

The Bradford pears lining the perimeter of Centennial Olympic Park were just beginning to show off their little white petals. Some of the buds were still swelling, nearly ready to pop. The pungently sweet scent from the trees wafted through the city air, doing its best to push away the smells of metropolitan civilization.

Sean strode down the sidewalk with his entourage in tow.

Alain sent Tusun and four of his best along for the ride. It was the second time Sean recognized the use of five men in a unit. He figured it was part of an ancient tactical strategy. One guy would lead; the others would support. He'd noted, too, the fact that the highest-ranking warrior didn't hide in the shadows like so many commanders from history, sitting high on their horses atop a hillside while their men spilled blood for king and country. This man didn't shy from combat.

There was a certain admiration Sean had for that fact, even though he knew, to a man, that each one of the Assassins would have to die. He had to wait, though, and pick the moment as he'd done so many times before. People weren't robots. That meant they were prone to mistakes. Everyone made them. It was only a matter of time —or so he hoped.

But these guys were the closest things to robots he'd seen so far.

Sean had fought terrorists, mercenaries, even trained soldiers before. He'd gone up against some of the best spies in the world during his time with Axis. These men from the Order of Assassins were a different animal. They'd been hardened by something more than ordinary training regimens, workouts, and sparring. He sensed it in a way only he could. It was subtle, almost invisible, but it was there.

He didn't know what it could be, though he had a few ideas. Men like these were likely scooped up in their darkest moments, when their lives had hit rock bottom. It was how terrorist cells and gangs operated. They found the stragglers, the weak ones in the herd that couldn't keep up or were too different to be drawn in by the mainstream. They were the forgotten, the castaways of society. Some were probably orphans. That was a common denominator for several higher-end special ops units. Even the Pony Express had preferred men without familial ties due to the inherent dangers involved in the job.

Recruiting for something like this organization wasn't about the danger; it was about instilling these men with a sense of purpose and belonging. They were part of something greater than themselves and would do anything for the men who'd given them that gift.

Sean hadn't batted an eye when Alain killed one of his own subordinates in the forest outside of Charlottesville. He read the situation immediately. Tommy, on the other hand, had been repulsed at the incident, wondering what kind of sick person would execute his own men for trying to save his life. The logic was off. Sean knew that, but he also understood the underlying thought process. Nothing was greater than the mission.

Axis wasn't dissimilar in that regard. He knew that if he had died in the field, the American government would have disavowed any knowledge of what he was trying to do, or even who he was. That was the deal. At the time, Sean hadn't cared. He'd even lied to his parents, telling them he was going into the military as an intelligence officer. It was a half-lie. He'd done intelligence work while with Axis, though not in the way he led his parents to believe.

A garbage truck rumbled by, leaving a trail of nauseating aromas wafting over the men as they made their way down the sidewalk toward the IAA building.

Sean held his breath for a few seconds to let the smell dissipate. The two men to his right didn't seem to notice. He assumed the three behind him had the same reaction.

It was like they'd been desensitized to just about everything the world could throw at them.

They neared the front entrance and rounded a turn. The building featured an overhang at the main doorway. Sean knew there were cameras in four locations, each in a corner to capture people coming in and going out. It was a security measure they'd included when the new headquarters was constructed after an attack that left the old structure nothing more than rubble.

He glanced up at one of the security cameras and, noting his guards weren't paying attention to his face, mouthed one word.

"Run."

Sean had no way of knowing whether or not Tara and Alex would see the message. They probably wouldn't since that feed was monitored by a security guard. He doubted Henry the doorman would see it either, but he had to try.

They reached the entrance, and Sean pulled open the door. He held it open to allow the others inside, but Tusun wasn't having it.

"After you," he insisted.

The man didn't need to brandish the gun he had within the folds of his jacket. Sean knew the implied threat. The other men were also armed with pistols, each weapon concealed inside their thin coats.

One wrong move, and the Assassins would cut Sean down without a second thought. They'd figure out the tablet and everything else later. These were pure killers. They wouldn't tolerate a single misstep.

"Good morning, Henry," Sean said as he walked into the building.

The older man was sitting behind his desk, reading the paper. In a digital age of instant news delivered straight to smartphones and tablets, Henry stood firm, sticking to the same routine Sean imagined he'd had for fifty years.

"Morning, Mr. Wyatt. Bringing some friends in to see the place?"

"Yes, sir. I'm just going to show them the lab and a few other things."

"All right then, Mr. Wyatt." He hesitated then cocked his head to the side. "You seen Mr. Schultz lately? He hasn't been around much the last week. I didn't know he was going out of town. He usually lets me know, not that he has to."

"Yeah, I think Tommy's working on something up in Washington. Seems like the Smithsonian needed him for something." Sean didn't stop, instead merely slowing his pace momentarily to finish the conversation. "Have a good rest of the morning, Henry."

"You, too, Mr. Wyatt."

Sean led the other men to the elevator and pressed the button. A ding signaled the lift was already there, and the metal doors slid open. The men stepped aboard, and Sean hit the button for the basement, where the lab was located. A moment later, the doors closed, and the elevator took them down.

The men moved out into the wide hallway. The ceilings were at least twenty feet high. Across from the elevator, a huge wall of glass rose up to the ceiling, braced every few feet by metal frames. The giant glass room contained computers, dozens of workstations and tables, desks, clay pots, sculptures, ancient tools, and myriad other things relating to archaeology and the research of it.

Sean walked over to the double doors leading into the clean room and pulled it open. "Step in, gentlemen," he said. "This is going to blow."

Tusun frowned, not understanding what his prisoner meant.

"It's kind of a cleaning station before you go in there, you know, to keep loose contaminants out of the area."

Tusun motioned for two men to go in with Sean. That appeared to be all that could fit at one time.

Sean shrugged and stepped inside with his two guards. He pressed a red button, and a machine fired up. It moved across a pair of rails above them, blowing air down onto the men as they stood on a metal grate.

The process took less than ten seconds, and then the door on the other side opened automatically. Sean stepped through with his guards and waited patiently while Tusun and the other two repeated the process. Once everyone was inside, he looked over to the corner and found Alex working on his computer.

"Hey, Alex," Sean said. He noted Tara's absence. That could mean a number of things. Maybe she'd gotten his message on the camera. Sean doubted it, but anything was possible. More likely, she was in the bathroom or out getting coffee. Maybe she was running a quick errand. Whatever the reason, Sean didn't mention it to his unwelcome guests, though he was immediately concerned she'd inadvertently walk into the hostile takeover and get shot.

She was savvy, though, and Sean knew if Tara noticed the five newcomers, she'd treat the situation with caution.

"Whatcha working on?" Sean asked as Alex looked up from his computer and realized Sean was with five strangers.

He didn't get a chance to answer. The two men with Sean immediately pulled out their weapons and pointed them at the young researcher.

"Don't move," one ordered.

"Okay," Alex said. His voice was oddly calm given the circumstances.

The two men nearest him rushed over to the corner and grabbed him out of his chair. They pushed him against the wall, face first, and frisked him quickly to make sure he was unarmed. Satisfied he was no threat, they spun him around and pressed his back to the wall.

"You don't have to be so rough with him," Sean said. "He's just an analyst for us."

Tusun stepped in front of Sean and glared at him. "Don't tell us how to do our jobs. Everyone is a threat."

Then he turned his attention to Alex, who was being held at gunpoint from two angles. "You. Where is the tablet?"

"The...the what?" Alex stuttered.

Tusun drew his weapon and moved across the room with huge, dramatic strides. He stopped short and pointed the pistol right at Alex's forehead. "Don't play stupid with me. Where is the tablet?"

"Oh," Alex said. "I thought you meant like a digital tablet. 'Cause there's one right there on the desk." He motioned with a tip of the head. "But you're looking for the other tablet."

Tusun's eyes narrowed. If he could have fired arrows out of them, he would have.

"Right," Alex went on. "It's just over there." He kept his hands up, but flicked a finger to his right.

Tusun turned and saw the flat piece of stone sitting on top of a worktable. He lowered his weapon, leaving his men to watch the young man.

Sean watched from near the room's entrance as Tusun walked over to the tablet. For a second, the man hovered over it, staring down at the thing with mesmerized curiosity. He reached down and worked his fingers under it.

"You really should use gloves if you're going to handle that," Alex warned.

An irritated look from the two men watching him told him to keep his mouth shut.

Tusun ignored him and picked up the tablet. His muscular fore-arms only strained slightly at the weight. He stared at the symbols for a moment before slinging the bag from his shoulder and down onto the table. He reached inside and pulled out a plastic case, roughly the same size as the piece of stone. His fingers worked quickly, opening two latches on the side of the case, and he flipped it open. Sean could barely see, but he made out black foam on the interior. At least the guy was going to be somewhat careful with the priceless artifact.

Tusun placed the tablet in the case and closed it. Satisfied it was secure, he stuffed it into his bag and turned back to Alex. "Where is the journal?"

"Journal?" Alex asked.

Tusun tilted his neck to the side. "We know you have it. Tell me where it is, or you will spend the rest of your short life in agonizing pain. Do you understand?"

"Agonizing pain? Yes. Journal location? No. We never had it."

"He's not lying," Sean interrupted. "Tommy and I kept that for ourselves. Besides, the only thing helpful in the journal were the clues. We already figured those out. We got you the keys. Now leave him alone. He doesn't have anything to do with this."

Tusun listened until Sean was done speaking before he turned to face his enemy. "When I want your thoughts, I will ask for them." His head pivoted around toward Alex once more. "You have notes, translations for the tablet. Where are those?"

Alex swallowed. "They're on that computer," he said, pointing a bony finger at the nearby workstation.

"In a file?"

"Actually, no. They're right there on the screen. You can print them out if you like."

"Do it," Tusun ordered.

"Okay, then."

Alex shuffled over to the computer and sat down. He started to click on the mouse when Tusun put a firm hand on Alex's shoulder and pushed down. "Don't get any foolish ideas."

Alex looked up with a clueless stare. His head shook rapidly back and forth. "Nope. I wouldn't think of it."

Then he swiveled back to facing the screen and hovered the mouse arrow over the files. The screen was filled with a preview of the translations he and Tara had been working on.

Tusun leaned over Alex's shoulder and pored over the file's contents. "Print that."

"Yes. Yes, sir. Sure thing."

He moved the arrow up to the top, opened the drop-down menu containing the print option, and clicked the button.

A big printer to their left whirred to life and a moment later pages started sliding into the receiving tray. Tusun motioned to one of his men. The guy immediately went to the printer and picked up the sheets. He handed them to Tusun, who gave them a quick inspection. Satisfied he had what he was there to collect, he folded the papers and stuffed them into his gear bag.

"Anything else?" Tusun asked.

Alex shook his head. "No, that was all the translation we got. It's not complete, though."

Tusun's eyes twitched. "What do you mean it's not complete?"

"We're close. Real close. There are just a few symbols we haven't been able to figure out yet. This is essentially a language that has never been seen before...well, not for several centuries anyway. The people who created it are long gone. There's no records. We're using quantum computers here, and it's still taken us days to get this far. Might take a few more, if we're lucky. The Rosetta Stone didn't cover everything."

Tusun exhaled long and slow. He hadn't anticipated this problem. Maybe the young research assistant was lying. The dumb look on his face suggested otherwise. This wasn't a person given to dishonesty. That clueless expression was a difficult one to fake; that much Tusun knew. He'd killed enough people like this to have seen it before, only to find out later they were being truthful.

If the translation was incomplete, that could cause delays. Alain wouldn't accept that. Time was running short now, especially with the other phase of the plan being carried out in the next twenty-four hours.

Then he had a sudden realization.

"Where's the girl?"

Alex's eyebrows shot up. "Girl? What girl?"

Tusun cursed himself. He was thorough; always had been. He never let any detail slip. It wasn't just during missions. Attention to the particulars in life kept things in order, prevented problems— problems like this one.

He'd known there should be two researchers in the room. Based on their surveillance, the two were almost always together, even when they left the building. They didn't live together, but it was clear that they were either close friends or that something else was going on.

Whatever the reason, she wasn't in the room. That was a problem.

Tusun reached down and wrapped his fingers around Alex's neck. "Tell me where she is, or I rip your throat out right now."

A muffled pop echoed through the room. Tusun flinched. His grip on Alex's neck eased. Tusun dropped to the ground and spun around on one knee. The nerves in his shoulder screamed with a burning, stabbing pain.

Another pop, and one of his men to the left fell to the floor, grasping at his neck. A third suppressed shot sent a gunman to his right sprawling over a desk. He and his men had been caught off guard; that much was clear. Getting the drop on Tusun was something that never happened, not since his childhood on the streets.

He didn't have to peek over the row of desks to know what was going on.

The girl had gotten the drop on them.

30

NEW YORK CITY

Sirens blared in the concrete jungle outside the walls of Tommy's prison. He didn't know how long he'd been sitting in the chair. Consciousness had really only returned to him a few minutes ago.

He'd been in and out for what he figured amounted to hours, but there was no way to tell for sure. He winced at a stinging pain coming from his cheek. The movement stretched his skin, and he felt something tight pulling at a wound. The caked blood covering the cut on his cheek cracked a little.

His scratchy throat begged for water. He swallowed, but the muscles barely worked.

He felt the tightly clasped zip ties cutting into his wrists. He still had circulation to his fingers. At least there was that.

Tommy raised his head and looked around the room, his eyelids still straining like they were tethered to ten-pound weights. He recognized the place. It was where the Assassins had taken him before putting him in another room to beat him savagely, and thoroughly.

That part he remembered.

The one called Alain stood in the corner and watched while his men did their work. The first few blows were easy to recall. Then his consciousness faded, and he didn't remember much else, other than being brought back to this room.

Sean was there; at least he thought he was. Maybe he'd imagined it. That would make sense since Tommy was now the only one in the room.

Where were the Assassins? Where was Sean?

Tommy tried to move his right foot, but his ankle was tied to the chair leg, as was the left. He exhaled through his nose. The air squeaked in his left nostril. It was mostly closed off, swollen from being damaged in the fight.

He let out a demented chuckle. Fight. It was hardly a fight. Fights were fair, at least in the fact that both people got a chance to defend or attack. Tommy could only sit there, taking the blows as the men performed their task without mercy.

He wiggled his fingers just to make sure they were all intact. He'd heard torture stories about people who'd cut off fingers and toes. Some went for the tongue or eyes, maybe ears on occasion.

Tommy hadn't suffered any of that. He wondered why.

Not that it would have mattered. He wouldn't have told the men what they wanted to know. Doing so would have jeopardized the lives of people he cared about. No amount of mercy was worth that.

He had a sneaking suspicion, however, that the treatment he'd received was only the appetizer. The main course, he feared, would be far worse.

He drew a deep breath and scanned the sparse room. A lone window with cracked glass was the only source of light beyond a single bulb hanging overhead. It was daytime; that much he knew. The gray sunlight pouring in signaled it was probably cloudy outside, but not raining, though. The pitter-patter of rain on the roof or against the glass was distinctly absent amid the cacophony of honking horns, sirens, and car motors down on the street.

There was also no way to know how high up he was, but it felt like several stories, maybe ten, based on the distance of the street sounds and the light coming in through the window. But what city?

It had to be a big one. It wasn't Atlanta. It could be Washington, but he doubted it. Only reason he considered it was the proximity of DC to where he and Sean had been caught.

The thought of his friend brought back the question to the front of his mind. *Where is Sean?*

The answer filled him with dread, creeping into his mind and planting its tentacles into every brain cell, choking out any calm he tried to grasp. Sean was being beaten, just as Tommy had been.

Or worse.

He snapped his head to shake away the thoughts. Sean was tough, resilient. Right at that very moment, he was probably figuring out a way to take out every member of the order and find an escape. That was how Sean worked. He was always looking for the opening, the narrowest of paths that he could forge into a chasm.

At the moment, Tommy wished his friend would burst through the door. Something told him that wasn't going to happen anytime soon.

There was a conversation, distant, almost ethereal, playing out in his head. It felt like fiction, a discussion that never occurred. He could hear voices—a few he thought he recognized and one he definitely knew. There were men, talking to Sean. They said something about a—

"The tablet," Tommy said out loud. "That's where they took Sean. To Atlanta."

The epiphany gave him hope. If they took him to Atlanta, he'd be okay. At least for now.

Then another thought popped into his mind. The kids, too, could be in danger. They had no idea Sean was coming there or about the men who were with him. Sean would have no way to warn them.

Worry cascaded into his gut, causing his stomach to turn and twist into a knot. He shook his body against the bonds, wriggling his wrists and turning his feet back and forth to see if he could get them loose. It was no use, though, and after a minute of struggling he stopped to catch his breath.

Blood pulsed through his veins, and his muscles swelled. Though to a casual observer it may not have seemed he'd done much, the effort against his bonds took a huge amount of energy.

His breathing slowed. He forced himself to calm down. "What would Sean do?" he asked himself. Sean would stand up, hunched over, and shuffle his way to the door, break it open, and kill every man in the building with the chair on his back.

Tommy knew he couldn't pull off that trick. The first guard he encountered would shoot him on sight.

That plan wouldn't work, but it did get him thinking. During his spastic struggle, he realized the chair wasn't fixed to the floor. It jiggled while he was jostling around.

Tommy leaned his weight to the left, and sure enough the two right legs raised up off the floor. He shifted back to center and let the chair sit on all fours again. An idea raced through his brain. He shimmied back and forth, causing the chair to turn a little so he could see the window. When he'd moved enough, he twisted his head to the side and inspected the glass. Most of the window was still in place, partitioned into several small squares, each separated by a metal divider.

Two of the panes, however, were broken in half.

He turned back to the door and listened intently for a half a minute. He didn't hear anything in the hall outside. There had to be at least one guard, maybe two on the other side of the door. He imagined the men were standing there with guns slung over their shoulders, staring at the wall, waiting for the next shift to come.

Tommy wondered why there was no one in the room with him, but based on the beating he'd taken and the way he was fixed to the chair, the men in charge must have figured he wasn't much of a threat.

The swelling and stinging wouldn't go away. First thing he was going to do when he got out of there, besides finding a way back to Atlanta, was find some ibuprofen and maybe an ice pack.

He took a deep breath and leaned to the side again. This time, as the chair's legs came up, he shoved his right foot down as hard as he could. His ankle slid along the metal leg, and a second later his heel struck the floor with a light thud. He froze for a second, his foot now free. Tommy's eyes shot up to the door. He stared at it for nearly a minute, waiting to see if anyone had heard what he'd done. No sound came from the hallway, but he waited another twenty seconds before moving again.

This time, he leaned the other direction, causing the left legs to come off the ground. He shoved his foot down hard again, though this one took more effort. The zip tie around his ankle was caught on something.

Tommy felt his weight tipping the chair over. He jerked his torso back the other direction to recover his balance. Gravity kept at it, tugging him down toward the floor. He gave one last heave and felt himself going back the other way. The chair's legs struck the floor with a bump.

He let out a sigh and took a second to catch his breath. Still no sound from the other side of the door.

He wondered what it would take to get their attention, though he already had a plan for that when the time was right.

Tommy leaned to the side again, more carefully this time. If he were to fall over, the guards would surely hear the crash. He'd only get one shot at this, and he knew he had to make the most of it if he wanted to get out of there in one piece.

The chair's legs hovered over the floor, and Tommy wiggled his foot around to loosen the zip tie and get it by whatever had impeded it before. He looked down at the leg and saw there was a tiny piece of metal sticking up.

"Of course," he said. He kept twisting and pushing his foot down until, finally, the plastic strip keeping his ankle to the chair slipped over the metal splinter. With his other foot free, he planted it on the floor and gently set the chair back on all fours once again.

He swallowed hard, this time his throat opening a tad more than when he first roused from his hazy sleep.

Still no sound of concern or alarm coming from the corridor.

Tommy pressed his hamstrings against the front edge of the chair and leaned forward. His arms and hands easily slid over the top of the chair back. His leg muscles strained as he stood up straight. They were weak, and his knees buckled like a newborn foal trying to walk for the first time. Had he been drugged? That would explain the fog and lack of muscle control. Those things didn't usually accompany a simple beating, at least in his limited experience.

His muscles adapted quickly, and he shook his feet a few times the same way he'd seen runners do just before a race. The blood returned to his toes and feet. Just standing up for a few seconds made him feel much better.

Tommy looked over at the window to his left. He tiptoed over to it and turned around. His hands were still tied behind his back, so he couldn't see what he was doing as he stood up on the tips of his boots and felt the window for the broken pane. It was a dangerous and tricky task. One wrong move and he could gash a finger or two. He doubted he'd get medical attention for such an accident in this place, so he exercised extreme caution as he felt the first pane, then the second, finally locating the third one on the right that was half missing.

Cool air poured through the opening and washed over his skin. He placed his thumb on one side and his forefinger on the other, then squeezed, pinching the pane as hard as he could. Then he jostled the piece of glass back and forth to break the seal keeping it in the frame. It took nearly thirty seconds before the thing started to come free. When it did, it snapped completely off the window. Tommy lurched forward, nearly falling on his face, but he managed to plant his right foot in front of him and steady his balance.

He let out a relieved breath, but he was far from freedom.

Behind his back, his fingers worked quickly. He turned the glass over and positioned the sharp edge against the plastic band binding his wrists. It was difficult work and put his hands into an awkward position that required several little breaks between cutting.

He moved his forefinger and thumb back and forth in a sort of twitching motion, which was all he could manage. The tedious task took more than five minutes of concentrated and persistent effort until, finally, the zip tie broke free.

His hands shot out to the side, and a renewed sense of relief hit him. Blood flowed more easily into his hands and fingers. Tommy looked down at his wrists and saw red indentions from the plastic bonds. He clenched his fists over and over again to assist the blood flow. Then he looked over at the door.

"Time to get out of here," he whispered.

He set the glass down on the floor and stalked back over to the chair. He picked it up and carried it to the window, set it back down, and took a deep breath. Then he exhaled and looked at the window with callous determination.

Tommy knew what he had to do. He was going to get out of this building or die trying. He preferred it be the former, but there was no way he'd just sit idly by and let his friends get hurt.

He wrapped his fingers around the back of the chair and picked it up. Then he twisted his body and swung it hard like a giant, awkward baseball bat. The legs struck the remaining panes of glass and shattered them, sending the shards down to the fire escape a few feet below.

That would get the guards' attention.

31

ATLANTA

Tusun dove under the table across from Alex and slid to a stop on the other side. He drew his gun in a single fluid motion and immediately checked behind him, then to his right and left. There was no sign of the shooter.

Sean saw the team leader disappear under a table near Alex right after the gunfire began. Sean's instincts were just as fast, if not slightly faster. He'd seen a silhouette moving in the shadows in the back-left corner of the room. Tara must have been working on something in that area when Sean initiated the cleaning sequence. It was clear she'd seen what was going on and thought it was fishy. Maybe she'd noticed his warning via closed circuit TV. Doubtful. If that was the case, she and Alex wouldn't still be sticking around.

No, Tara had seen the men approaching through the clean room and realized something was amiss. There was no time to warn Alex, who was busy working on the other side of the room. Plus, there was the chance the dangerous-looking men with Sean would have heard her.

So, she'd waited, lurking in the shadows behind a desk and stacks of paperwork until the chance presented itself.

Sean had taken it upon himself to teach the kids some of the things he knew about clandestine field operations. They'd become excellent marksmen over the years, and were handy in a fight. Both of them were eager to learn and spent hours with Sean in a training room he'd set up on site. Their skills in hand-to-hand combat grew with every week. They got so good, in fact, Tommy was now sending them out on short recovery missions. Nothing crazy, so far, but he knew they could handle it.

The world Tommy and his agents lived in was a dangerous one. It was one of the reasons he'd brought Sean on board. He knew Sean had a certain toughness about him, not to mention high-level government training. That sort of thing could come in pretty handy when a group of thugs was trying to jack a priceless artifact from a transport or even on a dig site. Up to that point, Sean and Tommy had only really needed the kids to use their newfound talents one time, in a fight in Japan.

Tara disappeared from view to get a better angle on the two remaining men standing by Sean, just like he would have instructed.

She'd also taken out the two farthest targets. Certainly doing so presented the possibility of missing and sending bullets bouncing around the room, but her confidence in taking those shots was commendable. Sean had always told Alex and Tara that if they were in a situation where the odds were against them, take out the targets farthest away first. Doing so had a disorienting effect on those caught in the middle of sudden gunfire, pushing them to react differently than those who went on offense.

It was something he'd shown them in history books, in tactical manuals, and even in a few movies.

Sean wasn't sure if Tusun was dead, but he was fairly certain the other two she'd hit wouldn't be joining the fight. Now there were only the two men closest to him remaining.

The closest one was to his right, a few steps away. Upon hearing the gunfire, he spun around to find where it was coming from. His biggest mistake was thinking it came from the doorway.

Within the giant glass-encased room, sound was amplified a little, but the acoustics displaced the weapon's report significantly, making tracking down its source nearly impossible without seeing the shooter.

As the confused gunman twisted around with his weapon raised, Sean dove into him headfirst, plowing his shoulder into the guy's gut.

Sean pumped his legs and kept driving the gunman backward until his tailbone hit the edge of a table with a sudden thud.

The guy grimaced but didn't give in. He slammed the grip of his pistol into Sean's upper back twice before Sean blocked the third attempt with a circus like contortion of his body.

Sean knocked the hand aside and jabbed the guy in the nose. The man yelped and did his best to whip the weapon around again so he could finish the fight.

Sean saw the move and reacted with a counter, throwing his elbow at the man's ribs. The blow sent a sharp, stabbing pain through his nerves. Sean elbowed again, hoping to make a clean break in the bones. The guy twisted just enough to take the blow in the abs, which sent a new rush of pain through his body. It was a good bet he had broken ribs, bruised at the very least—an injury that was far from painless. Now he'd have an abdominal contusion to boot.

Still, the Assassin managed to stay in the fight. He blocked a left jab Sean thought he could sneak in, and drove his fist into Sean's jaw, snapping his head to the left.

Sean staggered back for a moment and worked his chin left and right to get rid of the pain.

A dozen feet away, the other remaining henchman was on the hunt, stalking the girl who'd surprised his entire unit. He let his partner handle Wyatt while he skirted to the nearest corner, ducking for cover behind a stack of crates. He poked his head around the corner of a box and scanned the area directly ahead. There was no sign of her.

The shooting had come from somewhere on the other side of the room. He cocked his head to the side, leaning out a few more inches, and saw a door. That had to be where she'd come from and, perhaps, where she was now.

He crouched low, creeping around the wall to his left, staying out of sight while he stalked his prey. Upon reaching the next corner, he stopped under a long metal table that was littered with sheets of paper, fragments of jars, and a collection of tiny stone statues.

The gunman looked around the table and could see all the way to the other end of the room, where Tusun was inching his way toward Wyatt.

There was no sign of the shooter.

He glanced behind him to make sure she hadn't circled around. The area was clear, though he knew that could change rapidly. He inched his way toward the door on the left. What lay beyond was anyone's guess, but his was, that is where the girl went.

Between rows of tables, he stopped and looked over his right shoulder. Wyatt looked to be winning a fistfight. What Wyatt didn't know was that Tusun was creeping up behind him. Wyatt might win the fight, but he would lose the battle in the end.

The gunman made it to the door and grabbed the latch from his low position. The door opened easily, and he stuck his gun through the crack, peeking inside. He frowned. It was a break room from the looks of it. He pulled the door open a little wider and slipped inside. There were a few chairs, an ordinary table in the center, and a counter with a sink. A coffeemaker sat in one corner next to a sparse collection of white mugs.

His hands swept the near corners first, and he immediately realized there was no one inside...unless....

He let the door close behind him and reached back to lock it with his left hand. No one was going to get the drop on him.

His eyes darted to one of the cabinets on the left. The doors were big enough that a small adult could fit in, maybe even an average-size person. He flung the first door open and found some cleaning supplies. Then he stepped to the next set of doors, and the next, repeating until he came to the last pair closest to the refrigerator in the center of the back wall.

He clenched his teeth and pointed the gun down at the cabinet. He bent down and jerked the door open. At the same moment, he heard a click as he stared into the empty shelves.

The trap had been sprung, and he was caught like a dumb animal. When he heard the clicking sound, he realized what had happened. He tried to spin around to defend himself, but it was too late. Tara stood in the doorway with her weapon drawn. The elongated barrel gave off a white flash accompanied by a muted pop. The bullet struck him in the chest, piercing his heart in an instant.

He feebly tried to bring his pistol around to reply, but she fired again, arms outstretched and holding the gun at length, almost as if she'd been practicing for this moment for years.

Tara's finger twitched as she pulled the trigger, driving the gunman back against the counter with round after round until his torso was riddled with metal and her magazine was empty.

He fell to the floor and onto his side, staring lifelessly at the floor.

Sean blocked his opponent's attempt to kick him in the groin, easily swiping the leg aside with his forearm. He countered with a punch to the man's gut. The second the guy doubled over, his face met Sean's knee. The nose crumpled, and the killer could do nothing more than grab at the broken appendage while Sean twisted around, wrapped a forearm around his neck, and gripped the side of his head. The Assassin struggled, but only for a second. Sean jerked the man's head at a gruesome angle. A pop sounded, and the body immediately went limp. Sean let him fall to the floor with a thud.

He breathed heavily for a second and stared at the body. He looked at his hands, blinking rapidly.

His mind swirled. He hadn't been given a choice. Regret? Maybe. Again, the choice thing. Or was it something else, something far more wicked in nature? He felt...no, that couldn't be it. Could it?

It was a feeling of power.

His thoughts were jarred by a familiar voice on the other side of the room.

"Don't move!" Tara shouted.

Sean spun around. The rush of adrenaline, the overwhelming sense of power, his thoughts, all came to a sudden halt. Across the room, near the door to the break room, Tara was holding out her pistol with her right hand, arm at full extension. Sean followed the gun's line of sight back to the center of the room. Tusun stood there with his left arm wrapped around Alex's neck. His right hand pressed a pistol to his hostage's temple.

"No!" Tusun shouted. "You don't move! I will execute him right now."

His head twitched between Sean and Tara, his nerves evident in his drawn face and bulging eyes.

"Give it up," Sean said. "You'll never get out of here. Cops have the place surrounded." He was bluffing. No police would know what had just transpired down in the IAA basement. Sure, it was possible that Henry had sensed something was amiss and made a call, but that was a stretch. More than likely, Henry was upstairs sipping coffee at his desk, watching reruns of some old television show.

Tusun shook his head. "Drop the gun, girl," he hissed. "I won't tell you again."

He left no doubt in his voice. The menacing tone said it all. This guy meant it. He was a killer, cold and pure. Executing Alex would be nothing more than stepping on an insect to him.

"Don't do it, Tara," Sean warned. He saw the doubt in her eyes, the conflict raging. She had the killer in her sights. All she had to do was pull the trigger. At that distance, missing the target was possible but not probable. She was a crack shot, a dead eye with a pistol, with long-range weapons as well. Sean had no doubt she could take out the man holding Alex. He also knew she'd never been put in this situation before.

Tusun observed the same thing Sean saw, the confusion on her face. He wasn't so sure the girl would put the gun down. So, he did the only thing he could. Killing the whelp in his arms would mean death for him. The second he pulled the trigger, she would respond in kind. Based on the fact she'd just taken out some of his men, Tusun knew she was capable.

Fear of death didn't keep Tusun from killing his hostage. Fear of failure did. If he died there, no matter how many of the infidels he took out, Alain wouldn't get the tablet and the mission would fail.

That was something he could not abide.

He shuffled his feet to his left, inching toward the clean room and the exit beyond. Tara turned gradually as the target continued moving across the lab. She couldn't get a clear enough shot, at least not in her mind. A section of the man's head was in view. But if she missed, Alex would die.

Sean watched helplessly as Tusun moved to the door, putting Sean between him and the gun-wielding woman. Now she definitely didn't have a shot.

Tusun backed up to the door until he felt it touch his shoulder blades. "Open it," he said into Alex's ears.

To his credit, Alex was keeping it together. He struggled against the strong arm around his throat, but not enough to cause the guy to fire his weapon—on purpose or accidentally. Alex only allowed the slightest sign of fear to cross his face. His eyes remained resolute, narrow to the point of anger. He wouldn't give this guy the pleasure of seeing him terrified.

"Open it, I said," Tusun repeated.

"It's okay," Alex told Tara. "It's okay."

He reached back and felt along the glass wall until he located the red button. He pushed it, and the door to the clean room slid open. Tusun backed into the intermediary room, and a second later the door closed again. Once they were behind the glass doors, Tusun's head turned from side to side, then up. He was looking for something, anything he could use.

The hostage had served his purpose, but dragging the man up the stairs and through the streets of Atlanta wouldn't be optimal. He needed to lose the excess baggage so he could move quickly, stealthily.

He found what he was looking for overhead.

A mishmash of wires hung from the moving part of the sterilization machine. The thing was like a big robotic arm that moved to and fro as it sprayed clean air on people entering the lab. The wires connected the arm to its power source and probably to a computer that fed it instructions.

They would do.

Tusun loosened his grip on Alex for a brief moment and jumped up. His fingers wrapped around the wires, and as he fell back to the floor the wires ripped easily from their housing. Tusun made quick work of them, tying them around Alex's neck in a makeshift noose.

"Don't go anywhere," Tusun warned as he stepped back, pointing his weapon at the back of the hostage's skull. He was careful to keep Alex between him and the other two still in the room. Sean took a cautious step forward but froze when Tusun wagged his weapon in a threatening motion.

Tusun hit the button next to the exit, and the door slid open.

Alex grabbed at the wires around his neck.

"Take a deep breath," Tusun said as he stepped out of the room. He pointed his pistol at the biometric panel and squeezed the trigger. The weapon let out a loud bang. The terminal exploded into a tangled mess of metal, plastic, and wires. Sparks flew out of it for a second, and then the door slid shut.

The robotic arm inside the clean room began moving backward, spraying sterile oxygen down to the grate below. As the arm moved, the wires were pulled up and back. Alex's face twisted as the wires squeezed his throat, cutting off the air to his lungs.

The robotic mechanism strained, pulling him off the ground and suspending him over the floor. He pried at the cords with his fingernails, but it was too tight.

Sean and Tara rushed toward the door.

"Alex!" she shouted. "Hold on!"

Sean made it to the door first and slammed the red button. The machine didn't stop. Something was wrong.

He'd seen Tusun shoot the panel on the other side. That must have caused some kind of malfunction in the system.

Alex's legs kicked wildly. His eyes looked like they were about to pop out of his head. His face reddened. They only had seconds before he'd lose consciousness, only a precious few more before he was dead.

"Shoot the glass," Sean ordered.

Tara didn't hesitate. She fired. The bullet punctured a hole in the surface, sending a spiderweb crack through the entire pane. She squeezed the trigger two more times, the rounds weakening the glass further.

Sean lowered his shoulder and barged through the door. Shards of broken glass splashed around him, shattering on the floor as he charged toward Alex.

He slid underneath the choking man and got on all fours. "Put your feet on my back!" Sean shouted.

Alex's legs weren't kicking as much. He was blacking out. Somehow, he mustered the strength to plant his heels on Sean's back. The support eased the strain on his neck. He desperately gasped for air as the wires slackened only slightly. He took the oxygen into his lungs in huge gulps.

"You okay?" Sean asked over the sound of blowing air around them.

"Just...a...second."

"Shut this thing off, will ya?" Sean said to Tara.

She was already on it, pulling cords out of a socket in the wall. When that didn't work, she pulled out a pocket knife and cut wires in half, as many as she could find. The machine suddenly shut down, and the air pouring out of the vents petered out.

Alex stood up straight and worked his fingers under the wires enough to loosen them from his neck. He pulled the tight loop up over his head and bent his knees, lowering himself to the floor.

He hit the metal grate hard, but it was more from exhaustion than anything else. His chest rose and fell heavily as he continued to catch his breath.

Sean patted him on the shoulder and stood up. He walked out the exit and glanced down at the destroyed biometric panel. Then he turned and looked toward the elevator doors.

Behind him, Tara was checking on Alex. Her voice overflowed with concern, "Are you okay? Can you breathe?"

The questions blended together into an incomprehensible stew of noises as the realization hit Sean.

Tusun was gone.

32

NEW YORK CITY

T ommy scurried back across the room, still gripping the chair firmly in both hands. He knew the guards must have heard that—if there were guards.

No chance he was that lucky.

Sure enough, he heard a set of keys jangling outside the doorway. He imagined the men were startled by the loud, abrupt noise of the window being broken. Tommy knew what was coming next.

The men would come through the door, rushing in to stop their prisoner from doing whatever he was doing, see the destroyed window, and figure he had jumped out somehow.

Tommy pressed his back to the wall just a few feet to one side of the doorway—and waited. He heard the key go into the lock while one of the men was shouting, probably at the other to hurry up. The lock's bar slid into the housing, and a second later the first guy burst through the doorway.

He rushed ahead with pistol in hand and full blinders on, focused exclusively on the window he believed Tommy had jumped through.

Tommy heard the footsteps of the second guard, and just as the man appeared in the doorway he swung the chair as hard as he could.

The metal legs smashed into the man's face with devastating effect. The chair shuddered but was undamaged. The guard's nose crumpled into his skull and dropped him to the ground even as his momentum carried him forward a few feet until he skidded to a stop, facedown on the floor.

The first guard had reached the window and was looking out when he heard the commotion behind him.

Tommy had already reacted, though, and threw the chair across the room like an Olympic hammer thrower. The first guard twisted around in time—but only to put his hands up in defense. The back of the chair hit him hard, the metal edges digging into the man's forearms and bruising the bones.

He grimaced from the pain as the chair clattered to the floor with several loud clanks. Then he stood upright and tried to aim his pistol. His reaction was too slow.

The second he threw the chair, Tommy reached down and took the pistol from the unconscious, or dead, man on the floor. The first guard never even had a chance to pull the trigger.

Tommy shot first. Once. Then again. The bullets struck true, dead center on the man's chest.

The guard staggered back, nearly knocked over from the powerful rounds. His back hit the wall, and he tried feebly to raise the pistol one more time to get a vengeful shot off, but it never came. Tommy squeezed the trigger again and finished the guard with a round through the skull.

He turned back to the man on the floor. Keeping his weapon aimed at the guy's head, Tommy knelt down and checked his pulse. There was none. A pool of dark blood had puddled around the guy's face, leaking from his nose.

"That was lucky," Tommy said. "Not for you, of course." He stood up and hurried over to the door, then remembered there was another full magazine in the first guard's weapon. He leaned around the doorframe and didn't see anyone coming, so he rushed back to the dead man under the window and retrieved the second pistol.

He stuffed it into his pocket and returned the door, checked the corridor in both directions, and then headed to the left.

He found a door at the end of the hall with an old sign displaying a picture of stairs. Tommy pulled the latch down and eased the door open. He heard footsteps coming up the stairs and closed it as quietly as he could.

Reinforcements were on their way. He knew that was a strong possibility. Someone had either heard the shots or radioed in that something strange had happened inside the prisoner's cell. Either way, trouble was coming. From the sound of it, there were more than a few responders.

Tommy scanned the hallway. The door to his room was still open, plus there were five other rooms—three on the left and two more on the right. All the doors were closed except one. He sprinted down the corridor and stopped at the one on the left that was cracked. He used the muzzle of his weapon to shove it open and found it was just a broom closet.

The space was shallow, maybe a couple of feet deep. Luckily, the only shelf in the little room was just over his head. He stepped inside and pulled the door closed a second before the one at the other end of the hall burst open.

Tommy held his breath for a second as if that might help him fit more comfortably in the tiny space. He waited and listened as the footsteps rushed down the hall. He was certain there were at least three men, possibly four, but he couldn't see.

The first of them ran by. Tommy knew where he was going, where they were all going.

A moment later, the others joined him, and shouting ensued.

"Check all the rooms! He couldn't have gotten far!" the man yelled.

Footsteps drew closer and then veered off to both the right and left.

Tommy knew it was only a matter of time before they checked his hiding spot. Might as well use the element of surprise.

He twisted the doorknob, pushed the door open, and stepped into the hall with pistol raised high. A guy was running through the doorway across from him when Tommy appeared like an apparition out of thin air. The man couldn't stop, couldn't even raise a hand to defend himself, before Tommy put a round through his forehead.

Tommy shoved the dead man aside as the body fell in a heap on the floor, and he fired twice more. The rounds pounded the guy inside the room, one to the shoulder and one to the gut. The power of the bullets spun the man around in a circle before he crumpled to the floor, writhing in agony.

The Assassin to Tommy's right reacted quickly and turned to fire just as his target dipped into the big room once more. The bullets zipped down the hallway, one plunking into the broom closet door, the other accidentally striking his comrade in the leg.

The wounded man screeched in pain and dropped to his good knee, clutching his thigh with both hands.

No apology came as a result of the friendly fire.

Tommy reached into his belt and grabbed the second pistol. He knew the last remaining guard would come into the room and sweep the nearest corners first. It was a standard tactic.

He put his back against the wall a few inches from the doorframe and slid down to a crouching position. He knew that when the guard came in, the guy would be standing upright. Staying low would give Tommy the slimmest of margins to surprise the gunman. At least that's what he hoped.

His back pressed into the wall, he tempered his breathing to make it inaudible. He listened for movement in the corridor but heard nothing for a minute. Then a floorboard creaked around the corner.

Tommy knew what was coming next.

With his cover blown, the gunman charged into the doorway. He swept his pistol to the right first, which was what Tommy had banked on since the guy was coming from the left.

Tommy sprang to the side and opened fire with both guns. The muzzles flashed amid a series of thunderous bangs.

The gunman saw the movement in his periphery, but it was too late. By the time he started to turn, five bullets tore into his torso and sent him stumbling back against the doorframe before he fell into the hall.

Tommy stayed on his back for a second with both weapons still extended. Streams of smoke swirled out of the barrels, mixing with the tendrils already hanging in the room.

Tommy gasped for a few seconds. The acrid smell of gun smoke filled his nostrils.

"Break's over, Tommy," he said to himself. "Gotta get out of here."

He rolled over onto his side and stood up. He pressed the release button on the first pistol and ejected the magazine into his palm. One round left.

He ejected it out of the magazine, which he let fall to the floor. Then he released the magazine on the second weapon and counted the remaining rounds before adding the lone bullet. Once the magazine was secure again, he stuffed the weapon into his belt and picked up any remaining guns from the dead men, tucking another one away and holding on to two.

For a brief moment, Tommy felt like he was armed well enough to take down a small government. He knew that wasn't the case. Even with multiple guns on him, those rounds wouldn't last long.

He'd have to be judicious with how he spent them.

The question on his mind now was how to get out of the building.

He hurried over to the broken window and looked out. The fire escape was an option, but not one he liked. The rickety metal landing and the ladders below didn't look like they could hold his weight. Dark-orange rust covered the hinges and railings in several places. The bolts holding things in place were also oxidized, and likely weakened from years of weathering and neglect.

No, the fire escape wasn't a great option.

Tommy rushed back to the door and stepped over the dead man whose body was half in the room, half in the hallway. A quick check to the left and right told Tommy the area was clear, but it wouldn't be for long.

He looked up into the corners of the dimly lit space, expecting to see cameras or some kind of security system. There were none.

That meant the reinforcements had either heard the chaos upstairs, or they were connected by radio. Maybe it was both.

Tommy bent down and found half the answer. A tiny earpiece was wedged in the dead gunman's ear. He took it out, gave it a wipe on his shirt, and tucked it into place.

A man was speaking in an urgent tone. "Team two, do you copy?" The accent wasn't foreign, unless it was Canadian, but it sounded devoid of any distinction.

"Team two, copy. Prisoner detained. Situation under control," Tommy said, disguising his voice to make it sound a little more gruff than usual.

"Copy that, team two."

Sweet. The guy bought it.

"What happened up there, team two?"

Tommy hadn't anticipated a lengthy conversation with whoever was on the other end. He struggled to concoct an explanation. "The prisoner tried to escape," he said, doing his best not to stammer. "Took out two of our guys. We have him now, though. Everything is fine."

He cringed at the last line. That didn't sound like something these guys would say. "Everything is fine?"

He shook his head.

There was a long pause before the other guy came back. "We're sending another unit up there to secure the area."

"Negative," Tommy said. "We have it under control. Secure the perimeter of the building in case there's...an attack."

No response came. Tommy stood there for a moment, waiting for the other guy to say something. Nothing.

They weren't buying his little ruse, and Tommy knew it.

His suspicions were confirmed a second later when he heard the man's voice come through the earpiece again.

"Swanson, Durbitoff, Carmon, Kone, sweep the top floor. Make sure the prisoner hasn't gotten out of the building."

Tommy clenched his teeth in frustration. No turning back now. It was either the fire escape or the stairs. Since the men who'd come up earlier had used the stairs, he figured if the building had an elevator it hadn't been usable in a long time.

He craned his neck and listened closely. No sounds of footsteps or voices echoed through the hallway yet. They would be there soon, though, and Tommy knew time was running out.

Reluctantly, he turned back to the mangled window and ran to it. The metal frames were still in place, albeit bent severely. Some were broken. The blow from the chair had knocked the thing loose from its locks, and now it hung free, slightly opened.

Tommy stuffed the two pistols in his hands down into the back of his waistband and hoped the four guns wouldn't fall out during the climb down. Only slightly satisfied with their security, he pushed the window the rest of the way out and swung his leg over the edge, making sure there were no remaining shards of glass sticking up that could cut him. A slice to the groin would be unfortunate, to say the least. He didn't see any dangerous pieces jutting up and grabbed the edge of the wall with his left hand to brace himself as he planted one foot on the wobbly landing and swung the other over the window ledge.

Cool air rushed over him as a gust of wind rolled in from the west. The fire-escape platform shook under his weight. He reached out and grabbed the railing as he shuffled his feet toward the ladder on the right. The metal grate underneath him wobbled, and Tommy felt his balance wobble for a moment as he looked down to the street below.

He was about ten stories up, as far as he could figure. He couldn't help but think of Sean's intense fear of heights. Tommy had always thought it strange that his friend could have such a near-superhuman way of doing almost everything but hated being in high places.

At the moment, Tommy understood the phobia completely. He felt his stomach turn, and for a second nothing was stable, not even the buildings around him or the street below.

He snapped his head once to clear the irrational fear. His knuckles whitened from the tight grip he had on the railing. "Come on, man. Get it together."

He moved faster and reached the ladder with a few more steps. It was held in place by a safety latch that looked anything but. The rusted clasp had all but eroded away and was now holding on by nothing more than a quarter inch of old iron.

Tommy grabbed one of the ladder rungs with one hand and pried the latch up with the other. The ladder released and screeched as it started its descent to the next level. Tommy tried to temper the speed of its movement by holding on to the top rung, but it did little good. He had to let go a second before the thing stopped with a loud clang. The platform swayed back and forth, causing another spat of vertigo to hit Tommy's vision.

He wavered but didn't lose his focus. Still holding on to the rail with a death grip, he spun around and placed his right foot on the top rung of the ladder and began his climb down.

The ladder shifted and vibrated with every step. Tommy did his best not to look down, as he'd advised Sean so many times before when the two were in a high place. On a ladder, though, that was easier said than done. He had to at least take a glance below every now and then to make sure his foot hit the next step.

Tommy felt his foot hit something more substantial than the ladder rungs, and he risked a look down to see the platform under him.

"One story down. That many to go," he said as he stared down at the next nine floors.

Shouting mingled with the sounds of the street below. The voices weren't coming from pedestrians on the sidewalk. They were coming from above.

He had no time to lose.

Tommy flipped the clasp on the next ladder and let it slide free down to the next level with a loud bang.

He couldn't afford to be cautious now. As he wrapped his fingers around the ladder's sides, he looked to the window above and saw a man poke his head out. Tommy knew what was coming next.

The guy leaped out onto the platform, causing the already unstable fire escape to shudder once more. A gun appeared in the man's hand, and he fired down at Tommy repeatedly.

Tommy loosened his grip and let himself slide down the ladder like a fireman on a pole until he hit the ground with a heavy thud. The bullets raining down from above pinged off the metal grate above. A few sneaked through, ricocheting off the metal around Tommy. He jumped across the platform and kicked the next clasp, freeing the ladder.

He no longer cared how high up he was. He just had to get away.

33

ATLANTA

Sean stepped back into the clean room and offered Alex a hand up. The younger man reached up and took it.

"You all right?" Sean asked, analyzing Alex to make sure he was fine.

"Yeah, I'm good." Alex twisted his head to the side and rubbed his throat where a red line stretched across the skin from ear to ear.

"You sure?"

Alex nodded.

Tara dropped the gun and wrapped her arms around Alex. Then she put a palm on each of his cheeks, looked into his eyes, and pressed her lips against his. At first, Alex was a little caught off guard. Then he relaxed for a second.

Sean cleared his throat. "Sorry to bother you two, but we have a problem. That guy just got away with the tablet and all your notes."

Tara let Alex go. He staggered back for a second and wavered as if he might pass out.

"I guess that clears up that question," Sean commented.

"What question?" Alex asked.

Sean pointed his finger back and forth between the two. "About you...two...doesn't matter. We have to get the tablet and those notes back."

"What about those cops?" Tara asked. "You said there were cops waiting outside."

"I lied."

"Then shouldn't you go after him?"

Sean shook his head. "It won't matter. He'll be out of the building by now. By the time I got back up to the ground floor, he'd be long gone."

"So, we call the cops," Alex suggested. "Get them to set up a city-wide net to catch him."

"Doesn't work that way," Sean said. "They'll send guys here first. Then they'll want to know what happened to all these dead bodies. They'll ask a ton of questions before they even lift a finger to find him."

"So what, then?"

Sean already had an idea. "Did you happen to look at the stuff you were printing out for him?"

"Yeah," Alex said with a nod. "Not that it was helpful. Just a bunch of numbers. There was no rhyme or reason."

"And the instructions were incomplete," Tara added. "Our computers were still working on the last few bits of information."

"I know the instructions," Sean said. "They've always been there, out in the open."

"They have?" the other two spoke at the same time.

"Yeah, but we're not going to activate the Ark. We have to stop that guy and his group of killers from activating it. That means we have to find it before they do."

"How?" Tara asked.

"You said some of those printouts were a bunch of numbers?" Sean asked.

"Yeah, but they're nonsense," Alex answered.

Sean knew better. He'd seen enough ancient clues, texts, codes, and ciphers over the years. One thing always rang true: there were no accidents, no mistakes.

If there was a sequence of numbers, they had been put there for a reason.

"Show me what you printed."

The three hurried back inside the lab to the computer station where Alex had been minutes before. Smoke still hung in the room from the firefight, hovering like a bitter apparition.

Alex slid into his chair and clicked the part of the screen that contained the sheet he'd printed for Tusun.

"See?" he asked, pointing at the monitor. "This is what we got from that series of symbols in the journal images you sent. It took awhile. We initially believed that these emblems represented letters. Turns out they represent numbers. Kind of straight, right? I thought maybe it could be a Fibonacci sequence."

"No," Sean said. "That's not it."

"Obviously." Alex tried to cover his tracks and not look stupid.

"Anyway," Tara interrupted, "we tried figuring what the numbers mean, but we still don't know for sure."

Sean stared hard at the line of twenty-four numbers. "Twelve and twelve," he repeated. "Twenty-four numbers, some repeating, some not. Odds, evens, no pattern." His brain went into overdrive. The digits swirled in his brain like a blizzard. His brow furrowed, and he leaned over the desk, hovering above the keyboard as he continued to gaze at the screen. "Divided by two, twenty-four is twelve. That's one of the sacred numbers from the Bible," he said. "Perhaps that has some bearing here?"

"It's possible. I mean, you're looking for the greatest biblical relic of all time, so that would make sense." Alex's voice echoed in the room for a moment and then died.

"They aren't biblical texts," Sean said, ruling that possibility out. "There would be colons and commas."

"Unless Lafayette was trying to throw people off by stringing them all together," Tara offered.

"No," Sean said with a shake of the head. "I don't think so. The books of the Bible have titles, words. I've never heard of a way to use numbers to identify texts in Scripture."

The room went quiet again as the three plunged deeper into thought. Every theory that came to mind didn't add up, so no one said anything for what seemed like an hour.

Sean stood up and stretched his back, putting his arms up high. He was sore from the fighting, the running, the gun play. He wasn't an old man yet, but there were moments when he felt like Father Time was catching up to him. Now was one of those moments.

His eyes wandered across the room. He noted the bodies still lying on the floor. Those would need to be dealt with sooner rather than later. A call to Emily would be in order. She could handle it, keep things under wraps. No need to alert the cops on this one, especially considering who these guys were. The less the police knew, the better as far as Sean was concerned. Not to mention he didn't want them poking their noses around his business. He did his best, whenever possible, to avoid contact with the authorities, partly because he —in a few ways—felt above them. It was also because he didn't like the tedium and incompetence they brought to investigations like this one.

Sean turned his head, and his neck let out a relieving crack. He was about to turn around and return to the code on the screen when his eyes caught something, an object, on the other side of the room he'd seen a hundred times—but had never thought much of until now.

A giant map of the world stretched out across the wall with push-pins stuck in every place IAA had retrieved and secured an important historical artifact. Sean felt himself moving, almost subconsciously, toward the map. Before he realized it, he was standing underneath it, looking up at the countries and continents of the world, surrounded by oceans and seas, divided by man-made boundaries.

"Sean?" Alex asked. He and Tara were still by the computer, watching him intently as he gazed up at the map. "You okay?"

Sean nodded absently. "What if," he said, "the numbers aren't a piece to the puzzle? What if they aren't something that leads to another clue? What if they're the map?"

He didn't see the puzzled looks cross their faces. They didn't yet see what he was talking about.

"What do you mean?" Tara asked.

Sean pivoted around and stalked back toward them. There was a renewed energy in his eyes, full of determination and excitement.

"Do you have a pen?"

"Um, yeah." Alex immediately began rummaging through the desk drawers, pulling out note tabs, paper clips, rulers, and other objects.

"Here," Tara said, finding one behind the computer monitor. She handed it to Sean, who then picked up a sticky note and began writing.

When he was done, he had two sets of numbers with a dash between them. He straightened and tapped the paper with the bottom of the pen. "See?"

The other two frowned as they looked down at the numbers.

"I don't get it," Alex confessed. "What am I supposed to be seeing again?"

Sean let a mischievous grin creak across his face. "How about now?" He added a few periods and two more dashes. "What does that look like?"

The realization hit Tara first. Her eyebrows lifted, and she smacked Sean on the shoulder. "Oh wow. I never even considered that before."

Alex caught up a moment after her. "Coordinates!" he nearly shouted. "The numbers are longitude and latitude."

Sean confirmed it with a nod. "Yep. Now do me a favor, and enter those first digits into the computer. Let's find out exactly where Monsieur Lafayette was trying to tell us to go."

"Way ahead of you, boss."

Alex's fingers flew across the keyboard, driven by the thrill of the chase, the ecstasy of discovery, and the possibility that they were going to finally unravel a mystery two thousand years in the making.

He hit the enter button, and the screen flickered, then changed. A map appeared, displaying a location every one of them knew. Alex zoomed in on it, and a familiar golden dome appeared on the satellite image.

"Jerusalem," Tara whispered.

"Where the Templar journey began," Sean added. "Now type in the other coordinates." He leaned forward, looming over Alex's shoulder as he hurriedly entered the next set of numbers.

Alex hit the enter key again, and once more the screen changed. This time, to a different location.

Every set of eyes gaped wide. Mouths dropped. Sean clenched his teeth.

He stood up straight again and swallowed. He could feel the pulse quicken in his chest, pumping blood through his extremities faster and faster.

"I can't believe it," Tara said.

"All this time, it was right there," Alex added.

"So," Sean said, "that *is* where they hid the Ark of the Covenant." His excitement faded in a moment. "We have to get Tommy."

The other two stared at him, waiting for an explanation. They'd been wondering where Tommy was but hadn't had a chance to ask.

"I don't want to put you two in danger, but I might not be able to do this alone."

Alex and Tara cast a sidelong glance at each other and then turned back to Sean.

"We learned from the best," Tara said.

"Yeah, Sean. You've showed us how to handle ourselves in a fight. We'll be fine," Alex added.

Sean's jaw set firm. He admired the courage they displayed, but he also knew they had no idea what they were up against. There was no telling how many more men the Order of Assassins had to throw at them. The dead men on the floor in the lab could very well be a drop in the bucket. He'd seen inside their headquarters, passed the cells in the hallways. There were dozens of them, probably more. Alain Depricot was amassing a small army of the world's deadliest covert fighting forces. Sean had a bad feeling that someone wasn't coming back alive. He didn't let that deter him.

"All right, kids," he said, finally. "Let's go get the boss. Then we find the Ark."

34

Tommy hit the platform of the seventh-floor fire escape and rushed to the other side to kick the ladder free as he'd done with those above. The gunmen overhead continued their pursuit, gradually gaining on Tommy with each descent.

The ladder rattled free and dropped down. It was still moving when Tommy grabbed it and slid down, his boots scuffing the ladder's edges along the way. Friction burned his palms and fingers, but he ignored it, desperate to get to the freedom of the sidewalk and the crowds below. These guys were bold, but they weren't stupid enough to carry a gunfight into broad daylight in front of thousands of witnesses.

At least that's what Tommy hoped.

He landed on the next platform and almost lost his balance, but righted himself with a hand on the rail. He was about to head to the next ladder when the window to his left burst open.

Glass shattered and crashed to the metal grate. A split second later, Tommy was struck by something huge. He didn't realize what it was until the mass drove him sideways into the rail.

His shoulder hit the metal hard and sent a fresh new surge of pain through his body.

He grimaced and then collected himself in an instant. An Assassin had barged through the window and tackled him high above the street. The man's plan of attack was far from perfect and had almost sent the two of them tumbling over the edge to their deaths.

Tommy recovered from the blow and pushed himself up from the grate underfoot. The attacker wobbled but stood up with a pistol in one hand. Tommy kicked his right foot around and struck the gunman's hand, knocking the weapon free and sending it sliding across the platform.

It was Tommy's turn to draw. He reached for one of the pistols in his belt, but the killer was on him before he could even touch the grip.

The guy jumped at him and drove his heel into Tommy's chest, sending him stumbling backward until he felt his lower back hit the railing. A quick look up told him the pursuer from above was still coming, though the man seemed less intent on firing his weapon into the mesh of metal surrounding Tommy. Instead, he was trying to catch up.

For the moment, Tommy had more immediate concerns. He reached down for one of his pistols again, but his opponent fired a jab and struck him in the jaw.

The world blurred again. The buildings around him started to spin. Tommy put up his fists to defend himself, but his coordination was knocked off kilter.

The Assassin stepped to him, obviously seeing the fight was all but over. He lunged at Tommy, leading with a right hook. Tommy did the only thing he could with his faculties being so off. He dropped to one knee and let the guy's momentum take him to the railing. The killer saw the move and attempted to knee Tommy in the face.

Tommy saw it coming and twisted just enough so that the man's knee whooshed by his head. Then Tommy leaned forward, putting the back of his skull into the guy's groin, grabbed the killer's right hamstring, and raised up with all his strength.

The Assassin knew what was coming but could do nothing to stop it. He shrieked for a second as he felt the safety of the platform disappear from under his feet with nothing but air surrounding him as he tumbled over the railing and down seven stories to the sidewalk below.

Tommy regained his balance and leaned over the rail. The fallen man was lying prostrate on the concrete. People were already rushing to see what had happened. Some covered their mouths in horrified shock. Others were calling for help to anyone around. Still more were pulling out their phones to call emergency crews. It was sheer luck no one below had been hurt, other than the guy he'd thrown off the building.

Tommy glanced up and saw the man above was also looking over the edge. His attention was only distracted for a moment before he renewed the chase.

Enough of this, Tommy thought. He climbed through the window and into the room beyond. It looked much like his makeshift prison upstairs, though this one had floorboards missing in several places, either rotted away or removed strategically by someone intending to do repairs.

He knew the guy chasing him would follow. That wasn't what concerned him. Tommy could deal with that one. It was the other two he knew were coming. Based on what the guy said in the radio, there were four men after him. One was dead on the street below. The other was out on the fire escape. Where were the other two?

He drew two pistols from his belt and rushed to the door opposite the window. He risked a peek around the corner and found an empty corridor that mirrored the one he'd been in on the top floor.

No sign of the other two gunmen, but he knew that wouldn't last. At that very moment, the guy on the fire escape was probably telling his comrades what was going on, giving an update on their prisoner's position.

Tommy started down the hall to the left, knowing the stairwell would be there. Then he had another thought. The men who'd gone up to the top floor would be coming down that same way. If they radioed for more reinforcements, he'd be caught on the stairs between the two groups. Even with all the rounds he had on him, there was no way he'd win that kind of firefight, not in such close quarters. The gunmen would either cut him down, or worse, they'd force him to surrender, meaning he'd have more torture to look forward to. And next time, it wouldn't just be a beating.

He skidded to a stop and looked back over his shoulder. The metal elevator doors were at the other end of the hall. They weren't roped off or covered with tape. There was no need for that if everyone in the building knew not to use it.

Tommy, however, wasn't looking for a ride down. He just needed a way to get out where no one would see him. Another realization struck him. At one point, probably during the brief fight on the fire escape, he'd lost the earpiece. He no longer heard the chatter from the men trying to catch him. He cursed himself, but it was a bump in the road, nothing to cry about.

There wasn't time to ponder the consequences. He started back the other way and nearly ran into the man chasing him as the guy rushed out the door. Tommy accidentally charged into him, plowing his shoulder into the guy's chest like a linebacker.

The gunman never knew what hit him. Tommy kept pumping his legs, wrapped his arms around the man, and then leaped into the air, forklifting his feet off the ground. The power of Tommy's momentum seemed to double his strength as he sailed several feet with the guy under him. One second, they were flying through the air. The next, the man hit the floor. His head smacked against the surface with a sickening sound. Instantly, the gunman's eyes went hazy, and his head twisted left to right as he fought the effects of what was surely a concussion.

Tommy looked down at his hand and wrenched the pistol from the Assassin's grip. He stood over the man and fired a single shot into his head. The man became still. Tommy glanced down at the pistol and dropped it on the guy's chest, figuring that between the rounds already spent on the fire escape and the one he'd just used, there weren't many left.

Tommy didn't pause. He knew to do so would mean his end. He'd been lucky just now, running into that gunman the way he had, but Tommy knew better than to rely on luck.

He rushed to the elevator doors and found the seam between them was cracked just enough to wedge his fingers inside. He pulled hard at one side and found the doors opened without much resistance. Once the opening was wide enough for him to fit through, he slid into the opening and reached out into the darkness.

No way Sean would do this, he thought, considering how high up he had to be.

A seven-story fall into a dark abyss would be a terrifying way to go, and a shame considering how far he'd made it thus far.

He held on to the door with one hand, gripping it as hard as his muscles would allow. If he could have crushed the metal, he would have. As he leaned out over the black deathtrap, he considered the possibility that maybe the cables were no longer there, that he was reaching for nothing but air.

A door at the end of the hall burst open. Tommy startled, his head instinctively twitching to look back in the other direction. When he did, his left foot carrying most of his weight slipped off the edge. He felt the horrifying sensation of falling for a second as he disappeared into the shaft.

As he fell forward, he waved his hands around in front of his body. His palm struck something metal, and he instinctively wrapped his fingers around it. The move slowed his fall. Grabbing the threaded cable with the other stopped his motion altogether.

He clutched the metal rope with utter desperation. When he looked back up at the ajar elevator door, he realized he'd only dropped a few feet.

Tommy knew he had to keep moving. Sooner or later, the men would check the elevator shaft. They'd pore over the entire building. The Assassins didn't strike him as the kind of group who'd leave any stone unturned.

He began lowering himself down into the darkness, one hand over the other, inching his way closer to freedom.

The sounds of footsteps echoed into the shaft. They came from above and below. He heard men shouting, some of them in different languages. Most of them were speaking English. He wondered how many men were in this organization. He'd taken out several. From the sound of it, there were still dozens searching for him, maybe more.

The entire time, Tommy kept moving down the shaft. He squeezed his legs and feet together to ease the strain on his forearms, whose muscles were burning. They felt swollen enough to burst through his long-sleeve shirt.

He fought off the unrelenting urge to let go by reminding himself of the rope climb in gym class when he was in high school. Most of the kids had been unable to make it to the top. Tommy was one of them. Sean, of course, had no trouble with it, but Tommy never was in as good a shape as his friend. Not until recently. He'd spent a good amount of time focusing on his diet, exercising, and strength training.

At the moment, all of that was saving his life because he knew, in his old condition, his muscles would have failed around the top of the sixth floor and sent him plummeting to his death.

Even with his newfound strength, his fingers were getting tight. The tendons in his arms stiffened. The exertion was simply too much.

He didn't know how far down he'd traveled, but gauged on the distance up to the slightly open elevator doors above, he figured he'd gone at least four stories—but it was difficult to say.

The sounds of men's voices grew louder, reverberating in the concrete shaft. Between the noises and the pain in his arms, he started letting his hands slip faster down the cable and hoped there weren't any metal splinters sticking out. A small problem, considering the circumstances, but one he'd rather not deal with. The last thing he needed was a tetanus shot on top of everything else.

The cable groaned as he worked his way down. With the increased speed, it swayed back and forth, moving a few feet to one side and then the other. Still, the movement made navigating the dark shaft that much more difficult.

Up above, the voices mingled with footsteps. He saw flashlight beams dancing on the wall opposite the door he'd come through just moments before. The men were coming to check the elevator shaft. The lights were far overhead now, but he still didn't know how much more there was to go before he found the ground level. He loosened his grip a tad, and his speed increased again.

His fingers and palms burned from the friction, but he didn't dare slow down. Suddenly, he bumped into the wall as the cable swung wide to the left. His grip loosened and he lost his hold.

Tommy's arms flailed wildly as he desperately tried to regain control of his drop, but it was futile. He felt the air beneath him. His feet kicked for a second, as if they could somehow grab ahold of the cable and steady his fall.

Then a jarring pain struck him in the tailbone. His back hit next. Then his arms and heels. He looked around but couldn't see anything. Was he dead?

No. That was a stupid question. He still had control of all his faculties. He'd landed on the floor of the elevator shaft after only falling six or seven feet. He looked up and saw the flashlights poking into the darkness.

Tommy scrambled to his feet and rushed to the same side of the shaft that the doors were open above. He felt around and discovered similar metal doors as before and pressed his back against them.

He managed to clear the field of view just in time. The broad beams of light shone down onto the floor where he'd just been a moment before. The dancing cable might have given away his escape plan, but there was no sign of him for the pursuers to find.

Tommy stared straight ahead, doing his best to keep his breathing to a steady, silent rhythm. He noticed the massive springs set into the floor, along with a few buffer plates. How he'd missed those was a minor miracle. If he'd hit his head on one of the objects jutting out of the floor, it could have been fatal, or at least rendered him unconscious.

The lights on the floor disappeared.

Tommy waited a second before he poked his head out and risked a glance up. The men were gone, probably to check the rest of the building.

He turned around and found the seam between the elevator doors and pulled. Dim light flooded the dark space around him. The smell of hookah smoke, onions, curry, and damp air filled his nostrils. As the doors opened wider, he saw the hallway just beyond. It was empty, though a chair sat next to a metal door at the other end of the corridor. The door had a sliding plate near the center top where people could look out to check who was attempting to gain entrance.

He didn't know where the guard was—more than likely helping the others try to find the escaped prisoner. Tommy wasn't going to take the moment for granted. Like his friend always said, "When the opportunity comes, take it."

Tommy burst from the elevator shaft and sprinted to the door. He pulled back the latch and swung it open.

City air rushed over him with a cool chill. Light struck his face from the gray sky above. He risked one glance back and then darted toward the street and the sounds of sirens rushing to the scene where a man had, apparently, jumped off a ten-story building.

35

NEW YORK CITY

Alain's boots clicked on the wooden floor beams as he stepped into the now-vacant room. His eyes immediately flashed to the twisted metal and shattered panes of glass of the window in the far wall. He walked deliberately over to the opening and poked his head through, looking down at the street below. The crowds had been pushed back by the police, several of whom were on the order's payroll. The name of the man who'd "jumped" from the top floor would never be known to the public, just another John Doe lost in the pages of tabloid newspapers.

The dead man wasn't the problem at the forefront of his mind, though it was certainly disconcerting that he and the others who'd been slain had fallen so easily to someone without their level of training, discipline, or sense of purpose. He was baffled by that, though he didn't let his men see.

The fact that Schultz had been able to escape his bonds, take down several of Alain's men, and managed to escape was proof that they were, perhaps, slipping. Doubt crept into the back of Alain's mind. Were they not as prepared as he once thought? Had they not spent years honing their skills, their minds and bodies, to achieve this great victory for the order? It was what they'd waited for, planned for, sacrificed everything for.

Now some rogue idiot had killed several of his men as if they were nothing more than mere thugs from a street gang—undisciplined, uneducated, undirected.

In the past, he'd have set an example. But the truth was that in the past, he wouldn't have had to. This failure would have never happened. He knew his master would have been disappointed. No, that word wasn't strong enough. He would have been repulsed, sickened by such a display, just as Alain was at that very moment. Alain punished himself, though, telling himself that such a breakdown would have never occurred under the master's watch.

A broken shard of glass clung to the warped remains of the frame, dangling for a moment. Some invisible force wiggled it free and sent it crashing to the floor to join the rest of the shards.

One of his senior members of the organization stood to the right of the doorframe. The man's long black hair was pulled back in a ponytail so tight that the dim light in the room seemed to shine off it. He was a man who'd come in just a week after Alain, picked up by the master on the streets of Seoul in South Korea. He'd been a strong soldier, unwavering in his discipline and fiercely loyal. Most of the men in the order were. The ones who weren't were sent on their way —to eternity.

"You want us to find him, sir?" the man asked.

Alain's mind had drifted so much that he'd nearly forgotten the other men in the room. Even with the ones he'd lost, there were still a dozen or so of them in the building. Then there were the men he'd sent with Tusun to Atlanta.

"No, Lee," Alain said, his head twitching slightly to the right. "No, let him go."

Lee's face tightened into a scowl. "Let him go?" He'd never questioned his leader before. This time, however, he didn't follow the line of thinking. "Sir, he could pose a threat."

"I'm well aware of the threat," Alain said. "Have a little faith in your brother Tusun. He will get us the items we need to complete the mission. Once we have those, I couldn't care less what Schultz does. There is nothing he can do to stop us."

Lee accepted the answer, albeit reluctantly.

Alain didn't let him see the anger that raged inside him. He was furious that Schultz had got away. There was nothing he could do about it now. New York was an immense city with tens of thousands of places he could hide. Finding him now would be like finding a needle in a stack of needles, even with his extended resources.

"What would you have us do, sir?" Lee interrupted his leader's thoughts again.

Alain was about to answer when the phone in his jacket started ringing.

He ignored the question and looked at the device, immediately recognizing the number.

"Do you have the items?" he asked, putting the phone to his ear.

"Yes, sir," Tusun said. He sounded distracted.

Alain sensed something was amiss. "What's wrong?"

"Wyatt got away, sir. His two associates ambushed us."

Tusun didn't try to make excuses. He didn't dare attempt to pass the blame. It was one of the things Alain liked about the man, and why he was the second-in-command over all the order. Tusun never beat around the bush, always giving a direct answer to everything.

He knew that Alain would be furious at the fact someone had got the drop on them, but lying would only postpone the inevitable. Truthfully, losing was losing in their minds. The way of the Assassins was to persevere, to always push toward victory no matter the cost. Loss of any kind was inexcusable.

Alain clenched his teeth. *How could this have happened?* For centuries, his order had been one of the most elite fighting forces in the world. They were rarely bested, and when they were it was a result of overwhelming odds, being greatly outmanned, or just the result of bad luck. It was difficult for him to comprehend how these two brigands had managed to slip through their fingers, and in a six-hour span.

"Where are you?" Alain asked, his tone even and firm.

"Driving, sir. I'm just north of Knoxville, Tennessee. I'll be in Virginia shortly."

"And you have the things we need?" He wanted to make sure he'd heard correctly.

"Yes, sir. I have the tablet as well as a sequence of numbers they printed out just before the ambush occurred."

Alain's forehead wrinkled ever so slightly as his eyebrows pinched together. "Sequence of numbers?" He motioned to Lee to be ready to take notes. The man complied, pulling out his own phone and opening a note app.

"Yes, sir. There are twelve digits. I don't know what they mean, and I wasn't able to obtain that information before we were attacked."

The last part of the sentence threw fuel on the fire about the whole scenario, but Alain doused it with every ounce of patience he could muster. "What about your men?"

There was a long pause. Alain knew Tusun never hesitated to give him information, even if it was bad. For a moment, he wondered if the connection had been lost.

"They're all dead, sir," Tusun confessed. "I'm the only one who made it out."

Alain's nostrils flared. The question kept resurfacing. *How could this have happened?*

Had he underestimated Wyatt and his friends? Underestimating an enemy was something Alain never did. He'd learned caution, precision, and respect for an opponent through years of training. This, however, was a clear indictment that he'd been slipping. Perhaps he *had* gotten soft over the years, despite sticking to their order's guidelines to the letter.

Alain stood at a crossroads. Either they would carry out the mission as if nothing had happened, push forward to the goal and leave Wyatt and Schultz out there to potentially interfere again, or they could reach out to every resource they had available to locate the two troublemakers and eliminate them.

The latter choice would alter their timeline, potentially slowing them down by days, even weeks. That wasn't an option. The president would only be gone for so long, and the window would be closed soon. If they were going to get into the White House, it had to be soon.

Alain thought of Darren Sanders, the pawn he'd used to open the door for them. Whatever means the man was going to use, it was a good bet it could only be used once.

"Sir?" Tusun brought him back to the conversation.

"Yes?"

"What are your orders?"

It was the first time Alain had fumbled through a decision since taking over the organization.

"What are the numbers, Tusun?"

"One moment, sir."

Alain raised a finger, signaling to Lee to be ready to take down the information he was about to receive from the caller.

Tusun rattled off the numbers and then repeated them once. Alain relayed them to Lee, who nodded when he'd confirmed the numbers in his phone matched those Tusun was passing along.

"Thank you," Alain said into the phone. "We will rendezvous in Washington tomorrow."

"Yes, sir."

Alain ended the call and crossed the room with great, long strides. He stopped next to Lee, who held his phone out for the leader to see.

Alain gazed at the screen, the long sequence making no sense to him.

"Do you have any idea what that means?" Alain asked.

"No, sir," Lee replied. He didn't even offer a guess.

"I thought not." Alain spun around dramatically, digging his toe into the floor and twisting on the opposite heel. His shoes clicked on the floor again as he marched deliberately back over to the window. He folded his hands behind his back at waist level and halted, once more looking out the window to the buildings beyond.

"There are twelve numbers, yes?" Alain asked.

Lee took a moment to count them and then confirmed them with a confident, "Yes, sir."

"Interesting." He rose up onto his tiptoes and then slowly lowered back down. "Divide them into two," he said, more to himself than Lee. Alain twitched his nose. "Read me the first twelve."

Lee did as told, reading off the first half of the numbers in a robotic tone.

Alain spun around and looked at one of the other two men in the room. "Look up those numbers," he ordered.

The man, a blond whose hair was cut almost to the scalp, gave a nod and immediately started tapping away on his phone. He stared at the screen for a second and then looked up with a disappointed expression on his face. "Nothing, sir."

Alain bit his lower lip. "Divide that string in two."

The man gave a curt nod and did as told. This time, he looked up much more quickly than the first. Alain knew what the expression meant.

"What is it?"

The guard took two steps closer and held out the phone so Alain could see it clearly.

It was exactly what he'd suspected.

Alain had a knack for solving puzzles and riddles. He understood ciphers better than anyone in the order. When he heard the series of numbers, at first he wondered if it was some kind of code, a hidden language that would reveal the location of the Ark. That wasn't so far from the truth.

What he hadn't expected was the location. All this time, he believed he'd pinpointed the location where the holy relic was hidden by the Templars so long ago. He felt certain it was under the presidential mansion in Washington. The evidence before him suggested otherwise.

It was a location he knew well, one that he'd even visited once on a cold autumn night. The media believed something was there, the Holy Grail, perhaps. Alain had come to the conclusion that it was a decoy, an elaborate scheme set up by the Templars to keep the Assassins and others perpetually digging deeper, wasting centuries and vast fortunes to find nothing but more and more teasers, clues that led to more clues in a never-ending wild goose chase.

Apparently, he'd assumed wrong.

He took his phone out of his pocket and called Tusun. The man answered in one ring.

"Yes, sir?"

"Change of plans, Brother."

"Change of plans?"

"It turns out we were wrong about the location. It isn't at the White House after all. It's in Nova Scotia." He waited for a moment to let the information sink in. "We're going to Oak Island."

36

ATLANTA

S ean and the kids cautiously made their way up the stairs, each armed with a pistol in case Tusun happened to still be around. It was doubtful—and Sean knew that—but he also knew caution was imperative.

He stayed several steps ahead of the other two as they rounded the last corner and arrived at the door leading into the lobby. Sean held back his hand to the kids. They halted and waited for his instructions.

Sean pulled the door's latch and cracked an opening, barely a few inches at first, just so he could get a view of the lobby. It was clear straight ahead. He swung the door open a little more, and scanned to the right, then left. No one there.

He raised from his crouching position and shoved the gun through the gap in the doorway. Stealthily, he crept into the lobby, swinging his pistol around one way and then the other. His shoes didn't make a sound on the floor. You could have heard a feather drop in the cavernous silence of the room.

Just as Sean motioned for the other two to move forward, the phone at Henry's desk screamed. Sean froze for a second, startled by the sudden noise. Tara and Alex stopped as well.

Sean looked over toward the high reception desk and saw Henry's head lean forward.

"International Archaeology Agency. How can I help you?"

From the sound of his voice and the sudden way he'd leaned up, it was clear Henry had been sleeping. Relief swelled in Sean. The killer hadn't harmed Henry. Sean didn't know why. Maybe the guy hadn't seen him. Perhaps he didn't consider the old security guard a threat. It didn't matter. Henry was okay.

"Oh, hey there, Mr. Schultz. Where you been?" His cool Southern demeanor carried in his tone. He punctuated the question with a hearty chuckle.

Tommy? Sean thought.

He threw caution aside and sprinted across the room, momentarily leaving Tara and Alex behind.

"Sean?" Henry said. "Yeah, I saw him come in with a bunch of guys a little while ago."

"Henry!" Sean shouted, approaching. "Is that Tommy?"

"Oh, here he is now, Mr. Schultz. He looks a little...." Henry saw the pistol in Sean's hand, and his mouth dropped open.

For a second, Sean thought he might let the phone fall to the floor.

"Mr. Wyatt, are you okay?" Henry asked. The frantic sound in his voice was rare to hear in the seemingly perpetually calm guard.

"Yeah," Sean said. Then he realized he still had the gun in his hand as he skidded to a stop at the desk. "Oh sorry. Had a...problem with the...smoke detectors downstairs."

Right on cue, an alarm started sounding. Sean's eyes rolled up to the ceiling and then flashed back to Tara and Alex. Alex hurriedly retrieved the phone from his pocket, typed in a few numbers, and disarmed the alarm from an app. The piercing sound ceased, and the cavernous lobby returned to relative silence.

"Smoke alarm?" Henry asked. "Shouldn't we evacuate the building?"

"No, Henry, everything's fine."

"You sure?" The old man cocked his head to the side, passing

Sean his most dubious glare. "You want me to call 911 or something?"

"No, Henry, it's fine. I promise. There's no fire."

Sean knew why the alarms were delayed. The new system inside their glass-encased laboratory hadn't been completed yet. There really were kinks in it. Sean was grateful the fire prevention system wasn't online yet. When it detected smoke or fire, it sucked the air out of the area to suffocate any flames. If someone was inside, they'd only have about thirty seconds to get out before running out of air.

"Hello?" Tommy's muffled voice came through the handset of the desk phone.

Sean reached out his hand and took the phone from Henry. "Thanks," he mouthed. "Tommy?"

"Sean. Good, you're okay."

"Yeah, we're fine. Alain's right-hand man got away, though. How'd you escape?"

"Long story. I'm calling from a department store courtesy phone." He didn't wait for Sean to ask why. "Please tell me you have the tablet and the journal. I'm assuming since I'm talking to you and not one of those goons that you have them."

Sean didn't answer immediately.

"Seriously. You have the tablet and journal, right?" Tommy sounded nervous—and angry.

"No, but it's okay."

"What?"

Sean hadn't heard his friend get angry very often. When it happened, though, there was no mistaking it. "Who took it?"

"There was a gunfight here at the lab. We took out all but one of their men. Tara got the drop on them." Sean looked down at Henry, who stared up from his chair in disbelief. "It's fine," Sean mouthed. "Tara did great."

Henry's head twisted slowly to the young woman who was now standing next to Alex near the desk. She rolled her shoulders as if what she'd done was no big deal.

"I'm guessing since you're so calm about all this, you have a plan. Please tell me you have a plan. You do have a plan, right?" Tommy's words spewed out of his mouth and through the phone's handset like a volcano.

"Yes, I have a plan. We managed to salvage a series of codes, numbers that were written down in the journal. We don't have the tablet, but we know where the Ark is."

Henry's eyebrows shot up, and his lips made a single movement. "Ark?"

Sean scrunched his face and briefly shook his head in a motion that was little more than a twitch.

"You did? I mean, you do?" Tommy asked, his tone changing instantly.

"Yeah. The numbers were coordinates for longitude and latitude."

"Incredible." Tommy's respect for the talents and skills from the Old World never ceased.

"Yeah, it is. Where are you?"

"I'm still in New York. I don't have any money; my phone is gone. I'm actually calling you from a courtesy phone here at Macy's."

"Macy's?" Sean had been to New York more times than he could count, but he'd never set foot in the department store famous for its sponsorship of the annual Thanksgiving parade.

"Yeah. I need you to come get me."

Sean heard the stress in his friend's voice. It was something beyond worry. He knew why. The men who'd captured the two of them could be anywhere. For all they knew, an Assassin was standing right behind Tommy at that very moment, waiting to put a knife in his back. They were able to blend into any group, virtually disappearing in plain sight.

"All right," Sean said. "First things first. You need to find a safe place to lie low until we can get there."

"Okay." There was hesitation in Tommy's voice, like he didn't know where that safe place might be. "Any thoughts? I mean, I have connections here in the city, but I don't want to put anyone in danger."

Sean knew exactly what his friend was talking about. Tommy's friends—more like acquaintances—were kind of high-society types.

They were philanthropists, collectors, and historical-preservation enthusiasts. While they may have been considered by many to be the social elite, those friends never acted that way. They didn't look down on anyone, instead trying to bring others up to their level. It was that kind of attitude and kindness that caused Tommy to have the inclination to avoid calling on them in this particular situation. The last thing he wanted to do was endanger good folks.

"I wouldn't want any harm to come to them either, Schultzie, but we have to get you somewhere safe."

A long pause cut into their conversation.

An idea popped into Sean's head, but he held it back for a moment. It wasn't one he liked, and he knew Tommy would like it even less.

"What about James Hadley?" Sean asked when he could think of no better options.

"The Mad Hadder?" Tommy's voice sounded sour. Sean could picture his friend in his mind, crinkling his nose, scowling, big wrinkles streaking across his forehead.

"I don't think you have many options. Unless you have other friends in the city I don't know about."

Tommy considered it in silence. James Hadley, affectionately known as "the Mad Hadder" by a few close acquaintances, was a relic hunter, a guy who chased down every treasure legend he could find. Sometimes he got lucky and found something of value, which he immediately hawked to the highest bidder.

Hadley represented much of what Tommy disliked about his industry, if it could be called that. Tommy didn't call Hadley a friend. He wouldn't even have a semblance of a relationship with the guy if it weren't for the fact that Hadley had tracked him down at a fundraiser once and clung to Tommy like a remora.

Funnily enough, it seemed Hadley held Tommy in the highest regard, considering him to be one of the best in the business. Strange since Tommy didn't do anything the way Hadley did.

Tommy maintained a high level of integrity. He didn't chase every lead that fell in his lap. And he certainly didn't sell anything he found, although to be fair the artifacts Tommy often dealt with had already been discovered. In those instances, he simply secured the item for transport to its destination.

Despite all those differences, Tommy felt like Hadley looked at him like he was some kind of rock star in the industry. On more than one occasion, Tommy had been chatting with other people in their field only to discover Hadley standing nearby, hanging on every word like some kind of deranged fanboy.

It wasn't the first time Tommy had a fan like this, but such adulation was, in his experience, rare.

"I don't know," Tommy said. "He's kind of a stalker."

"Which is why he'll make the perfect person to hide out with until we can get there. It'll only be for a few hours, six or seven tops. We'll get the jet ready and be there in no time."

Tommy sighed dramatically into the phone so Sean could hear his exasperation. The truth was, Sean wanted his friend to be stuck with the Mad Hadder.

The Hadder's backstory, seemingly originating from the Maghreb, aka Northwest Africa, suggested that Hadley had once been captured by a roving group of bandits. From the sounds of it, Hadley had made an improbable and daring escape. Along the way, he managed to find and recover several important pieces from an ancient Assyrian temple.

The artifacts were sold at auction, and Hadley received accolades for months over the affair.

Sean doubted Tommy was jealous of the incident, since he most likely realized that most of the tale was exaggerated and the Hadley discovery was probably dumb luck. Still, there was something funny about the possibility of Tommy being stuck with the guy for several hours.

So long as Hadley didn't take it too far. Sean's hilarious visions changed to something far more disconcerting, like Tommy being strapped to a bed and having his ankles hobbled.

Sean cringed at the thought.

"Okay," Tommy said. "I'll do it, but that doesn't mean I have to like it."

"No one's asking you to."

"You're insufferable. You know that?"

Sean giggled. "All the years I've known you, I think that's the first time you've used that word to describe me."

"Just be at Hadley's as soon as you can. Let's hope when you get there you don't find me in his freezer."

"I'm sure you'll be fine. He doesn't strike me as a cannibal. Stalker? Yes. Cannibal? No."

"Thanks for the encouragement," Tommy joked. "Fine. I'll call Hadley. Just hurry up. The less time I have to spend with that nut job, the better."

"You do realize that you're not really giving me any incentive to get there faster, right?" Sean held back the chuckle that nearly escaped his lips.

"Maybe the gang of deadly Assassins looking for me will give you a little motivation."

"And the fact that they stole the stuff we need to figure out this whole riddle. We'll be there as soon as we can. Just hang tight."

"Will do." Tommy was about to hang up the phone when he stopped. "Oh, Sean?"

"Yeah?"

"Where did they take the tablet?"

Sean felt an old, familiar feeling surge through him. He hesitated to call it the thrill of the chase, but that's what it was. It hit him now and then when he and Tommy discovered something, when they unraveled a clue, or when they sensed they were close to something big. This time, the bag of feelings was mixed. He knew about the location where Alain and his men were headed. People had died there in futile attempts to recover what they believed was a great treasure buried in the ground. Fortunes had been lost. There was no reason to think that they would be able to succeed where so many others had failed. That didn't mean they weren't going to try.

When he spoke, Sean's voice was monotone, leaving all drama behind. "Oak Island."

37

WASHINGTON DC

Today was the day Darren Sanders would take a bold step toward the Oval Office, both literally and figuratively. He laced up his shiny Italian shoes then slipped his blue pinstripe jacket over his white shirt. He loved pinstriped suits. He didn't know why, though he suspected it was because they made him look powerful, like the CEO of a billion-dollar multinational corporation. Except soon, those types would be bowing before him.

He looked into the mirror and sighed. *It isn't too late*, he thought. He still had a chance to back out, run away from all this. What if he got caught? That question was the sole mover of the mountain of doubt inside him. He didn't want to go to prison. If someone happened to catch him in the act—well, Sanders didn't want to think about it. What he was about to do would come with some of the worst felony charges possible, at least for someone like him. He'd be better off being arrested for murder. At least then the other inmates would have to respect him on some level.

Sanders shook off the thought. No one was going to catch him. He was just getting cold feet about the whole thing. The plan was perfect. If someone happened to walk into the break room while he was doing his thing, he could blow it off as an accident. That was the genius behind it all. The best crimes looked like accidents. He'd known that for a long time. It was how he'd gotten rid of Cindy.

She'd been a good personal assistant, ambitious and beautiful. From time to time, he'd caught a whiff of her perfume on another woman passing by on a random sidewalk or in a department store. Every time, it was as if her ghost was tickling his senses once more, haunting him with a feather of guilt.

They'd been a good team. Sanders had wanted her but played it safe until he knew she reciprocated. After all, she was only twenty-four years old, and he was more than double that. What could she have wanted with a man like him other than perceived power and money? She said and did all the right things to make it seem as if she was genuinely attracted to him. Maybe she had been in some strange way.

If that was the case, however, then he wouldn't have found her with a guy twenty years his junior.

That day, the gray sky above had stirred like gruel, dumping sheets of rain on the city. Sanders had a key to her place and let himself in. He never bothered to knock. That's what the key was for.

Then he'd heard the noises upstairs. The moaning. The grunting. The unmistakable squeaking bed frame.

Sanders wasn't hurt by her actions. If anything, he understood all too well. That didn't mean he wasn't jealous. Cindy was his property. Not some young punk's whose only concern was the latest hit song or wondering how many likes his last social media post received.

The thought had burned inside him. The fire inside him had grown with every sound echoing down from the second floor. He blinked rapidly, and his feet began moving, almost without his knowing.

Before he knew it, Sanders was standing in front of the kitchen stove. It was one of those gas numbers like the chefs on television always used. They never bothered with the electric ones. No one had time for that. Much like Sanders didn't have time for dealing with insubordinate little tramps.

Maybe it had been the bourbon coursing through his veins.

Maybe it had been the sound of the headboard hitting the wall upstairs. She yelped loud enough for him to hear, in a way he'd never heard when she was with him.

Sanders stood in his own living room, recalling what he had done next.

He'd flipped on one of the burners, without letting it ignite. For a second, he considered turning on all of them, but that would be a dead giveaway. Investigators would see that as odd and immediately begin looking into foul play. One burner, though: leaving one on was easy enough to believe it was a mistake, a simple accident that resulted in tragedy.

Sanders knew what would happen. Cindy always loved to have a cigarette after sex. It was like clockwork. Sometimes he wondered if it was her way of washing away some kind of disgust with something more disgusting, but during their time together she'd done it without fail, religiously.

He turned and left the house, closing and locking the door on his way out. There were no cars driving by at that time of night on the sleepy suburban street. No one would see him leaving.

Sanders looked in the mirror near his door and tightened the tie just a little bit more as he recalled the reports of the gas explosion at Cindy's house. He'd noted them with the same callous, almost disinterested lack of affect he displayed when signing off on a bombing in Afghanistan.

He handled the kind gestures, the apologetic emails and phone calls, and the sympathy cards with a genteel grace that could have won him an Academy Award. Inside, he was glad she was gone, consumed in a fiery explosion along with her punk lover.

Sanders never even looked up the man's name. He didn't care. They were gone and the deed was done.

He stepped out onto the front porch and took in a deep breath. If he could do that, this was a walk in the park. No one had to die today. At least he hoped that was the case. All he had to do was go to the break room in the White House, put some popcorn in the microwave,

and let it do its thing. It was the perfect plan, and plausible deniability was built right in.

"Good morning, Cliff," Sanders said to the man waiting at the
bottom of his front steps.

The guy wore a plain black suit and matching tie over a white
shirt. Sunglasses rested on his nose despite the early morning darkness and the cloudy sky above. Cliff had been with Sanders for a long
time as his security guy. Of course, there were others who rotated
through at night, but Cliff was usually the one keeping watch during
daylight hours.

"Good morning, sir," Cliff said with a nod.

One thing Sanders greatly appreciated about the man was his
ability to keep secrets. If he'd wanted, Cliff could have divulged all
kinds of information about Sanders's personal life. While he wasn't
present during Cindy's murder, there were plenty of other events the
media would have a field day with if Cliff were to betray his boss's
trust. Of course, to do so would mean career suicide. The security
circles were tight, especially in Washington. Everyone who took a job
in that line of work knew the score. Each man and woman understood their roles. In exchange for their discretion, they were well
compensated. Many would retire with a tidy sum of money stashed
away for their later years.

"To the office this morning, sir?" Cliff asked while ushering the
secretary of state to his vehicle.

"Actually, I need to drop by the White House for a minute."

Cliff opened the back door to the SUV. "The White House? The
president is leaving in the next hour to head out of the country."

"Yes, I know." Sanders anticipated this resistance, even from his
loyal protector. "I have a meeting with a few members of his cabinet.
Shouldn't take long, maybe an hour."

He slipped into the back seat. The leather felt warm from the
built-in heaters. He knew Cliff would accept the lie. Sanders had only
been forced to be dishonest with the man a few times. This occasion,
however, required deceit. No one could know what he was planning.

When they arrived, the guards at the White House gate cleared the SUV to pass through. Cliff slowed down and let his charge out at the side door leading into the wide hall on the main floor. Sanders knew the routine. Cliff would go park and wait in the SUV while Sanders took care of business. Now that he was on the White House grounds, he was safe. He was inside the fences of one of the most secure buildings on the planet. He'd be fine.

Sanders made his way inside and nodded at some of the security detail and cleaning crews busily vacuuming and dusting.

No one batted an eye at his presence. Why would they? He was a high-ranking government official and one that the president trusted. He'd been there more times than he could count. No one would think he was there to commit arson.

It was a simple enough crime. No one had to get hurt. He doubted the fire that would damage the break room would get any farther than that. The blaze would be contained within minutes, injuring no one and leaving nothing but a fairly mundane cleanup, a task that would be handled by his mysterious new friend.

Sanders worked his way through the corridor, the foyer, and then to the stairwell leading down to the break room and the other areas beneath the mansion.

One polite maid gave him a nod. She was wearing a surgical mask like he'd seen so many people do recently to avoid the flu. Apparently, his little ruse to get most of the crews sick had worked. Many were probably vomiting or lying in their beds with what they believed was some kind of food poisoning. It had been an easy enough thing to accomplish. A few spritzes of germs in the cafeteria, and voilà.

At the bottom of the stairs, he walked by a few interns and administrative assistants, giving polite nods as he passed before stopping at the doorway into the break room. He leaned forward, tilting his head to the side as he took a peek. It was empty. The young ladies he'd just passed must have only left a moment before. Timing, it seemed, was on his side.

Sanders stepped into the room and paused for a moment, considering closing the door behind him so no one would see his actions.

He shook off the thought. He wasn't doing anything wrong, just microwaving some popcorn. No big deal. No reason to hide that. Closing the door would raise more suspicion than anything.

He strode with purpose over to the counter and opened one of the cabinet doors. The only thing in there was a sparse collection of random coffee mugs, some paper cups, plates, and extra sugar and nondairy creamer. He closed the door and opened the one to the left. Still nothing. A sudden concern rushed into his head. What if there wasn't any popcorn here? He'd considered bringing some, tucking it away in his suit jacket, but that would have been annoying and could have raised suspicions. Would a bag of uncooked popcorn really be worth Secret Service scrutiny? Maybe he was being paranoid.

He racked his brain to recall where the person had found a bag the other day. Then he remembered. He reached over to another door and tugged the handle. He found the box of popcorn sitting inside and was relieved to see there were still two bags left.

Sanders grabbed one of the bags, ripped the plastic off, and opened the microwave door. He glanced back at the entrance to the room and waited for a second, listening intently to hear if anyone was approaching. He didn't hear a sound.

Relieved, he swallowed and placed the popcorn bag onto the spinning tray and closed the door. Popcorn usually took a couple of minutes to cook. He figured he'd play it safe and set the timer for twenty-two minutes. That way, if anyone somehow pieced together that he'd been the one responsible for the incident, he could say he thought he hit the two and must have accidentally hit it twice.

Again, plausible deniability.

He was about to hit the start button when he heard a clicking sound coming from outside the break room.

Sanders sighed, irritated at whoever was approaching. *Of course it couldn't be this easy,* he thought.

He hit the cancel button on the microwave on the off chance that whoever walked through the door might notice the time he'd entered on the keypad.

The footsteps drew closer, louder with every second.

A familiar face appeared in the doorway.

"Cliff?" Sanders asked, befuddled. "Why are you in here? You usually wait in the car."

"Sorry, sir. I didn't get my coffee this morning, and thought I'd come down for a to-go cup. I hope you don't mind."

Sanders played it off as best he could. His head gyrated nervously as he tried to shake it back and forth. "Mind? Why would I mind? By all means. I understand needing coffee as well as anyone."

"Thanks, boss," Cliff said. He took a few long strides across the room and drew close to Sanders.

"I could have brought you a cup, you know. Anytime you need anything, just ask, Cliff. You and I go back a long time. Always happy to help you."

Cliff offered a tenuous smile at the offer. He knew Sanders was being sincere. For all the politician's faults, the two had a good working relationship. There was something, however, in Cliff's expression that was different than normal. Sure, he was in an industry where smiling wasn't commonplace, at least not in his professional life, but the two had known each other for years. Now and then, Sanders would crack a joke or say something that would unexpectedly generate a grin from his bodyguard.

This smile was different, almost as if he really appreciated the offer. Or was it something different?

Sanders's mind raced through his index of memories for a similar expression. The only thing that kept coming up was a look some of his former girlfriends had given long ago, moments before they had said the famous words: "We need to talk."

Cliff wasn't breaking up with him. That much was true. Was he going to quit his job?

Sanders's intuition about body language and facial expressions wasn't as attuned as some, but it was better than average. Something told him that Cliff needed to get something off his chest, but what that was Sanders didn't know.

"You okay, Cliff? You look like something's bothering you."

"No, sir," Cliff regained his composure. Either he realized he was giving off a weird vibe or there was nothing wrong to begin with. "Just need some coffee. My day doesn't get going without it."

"Well, here. Let me get you a cup."

Sanders opened the door he'd looked into previously, remembering where the paper coffee cups were stashed, and reached up to take one. His torso twisted slightly as he took hold of it. His fingers wrapped around the rippled foam exterior of the cup. He started to take it down when he caught a sudden movement out of the corner of his eye. Then he felt something cold and hard press against his left temple.

He frowned, his eyebrows pinching together hard enough to crush a walnut between them. "Cliff, what are you doing with that? Is this some kind of a weird joke? That thing could go off."

The muzzle pressed deeper into the politician's skin, pushing hard on the bone beneath.

Sanders tried to turn to look into Cliff's eyes, hoping to get some kind of understanding as to exactly what was going on with his usually sane bodyguard.

"Cliff, seriously." Sanders knew the weapon was loaded and chambered. His security guy always kept it that way.

Cliff said nothing.

Sanders's discomfort swelled to irritation, bordering on anger. "I am not screwing around, Cliff. Put that weapon away. You're freaking me out." He tried to wriggle free, but Cliff held him tight with his free hand gripping the secretary of state's shoulder like a clamp.

"What is this about, Cliff? Did they tell you what I was—"

The gun fired with the slight twitch of Cliff's trigger finger. The cabinet and refrigerator instantly stained red and pink.

Cliff lowered the body to the floor, letting it come to a rest in a sprawling heap. He placed the weapon in Sanders's left hand, making sure the index finger was perfectly fitted into the loop that housed the trigger. Cliff removed his latex gloves and stuffed them into his back pocket. Alain would be pleased. Learning that the real location of the Ark was on Oak Island meant Sanders was an unneeded pawn and one that had to be sacrificed.

Cliff hurried back over to the door and rushed toward the stairs. Security would be on their way within seconds. Cliff had no intention of getting caught. He ran past the cameras without a second thought. They would do no good. He'd been wearing his disguise for years now, every time he picked up the politician.

He stopped at the stairs and waited for a moment until he heard footsteps. "Help!" he shouted. "I need backup down here! The secretary just shot himself!"

38

NEW YORK CITY

Sean rapped on the door in a rhythm he'd used for nearly twenty years. It wasn't a secret knock or anything like that. It was just something he liked to do. Maybe it was a calling card of sorts. He didn't know. Now it was more habit than anything else.

It took less than a minute before the door's half-dozen locks began clicking as the paranoid resident on the other side busily set to work to let his next guests in.

The door swung open, and a stone cold face stared out a Sean.

"Hello, Sean," James Hadley said.

"Hey, Jimmy." Sean clapped the guy on the shoulder and walked right by him, shoving him aside as he did so.

"Don't...call me that," James said, clearly irritated but far too afraid to do anything about it. It didn't take a genius to see which of the two was the alpha male.

James Hadley was a scrawny guy, a few inches under six feet and maybe 160 pounds dripping wet. His brown hair was shaggy, not unlike Sean's except for the color. His face displayed a few days' worth of stubble, though probably not for the reason Sean's did. Sean kept the five o'clock shadow as a preferred look. He got the feeling

Hadley was just lazy about hygiene. As Sean stepped into the younger man's apartment, that suspicion was confirmed.

The layout of the place was like many other apartments Sean had seen or lived in over the years: a small kitchen on the left, a living room straight ahead and to the right sharing the same open floor plan. Then there was a short hallway to the left with a bedroom on the right and the master at the end. The dark hardwood floors were difficult to see under the stacks of boxes and magazines strewn across it; the latter were mostly for console and computer video games.

Sean held the door open as Tara and Alex passed through.

"Who are they?" Hadley asked, suddenly suspicious.

"They're friends of mine and Tommy's," Sean answered. "You got a problem with that?" Sean made sure their host understood who was calling the shots, not just in this scenario but generally. Hadley had heard of Sean's exploits. He knew the former agent was still just as deadly as he'd been when he was Hadley's age. That threat loomed like an aura around Sean, an aura he did little to try to hide.

"Nope," Hadley said. "No problem."

"Tara, Alex, this is the Mad Hadder," Sean said, sticking out his hand as if showing off a new car.

Hadley cringed at the moniker but managed a timid, welcoming nod. He had no intention of correcting Sean and telling him he didn't like that nickname. "Tommy's in the back getting ready. I had to get him some clothes. He didn't think it was safe to go out on his own, but I wasn't going to let him keep wearing the same stinky stuff he had on when...when he escaped wherever it was he escaped from."

"So, he told you?"

"No," Hadley nervously shook his head. His voice had a constant quiver to it, like he was on edge all the time. Maybe it was insecurity. Perhaps he was on drugs. Sean didn't care. He figured it was just the way the guy talked. "No, I figured that part out. You don't get beat up like that and then come looking for a place to hide out unless someone is after you. I put two and two together when he asked if he could lie low here for a day or so."

Sean was impressed. He knew Hadley was smart. That much was

easy to assess. Sure, he'd had some good luck along the way that helped him find a few priceless artifacts, but the guy was far from stupid. His intuition in this case was spot on.

"And I appreciate your kindness," Tommy said from the other end of the hallway. He appeared a moment later, pulling on a hoodie over his T-shirt. "Thanks for the clothes, too, Hadder. Nice to get a shower and something clean to wear."

"Anything for you, Mr. Schultz." There was a creepy air of admiration in Hadley's voice, and the nervous crackle from before had disappeared.

"I told you, call me Tommy. Okay?"

Hadley swallowed and nodded. "Yes, sir. Whatever you say...Tommy."

"That's better." Tommy turned his attention to his friend. "Glad you made it out of Atlanta alive. I hope the lab is okay."

"It's fine," Sean said. "And we're good—thanks to Tara. She did some fancy shooting back there that saved our hides."

Tommy raised an eyebrow. "Not the first time." He changed the subject seamlessly. "So, we're heading to Oak Island." It wasn't a question. "I wondered about that. I always wondered if anyone would find something there. That pit is far too elaborate to be nothing more than a decoy."

"Or put there by nature," Hadley added.

"Correct."

The affirmation caused Hadley to blush. "So, what time do we leave?"

Sean winced. "Um...here's the thing, Hadder. We have to do this on our own. We can't risk...you getting hurt in the process. This is going to be dangerous. We're dealing with an ancient society of killers here."

"You guys seem to be okay. And the two of you were captured by them at one point." He pointed at Tara. "If she can take them on, so can I."

Tara scowled at the insinuation but kept her lips pressed tightly together.

"Easy, tiger," Sean said to Hadley. "She's well trained. I'd hate to let her loose on you."

Hadley sensed the threat and said nothing more.

"And at any rate," Tommy jumped back in, "I have a special assignment for you."

Hadley's spirits rose with his eyebrows. Sean, too, seemed surprised at the comment.

Tommy ignored his friend's questioning glance.

"Yep." He pulled a piece of paper out of the jeans Hadley bought for him and handed it to the younger man. Hadley took the paper and unfolded it. There was a sequence of numbers written down on it.

"What is it?" Hadley asked.

"That, my friend, is a cipher. The original is still in the lab in Atlanta, but I kept it up here," he tapped his skull, "in case I ever got a chance to bump into you again. I figure someone with your intellect can figure it out. If you do, I think it might be the key to unlocking an ancient treasure somewhere here in the United States."

Sean bit his lip, doing his best to keep quiet.

Hadley's eyes opened like twin volcanoes, ready to spew. His guests could see the excitement bubbling up inside him. "Are you serious? You want me to work on a project with you?"

Tommy nodded. "Just get to work on figuring out that translation. You know how to find me."

Hadley's head eagerly bobbed up and down. "You bet."

Tommy motioned for the others to leave and followed them out the door. He paused on the threshold and looked back at Hadley, who was staring at the paper, his head already running through a million possible answers. "Thanks again, James. I appreciate your help."

"Yes, sir. Anytime…Tommy."

Tommy closed the door and let out a sigh. He looked at Sean with daggers in his eyes. "Don't ever make me do that again," he hissed.

"Have a good time with your buddy?" Sean asked with a wink. He turned and started down the hallway with the kids in tow.

Tommy hurried to catch up. "You have no idea how annoying that guy is, especially living with him."

"Living with him? You were barely here less than a day, Schultzie. It couldn't have been that bad."

"He eats cereal for dinner, Sean. And you saw his place. It's a pigsty."

The group made their way down the stairs.

"The Assassins didn't find you, though, did they?"

"No," Tommy relented. "It was a good idea. It just sucked to be there with that little creep."

"You know, he's a big fan," Alex said, finally speaking up for the first time since getting his boss back.

"You think, Captain Obvious?"

Alex chuckled. "What was that sheet of paper you gave him anyway? Did you really have some code you discovered? I don't remember you mentioning anything about that to us."

Tara agreed. "Yeah, what's up with that?"

They rounded another corner in the stairwell and continued down to the ground floor. Tommy shot a look up above to make sure Hadley hadn't followed them to listen in on their discussion.

"You ever give a guy a fake name and number just to get him to leave you alone?"

A smirk spread across Tara's face.

"Well," Tommy said, "I just took it to the next level."

They emerged from the building and crossed the street to the SUV Sean had rented from the airport.

"What's the status on the bad guys?" Tommy asked as he climbed into the front passenger seat.

"As far as I know, they're already in Nova Scotia. It won't be easy. These guys are pros' pros."

"Yeah, but you have a plan, right?"

Sean confirmed the answer with a nod. "Yeah. I have a plan."

39

OAK ISLAND, NOVA SCOTIA

Alain ended the call and put the phone back in his coat pocket. A chilly, howling wind blew from the west, sending a blast of cold air across the few parts of skin not covered by his thick winter gear. He winced behind his sunglasses. None of the other men noticed, which was what he'd hoped.

They were all hardened against the elements and trained not to show even the slightest discomfort. The spitting rain hit their coats like liquid BBs, splashing and rolling off the waterproof fabric with no effect other than the irritation of being exposed to the elements. The gray soup above offered no relief in sight, which meant Alain and his men were going to have to simply deal with it.

There were no workers in sight on this day. The crews that spent so much time trying to figure a way down into the pit to extract its secrets were gone. The temporary office building the owners had set up in the middle of the island was devoid of any activity. No cars were parked in front of it, another sign that Alain and his men had the place to themselves.

Getting through the protective fence had been easy enough. There had been a guard—now dead—blocking their way. He'd been less trouble than an insect crawling around on a kitchen counter.

Alain stood with his back against the main building and stared out across the meadow at the giant hole in the ground. Two cranes were set up on opposing sides of the pit, surrounded by several other huge machines. Some dangled cables into the depths of the hole. Others had huge metal pipes attached to giant metal arms that loomed over the site.

"Is it done?" Tusun asked. He stood close to Alain, nearly touching shoulders. He didn't shiver or show any signs that the cold was bothering him, even though Alain knew it had to be.

"Yes. Sanders is dead. Apparent suicide. Our man in Washington got out safely and is on his way back to New York to join the others."

Alain brought several men with him to Oak Island but kept some in reserve back at their headquarters to guard the place. Many of his men had been killed in the last few days, something that hadn't happened in a long time—not since the Templars had ravaged their ancestral lands so many centuries ago.

"What's the plan, sir?" Tusun asked. It was something he'd been wondering about during the journey to the island.

Men had been trying to unearth the secrets of the pit for a few hundred years. Tusun knew that. His leader wouldn't be so brash as to think he could simply show up and the hole would magically reveal all to them. Alain had to have something in mind.

"Medar," Alain said, turning his head to the left. He planted his eyes on the shortest man in the group. Medar only stood a few inches over five feet. What he lacked in height, he made up for in ingenuity and tenacity. He was a fierce warrior and had been as successful in his missions as any other brother in the order.

"Yes, sir," Medar said, approaching with an eager but firm look on his face.

"You brought the suit?"

"Yes, sir."

"Good. Get ready. You're going in."

Medar trotted back behind the building to one of the SUVs parked there.

"What's he doing?" Tusun asked, still in the dark with the whole plan. Had he been able to make the journey in its entirety with his superior, he could have gleaned more information.

"We're going to drop Medar into the pit. Last we checked, the hole hadn't collapsed in recent months and is full of murky seawater. He won't be able to see much, which is why we've equipped his dive helmet with a special lens that renders objects in a digital view."

"Like virtual reality?"

"Exactly," Alain said with a nod. "The helmet is equipped with sensors that detect solid objects within the water. While his naked eyes will be all but useless down there, he'll be given a full digital rendering of anything below. That will enable him to reach the bottom of the shaft and, hopefully, recover anything that's down there."

Tusun frowned. "But the pit's bottom collapsed again months ago, didn't it?"

"Which is why I've equipped Medar with a special tool for that job. When he finds the bottom, he'll use that tool to dig through to the next level."

"Tool?"

"It's essentially an auger but designed specifically for this kind of task."

"Sounds dangerous." The irritated look from Alain caused him to pause. "Sir."

"Medar will be fine. He'll have plenty of air in four micro tanks that will enable him to maneuver in the tight confines of the shaft along with the auger. Many people have come close to reaching the bottom of the pit but always failed. Where they failed, we will not. Their issue was sight. We now have the technology to see without seeing."

Tusun continued to process the information. "Sounds like you thought of everything."

"I did think of everything, my good friend. You and I both knew that this location could be the resting place of the Ark. I knew it was a possibility long ago but wasn't willing to commit to it until I knew for certain. The idea of the Ark being here isn't a new idea. We made preparations for this long ago. Chance always favors the prepared mind, Tusun. That's why I had these tools created just in case."

Tusun gave an understanding nod. Now it made sense. "That's why you're in charge, Alain." Inside, though, questions simmered. One kept rising to the top: *What else is Alain not telling me?*

Alain accepted the compliment with a stoic, tight-lipped grin.

Several minutes passed before Medar returned wearing a gray dry suit. The water in the shaft would be far too cold for an ordinary wet suit. The dry suit would make plunging into the vertical channel a little trickier due to its bulk, but Alain was confident his man could do it. That's why he'd chosen the smallest of the bunch.

Alain turned to one of the other men. "Move the truck into place."

One of the men motioned to the driver of a heavy-duty pickup truck that had remained near the exit. The diesel motor rumbled then whined. The driver maneuvered the vehicle around until the tailgate was facing the opening to the shaft.

Alain waited until the truck was in place before he turned to the men surrounding him. Some were standing in the frigid rain. A few were next to him in the relative shelter of the building's overhang.

"Today," he began, "we take what is rightfully ours, something that our enemies have held on to for far too long."

The men roused into a cheer.

"Centuries ago, our forefathers fought the Templars in a holy war. They fought for justice and truth. But they were misguided."

Tusun's ears pricked. *What did he just say?*

"Their mission," Alain continued, "was dedicated to religion, to a cause they believed to be given them by almighty Allah. Perhaps they were right. Maybe Allah did commission them to this purpose. I, however, believe that you have suffered enough. You, my brothers, born from poverty, crime, and some of the worst places on Earth, deserve a taste of glory. We have all lived in servitude, and our brothers before us did the same throughout history. While I hope we have been blessed in our mission, I believe it is time that you reap the rewards of your sacrifice."

He looked out at his captivated audience, meeting the eyes of every man there with resolute conviction. All except Tusun.

"With this weapon, we will be the unchallenged power in the world. Nations will fall to their knees before us and give us whatever we desire to spare them from utter annihilation. You, my brothers, will be the wealthiest men on Earth. You deserve it. You have suffered enough. We honor our fallen with what we do now, by elevating the Order of Assassins to a level of power never before known on the planet." He paused and then nodded to Medar. "Let's begin."

The men rallied with applause, shouting cheers and praising their leader as they turned and made their way over to the shaft opening. Only one lingered behind, staying next to Alain.

"Sir?" Tusun said, snatching his superior's attention from the unfolding scene. "What are you talking about? We are servants of Allah. This...this speech you gave, it isn't right."

Alain's head snapped to his second-in-command. "You question my authority?"

Tusun clenched his jaw. "If it is against the will of God, then yes, Brother. I do. These things you say are...worldly. We were not meant to be of this world. Our sights must be higher. Our mission is to purify this place and bring humanity to a greater truth. It has always been so."

Alain heard the man's words and nodded. "Yes, Tusun. You're right. That was our original purpose. Haven't you sacrificed enough? Haven't our men? We came from nothing and have become one of the most powerful fighting forces in the world. Don't you want to have a taste of something good while we're here? Governments will pay us billions to keep from wiping them off the face of the earth. Once we've collected our ransom, then we can focus on the will of Allah. I, for one, am tired of a life of sacrifice. I'm ready for a taste of opulence."

Tusun frowned. His head turned back and forth slowly. The look of disgust he gave his leader said enough. His eyes searched Alain for a sign of hope, for any chance that all this new information was just a joke of some kind. He found none.

"You have lost your way, Brother," Tusun said. "This is not why we exist, to seek worldly pleasures and wealth. Our treasures await in heaven."

Alain turned back to look at the men who were busy making preparations for Medar's dive.

"I'm sorry to hear that, Tusun. You've been a loyal friend all these years. You, more than most, deserve a reward."

"Like I said, Brother," the word carried venom, "my reward is in paradise."

Alain pouted his bottom lip and nodded. "Very well. Then, by all means, have it now."

He twisted toward his comrade. The movement was subtle, but Tusun didn't anticipate it. A muted pop came from the pistol in Alain's hand. The storm and the noisy work going on by the pit covered up the rest of the sound. Tusun dropped to his knees, clutching the bleeding wound in his chest. The whites of his eyes burned bright with a fire of rage and surprise. Then he toppled over onto his face at Alain's feet.

Alain ticked his head to the side, staring down at the body. "Shame you couldn't see things my way, Brother. I suppose we'll both receive our rewards today."

He stuffed the weapon back in his coat and skipped down the steps, onto the gravel. The long cable was already hooked to a carabiner on Medar's harness. His air tanks and helmet were in place.

Alain strode over to the truck and flung open the door. One of his men was in the passenger seat with a laptop. The screen displayed the digital rendering of what Medar's helmet was transmitting.

"Everything ready?" Alain asked.

"Yes, sir."

"Let's proceed."

Alain narrowed his eyes against the blowing rain, leaning forward as he walked to the back of the truck. "You ready?" he shouted to Medar.

Medar gave a thumbs up.

"You're good to go, then. We're going to lower you down until you get to the water. Once you reach the surface, we'll give you slack."

Medar nodded.

The man in the dry suit walked over to the lip of the shaft. A metal ladder was fixed to the side, dropping down to a platform below. The scaffolding looked like it had been there a long time, possibly decades.

Medar took a deep breath and started to bend down to grab the loops at the top of the ladder. His body suddenly jolted, as if hit by some invisible force. He stood up straight again and turned to Alain, looking at him with a puzzled, pained expression. Then his head dipped, and his eyes found a hole in the dry suit. Crimson oozed from the tattered opening within seconds. Medar's eyes blurred. He blinked against the coming darkness, but it was in vain. His legs buckled, and he fell forward into the shaft. The cable went taught. His body jerked from the abrupt stop, then twisted and turned, bumping against the shaft's wall.

Alain and his men reacted instantly. His first thought went to Tusun, but a quick look to the porch told him his second was still there, unmoving.

The men fanned out as they'd done so many times before. Alain dove for cover under the pickup truck a second before a cacophony of gunfire erupted amid the sounds of wind and pouring rain.

He rolled to a stop, the gravel cutting into his skin. He ignored the minor pain and drew the weapon from his coat. Bullets smashed into the truck body and tires. Bits of gravel exploded around him.

Alain immediately realized the bitter, irritating truth.

They were under attack.

40

OAK ISLAND

"Hold your fire," Sean said into the radio clipped to his jacket. "Take cover again."

He knew Tommy and the other two would do exactly as he said within a fraction of a second.

They'd arrived at the scene too late, though he'd anticipated as much. Sean knew there was no way to catch up to Alain and his men. Preparation time, it seemed, had allowed Sean and his friends to at least get there before the Assassins began their operation.

He'd noted the pickup truck carrying the cable spool and immediately knew what it was for. He wasn't sure how the man in the dry suit was going to get deep enough into the pit to find anything, but that wasn't Sean's concern. The guy was the easiest target due to the suit's color.

Sean had punched a round through the guy's chest from a hundred yards away. He'd surprised even himself with such an accurate shot in these conditions, though he knew that wouldn't have been possible from much farther away. Only the best in the world could do such a thing, and Sean knew he wasn't that.

Once the man in the dry suit fell into the shaft, Tommy and the kids opened fire from their positions.

The four attackers had found the dead guard when they arrived at the island's gate. Sean was somewhat surprised Alain hadn't left anyone to guard the earth bridge to the island, but the Assassin was overconfident to the point of cockiness. Or maybe he was simply one of those people that had the strange desire to get caught. If not caught, perhaps he just wanted a fight.

Either way, Sean wasn't going to let the opportunity slip away. He'd considered going in by boat, but rough seas would have made that difficult, even dangerous. They would also have been easily spotted in a vessel tossing around in the tall swells, despite the cover of night.

Sean crouched down behind a big rock on the edge of the shore. The raging water splashed on the pebbles and stones behind him. He blinked rapidly to keep the steady downpour out of his eyes, but it was an effort in futility and reinforced how fortunate he'd been with his kill shot.

Alain and his men didn't panic. They'd reacted quickly, spreading out and seeking cover from the ambush. The leader dove under the pickup truck along with one other gunman. Tommy and the two kids peppered their position with bullets until Sean gave the cease-fire. Then the island returned to the constant drone of rain.

The plan was to wait for the authorities to arrive, though there was no telling how long that would take. The local police wouldn't be much help. The town only had a few cops on the payroll, and they were ill equipped to deal with a threat of this magnitude.

Sean looked out across the bay. No sign of the cavalry. He glanced back over his shoulder. No headlights bobbed along the road leading to the bay.

He knew Emily had made the call to the agencies that could best assist them, but there was red tape, chains of command, and intel that had to be evaluated before those in charge would make a decision. Sean didn't want to sit out here for hours. He knew their siege could only last so long. Eventually, Alain and his men would strike back.

"What should we do?" Tommy said into the radio.

"Just keep an eye on them, Schultzie. If one of them moves and you have a clear shot, take it. Otherwise, don't give away your position. Our best chance here is to wait on reinforcements. We just have to keep them pinned down."

Tommy knew the plan. They'd discussed it before arriving. Still, conditions seemed to be getting worse, and there were more enemies than they'd anticipated.

Sean stayed low behind his rock. He peered out at the clearing where massive machines surrounded the pit. All of the Assassins were out of sight now, each probably waiting for a mistake by one of the attackers.

But Sean, Tommy, and the kids had the area surrounded; one positioned at each corner of the island to ensure none of the Assassins could escape.

A few minutes passed, and no one moved. Something was wrong. Why weren't Alain's men scrambling to make a move? They wouldn't just sit there for long. Would they?

Sean got his answer within seconds of the question popping into his head.

Several tall light posts cast an eerie orange glow on the area. Sean saw an arm move in a dramatic arc. Then he caught a glimpse of something flying through the air toward the driveway between him and Tommy.

Sean knew it was a grenade of some kind, though he wasn't sure if it was an explosive, a flash bang, or a smoke bomb.

He ducked down and waited. A searing white light flashed into the sky, accompanied by a loud pop.

"Flash bangs," Sean said into his mic. "Stay down. They're trying to draw us out."

"Roger that," Tommy said.

Sean peeked around his rock and saw more of the Assassins tossing grenades from behind trucks, machinery, and stacks of metal containers.

"Here come some more," Sean warned.

This time, however, there was no pop, no flash of bright white light. Sean frowned and risked another look into the clearing. He realized in an instant what the Assassins were up to.

The canisters opened in a wide circle that surrounded the pit and all of Alain's men. Gray smoke poured out of the devices, enveloping the entire clearing in a hazy shroud. Sean's visibility diminished to the point he couldn't even make out the outline of the pickup truck.

"Smoke grenades," he confirmed the obvious.

"I can't see anything," Tommy said.

The artificial fog was blowing all around him.

A bad feeling sank into Sean's gut. He knew what Alain and his men would do. The Assassins realized they were surrounded on the perimeter. The only way to win the fight would be to breach that perimeter and take out the threat, working their way around the shore until the ambushers were dead. The smoke from the grenades was being blown to Tommy's position, giving the Assassins the perfect cover to reach the edge and begin their systematic executions.

"Tommy, you have to move," Sean said, his voice suddenly urgent.

"What? You said to—"

"Get out of there. Now!"

Sean stood up, exposing himself to the gunmen. He looked out to the right where Tommy had been hiding behind a similar rock. His friend was gone, engulfed in a cloud of smoke. Sean turned his attention back to the center of the clearing. The killers would be on the move, slipping to the shore under the cover of man-made fog.

He had to act fast. While he knew Tommy wouldn't ignore his urgent order, there was still more danger. Even if Tommy was safe, Tara and Alex would be watching from their positions, unaware that the gunmen were circling around to take them out.

Sean couldn't let that happen. He wouldn't.

He burst from his cover and pumped his legs. Rain splashed against his face. Gravel kicked up behind his boots. The rifle in his hands dripped with water. The first canisters were running out of fuel and the stream of smoke dwindled.

He caught sight of movement to the right of where he figured the pit was located. Then glimpsed a man running from the pickup truck.

Sean raised his weapon, still on the run, and fired. The gun recoiled against his shoulder as he fired again and again. He didn't know if he was even coming close to the target. That didn't matter. He had to draw their attention away from Tommy and the others.

"They're moving to the shore, following the smoke screen," Sean said into his radio. "Fire into the smoke. Look for any signs of movement."

41

OAK ISLAND

Alain heard the shots from behind and skidded to a stop in the gravel. One of his men ran by, heading toward the shore, and stopped next to him.

Something was wrong. If it was Wyatt and his friends, they'd have positioned themselves along the edge of the island to prevent escape.

These new shots were coming from much closer.

That could mean only one thing. Wyatt was moving in.

Were these amateurs trying to squeeze the noose, like a python constricting its prey?

Surely not.

Suddenly, one of Alain's men stumbled and fell to the ground. Alain took a knee and saw the mortal wound in the guy's back.

Alain winced.

His moment of painful regret didn't last long. More gunfire erupted from seemingly everywhere around him. Bullets whizzed by. One struck the ground next to his left leg. He jumped but didn't panic.

He looked back toward the shore and saw two of his men cut down, staggering forward as their momentum carried them to the ground.

How could this have happened? Wyatt and his little group of untrained, undisciplined companions had gotten the drop on them. Alain wondered if his own confidence was to blame. No. He'd done everything as his master would have, to the letter.

He heard his men returning fire, their weapons echoing like roaring thunder across the island and the surrounding bay. They would be slaughtered, undone by their only means of escape in the shroud of smoke.

A dagger of pain stabbed at Alain's heart. He loved his brothers. He didn't want to leave them behind, but he had no other choice. The keys would still be in the pickup truck. He could escape. There were still a few canisters dumping smoke into the air. If he hurried, he could make it.

Alain didn't think any longer. He sprang from his position and retreated back toward the truck. He couldn't see more than a few feet in front of him, but he knew he was going in the right direction. He started seeing shovels and other tools he'd passed just moments before, lying on the ground. The firefight continued behind him, though with every passing second there was one fewer gun in the battle.

He saw a yellow power cord lying on the ground and knew he was close to the truck. He'd seen the same cord a few moments prior. As he was about to slow his pace to prevent running head-long into the truck, a figure appeared in the haze right in front of him.

He ran into the apparition and fell onto his back, like he'd just hit a wall.

His weapon jarred from his hand and hit the gravel with a clack. He felt around on the ground, sifting through the loose rocks with his fingers.

Then he saw the body hovering over him. It was Sean Wyatt.

Sean looked down at the man. Adrenaline coursed through him. He held the assault rifle in his hands with the barrel pointed down at Alain's head.

On the other side of the gravel lot, Tommy slid another magazine into his weapon and squeezed the trigger. The last traces of smoke blew clear, and now the remaining gunmen scrambled for cover.

He took out two more Assassins and emptied his magazine trying to eliminate one more. The man dove behind a jeep parked off to the side.

Tommy rushed out of his cover behind a stack of pallets and rushed toward a steel drum in the clearing. Another gunman appeared to the right. Tara spotted him and whipped her weapon around, unleashing two rounds that hit the guy in the gut and chest.

Tommy leaned around the barrel and was greeted by a flurry of bullets. The rounds struck the drum, plunking into it and rattling to the bottom. Tommy ducked back for cover and motioned to the other two to circle around. Alex took the lead, rushing around the edge of the clearing with Tara right behind him. Tommy waited a few seconds then stuck his weapon around the drum and squeezed the trigger. The gun clicked three times before he remembered he'd spent the magazine's contents on the last few targets.

He cursed himself under his breath and tossed the weapon aside. He still had the pistol in its holster and two additional clips on the belt.

He took out the gun and poked it around the edge of the drum. The enemy opened fire again before Tommy could get off a single shot. Instead, he withdrew once more, hoping none of the incoming rounds would hit his hand or wrist. He gulped and breathed heavily.

"I hate gunfights," he said to himself as he dug his heels into the gravel.

He raised the pistol over his head, aimed it in the direction of the gunman, and squeezed the trigger. The gun popped four times before he pulled it back down. Tommy had no idea if the rounds were even close to the mark or not. He didn't care. His only purpose for firing was to buy Tara and Alex enough time to flank the gunman and take him out.

Thunderous gunfire boomed from Tommy's left. He peeked around the steel drum enough to see Tara and Alex firing at the last Assassin. From his position, Tommy could see the guy spin around and try to defend himself, but his reaction was too late. His body snapped in different directions with every bullet that struck him until he fell backward onto the gravel and stopped moving.

Tommy breathed heavily and then climbed out of his spot. He looked over at the kids with relief in his eyes and gave them a wave. He heard something behind him and spun around, ready to shoot at whoever was coming. There was no one near him. The sound he heard was Sean across the clearing, tossing his rifle to the side.

Sean stared down at Alain as his gun rattled on the gravel and came to a rest. Then Sean removed the pistol from Alain's holster, loosed the magazine, and flicked all the rounds out of it, rendering the weapon useless.

"Get up," Sean said.

Alain's eyes narrowed, and he scrambled to his feet. He didn't take a defensive posture. No martial arts stance or boxing position. It was almost as if he hung there, in the rain, a tree in the storm.

"It's just you and me now, Alain," Sean said. He put his hands out wide. "All your men are dead. Your quest is at an end." He caught a glimpse of Tommy approaching with a handgun extended with both hands. Sean gave his friend a quick shake of the head and held up his palm, signaling that this fight would end the old-fashioned way.

The kids trotted up but halted a few dozen yards away at the sight of Sean's instruction.

"This is between me and him," Sean said.

Alain shook his head. "You don't want to do this, Wyatt. You can't win."

"Neither can you."

Alain offered a shrug. "Maybe. I kill you, and then your friends here kill me. Fair enough, but I'm gonna take you with me."

He lunged forward and punched at Sean's face with a tight fist. Sean ducked left and used his left hand to strike Alain's wrist. The attacker's hand shot down for a second, and Sean reached to grab it, using a move he'd done so many times before to break an opponent's arm. Alain sensed the counter, however, and kicked backward at Sean, hitting the opponent's knee with the heel of his boot. Sean grimaced in sudden agony as the cartilage and ligaments stretched inside the joint.

He dropped to his good knee and managed to block another kick from Alain's other leg, grabbing the ankle and lifting it high in a swift motion. Alain flipped head over heels, landing on his back with a sudden and jarring thud. A few loose pieces of gravel trickled out from under him. He blinked fast, trying to shake off the stunned feeling in his mind, and rolled to his side, ready for another attack.

Sean was still reeling from the needling pain in his knee. He managed to push himself up off the ground and take a step toward Alain. Forward movement was fine, but he had a bad feeling one of the ligaments was torn, which would make lateral moves problematic.

Alain surged forward again. This time, his fists flew at Sean's face and gut like jackhammers. Time and again, Sean blocked and countered but couldn't land a blow. Finally, one of Alain's attacks sneaked through and landed on Sean's jaw. His head rocked back. Then he took a shot to the abdomen, another to the cheek. Again and again, Alain pummeled him, driving Sean backward in what looked like a drunken retreat.

Sean felt something against his back and realized he'd hit the hood of the pickup truck. Alain reared back and launched a haymaker. His knuckles drove into Sean's jaw and sent him sprawling onto the hood, only to slide off a second later into a heap on the ground.

Alain loomed over him, breathing heavily from the exertion. Sean lay still for a moment, and Tommy wondered if he was unconscious —or worse. He aimed his weapon at the back of Alain's skull and tensed the trigger with his index finger.

Tommy couldn't take seeing his friend get the beating of a lifetime, but it was what Sean asked for. He felt like a boxing trainer, standing outside the ring and holding a towel that could finish the fight if he just tossed it over the ropes. Something kept him from doing it. What it was, he didn't know.

"Is that it?" Alain asked. Spittle sprayed from his lips and mingled with the rain. "Is that all you have for me, Sean Wyatt? I'm glad you killed my men. I don't need weaklings working for me. If they could be so easily bested by you, I'd be surprised if a little schoolgirl couldn't take them out. Perhaps I've been too easy on them. I suppose it doesn't matter. We're all dead men anyway. The second I end your life, your friend back there with a gun pointed at my head will take mine. An eye for an eye. Fitting, isn't it, seeing that we're all after a biblical relic? A biblical parable for a biblical treasure."

He turned his head and looked at Tommy over his shoulder. "What are you going to do with the Ark once you have it, eh? Take it to your museum? Put it in your lab to study it? Or are you going to sell it to someone? No, that isn't your style. You like the fame and glory, don't you? That's what you're all about. You're going to prop it up in that little building of yours in Atlanta for all the world to see. The great Tommy Schultz and his agency will show off the greatest find in all of history."

Tommy sneered but said nothing.

"You're no different than me," Alain said. "All of you. You're so high and mighty, but you all want the same thing. You want the world to kneel before you and beg for scraps from your table."

"That's not why we do it," a voice grumbled from behind Alain. He snapped his head around and saw Sean standing there with blood trickling out of his nose and from the corner of his lips. His face was swelling. One of his eyes had a big gash under it and was nearly swollen shut.

Alain chuckled. "And here I thought you were dead. You will be soon enough. And then I suppose I'll join you."

Sean shook his head. "No."

Alain punched hard at Sean's head, but this time Sean dodged it by an inch and swung his elbow into Alain's kidneys. The Assassin fell forward and hit the truck's grill, but he didn't fall, instead pushing away from the vehicle and launching himself back at Sean for another attack.

His fists were a blur, using a combination of boxing and kung fu. Sean blocked, parried, and deflected every one, now letting the attacker wear himself down. Alain grew frustrated and angrier. He swept his leg out to strike Sean in the other knee, but Sean spun clear. Alain saw the move, planted the first kicking foot into the gravel, and jumped into the air, whipping the other heel around in a Brazilian roundhouse. Sean ducked the kick and punched hard with the heel of his hand, landing the blow in Alain's sternum.

The strike knocked the wind out of the Assassin and dropped him to his knees, and he clutched his abdomen to get precious air back into his lungs. He gasped and heaved, but none would come.

"Speaking of being on your knees," Sean said.

Headlights appeared at the other end of the land bridge connecting the island to the mainland. Blue lights spun on some of the approaching vehicles. Sean and the others knew that the ones without emergency lights would be Canadian special agents. Their sirens couldn't be heard yet over the howling wind and the rain splattering around them.

Alain finally caught his breath and saw the lights in the distance.

Sean lowered his fists and relaxed for a second.

"Friends of yours?" Alain said with disdain in his tone.

"It's over," Sean replied in the smuggest tone he could muster. "Your order is done. Your men are dead. You're going to jail."

Alain snickered. "Not likely, Sean. I have connections you couldn't dream of. I'll never spend a single night in a prison cell. I'll be out before you know it, and when that happens I'm coming after you."

Sean let a grin crease his bloody lips. "I don't think so."

Sean felt the same odd rush course through him that he'd sensed before when he killed one of Alain's men with his bare hands. It was ancient, barbaric, the urge to kill. He tried to fight it, but the look on Alain's face begged him to do it. For all his bragging, Alain probably knew his best option was death, right then and there.

Bloodlust flooded Sean's mind. He thought of everything this man had done, all the people he'd killed that Sean didn't even know about. There were probably hundreds, some of them innocent. He could see it in Alain's eyes, those cold, vapid orbs that held no regard for life.

Sean stepped close and raised his hand, opening the palm to the sky and exposing the bridge of it to Alain. "You know, when this part of my hand strikes your nose, it will drive the bone into your brain and kill you almost instantly."

Alain's teeth flashed like a shark swimming in a bloody ocean. Sean grabbed the back of the Assassin's head, gripping his soaking-wet hair and tilting the skull back to make the nose an easier target.

"Sean?" Tommy said. "What are you doing? The cops are almost here. Let them take care of it."

"No, Tommy. I want this."

"Sean, don't."

A sickly laugh escaped Alain's mouth. "Go ahead, Sean. Do it. Take my life and become one of us."

"Don't do it, Sean!" Tommy shouted above the rain. The sirens now mingled with the sounds of the storm. "It's what he wants!"

"It's what I want, too, Schultzie," Sean said in a tone his friend had never heard before. It was full of wicked delight. "It's what I'm good at. It's what I enjoy."

"Sean?"

He raised his hand higher, feeling the rush of the kill pumping through his veins. Then he let go of Alain's hair and kicked the man in the chest. Alain went sprawling onto his back, legs bent at an awkward angle.

Sean lowered his right hand and gasped for air. He crumpled to the ground, bracing himself with his left palm.

Alain's laughter heightened. Tommy looked down at his friend, momentarily distracted. He didn't see Alain reach into his belt underneath his jacket and pull out a small pistol.

"Time to die, Sean Wyatt." He raised the pistol. Tommy saw it a second too late and whirled back to the target.

A weapon fired, but it wasn't Tommy's or Alain's.

The side of Alain's head burst, and the man dropped to the ground in an instant, dead.

Tommy rushed over to the body and kicked the gun away, a pointless gesture considering the wound to the guy's skull. Then he looked around for the shooter. His eyes darted to Tara and Alex, but they shook their heads. Then Tommy saw the man lying on the porch forty feet away. He was facedown with a pistol in his hand, arm extended. A thin trail of smoke wafted from the muzzle and disappeared into the rain. Tusun closed his eyes and allowed the last breath to leave his lungs.

Tommy tossed his pistol aside and knelt down next to his friend, putting his arm around him. "You okay, buddy?"

Sean was shaking. His hands, head, lips, everything trembled.

"No," Sean said. "I'm not."

Tommy frowned as the kids hurried over to join them. "What was that all about, man? I've never seen that side of you before. It was like—"

"It was the real me, Schultzie." Sean's voice shook. "I'm a killer. And I like it."

"No, you're not, Sean. You left that life behind. It's okay." Tommy embraced his friend with one arm, kneeling awkwardly at his side.

"I never left it behind, Tommy. Something inside of me...enjoys the killing."

It was the single most disturbing thing Tommy ever heard out of his friend's mouth.

"No," Tommy said. "You could have killed Alain, but you didn't. You stopped yourself."

Sean's head still shook side to side. "It feels so powerful. So...so strong. I feel like—"

"Like a god?" Tommy finished the sentence.

Sean looked up into his friend's eyes. "Yes."

Tommy nodded. "I know, but in the end, you did the right thing. You spared an evil man's life."

Sean gave a nod and then looked back at the soaked gravel between his feet. "I don't want to kill anymore, Schultzie. I've become a monster. I don't want to be one."

"I know, buddy. It's okay. We can deal with it." He cradled his friend's head and stared him in the eyes. "Together. Okay?"

Sean nodded after a second of thought. "Okay."

42

WASHINGTON DC

Secretary of State Darren Sanders was given a hero's funeral. The nation mourned the leader in the press and across social media. Tributes were paid on nearly every television station, web site, and print publication.

The truth about his death was never released.

The story given to the world was that he was found unresponsive in the break room of the White House, the result of a massive stroke. It wouldn't do to have the enemies of the United States knowing that a secret order of killers had managed to breach security and get into the president's dwelling.

President Dawkins delivered a moving speech during the memorial service. Tears welled in nearly every eye as he praised Sanders for his ambition, tenacity, and the courage to always speak his mind even if the opinion clashed with the most powerful man in the free world.

Sean and Tommy had been invited to the funeral by the president, an invitation no one could turn down, though Sean wasn't sure why their presence was requested.

He stood toward the back of a huddled mass of people as a priest performed the last rites, motioning his hand over the casket. Sean knew very few of the people in attendance would understand the Latin slipping from the priest's lips.

Tommy introduced Sean to a new line of weapons he and the other agents in IAA would be using from then on. They were non-lethal, high-tech weapons that could take down enemies as effectively as normal guns, without the need to kill. While Sean knew that the time might come when he might have to take another life, it made him feel better that it didn't have to be the first option. For now.

He'd begin seeing a therapist the following Monday to work through the feelings he'd had during the events of the previous days. It was only the second time in his life he'd seen a shrink.

Sean squinted his eyes against the bright sunlight. For a funeral, the day was anything but dreary. There wasn't a cloud in the azure sky above. The blazing yellow sun covered the congregation with a warm blanket of light, cutting away the last remnants of winter.

"Good group of people," Sean whispered to Tommy. It was the second time he'd made the comment: once here, once at the church where the primary service was held.

"Yeah, you mentioned that." Tommy breathed, trying not to draw attention to himself.

An older woman in a black dress with a crimson jacket glared at him over her shoulder, giving Tommy her best shushing librarian look.

Tommy's eyes flicked up to the sky, and the woman turned around. He wanted to punch his friend in the shoulder. Sean had always gotten him in trouble, ever since they were kids.

Some things, it seemed, never changed.

"You just got me in trouble again," he said, leaning close enough so that only Sean could hear.

Sean's lips creased to a wide grin. "Sorry." He fought off a chuckle. Laughing during a somber moment such as this would be against almost every social convention.

He instead focused on the crowd of people hovering around the grave. Most of them were fellow politicians. Sanders, it seemed, didn't have much family, if any. He had no kids, no wife, and his parents had

passed long ago, or so Sean assumed. He did have plenty of coworkers, however, and they'd come out in droves, even his enemies on
Capitol Hill. Those, Sean assumed, were there for the public, a little
trick to boost their approval ratings to the constituents.

The two friends stayed until the priest finished the last rites, and
then they turned away as the casket was lowered into the ground.
President Dawkins was near the front of the gathering, standing close
to the grave. His security detail was surrounding both him and the
property, perpetually on high alert.

Sean and Tommy would talk to Dawkins later, or so Sean
thought. They'd become good friends over the years, which was a
little crazy to think about; that the president was a personal friend.
Not many people throughout American history could say that.

The two were walking back to their car, making their way through
the maze of headstones, when Dawkins's voice surprised them both.

"Fellas?"

Sean and Tommy spun around, both recognizing the commander
in chief's voice.

"Yes, sir?" they said at the same time.

"At ease, soldiers," Dawkins said with a grin. "It's me."

"Sorry. Lot of people around, sir," Sean said. "Force of habit."

Dawkins gave an understanding nod. "I have a friend that would
like to meet you."

"A friend?" Tommy asked.

Dawkins's head bobbed once. "Yes. He's in that limo over there."
His hand extended and pointed at a long black limousine parked on
the edge of the pavement.

Sean frowned. "What's this about?"

"He's a good friend of mine, Sean. You can trust him."

Sean realized his tone had sounded a bit suspicious. It was a total
accident. Or maybe he was always like that. "Sorry. Another force of
habit."

"No worries," Dawkins said with a grin. "I know your car is here,
but he'd like to take you for a ride. There's something he wants to
discuss with you. Apparently, it's pretty important."

Sean and Tommy continued staring at the limousine, wondering who was behind the dark-tinted windows. Sean shrugged. "Okay, sir. But if we end up with concrete boots at the bottom of the Potomac, I'm going to be irritated with you."

Dawkins laughed. "You'll be fine; I assure you."

The two strolled over to the limo and paused on the edge of the grass. The back door flung open, and they saw a pair of legs in black pants on the other side. An older man with slicked back silver hair and a tanned, smooth face leaned forward.

"Gentlemen? Please, get in."

Sean's alarm bells were going off in his head, but he'd been given assurance by the president that all would be fine. Dawkins wouldn't mislead him.

They climbed into the car, and the driver rushed around to close the door. It slammed shut as Tommy wriggled into the leather seat across from their mysterious host.

"I must say, it is an honor to meet the two of you." There was no insincerity in the man's voice. His tone was pleasant, sprinkled with just enough rasp to make him sound more masculine.

"I'm sorry," Sean said. "What's your name?"

The man smiled a broad, pleased smile. "My name is Daniel Jacobson." The car started moving, and soon they were out on the main road.

"What's this about?" Tommy asked. "Are we in some kind of trouble? You don't work for the IRS, do you?"

Jacobson's grin stretched farther. "No. I'm not with the IRS. Are you having some kind of trouble with them?"

Tommy shook his head. "No, but no one really knows they are until they're told they are."

Jacobson chuckled. "Very true. No, I'm not with them. I represent another organization."

Sean's brow furrowed. "Another government agency?"

"Not exactly."

He let his answer linger in the cabin for a few seconds before he went on. The driver turned to the left and continued down the next street.

"I'm with an organization you probably know about on some level, though I suspect what you know is what most of the population knows."

Sean and Tommy both leaned forward a couple of inches. Their interest spiked.

Jacobson went on. "I am the head of the Fraternal Order of Freemasons."

The two friends frowned and sat back in their seats.

"I thought the grand master of that order was someone else. His name escapes me, but I've seen him on television. He did a special on the History Channel once, answering questions about the temple and all that."

"A ruse," Jacobson said. "All part of a greater plan. That man, Mark Westmoreland, does play an important role in our organization, but it is an illusion. Smoke and mirrors."

"Why?" Sean blurted. "You guys up to no good?"

Jacobson's smile softened, and he shook his head. "Not at all, Sean. Quite the contrary. We're up to the greatest good of all."

"And what's that?"

"Protecting the greatest weapon ever made by man."

The two guests leaned up again, waiting for him to say it.

"We're the guardians of the Ark of the Covenant."

Chills ran through Sean and Tommy. Their skin instantly broke out with goose bumps. The hair on their necks raised.

Jacobson sensed their emotions and thoughts. "I know it's a lot to take in. Which is why I wanted to bring you here."

The limo turned into a driveway connected to a gray nondescript building. A garage door opened, and the car pulled inside. Sean looked out the back window as the door closed behind them. They were on the outskirts of the city, close to the river. That was all he knew.

"You'll be fine, Sean. I know you like to have a grasp on your surroundings in all situations. You're not in danger. I have something I want you to see."

Tommy's hopes vaulted into the stratosphere. "The Ark?"

Jacobson guffawed. "No, unfortunately, that won't be possible. And quite frankly, it's for the best."

The door opened, cutting off his next comment. He stepped out and waited until the other two joined him in the garage.

The vast space stretched at least a hundred feet to the back wall and was at least that wide, capable of holding dozens of cars. Maybe more.

"What is this place?" Tommy wondered.

"This," Jacobson said with hands out wide, "is where we keep the archives."

"Archives?"

"Of the order."

He led the way to the other side of the room where two steps met a door. The driver was already standing there, turning the knob to let them in. The men made their way inside and were greeted by a stunningly bland hallway. The gray walls were dotted with simple brushed metal sconces but featured no pictures or shelves of any kind. For an archive, this place seemed more like the hall of a hospital or an asylum.

Jacobson turned to the right and started walking. His shiny leather shoes tapped on the concrete floor with every step, echoing the sound down the corridor.

"You two are probably wondering why you're here, yes?" Jacobson asked.

"Yes, sir," Sean confirmed as he and Tommy hurried to keep up with the man's long strides. "That's an understatement."

They reached an arch in the wall to the left and passed through. On the other side, the next room was just as bland as the first, except the vaulted ceiling was three stories up and there were rows upon rows of books. On the main floor, directly in front of the three men, were a dozen airtight glass vaults. Each had a vent protruding from the top. Inside, more shelves contained books that looked as old as time, along with scrolls, other various artifacts, and some metal boxes.

Jacobson stopped and looked out at the room with a hint of pride in his eyes. "We've been keeping the location of the Ark a secret since shortly after it was brought to the New World. It has been safe all this time, until recently, when a threat arose."

The guests said nothing.

"The Order of Assassins has been after the Ark since their beginning. When the Knights Templar discovered it under the temple in Jerusalem, they knew it would become a target for the enemy. The Assassins came from a long line of jealous men. They believed it was their birthright to possess the Ark, part of a promise given to Abraham's first son, Ishmael, that God would make of him a great nation. They've been trying to not only level the playing field ever since but to dominate it. For thousands of years, there has been a balance to the great conflict between the sons of Abraham. The Ark holds the power to destroy that balance."

Sean and Tommy listened intensely.

"The Templars," Jacobson continued, "knew that not even they could possess the Ark. Its power was too great, and they believed in the balance, even if it meant the war between the factions would never end."

"So," Tommy finally spoke up, "the Knights Templar became the Freemasons?"

Jacobson flashed what had quickly become a familiar grin. "No, Tommy. The Knights are gone. Their order has all but vanished. Many years ago, one of our order learned of the location of the Ark. He took it upon himself to unearth it and bring it to a place where it could never be found, where it would forever be safe."

Sean frowned. He and Tommy both had a million questions running through their head.

"Over here," Jacobson said, with a hint of mischief in his voice. He motioned for the two to follow him to a door off to the side of the vacuous room.

They walked across the expansive floor and entered a small

chamber where more books lined the walls. A large, shiny table stood in the center. On the back wall, the shelving stopped, and the surface was bare except for one thing: a painting. It featured the first president of the United States presiding over a ceremony.

"October 13," Sean whispered. Chills coursed through him. Tommy experienced the same.

"That's why Lafayette wrote that date in his journal."

Jacobson confirmed the statement with a nod.

"October 13 was the date the Templars were nearly wiped out in France."

"And the date," Tommy added, "that George Washington laid the cornerstone of the White House."

"Correct," Jacobson said.

"I don't know why we didn't see the connection before."

Tommy was dazed by the incredible revelation.

"But it makes perfect sense," Sean said.

"Absolutely," Jacobson agreed. "Washington knew that, sooner or later, someone would stumble upon the hiding place of the Ark. As elaborate as the Oak Island trap is, someone would eventually figure out how to bypass it."

"So the Ark *was* there?"

"Yes. Washington knew it wouldn't be safe there forever." Jacobson paused. "But the White House is one of the most secure pieces of property in the world."

"Except for 1812," Tommy chimed.

"Yes. The British nearly ruined Washington's plan, though it is doubtful they had any idea what lay beneath the mansion."

Sean was almost in a trance. "It makes so much sense now. One nation, literally under God, protected by the most powerful relic of all time."

"Indeed. Washington believed that the Ark would not only be safe there but that by possessing it the United States would become the most powerful nation in the free world, a light to the rest of the planet. It would seem, for the better part of our young history, that his assessment was correct."

The room fell into silence. Sean and Tommy kept staring at the painting of the laying of the White House cornerstone.

"A nod to the Templars," Jacobson said, a heap of admiration in his tone. "He chose that date specifically to honor them."

"Honor," Sean said. "Why do you honor us with this knowledge? Aren't you afraid we'll go out and tell the world? You've kept this secret for so long."

Jacobson sighed. "No, I'm not worried. You see, you can never leave this place again."

He waited until sudden fear crept into his guests' eyes. Then he burst out laughing. "I'm messing with you."

Tommy and Sean began laughing uneasily.

"I am bestowing this knowledge upon you because you two helped defeat enemies of the order. You defended the Ark against evil. For that, you have earned the right to know the truth. It is the way the Templars would have wanted it. And it is the way I choose."

Sean and Tommy swallowed hard. There were so many questions they wanted to ask but didn't know where to start.

"Unfortunately, I have to be going. I'm a very busy man."

"We can imagine," Sean said.

"However, I am going to give you one final gift before my driver takes you back to your car."

"What's that?"

"You may have one hour here in our archives. Not a second more. Search for anything you desire. I trust that you will take the same care of our records that you have with everything else in the historical realm."

Jacobson walked out of the room and headed toward the main door, leaving Tommy and Sean with mouths hanging wide open.

"So, you're just going to leave us here?" Tommy asked.

"For one hour," Jacobson held up a finger and kept walking without turning back.

He disappeared out of the main chamber.

The two friends kept staring at the door until they were certain he wasn't going to come back.

Tommy looked across his shoulder at Sean. "Dude, can you believe this? This is incredible!"

Sean shook his head. "No," he said in a reverent tone, "I can't."

Tommy walked out into the big room and spun around, trying to figure out what he wanted to see first. He nearly ran over to one of the giant glass vaults and stared inside at the shelves of volumes, documents from ancient times long forgotten.

Sean stood alone for a moment. He took in the contents of the room with astounded appreciation.

"You okay?" Tommy asked, noticing something was off with his friend.

"Yeah," Sean said. "I'm good. I just think...I dunno, some things are better left to the imagination."

Tommy frowned. "What do you mean?"

"I mean, all these secrets kept in this place, protected for centuries by these guys. Honestly, I think they should stay secrets."

Tommy understood what his friend meant. "The best part of Christmas is not knowing what's behind the wrapper."

"Right."

"And when you try to peek, it's disrespectful to your parents and to yourself."

"Right again."

"So...what do we do?"

Sean flashed his normal, mischievous smirk. There was a glimmer in his eye. "We leave the mysteries that have already been found to those who protect them. And we search for the ones that are still out there."

THANK YOU

I just wanted to take a second to say thanks for reading my book. You could have chosen to spend your time with a million other stories and you chose mine. For that I am honored.

If you are new to my stories, swing over to ernestdempsey.net to join the VIP Reader List. All you have to do is enter your email to join the VIP group. You'll also get exclusive content like video interviews, free unedited chapters, and much more! Plus, you'll receive a FREE short story that isn't sold anywhere in stores.

Once again, thanks for reading this story. Please take the time to leave an honest review on your retailer of choice. Those reviews are helpful to other readers and to authors too.

Have a great day!

Ernest

AUTHOR NOTES

This story was an absolute blast to write. As with all my works in regards to history, there is a good bit of fiction and some truth all mixed together.

As to the story itself, no one really knows what happened to the Ark of the Covenant. The Bible documents a great many details about this relic from the time of its creation until the period when it was moved into Solomon's Temple.

The archives I mentioned at the end of the story are completely fictional, at least to my knowledge. There could certainly be a secret location like that, but if there is I don't know about it.

The information about Missouri in the beginning of the story is accurate, though it isn't known if Jesse James left a treasure or anything else hidden somewhere in Centralia.

The places I mention in Fredericksburg and Charlottesville are well-known historical locations that can be visited by the general public, though I changed a few details about the layout of the area to suit the needs of the story. Shenandoah Valley and the surrounding area his breathtaking, however, and I highly recommend a visit.

The characters in the beginning of the book are a figment of my imagination, though I do believe such people certainly existed.

It is well-known that Jacque de Molay was the leader of the Templars around that time, however I don't believe he would have been directly involved withs secreting away a powerful relic.

Most historians agree the current version of the Knights Templar doesn't have a direct connection to the fabled knights of old.

There are, however, some very interesting parallels between the original knights and the current-day Masons.

While we will never truly know how deep the rabbit hole goes with any secret organization, it's certainly fun to speculate.

I spoke with numerous Masons during the writing of this book to make sure I didn't include anything that might come off as offensive to their organization. Both the Order of Freemasons and the Knights Templar do incredible amounts of charity work and I would never want to show them in a negative light.

In regard to the ancient order of Assassins, this group was, and could still be, very real. They disappeared into the shadows long ago, though their name continues to be used to this day when someone's life is taken in a underhanded, stealthy manner.

The war between the two factions was certainly real. We may never know the true extent to which each organization went to exterminate the other. We do know that they were both elite fighting forces engaged in what each believed to be a righteous and just cause. That sentiment alone has fueled the fire of war for far too long.

Again, I hope you enjoyed the story and will check out more of the Sean Wyatt universe in the future.

OTHER BOOKS BY ERNEST DEMPSEY

For my friend Brandi.

ACKNOWLEDGMENTS

As always, I would like to thank my terrific editors for their hard work. What they do makes my stories so much better for readers all over the world. Anne Storer and Jason Whited are the best editorial team a writer could hope for and I appreciate everything they do.

I also want to thank Elena at Lı Graphics for her tremendous work on my book covers and for always overdelivering. Elena definitely rocks.

Last but not least, I need to thank all my wonderful fans and especially the advance reader team. Their feedback and reviews are always so helpful and I can't say enough good things about all of them.

Made in the USA
Middletown, DE
13 May 2020